SLIT THROAT SAGA

TESHELLE COMBS

This story is currently available in serial format on the Kindle Vella platform.

To the kid who was too afraid to be yourself.
You're still you. It's not over.

Ep 1

It's My Story, I Can Lie If I Want To

Life Tip: Never wear your best footwear to public executions.

I pushed the cloth soles of my shoes into the tiny bits of loose gravel on Ender Stream. The discomfort helped me concentrate. *Focus, Nex.* But it was difficult to steady my mind on the one thing I was trying to ignore.

The people—friends and family, neighbors and strangers—crowded alongside me, shoulders bumping, the fabric of my sleeves rubbing against theirs until every inch of me was pressed against someone else. *We are the same.* That's what I was taught to think at times like these.

The reality that there was no escape from the ocean of people overwhelmed me. My heart began to race as my toes were crushed under well-meaning heels and my head knocked about by the waves of oblivious chests and shoulders. Until someone shoved, clearing a few inches of air around me and then resting a warm hand on the small of my back, pulling me to the right.

"There you are," he said, kissing my temple. "I thought I lost you for a moment."

He had indeed lost me. It was too difficult to keep track of anyone at such an event, much less someone with a small frame like mine. But, like always, Onur found me when I needed him. Usually, if he came close to me as he did then, I would lean in, relieving myself of some of the weight I carried. But during an Ending, I couldn't bring myself to relax, not even for a second. Not even with my best friend.

Onur kept up his duty, bless him, elbowing to box out the people who crammed into us. He had always been that kind of person. A protector. I hoped in earnest that he attributed my obvious nerves to the throng and not to anything else—to anything more sinister, more deadly.

"This is going to be a big one," he whispered, and I couldn't tell whether the airiness of his words signified anxiety or thrill. His blue eyes studied me briefly, then he used his thumb to rub a bit of dust from my nose. How he could tell bits of dust apart from my multitude of freckles was one of his mysteries. He pushed a large man forward, preventing him from standing square on my feet.

"Must be someone popular for so many to attend. Do you know who it is?"

My mouth was dry, and I knew my words would sound sticky, so I swallowed hard before I tried to speak. "Not personally, no. A woman, though, I think."

It was very often a woman these days. Most of the men had been eliminated in earlier decades, as far back as the Negative Forties and Fifties. Some think it was because the men sacrificed themselves to protect their women—the ones who could carry babies and keep their kind alive.

But I had a different theory. See, men, while courageous and strong, are also brazen and loud, brash and unthinking. Women...women are clever. Cunning. They are used to hiding parts of themselves. Under fabric and long hair, under feigned weakness and fainting spells. Women are not cowards. They are careful.

The Fight had been going on long enough, however, that the women were being found just as the men had been. One by one. Painfully. Perfectly.

The murmuring of the crowd deafened me. I wondered briefly how many humans were present at this Ending. A hundred thousand? Maybe more. I could see nothing over the backs of so many but I knew that would change once things got started. This was far from my first Ending. And it would not be my last. Unlike others, I could not afford to skip them.

Someone somewhere began the toning call: a simple hum that would go unnoticed by most. But someone else would hear and add their own voice. So it would go until three or four joined, and then ten, and then a hundred. When the sound rose high enough, I knew I needed to join in, to hum the note with my people. I did not want to. I wanted to keep silent. To let the hum pass over me, knowing that no one would really be able to tell if I abstained. Yet. Yet I loosened my jaw and let the sound resonate within me. A low hum that mixed with thousands and thousands more just like it. *The same.*

We all turned our attention to the elevating platform in the center of the square, our eyes lifted though there was nothing to see quite yet. Only a single wooden pole in the middle of a plain wooden deck, several feet above us and growing higher until it reached a balconied building.

The noise we emitted crescendoed until, all at once, it did not. We were ready. Silence came like rushing rapids, thick and full. I always felt like it would drown me, the silence. It made my head pound and knees shudder. It didn't help that my people seemed so pleased by it. Reverent, even. As if God had come down as the platform went up.

The moment of silence gave way to a new sound. One that filled my nightmares. Fabric shoes dragging across wooden planks. One would think it impossible to detect such a simple noise from so far away, but it filled up my ears every time I heard it. The feet thrashed, resisting, trying to find a way to run, to escape, to survive.

Sometimes those destined for the platform were dragged out of the House Of Certainty by tied wrists, their bodies flailing like fish out of water as they went. Sometimes it was by their feet, and their hair swept the dust from the platform like they were doing some strange neglected chore. But my least favorite—the one that haunted me when I closed my eyes, when the quiet of night tucked me into bed each evening—my least favorite was the one before me right then.

A girl, younger than me by a few years it seemed, with a Moral's muscular arm around her neck and her struggling body pressed against his to keep her from wriggling away. Her airway restricted, her eyes bulged and lips sputtered. She said nothing. There was nothing to say.

The Moral, face hooded in customary dark wool, used a gloved hand on her throat to force her back to the pole. She tried to rip at his arm, at his face, but the leather of his uniform kept him safe. Another came forward to bind her hands and legs behind her back and around the pole with twisted vines. A tradition. Vines for purity.

The hum began again, and my own voice made my nose buzz as tears came to my eyes. We stood watching as the Best Of Us stepped forward in his clean-cut cotton suit. He raised his yellowed hands, not to silence the hum but to encourage it. And then his white beard gave way to a smile.

"My people," he said, yelling over the toning, "let's celebrate. For today, the one who breaks the laws of nature, the one who moves the unmovable, the one who tests the very hands of God, will be set back on the right path. The Fight is not in vain."

He turned with a flourish to watch with us all as a translucent synthetix blade, held tight in the Moral's fist, sliced across the throat of the girl. A gurgle, then her blonde head flopped forward. Her blood gushed brilliant red. One would think it meant that the Fight was mistaken, that she was just like everyone else—a normal human with no unearthly capabilities, no deadly tendencies. Her blood seemed pure and red, filled with iron just like it should be. But after a few seconds, as her strength faded, the red diluted and her blood ran clear as a mountain river.

She was Meta. Just like they thought and I'm sure as they determined when she was confined in the House of Certainty for questioning. No true metal in her veins. No metal in her whole body. Not even metal in her mind. Instead she could pull it to her. She was a magnet. An abomination. And if left uncaught and unkilled, her kind would destroy the world.

Slit Throat Saga

The people—my people—cheered along with the Best Of Us as the Meta's watery blood poured over her small breasts, down her loose linen shirt, over the wooden platform, and through the street. It always amazed me how long Meta could bleed, how much life they held in their bodies. We all waited until the flow pooled beneath our feet, Ender Stream blessing us with one final reminder: *If you are us, you live, and if you are them, you die.*

"Well, Nex," Onur said with a little sigh as the crowd began to disperse, shoes squelching in the remains of the Meta girl, "what must be done is done." He brushed my thick, silver curls behind my ear so he could kiss my temple again, his favorite habit. His pale skin seemed to shine against my dusty red complexion. He looked tired, but he smiled. "We should get something to eat, yes?"

I smiled back at him, turning and tiptoeing so I could reach his lips with my own. His were soft and yielding, warm and inviting. Mine were not quite as full, not quite as tender. I met his eyes, ensuring that my gaze said exactly what I needed it to. *All Fight, no fear.* "Yes, let's eat. We can say cheers to the next one to be found."

I stepped through the Stream, one hand tight in my love's. The other hand I kept stuffed in the pocket of my cotton dress, clenched, but not so firmly that my fingernails might draw blood from my palm. That would not do. For the Stream soaking through my shoes was no less damned than the blood coursing through my veins.

Careful, Nex.

Careful.

Ep 2

Dinner Is Non-Negotiable

Life Tip: When in doubt, check for puncture wounds.

The booths at our favorite place looked more inviting than expected. I had no idea how badly I wanted to sit down until the option was in my view, with soft red cushions and a plush back to lean against.

"For two," Onur said, waiting for the seater to hurry off and secure a table on what must have been a very busy late afternoon. To my surprise she returned almost immediately, bowing slightly as she mumbled an apology for the wait. Silly me. For a second, I forgot who I was with.

The seater made sure our table was spotless before allowing us to slide into the booth, side by side. I rested my elbow against Onur's, pretending to peruse the menu. I ordered something as normal and uninteresting as possible, my go-to strategy for blending in. Onur ordered the Calisto—some seafood-esque dish reserved for refined palates like his. The seater hurried off, nearly knocking over the tray of drinks in another seater's arms as she rushed away.

"Why do they always act like that?" I asked, feeling for the harried staff.

Onur leaned back, putting his arm over the top of the booth seat so he could peer sideways at me. "You have that effect on people."

I scoffed. "Me? Ha."

He examined me with his head tilted to the side, his cautious blues betraying his depth of consideration. "Yes, you. What on Aarde else could it be?"

I held my hands up, genuinely puzzled. "My dear, I am the most ordinary person in the whole City."

He smirked. "Okay, Primary *Aerixon*."

I rolled my eyes at him. "Oh *that's* what you mean? That has nothing to do with *me*. Besides, you're just as highly ranked, beautiful."

He blushed, pink coloring his pale neck and cheeks, and averted his eyes. "Beautiful, yes. Highly ranked, no."

A quiver of panic in my chest. I put my hand over his. The Vanes and Aerixons had always ranked together. Our parents had been friends since primary rank. Not only would I miss his company if we became unevenly matched, but it would be difficult to be paired together for a house unit in the future if the disparity between our current houses was too severe. That, and...having someone high-ranked who believed me to be completely and harmlessly human meant less peril and more security.

"Onur," I squeezed his hand, trying to catch his eyes. "Onur, what happened?" I knew my parents hadn't ranked ahead. The only explanation would be that the Vanes had somehow fallen behind. But how? Why? *And why hasn't anyone told me until now?*

Onur blushed even harder. "I thought you knew...."

I shook my head, my silver curls misbehaving, flying too wild around my face. "Tell me."

He inched closer, a secret about to ensue. "You remember a few months ago, that girl we Ended who ran red nearly the whole time?"

I nodded again. I particularly did not like that Ending. It took over an hour. The girl would not die, and so she could not have been normal, but she also would not run clear, so she could not have been Meta. It was quite the ordeal, her red blood staining the shoes of thousands and marking Enders Stream for weeks. But in the end, strung up on that pole, she ran out of red, just like all the other Meta before her.

Onur moved even closer, his voice barely detectable, his cool breath tickling my ear and raising goosebumps along my forearms. "You already know that a Meta who runs red is just using whatever iron they can find to darken their blood. They might have stored it beneath their skin or in their hair. Even in their eyes. But they can't keep up the ruse forever.

"Well this one...this one pulled iron from...unexpected places. That's why it took so long."

I almost—*almost*—blurted out that she pulled the iron from human blood straight into hers, but I forgot I should not know that, that most people could never fathom such a horrible idea. But I knew it was possible because...I just knew it was possible. I could feel it. The whisper of all the iron in all the blood in the whole restaurant. It was as real as the words Onur breathed against my skin. I knew it could be done, and I knew it should not be done. A rule written into the very fabric of me. But none of this could I ever let Onur know. Never—not once—had I ever spoken to anyone about the truth of me. So I played dumb, as one does, and let my love explain on.

"This Meta was able to pull iron from human blood—from *our* blood."

I nodded—*no not just a nod, Nex, this requires more reaction*—I gasped, pausing so it seemed I was letting it sink in. "But what does that Meta have to do with the Vanes' rank?"

"My father was the one who interrogated her in the House Of Certainty. So, naturally, the Fight wanted to know how he had missed such a unique ability, such a...potent curse."

"But...he did not know?"

"No, of course not!" He frowned at me, a little offended. "He did not know she could do such things, nor that such things were even possible. Regardless, he did not catch it in interrogation, and a spectacle was made during the Ending. So he is being punished not for his guilt, but his incompetence."

I wrinkled my nose. "How can he be held responsible for missing something no one knew existed?"

Onur shrugged, letting go of the topic as the food came out. "I don't know, Nex. Honestly, I don't. But I'll do my best to raise us up again. Don't worry."

I ran my fingers through his pale-blond hair. "I never really worry about you, Onur. It would be a waste of my effort."

He smiled at that, and leaned in, his lips close to mine but then pulled away awkwardly, clearing his throat and darting his eyes behind me, signaling that I should turn around.

I did so, to find a very tall, very tense machine of a man leering at my back. My jaw clamped shut, as was my usual response to Joacin Aerixon, the one I called father, the one who found responsibility for me his greatest burden.

I bowed my head in customary greeting. "Pattern, hello," I said. First address, as in the opening of a conversation, didn't need to be formal for other houses, unless there was some ceremony or official gathering. 'Father' did fine for most parent-child relationships. But not for the Aerixons. First address was first address, even at a casual restaurant with my love present.

"What on Aarde are you doing here?" my father said. When he talked, his voice squeezed out of his throat, like even his speaking muscles were wound tight. "Do you have any idea what time it is, Nexus?"

A guess perhaps? "Ummm...evening time?"

He did not think I was clever. He was probably right.

Onur gave the faintest, quietest whisper from his seat in the booth, "Dinner time."

But my father heard it anyway, and inclined his head toward him. "Thank you, Primary Vanes, for your support of my daughter. It is indeed time for dinner." He gestured for me to rise from my seat, but I motioned to the steaming plate of food, untouched, before me.

"But, I just got my—"

"Dinner is non-negotiable." He clasped his hands loosely in front of himself. "You will respect my expectations. And of course, you will not displease your mother."

My body involuntarily reacted, and I bumped the table with my knee, causing the utensils to clatter. I feigned recovery, shoving my hands in my pocket to calm me down. "Mother is...here?"

My father eyed me knowingly. "Preparing the third meal herself."

"Mother is *cooking*?"

My father sighed. "Do not be late, child." He swiveled sharply and left, his dark cloak floating behind the sound of sturdy footsteps left by synthetic boots. Seaters and guests alike skittered out of his way.

I flopped back into the booth and leaned all my wait on Onur. "Shit."

"Nex?" Onur said sweetly.

"Hmmm?"

"I love you but...get out of here."

He was right. *What am I doing?* I hustled to my feet, my legs wobbly from hunger, and took one last kiss. "Eat my food for me?"

He sighed dramatically. "If I must...anything for you, darling."

I squeezed my way out of the stuffed restaurant and onto the street, calculating the quickest way home from Ender Stream. Probably back streets. It was still early enough that they were safe. I wound my way east, nearly running, twisting through the alleys that hemmed in the central City area.

I wasn't paying enough attention to where I was going. That's how I ended up on the ground. At least, that's what I told myself. Dahn Vanes cursed, righting herself and dusting off her overbearing skirts.

"Good god, Nexus, why are you running through the streets? You could have killed me."

I sighed, letting my legs flop all the way to the ground while I caught my breath. "I don't think being bumped constitutes mortal peril, Dahn. But I am sorry I ran into you." *In more ways than one.*

"You haven't answered my question." She straightened her already bone straight scarlet hair with delicate hands. "Why were you running? Not that you were doing it very skillfully."

Sometimes I wondered why Dahn hated me, especially since we were very close friends growing up, but then I remembered her catching me with my arms around her brother's neck when we were twelve and I didn't have to wonder anymore.

"If you must know, my mother is home."

"Oh dear." Dahn glanced at the sun for the time. "You're already screwed."

I pulled myself up to my feet and then doubled over, a gasp hissing from my lips. Something...a sharp pain in my side when I tried to straighten up.

Dahn's face changed from haughty to concerned. She moved toward me. "Nex, what's wrong?"

I slapped her hand away. Instinct. Years of well-conditioned fear response. Because what I felt trickling down the skin just above my hip, just inside my thin cotton dress, was my own blood.

"It's nothing. Just running too hard. Got a stitch." I straightened up even though it hurt like hell and shrugged. "You can go back to being mean to me now."

She glared as she pushed past me, her head so high she might have caught a neck cramp. As soon as she was gone, I looked down at the source of my pain, quickly, so no one

else would notice. The streets were still bustling after
the Ending.

It looked like I'd spilled a glass of water on myself. Like
a common accident. But I knew what it was. I was bleeding.
And I was doing it all wrong. *How could this have happened?*
What did I do? I glanced around me but I saw nothing that
would explain why my skin had been so deeply penetrated,
enough to draw so much blood. The pain throbbed through
my whole torso.

I decided to hurry home. I could figure it out on the way.
People would not see a water stain and think, *oh that girl is*
bleeding. They would think I had spilled. That I was clumsy.
That a bit of Ender Stream had splashed on me, even.

But the closer I got to home, the more the injury hurt. The
throbbing turned to an icy sting that radiated up through
my chest and around to my spine. I could even feel it in my
legs, like a frosted giant breathing into my very bones. The
thoughts that should have been filling my head, like how to
prepare myself for dinner with my mother, were replaced
with an all consuming, "Ow ow ow ow ow," and then, right
before I ascended the stairs to our flat, the worst kind of
thought to think about one's condition: *Something is wrong.*

My body convulsed as I stood outside our front door, the
light of sunset gracing my back, contemplating whether I
should twist the doorknob or simply jump from the second
floor and hope I splattered. But the door wrenched open and
my sister, suddenly nose to nose with me, gave a little squeal.

"Nexus Aerixon, have you lost your entire mind? You're late!"

I nodded. "I didn't know...." And a groan almost came out
with it.

Priyaa looked me up and down, holding my shoulders and, unbeknownst to her, propping me up. "What...what is happening to you? Why are you all sweaty and flustered?"

"I ran here."

"That was a terrible idea, Nex," she hissed, glancing over her shoulder.

"But I was late."

"Yes, I understand that, but now you are late and sweaty and flustered."

And I'm about to fall over. That'll cause a stir.

She gestured to my dress. "Why are you filthy?"

"Because I ran all the way here, Priyaa." I gestured back to her, using irritation to hide my breathlessness. "Why are you perfect?"

She sighed, backing down from her tirade. "I don't know, Nex. It's just not that difficult for me."

"Wow, oh good. Thanks for that."

She grinned, her red skin, though not freckled like mine, glowing beneath golden hair. "You are most welcome. Now, go clean yourself up. I'll stall."

I tried to get past her but she wouldn't budge. "Don't be dumber than you have to be, Nex." She motioned behind me. "Through the window. You'll get caught otherwise. Now hurry up."

I kissed her cheek as I turned to leave the little sister who should have been the eldest and made my way to the back of our complex. Scaling the wall to my second story window would not be easy. Normally? A cinch, though not tempted in the light of day. But the pain made me want to curl up and never move again. Like menstrual cramps, but if they were sentient and trying to eat me.

I leaned my head against the vined and stuccoed wall for just a second, trying to calm my breathing and gather some resolve. I had to climb up. Had to. Fricking Viveka Aerixon was preparing a meal with her bare hands, and I would have hell and more to pay if I was not there to digest it, and punctually so. *I must respect her expectations.*

A few more breaths, and my usual mantra: "Help me, God." And I gripped the vines and started up, one inch at a time. Halfway there, I felt the world spin, flashes of black and chilling white all my eyes could detect. I would fall. I knew I would fall. Everything in me got cold and my muscles lost their strength. I would fall and break my leg and they would find me hemorrhaging on the brick terrace and haul me to the House Of Certainty and question me and drag me to the platform and hum and smile and slit my throat and Onur would say, "What must be done is done," and then my house would have dinner without so much as a 'tsk tsk'.

Or...I would hold tighter, gripping the vines I could no longer see and pulling until my palms felt the smooth edge of my window sill. I'd left the window cracked, for easy entrance and exit—this was not my first break in. Once I made it over the ledge, I collapsed onto the wooden floor of my bedroom. It was only then I realized how much I'd bled. My entire dress was soaked from the belly down. Even my shoes could have been wrung out if I'd tried. I thought for a moment that maybe I would die in my room. Then I thought...maybe I would not.

So I reached under my dress and examined the wound. It was tiny. A little larger than a pinprick. As if caused by a nail or a screw. *Maybe I scraped myself? But on what? And why the pain?*

I crawled over to my closet and tossed my clothes around until I found a scarf I'd never worn that my elderly neighbor gave me many holy days ago. I tied it tightly around my waist, hoping to end the bleeding. I figured, from what I'd seen at Endings, that I had a lot of blood left to lose.

I found a new dress, one of my mother's favorites with the white lace and the crisp hem, and pulled it over my head. I brushed my hair, dropping the paddle a few times, then splashed and dried my face. I felt no better, but no worse.

Downstairs. I was the only one unseated at our dining table. Many faces observed me, some scowling and some concerned, including Dahn and Onur Vanes', respectively. In fact, all the Vanes were present at our table, including Clay, the youngest Vanes. How on earth they all made it to my table before me was beyond me. And with no forewarning. *How long have I been upstairs? Did I actually pass out?* Regardless of how they'd arrived at our table, I was surprised— and not the good kind.

"Oh..." I said, which was, let me tell you, not what I was supposed to say. My mother stood up so abruptly that she startled me.

I clasped my hands in front of me, elbows straight yet loose, feet together, and bowed deeply. "Matrix, hello." My bending at the waist almost made me throw up, but I hid it with every particle of restraint I possessed. *Hide, Nex, hide. For the love of god, hide.*

"We will discuss your presentation during this house event at a later time," she said, her tone curt enough to slap me in the face. If one could decode her meaning, it would translate to something like, "You are in the *deepest* shit." And she sat down and began to eat, signaling that we all do the same.

"I would be elated to be the object of discussion," I said. We weren't ready for house dinners unless we had customary lying close at hand.

I sat too hard in my chair—sort of fell into it—largely because I blacked out just a tad. Onur didn't take his eyes off me. He knew me better than anyone seated. He waited until my parents weren't looking to mouth the words, "Are you alright?"

I gave the slightest nod, but it didn't fool him. "How are you here?" I whispered even quieter than he had.

"You look pale," Dahn said too loudly, chewing my mother's rather dry roast as if it were heaven on a plate.

I stared at her, trying to appear emotionless. "Thank you, Dahn," I responded. "I do what I can."

My mother set her utensils down. "While it is joyous that we are together this eve"—I looked around to see whether I detected any joy; we looked like prisoners of war—"I am here to inform you all of a grave happening."

More grave than family dinner?

She stood, her prim attire creased to perfection, her synthetic boots making no sound as she stepped away from the table. Priyaa and I got our red skin from our father. My mother stood so pale, she was nearly gray. She and I shared eyes, though, also gray and stony. Those eyes flicked over to me as if she could tell I was not paying attention.

She returned to the table and deftly set a device in the center of it. "This," she said carefully, "is a wonder of our modern age, given to us by the Best of the Best."

We all interjected with a unified refrain at the mention of his name, "How wonderful," even though we knew he himself did not invent it.

The device was synthetic and glass, clear enough to see a blue liquid contained within. She went on. "This will aid the Fight as nothing else ever has. It's proven to cause great discomfort to Meta, no matter their strength or resilience, but no such discomfort to our people."

A cluster of murmurs. Such a thing was indeed a wonder.

"Discomfort?" my father asked. His lips were pursed, his hands very still atop the table. He was angry. Probably because my mother had not shared her development with him first.

"Yes, Joacin. Extreme discomfort. Including pain, insatiable vomiting, stiffness of muscles, paralysis, blindness, deafness, and, depending on dosages or susceptibility of a host—death. Though it is difficult to dose that high without causing harm to our people as well."

Edwidge, Onur's mother, spoke up next. "This is marvelous, Viveka, simply marvelous. How will such a thing be used to help us?"

My mother, her arms clasped firmly behind her back, nodded matter-of-factly. "Excellent question, dearest friend. It will be used in many manners, in many ways, for many reasons. No longer will we rely solely on hearsay, rumors, and questioning to find their kind. We will flush the Meta out of hiding. And it will be wondrous."

Slit Throat Saga

The dress I wore, my mother's favorite, had no pockets, no place for me to shove my hands to keep them steady. I wanted to reach for Onur, but it was not allowed at dinner. Besides, he might have noticed how cold and trembling I truly was.

Instead, I chewed my roast in silence, pretending to admire the fearsome device mere inches from my plate, and trying not to bleed out at the table. When I did glance up, it was to see Dahn smiling at me, her eyes glinting even in the candlelight.

Ep 3

Yes, Mother Dearest

Life Tip: Bring a sharpener.

Priyaa snatched the novel out of my hand before I knew she was standing in front of me. I didn't mind losing my place in its pages, though, since I hated reading and only did it to look studious and to avoid conversation. I just held the book open and daydreamed mostly. It's a wonder people didn't notice I never turned the pages.

"Our mother is calling you," she said.

I didn't budge. It had been a couple days since I almost died at house dinner, so it was about time my life was threatened anew.

"Now?" I replied.

She clapped her hands in front of my face, her golden braid slipping over her shoulders. "Nex, yes, *now*. When has our mother ever called for you any time other than *now*?"

I sat up with a sigh. "You're right, Pri. I should have already mastered the ability to materialize before her at the mere inkling of her expectations."

Priyaa smirked. "You'd probably do it wrong."

"Like...so?" I grinned, pouncing on her and knocking her over onto the settee.

"Okay, okay, off. Off! You'll ruin my whole look!" I ignored her plea. "Nexus, you monster!" But she giggled when she said it.

"Nexus." The voice came from the sitting room doorway. It fell flat like a stone, but it gave me chills. I scrambled to my feet, yanking Priyaa up with me, and bowed.

"Matrix, hell—"

"Follow me," she said, cutting me off.

I followed, trying to walk in the most soundless way, as I knew she was aggravated by my noisy footsteps. Also me. All of me in general aggravated my mother. Her shoulders were impossibly straight, her back erect. Even though we were the same height, she seemed several inches taller. A colossus trapped in the body of a petite woman.

She stopped and swiveled, as most Fenders Of The Fight did habitually, and folded her arms behind her back to address me. "You will gather the required items, and we will make our way."

"Ah, yes. Okay...um...very well." *I am already somehow in trouble, aren't I?* "What...which items will I be needing?"

She would have scowled at me, but I had a theory that she was the victim of some terrible accident that decreased her facial mobility. She simply stared before speaking, her disdain evident in the burrow of her gray eyes. "A pencil and paper." She paused, but it took me a second to realize I was supposed to have moved. "Retrieve them. Now."

As soon as I was out of her sight, I switched from a somber march to a sprint for my room. Priyaa followed me, her bare feet smacking against the wood floor. "What is happening? Why are you running? What did she want?"

"I am to follow her to...somewhere. But first I need a pencil and paper."

Priyaa's brow furrowed. "Follow her? Like...going somewhere together? The two of you?"

I scrambled, flinging about desk items, praying that a pencil existed in the realm of chaos known as my bedroom. "I have no idea, Priyaa, but this is bad. This is terrible."

My sister disappeared and reappeared, pushing her own pencil and notebook into my hands. "Look at me, you nut."

And I did. Her brown eyes were calm, void of the disdain my mother's held when she looked at me. "Nex, you are going to be fine. Say it back to me, just like that."

A rattled breath, and then, "I am going to ruin everything and blame it on you."

She lunged forward, pretending she was going to bite my nose off, and then kicked me out of the room.

My mother was already outside, her layers of clothes pulled tight across her chest in perfect pleats and then billowing about her legs, revealing her legs in sharp black leather. Her dark hair was tucked into a neat, low bun, not a strand out of place.

I put a hand to my dancing curls, realizing that I'd taken little care for my appearance, especially with the pencil location debacle. I felt myself blush, glad it wouldn't show on my complexion. "Is this...am I decent, mother?"

"Of course not," and then she turned and headed down the stairs to the street. I figured I should follow, two of my steps to one of hers. We circled around back to her transport and got in. I only fumbled with the seat belt for a moment before it clicked into place.

It was rare for us to take a transport in the City. Well...it was rare for me, and actually quite usual for my mother. She traveled often. I rarely left our City square. With a few clicks of her fingers, she programmed a location into the transport receiver and I was sneaky enough to catch the address: House Of Houses.

House Of Houses? What on Aarde would I be doing there? I had never been. In fact, not many I knew had ever been. For most houses, one had to have a reason to enter. Basically, either one was invited or one was detained. *At least it's not the House Of Certainty*, I thought, exhaling way too loud in the passenger seat.

I wanted to ask why we were headed to such a place—I wasn't quite sure what the House Of Houses was for—but I let the burning questions lay to rest on my tongue. We said nothing the entire drive, about two hours. Just silence and the soft whir of the synthetix motor propelling us along.

We pulled up to the building, and a seater took my mother's transport to park it for her, I figured, and we went inside the largest multi-panel doors imaginable. They were made of glass. That was my best guess since they shimmered in the morning sun, narrowing to a point like one face of a very tall pyramid.

No one questioned my mother as we entered the building, though everyone else, Fenders and civilians alike, had to present their arms for identification at the doors. The ceilings and walls of the House were enormous, stretching and turning into strange angles, reflecting light, some with circuitry glittering throughout them. Even the floor was made of synthetix and glass. It was like being inside a giant, comprehensive computer. It would have felt alive if it weren't all so cold and calculated.

We rode an elevator that took us downward. Very far downward. Until I felt a little queasy. The lights were dimmer there, and the air smelled more of wet earth. *Subaardean level for sure.* There was no one else around. Not like the bustling main level, where hundreds of Fenders in suits like my mother's walked about with decided purpose.

Here were only a few tables, each with a light source above it, and some uncomfortable-looking chairs. Even the walls were black—no glittering lights or wiring.

My mother motioned to the nearest table. "Sit."

I obeyed, trying to hold very still while I did so.

"Your task is to sketch the architectural design of the main hall of the House Of Houses, which you just walked through a moment ago. You may take as long as needed. Be as accurate as you think is possible. Do not get up for any reason unless you are finished."

"Sk-sketch the entire—?"

"That is what I said."

And just like that, she swiveled and left through the way we'd come.

Fantastic. I tapped my pencil on the table, reviewing events in my mind. They were as follows: with no warning, my mother, who hated me, factually, brought me to the House Of Houses, sat me down, and told me to accurately sketch a building I had only seen in passing, one time ever, that very morning. No tools or resources provided. No guide. No opportunity to go back up and see it again.

I knew better than to disobey and find someone to ask questions. The questions came anyway...I had done so poorly on all my tests in primary as a child. Art? Failed. Composition? Nope. Math? Abysmal. *So why me? Why now? Why this?*

But questions and failed grades would not complete an impossible sketch for my impossible mother. I'd have to screw that up all on my own.

I began with the basic conical structure of the entryway, replaying the steps we took to get inside in my head. It was not long before I was lost in the work, my pencil scraping against the paper until...well, until my pencil broke.

"Oh my good god, *WHY?*" I said out loud to no one. *Why, why, why? Why?* I tried to peel away the wood of the pencil tip with my fingernails to reveal enough pencil point to finish my drawing. I was concentrating so fervently that I didn't realize how long my fingertip had been pressed against the tiny, almost invisible bit of lead, only taking notice when I heard a whisper. I dropped the pencil.

"Hello?"

I looked around, but I was still alone. No one. So I picked up the pencil and tried again, scratching at the tip. And there it was again. The faintest whisper. No words. Nothing intelligible. Just...whispering.

I pulled my finger away from the pencil, and it stopped. Back to the lead, and I heard it again. Repeat of this experiment about fourteen times before I decided to rip the pencil in half to get to the rest of the lead in the center. I tore, wood splintering, until it lay there in a bed of wood...a gray-

black cylinder, matte and textured. *Metal.* After a second—
or maybe it was minutes—I realized I could hear its whisper
louder. So similar to the hum of iron in the blood of my
people, but...different.

I touched it. Ran my index finger along the length of it.
Shivers wracked my spine. I thought perhaps a moan even
left my lips. The lead whispered even louder, like a cat
purring at its owner's caress.

"Hello," I said, again out loud, but this time not to no one.
Or at least not to nothing. "What should I do with you
now?" *Hide it? Throw it across the room? Smash it into dust?*
They would ask me why I broke the pencil, why I did not
simply set it down and wait for assistance. And what would
I say? What would I do then?

Truth? There was nothing in that moment I wanted more
than to take the lead home with me. Not just home with
me, no...everywhere. *It should be everywhere I am. All the
time.* And just like that, the lead lifted out of the pencil's
remains, disintegrated into the finest powder, and buried
itself into the pores of my skin.

Oh, and that's when the elevator hummed to life.

Ep 4

Good Girls Get Good Grades

Life Tip: The Thinky Grumps are friend, not foe.

It was not my mother who walked out of the elevator doors. I scooped the pencil shards under my table and stood, bowing at the strange man.

Obviously a Fender by the look of his attire, he acknowledged my bow with a nod—something my mother had never bothered to do. He observed my surroundings with a vigilant eye before he spoke, his hand outstretched.

"Your work for my review."

As I reached for the paper with the sketch—the sketch, might I add, that I had not reviewed myself and of whose quality I was quite ignorant—I realized I was brandishing the very arm that could cause my demise. But the worry was fleeting. I felt more confident, for some reason, with the metal in me. Though I did wonder if the Fender could hear the vibration of the lead in my blood vessels. *He looks ancient*, I thought. *Maybe he's deaf.*

He scoured the paper, turning it this way and that in the dim basement light. His eyes, shadowed by wiry gray eyebrows, flicked to me, to the paper, and back to me. His emotions were buried in the grooves of the deep wrinkles on his face.

"How have you done this?" He asked, holding up my sketch.

"How?" I shifted my weight, a habit of which my mother did not approve. "I did exactly what I was told."

The Fender turned one hundred and eighty degrees without warning, causing me to jump backward. "Follow me," he said, his voice as gruff as the weathered skin on his face. And I obeyed, as I should. In the elevator, without another word, me fidgeting with the seams of my pale-blue cotton dress, and him motionless as he reviewed my paper once more.

We walked down a gleaming hallway, where the circuits within the walls sparked and danced, energy zooming from one point to another. At another stupidly tall door, the Fender took a card from within his lapel and scanned it at the lock. The door beeped, sighed, and let us in.

I hesitated before stepping past the threshold. Maybe it was the knowledge that illegal metal was practically giggling beneath my skin. Or maybe it was the low throb I felt in my midsection—a reminder of the mysterious puncture wound from a few days before. But, in the end, I had to go in, and so I did.

The room glowed and hummed as we entered, as if registering our presence, or at least witnessing it, and then returned to normal. My mother paced before a mirror that covered the length of an entire wall. The mirror was covered with scribbles, and my mother was accessorized: a stylus in her hand and a frown on her face.

I know that look. When we were much younger, Priyaa and I called it the "Thinky Grumps." Our mother would come home from long work trips with the Fight still on her mind. She would scatter papers and communications all over whichever room she possessed. There was no interrupting her when she got like that. She didn't eat, she didn't talk, she didn't parent. She just worked.

I stood there in what I guessed was her office thinking about the Thinky Grumps, when the Fender who escorted me flashed me what I guessed was a look of disgust for not greeting my mother properly.

Only, he was unaware that she hadn't noticed either of us, so my greeting would have been wasted. I knew the rules of Thinky Grumps, and they superseded any other customs. Actually, if one were clever, such rules could be used to one's advantage. Basically, I did not have to climb the vines outside my window to see Onur at night if my mother didn't know I existed.

After a few solid minutes of standing there waiting for my mother to see us and observing the Fender man—literally, by any calculations, inching closer to death by the second—I took the lead. There was, after all, one trick that usually worked for such occasions. Except for when it didn't.

"That is definitely the solution," I said rather loudly. Didn't matter what she was trying to solve. Just needed to affirm it.

Still not noticing us, my mother mumbled, "Yes, I think it might be." And then, just like that, she came back to herself, smoothing her already creaseless outfit with precise palms. "What is it?" she growled, except her voice never grew tempered.

"She has completed the task," the Fender said. I noted a hint of disbelief in his tone that I couldn't blame him for.

"As I expected." My mother all but snatched the paper from the Fender. She glanced at it for not even a second. "How accurate is her replication?"

"Very accurate."

"How certain are you?"

The Fender seethed. That would be the word for that reaction. A sort of simmering anger, emitted but not expressed. "Very certain, Fender Master Aerixon."

She tossed the paper over her shoulder onto the floor. "I will, of course, take your word for it, Braggs. I am no scientist. And certainly no artist."

Two things here. First, the Fender—Braggs—just said my sketch was...very accurate? How could that be Aardely possible? And second, did my mother just say she is NOT a scientist?

I looked around the room with its impressive wiring and glittering technology. I visualized the concoction she'd set on our dining room table, meant to kill anyone without metal naturally in their veins. Anyone like me. In fact, all my life, I thought my mother to be a scientist—an inventor of some sort at least, if not a genius.

If my mother is not a scientist, what is she?

If my mother is not a scientist, what am I doing here in the House Of Houses?

"Shall we put her to work, Fender Master?" Braggs, though still hinting at disbelief, still stinging from my mother's offenses, was obviously eager. "Clearly, she is a talented replicator. I'm sure there are other gifts we can extract from someone so young. On behalf of the Fight of course."

My mother scoffed. "It is all on behalf of the Fight. And youth has nothing to do with it. She is useful. She will be used." She shook her head, clasping her hands behind her back. "And here I thought she might have been tossed in with the Feelers. Or forgotten among the Wizens. Too thin and clumsy for a Moral.

"But, I am vigilant. I detected this quality in her despite her lack of...decorum. She will make a fine Former in the end. A rank to be coveted may be hers after all." She angled her sharp chin toward me, and I tried to stop rocking on my heels when I realized she was actively looking. "Does this please you, Data?"

Does it...please...me? Never in all my life had my mother ever asked me a thing like that. And certainly not using the formal word for 'daughter.' Not that she didn't care about what I wanted, which God knows she did not. It was as if pleasure was not a factor for her. It did not exist as a concept. Perhaps it was why I could never please her. She simply could not be pleased.

I bowed deeply, because—well...*because*—and then met her eyes. "I will respect your expectations, Matrix."

And, I kid you not, Fender Master Viveka Aerixon almost—*maybe*—didn't seem like she vomited in her mouth when she nodded her head in acknowledgment.

Ep 5

With Sprinkles On Top

Life Tip: Ice cream and imminent death are not flavor-compatible.

"A toast! A dozen toasts!" Onur put his hands on my waist and hoisted me so high into the air I thought everyone on the street might see up my dress.

"Put me down, Onur," I yelped. "Are you trying to get me reprimanded?"

He kissed me before he did as I asked. A long one, parting my lips with his so I tasted the tip of his tongue. It was not allowed to kiss so passionately in the middle of the City, especially if we were not yet Housed together as a couple. I'd never seen Onur grin so big, though, and I'd known him my whole life.

"No one will reprimand us. Not today, Nex. Today is special."

I was a little giddy on my feet when he released me at last, but luckily the street was not crowded enough for me to bump into anyone. I wanted to keep strolling down Vessel Road, a quaint, historical part of town about a half length from Ender Stream, but Onur wasn't ready to move on just yet. Instead, he scooped my hands up in his. For a second,

I thought he might twirl, which I admit would have been adorable given his broad shoulders and long, sturdy legs.

"Nex, how are you not more excited? You went to the House Of Houses! Like...*inside*. And you earned a rank"—he snapped his fingers, releasing my hand only for a moment— "just like that."

I nodded. "Yes I know, Onur. I am the one who told you what happened."

He did a twirl, and I with him since my hands were still sequestered. My cloth shoes skidded along the cobblestone, and the dusty shops blurred into a haze before my eyes.

"And now you are going to be a Former. A *Former!* How did this even happen? I didn't know you were so...so talented!"

I would have said I was also surprised...if I had any words amidst the spinning. To my fortune, a gentle hand belonging to one Clay Vanes, lightened on her brother's forearm. At only twelve, Clay was my hero. Mostly because she could do things like that. Stop commotion with one carefully-placed, delicate little hand.

"She's had enough of the revelry, Onur," she said. I even liked how Clay talked. Like velvet against the cheek. Like the softest breeze on a balmy evening.

Onur sighed, still smiling. "Yes, you're right of course, Clay. I'm just...I can't believe it."

I bit my lip, but the words came out anyway and with a strong flare of sarcasm. "Really super unbelievable that I could achieve something, huh?"

"Oh don't be upset, Nex. You'll ruin the best day ever." He circled behind me and steadily pushed me, steering me down the street and toward one of the shops—brightly lit with its glass door propped open. "I know; let's get celebratory ice cream."

I was not in an ice-creamy mood, but I smiled at the counter and requested extra caramel drizzle on my cone. Onur ordered for Clay and handed her a smooth ball of mint ice cream in a paper cup. "I'll get us a table," he said, paying with his arm chip and practically skipping off.

Clay frowned down at her cup. "I did not want this." She outstretched her hand. "Do you want mine?"

"Nope. Do you want mine?"

She sighed and dug her spoon into her treat. I studied her as she studied her brother from across the shop, her irises quivering as she took in his movements. Of all the Vanes children, Clay had my favorite eyes. Dahn's were quick and cunning. Onur's were brooding and steady. But Clay had wide, blue eyes, almost circular, set deep in her face. They were always changing, always moving, always seeing. That's how I knew the quietest Vanes had the most to say.

"Have you ever seen him like this?" I asked her. "So happy?"

"He's not happy. He's relieved."

"Relieved?"

"Yes. He was worried about you."

I licked my caramel before it could drip down my knuckles. "I am not that hopeless of a cause, am I?"

Clay snorted a laugh. That was another thing I loved about her. That laugh. "Nothing about you is hopeless, Nexus. He wasn't worried about *you* you, he was worried about the two of you. Whether you would rank together. Whether what you want for each other will align with what the Fight wants."

What do I want for us? To have a house together. A home together. To rank well and live well. To hide what I am and to lie for decades until my cycle ends peacefully and I die with my secret. To never be myself, ever, not once. To never know what that even means.

"Does this ice cream taste weird to you?" Clay said, breaking my train of thought. "It's...I don't know. It's a little off."

I took a big bite off the top of mine. Clay was right. It was weird. *No, it's worse than weird.* It made my tongue feel strange. I examined the cone as we made our way to Onur's procured table but found nothing amiss. *Maybe the milk they used to churn it has soured?*

Onur patted the seat next to him. "Hey, Nex you remember Fren and Hab from training, right? They want to sit with us. I told them about your rank. They're grabbing ice cream and coming over."

Fren and Hab were friends of Onur's. They'd played athletics and battle strategy together. I didn't know anything else about them really, other than their relationship status. They'd never wanted to talk to me before that moment. I had always been Onur's partner. *Now I'm Onur's partner who is also a Former.*

I had never heard Onur talk so much. There really wasn't time to tell him that I felt unsure about my new role in the Fight. That primary rank was usually something people aimed for, wanted, strived toward. Not something that happened to them on a random morning with no warning. I didn't have time to tell him I didn't think I was good enough, that I wasn't sure I was good enough at anything, much less being a Former.

And what even am I going to do as a Former? Design build-ings? Replicate blueprints? Make computers? Program lighting? I was in over my head. And all Onur could do was brag about it.

Didn't matter much whether I had time to say anything, though. Something strange was happening to my tongue. A numb sensation spread over it, and then it began to throb. Much like the pain I felt in my midsection during my mother's dinner.

"Excuse me," I mumbled, and straight to the bathroom I went. By the time I got into the pristine restroom, I was no longer okay. I didn't know which was worse: violently void-ing the contents of my stomach or the sweat dripping into my eyeballs while I leaned over the toilet. The episode lasted a few minutes too long, my innards gurgling and twisting in pain until I thought my knees would give out.

I slumped to the floor, praying to God that no one came into the bathroom to witness me. The lead in my forearm vibrated, each atom buzzing until I had no choice but to pay attention to it. I put my hand over the area, even though I couldn't visibly see the lead, and I closed my eyes. I knew then, somehow, a truth. *Someone did this. It is not a coinci-dence. I do not have some strange ice cream illness. Someone did this. And they are trying to kill me.*

The lead buzzed hard enough to sting my fingers. My ab-domen clenched, my legs shook, and my skin flashed between ice cold and feverish hot. *Help me.* I tried to inhale, but I realized I could only hold my breath tight, as if the pain were taking over my lungs. It would spread to my heart. I could feel it coursing through me. Hunting me. Hunting Meta.

Help me.

And the metal heard me.

It shot out like water, moving fluidly within my body. I could feel—almost see really, but without looking—the particles of lead find the particles of a bluish plasma. It wrestled the plasma, containing the blue within itself, pulling it out of my blood stream like a sponge absorbing water. The lead squeezed itself tight, ringing the blue plasma out of me. I threw up one last time, and at last, the blue poison left my system.

I stared for a minute before flushing. It was the same. The same blue concoction my mother had placed on the dining table that night. The same blue concoction that must have been introduced to my system on the day of the last Ending, as I was on my way home to that dinner. *And again now, here. But how? And who?*

I remembered Clay mentioning the strange taste of the ice cream and yanked myself upright. *What if she's been poisoned as well?* I splashed and dried my face and hurried out of the bathroom to find Clay and Onur chatting with our training friends. Well, Clay, being much younger and not yet graduated from training,and also simply being Clay, merely sat without speaking, her ice cream half eaten and her stomach lining still seemingly intact.

I scooted back to my seat, trying to look normal, while thanking the lead inside me for saving my life. *Unless I'm delusional and none of this is real. Maybe I just have the flu. Maybe a Feeler should have a look at my psychological state? Or maybe a Wizen could study my anatomical issues?* I always thought Clay would make an excellent Feeler or Wizen. Maybe she could tell what was wrong with me.

But before I could wrap my head around anything else, one of our training friends, Hab—a rowdy boy with dark skin and a usually flashy smile—folded over his ice cream cup and hurled harder than Aardely possible. And he didn't stop. Not for a long time. Not until someone thought to call the Morals. Not the Wizens, with their medical gear and clinical knowledge. That's who they should have called for a sick teenage boy. No, instead they called the Morals, with their thick black woolen hoods and enough weapons to slay a mythical beast.

We all watched as a beefy Moral clubbed Hab on the back of the head, knocking him face down into his sick and his ice cream before he crumpled to the checkered floor.

No one said anything for quite some time as we tried to piece together what was going on. Fren, Hab's partner, softly wept at the table next to the overturned, empty red chair Hab had inhabited moments before. Clay rubbed Fren's back, soothing his grief and what would surely be the End of his love's cycle. Onur got up to ask the owner of the shop what on Aarde had just happened.

And me? I stared at the blue plasma that dripped off the table where Hab had sat and onto the floor near my feet. The lead hissed a warning from its home in my forearm, and I curled my toes inside my shoes.

This was one stream I would not be soaking my soles in.

Ep 6

How The Goddess Of Storm Was Made

Life Tip: If you don't know who you are, guess.

After a night of restless sleep, I woke up to a knock on my bedroom door. My eyes still pressed shut, my face smashed into my pillow, I groaned a slurry, "Please no," to whomever it was. My stomach was still trying to break loose from my body. I needed rest. Maybe a hundred years or so of solid rest.

"Nexus," Priyaa hissed through the door, "what in the City is going on in there? The whole house can hear you."

I almost threw out my neck by sitting up too fast. It took my eyes a moment to calibrate and absorb what was occurring in my bedroom. Something—something dark gray and textured—was zooming about my room, bumping into my lamp and knocking it over, ripping through pages of books, slicing long shallow grooves into my floorboards.

"Oh my living god." A sharp inhale. "What are you *doing*?"

The lead stopped moving at the sound of my voice, hovering in place above my desk.

"Go back to normal," I whisper-shouted at it. "You're going to get me Ended! Are you insane?"

The lead cooed, formed a narrow cylinder, and fell to the desktop with a soft clatter.

I just asked an inanimate object if it was insane. Who's the crazy one here?

Priyaa, her face obviously squished against my door from the sound of her muffled voice, whispered, "Who on Aarde are you talking to?" She gasped. "Is Onur...here?"

"No," I pretty much yelled. "Onur is not here. No one is here. Except me. I'm here. But that's it. Just me."

I leaped from my bed as if I were going to do something dramatic, but really, I just stuck my fingers into my hair and spun in a tight circle, surveying the damage done to my room and imagining Morals clobbering me like they did Hab at the ice cream shop the night before.

Priya jiggled the synthetix door handle to no avail. "Let me in, then, if no one is there, as you so suspiciously insist."

"Can't." I started scooping things into piles, making more of a mess, but hopefully hiding the more obvious signs of metal coming to life and battling my living space.

"You *can't* let me in? Why not?" I heard her stomp her foot. "Why not, Nexus? What is going on?"

"I"—this I yelled, dragging my carpets around to cover the scratches on the floor—"am practicing my forming. It requires the utmost concentration. I cannot be disturbed."

"Since when is concentration so loud?"

"I am also...gas."

"You are gas? That's a new one."

"I *have* gas, Priyaa, if you must know every detail of my life." At least that one was not a lie. My stomach cramps sharpened in response. "And I am working on ridding myself of the issue. So I do not wish for your, or anyone else's, company. I am *very* gassy. Very. And I want to be left alone. Do I have your permission to be gassy in private?"

"You know what'll make you feel better, Nex? More sarcasm. Then maybe you'll fill up with air and explode the whole City. Idiot."

And she left.

I figured it was a good time to lie all the way down on the floor. Just for a minute. I felt terrible from my apparent poisoning—my mother's brand of poison, just for the cherry on top—and I felt even worse for yelling at the metal that saved my life. That, and my body seemed weaker without it. I was aware of how vulnerable I really was. How empty. How alone.

I sighed and looked over at the desk. "I'm sorry I yelled."

No response.

"Please. I'm sorry. Come back."

Nothing.

I got up and pulled myself over to where the lead lay lifeless. I touched it and enjoyed the familiar thrumming, like a low, whirring heartbeat. I got to eye level, just me and the metal. Honestly, I couldn't see anything wrong with the stuff. Not inherently. Not...morally. It could destroy things, yes, but clearly, it could also protect. It was complex. Dynamic. Just like people. *Just like me.*

"Hey, listen. I don't know...well, anything. Truly. I am completely ignorant. An utter fool—well that's not true, I'm actually pretty quick witted. But possibly legitimately crazy." I massaged my temples. "I digress. Back to the point: everyone I've ever known says you are evil. But no one ever says why." I licked my dry lips, wondering if the metal understood anything I said. "So...I guess I'm asking...what do you say? About who you are?"

Still nothing.

I picked up the cylinder of lead and held it in my palm, inches from my nose. "Alright, fine. You know what *I* say? I say let's give each other another try."

With that, the lead split into particle dust and disappeared inside the skin of my palm, gliding through me and settling back into its home in my left forearm.

Another knock on my door, but this time, a much less frazzled Nex answered. "Who is it?"

Priyaa's tone was different. "There is an Ending. We must attend." She paused. "The gas can come too."

My heart lurched despite her joke. "Today?" They were usually scheduled far in advance. Fenders loved their order. Why are they rushing ahead?

"Today." Priyaa cleared her voice. "And our mother wants to see us before we go."

I had not done the wash and had no dress for the Ending, so I pulled on the same cotton frock I wore to the House Of Houses. The hem was just above my knees, the pockets deep and sturdy. I yanked a brush through my catastrophe of silvery curls, willing them to settle down around my shoulders—they did not respect my expectations—and washed my face. I knew I needed a full bath, but if I sat in a tub of water with no one around, I would have let myself cry, and there was no time for crying or baths or selfs.

I tripped on the last stair, quite naturally, might I add, and stumbled into the living area, caught at last by my father's grimace.

"At least you are presentable," he said. He nodded to Priyaa as she floated in behind me, her waist more narrow, her hair more tamed, her dress less wrinkled.

My mother came out of her room with more of a flourish than usual. She held out a syringe of sorts for us to see. Within it sloshed the blue plasma.

"With this invention, brought to us by the Best of the Best—"

"How wonderful," we replied in unison.

"We have discovered a Meta in our midst in record time, with almost no margin for error. It was—and will continue to be—distributed throughout the City via consumption, among other methods of delivery. Step by step, we will set everyone on the right path again. And one day, the Fight will be won."

"This is mesmerizing, Viveka," my father said, nodding. "Truly incredible work. You make our house proud."

My mother ignored the compliment, folding her hands behind her back, the syringe still within her grasp. "I would like to announce, before we participate in the Ending of the Meta, that our very own Nexus will begin work on a prototype for mass aerial distribution of our serum. Our house expects her to excel and to go beyond her capabilities as a Former. Of course, our expectations will be duly respected."

I bowed deeply. "I am honored."

"Yes. You are."

My father gave the slightest nod—a sign that his disdain for me had been downgraded to a strong dislike.

"Now," my mother said, "let us go to Ender Stream and do what must be done. As soon as the Ending is over, Nexus will report to the House Of Forms to begin her work. Soon, rightness will rain down on every Meta in the City, falling from clouds of truth and justice. And Former Nexus of House Aerixon will be the one who wields the storm."

Dahn Of The Dead

Life Tip: Do NOT take fashion advice from the Best Of Us.

"You're always hogging her, Onur, give someone else a turn."

Dahn Vanes slapped her brother's hand away from my shoulder and looped her long, slender arm around my neck, tugging me toward her and away from him. I was short enough for her to smash my face into the side of her boob—what she called a hug. She released me in a hurry, though, sticking out her tongue and pulling strands of silver hair from her mouth.

"You do have such unapologetic hair, Nexus."

I hid my grin and thanked my hair. "Sorry about that, Dahn."

"No matter," she said. "You and I should hang out for this Ending. Onur sees enough of you. It isn't fair."

I blinked at her. "What now?" We weren't friends. Far from it. We couldn't even pass for frenemies most days. I would have labeled us as nemeses had anyone actually ever asked. Which they would not have. That's how obvious it was.

She chuckled. "You're so funny."

"No I'm not."

She tilted her head at me, letting her glossy, scarlet hair cascade over her shoulder, so she could toss it back, the smell of moonflower shampoo smacking me in the face, her waist-long tresses glittering like ruby obsidian in the morning sun.

"Good god, Dahn. A bit much."

She shrugged and sighed. "I know." I rolled my eyes hard enough to see the whole City right from where I stood. Dahn didn't notice though. She was busy paying attention to herself. "How sad that these things must happen, don't you think? And to such a handsome young man, still unpartnered. Why is it always the beautiful ones who suffer? Poor Bab."

I wrinkled my nose as she put her arm over my shoulders again, essentially incorporating me into the pose she was striking. Like I was a prop. "Did you just call him...Bab?"

"Hmmm?" She was eye-flirting with some guy across the Stream.

"You called him Bab. His name is Hab. Hab."

It was her turn to wrinkle her nose, still eyeing the flirt. "That's a weird name, isn't it?"

Well, this is fun. As more and more people drifted in around us, I scanned the crowd for Onur. Or really anyone who might show mercy and save me. Onur was scanning the crowd for me as well, and when our eyes met, about one hundred lengths apart, I mouthed, "Help me," and he mouthed back, "How?" with an adorable shrug. And since I didn't have an answer, that was that.

People pushed in, forcing Dahn and me even closer together. I had no choice but to lean into her. Her body was taut. Not just thin, but muscular. *She must do a sit up every time she thinks about herself.*

"What was that?" Dahn said.

I clamped my mouth shut even though I knew I hadn't said anything. "Nothing."

"Oh." She smiled, clapping her hands, her arm still around me, so my head bobbled around like a buoy at sea. "We're starting! I just love these. The energy is electric. Plus, everyone is always in attendance, so it's the best place to network. Those ranks don't get themselves, you know."

She loves these? People...love these?

I stuffed my hands into my pockets, and my metal swirled in my arm. *You won't like this,* I thought, hoping it could hear me somehow. *But please don't do anything about it. You'll get us Ended.* It would be a short walk to the platform from where we stood on Ender Stream. I didn't have to use my metal to be killed; I didn't have to do anything at all. Hab, after all, was only guilty of eating ice cream. To be on the wrong side of the Fight, I only had to be me. To be Meta.

The hum began, swelling up and over our heads, crashing into solid silence like an ocean surge into a cliffside. As a Moral carried him out from the House Of Certainty and onto the platform, I wondered if Hab could hear our voices, the voices of people who, just the day before, would have called him by name and told him he was a blessing to his house.

"There he is, poor soul," Dahn cooed. "I mean...if he even has a soul. Do Meta have souls? Or are they born without those?"

Guilt writhed in my chest for not paying him any attention at the ice cream shop. Someone who was just like me, hiding in plain sight right across from me. Feeling afraid, probably. Feeling alone. And now, feeling his shameful End inches from his throat. He even looked like a different person on that platform. His once smooth, brown face was puffy and bruised. It even seemed like he was missing an eye. My emotions swirled—despair that his jaw was obviously too swollen for him to speak out and relief that he appeared barely conscious for what was transpiring.

The Best Of Us swooped onto the platform, wearing not a suit this time, but a sort of white gown with billowy sleeves. His neck adorned with pearls, he twirled, and his white hair fanned into the air. To end the move, he struck a pose that could have rivaled Dahn's. I sensed the spirits of the people lifting at the sight of him. He truly was the Best Of Us, trained to be the face of common hope and superficial guidance.

He yelled a lot about what we were preparing to do to Hab and why, the usual. Meta were the enemy, and we had to stop them from destroying us all. And then Dahn gripped my upper left forearm with such force that I was sure she would snap my radial bone in half. I wanted to yell that she should let me go—especially since my metal was trying to remain calm inside me—but raising my voice right then would have been considered dissent. And dissent warranted an overnight stay at the House Of Certainty for questioning.

I peeked at Dahn, and her face betrayed no emotion. She was as blank as she was beautiful, her high cheekbones catching the morning light, her dark eyes unwavering as she beheld the scene before us all.

But she did not release my arm. *She knows*, I thought. *She knew in the alley when she punctured me with the blue serum and she knows now.* My heart pounded, no doubt rushing metalless blood throughout my body. But as Dahn gripped me, the metal in me purred, scooting closer to where her fingers indented my skin.

I turned back to the platform, to the synthetix blade glinting in the sun and the Moral having to lift Hab's already lowered head, since he had clearly faded to the blackness. I did not flinch—I did not move—as Dahn slid her hand down my arm, stopping once her palm was pressed to mine, our fingers interlaced. She squeezed, and so I squeezed.

It made me wonder...in all the City...how many were secretly holding hands to make it through.

Ep 8

Say Hello To The Storm

Life Tip: Be polite to talking sidewalks.

I am really moving up in the City. That's what I should have been thinking when Onur picked me up in his father's transport, with its sleek synthetix sides and darkened windows. Once I got into the passenger seat, he tapped on the console and set coordinates for the House Of Forms.

We said very little for the first part of the drive. Onur tapped on the steering wheel as the transport directed itself to our destination. I twisted threads from the seams of my pockets. Every once in a while, I pulled a bit of lead through to my fingertips and swirled it, allowing the soft, gritty texture to distract me. Onur wouldn't notice if I kept my hands hidden. It calmed me like nothing else.

"I feel like you're mad at me," Onur blurted out. A hint of pink spread up his neck. He didn't usually pick fights, if that was what we were doing. Fighting.

"I'm not mad at you. Why would you think that?"

"Well, you didn't stand with me at the Ending, for one. And Hab...." His words cut short.

I hadn't put it together. Hab wasn't just some guy I went to training with who I ignored at an ice cream shop. Hab was Onur's friend. And I let Dahn use me when Onur needed me. I inhaled, wallowing in my ignorance.

"I should have been more sensitive, Onur. I'm so sorry."

He exhaled. "It's okay, Nex. I forgive you, of course."

"There's something else though?"

He shook his head. "No, now I feel silly bringing it up."

I chuckled. "Tell me anyway." And I held out my hand for him to grab onto.

He took it, rubbing his thumb across my knuckle and leaning his head back, closing his eyes while he spoke. I realized he looked tired. Dark circles under his eyes, his skin even paler than usual. I probably hadn't *actually* looked at my love in days.

"I didn't know how to tell you...but...I ranked."

I sat up straighter. "You did? Wait, what? How? When?" I kissed his hand, still clutched in mine. "Onur, you should have told me right away. This is amazing! Tell me everything."

A shadow of a smile. "You remember my father's rank lowered? From Fender Above down to Second Fender? Well, I was interviewed...about a week ago. And"—he cleared his throat, and when it didn't work, cleared it again—"and I will be filling his vacancy."

I hoped he didn't feel how cold my hand went in his. "I don't think I understand. How can that be? A son ranking higher than his own father? Can that even happen?"

"Apparently it can, in certain circumstances. I don't know if you noticed"—and he flashed me his blazing smile, though it did not reach his eyes—"but I am rather brilliant."

"Of course you are, Onur. And I'm happy for you. But what will happen to Richter?" The man was as close to an uncle as I had. He never had much to say, and where most found that disinteresting, I found it delightful.

"My guess is that he will continue to serve as a Second Fender. And I can better look out for him from my position as Fender Above. And look out for you, as well. You know...if I am so lucky as to be granted permission to have you one day." His straight blond hair fell into his eyes when he sat up. "I would have said something sooner, but I didn't want to take your spotlight."

I nodded, my mind still reeling. All in the span of a week, I had been given my primary rank with no warning, an Ending was called with no planning, and Onur had been given his father's role in the Fight with no precedent.

"We're here," Onur said, his voice cutting my thoughts to pieces. He leaned in and put his lips on mine like always. Slowly at first. But then with more force, more than he had ever used before. He went until I felt like my lips might swell. I pulled away, if only to see his eyes, to find some insight into what he was thinking, feeling. But they were the same eyes as always, blue and steady. He wiped just beneath my bottom lip and tried to smooth a stray curl of mine. It sprung back up out of place.

"You'll do great," he said.

I fumbled for the door handle, flustered by whatever kind of kiss I had just received, and stepped out of the transport. It wasn't until then that I realized all of my lead was in a ball in my fist and that I had been squeezing it fiercely enough to bruise my palm.

Okay. Focus, Nex. I stood alone outside a gleaming tower of modern architecture. The building stretched higher than any I'd ever seen, twisting around itself in a looming spiral of shimmering synthetix. I took a step toward it, and the pavement beneath my feet illuminated with a buzz, sending my startled metal flying back into my arm.

"State your name and purpose," the pavement square said to me in a formal, computerized voice.

"Uh...."

"There is no record of an 'Uh' in the Former database."

I shook my head. "No no. I mean, my name is Nexus Aerixon. And my purpose is...."

Oh god in Himinn, what is my purpose? What am I doing here? I couldn't figure out what to say, so I just stood there, the wind flapping my skirt and sending my hair careening over my face in a consistent yet spiteful manner.

"Proceed, Former Aerixon," said the ground.

"Oh. Right. Thank you, I suppose." And yes, I bowed to the pavement. But no one knew that except me. And maybe the pavement.

I entered the building through a door that swirled when I pulled the handle. The door itself was divided into planks that each spun on an axis. It resembled a byrd unfurling its wings. Or a drakon. I was enraptured by the engineering of the door. I pushed and pulled it for a good thirty seconds before the man waiting on me said my name loud enough for me to hear him.

I bowed. "Forgive me."

The man, wiry and small, wore Former attire: a white coat, buttoned to the throat, that reached down to the tops of black synthetix shoes, and white leather gloves, his long black hair back in a sensible braid.

"You are late," he said.

"It was unintentional. I humbly apologize."

"Are you aware of your purpose here, Former Aerixon? My intel informs me you did not state it at the door."

"I am...vaguely aware. More detail would be greatly appreciated."

"I see." He folded his arms behind his back, much like a Fender would, only he had his right hand hold his left elbow, the left hand hanging loosely. "Detail is very important to Formers. A Fender says only what they want you to know. A Former says everything, whether you want to know it or not. Therefore, I will brief you as one Former would another. Do you understand?"

I nodded.

"Verbal responses make for clearer communication."

"Yes, I understand."

The man looked me so keenly in the eye that it made me nervous, as if he were invading my privacy by conversing so intently. "Though you are a Former and hardly even an initiate, you will work on technology usually reserved for Formers Above or higher. Our directive from the Fenders is that you would begin work on an aerial device of great capacity, one with the purpose of releasing a powerful Metatoxin over the entire City. You will not work with a team, as most Formers do, but will accomplish this task alone, with only my occasional oversight. The entirety of your work is to remain confidential. This includes everyone except for me, your direct superior. Do you understand?"

"Yes, I mean...that was as clear as you can be, I think."

"You should request more clarity if you do not understand," he explained. "I was referring to the confidentiality requirements. No one is to hear of your task. Not any detail. Not anyone. Not Fender, nor Feeler, nor Best Of Us. No one."

Not Onur. Not Priyaa. Not Clay. Not my—

"What if my mother, Fender Master Viveka Aerixon, inquires?"

I was used to disdain from the Fenders to whom I frequently spoke. But this Former merely answered, no disdain included. "Your mother may not hear of this. Nor your father. No one."

"Then I understand." I decided to try my luck and actually ask something. I tried not to wince for his reaction, but to remain collected. "I do have a question, though."

"Withholding a pertinent question is frowned upon in the House Of Forms. Ask if you believe it pertinent."

"Alright. I would like to know why I am the one assigned to this...device. I've never formed anything before, and my grades were not high in training. So why me?"

"I do not have the answer. The House Of Houses sent you here. We will have to see why, won't we? I will show you to your station." But before he led the way he paused, glancing at the magnificent door. "My guess, if I was to allow myself one, would be that you are curious enough to question and reckless enough to try. That would make you an excellent Former indeed. But we will see. All theories must first be proven."

Along the corridors were laboratory rooms. In them, Formers, young and old, hunched over blueprints, sketching atop them, or scribbled on mirrored walls. Some were enthralled in heated debates. Others wore mufflers on their ears to focus on what looked like advanced machinery, sparks flying as they concentrated. Though the building itself did not buzz and swoosh like the House Of Houses, the Formers seemed invigorated by their work.

"It looks...fun," I said as I walked past them all.

"Forming is not as cold and joyless as others may think. We do not simply build structures; we innovate. It is a passion for most Formers. Perhaps it will be a passion for you as well."

My station was at the very end of the longest corridor, with no other rooms nearby. The ceiling light beamed on, just like the pavement came to life when I stepped on it outside. As soon as I could see clearly, I froze in place. In the center of the room was a machine larger than a transport. Larger than my entire bedroom. It had rotors atop it, and circuitry scrawled along its synthetix exterior. Clearly unfinished, portions of it were splayed open, wires twisting to the sky much like my curly hair.

"It is called Stur. And it will change the world. But first, it must be made whole. Not a simple task." The Former bowed to me. "I will leave you to your initial findings and check back in a few hours. The House helper may assist you with locating tools. Simply ask for what you need. She is called Formula. And the last bit of information for you will be my name. You may call me, Drenge. No need for my title, as it only slows communication. Simply Drenge will do. Do you understand?" He wiggled his thin mustache when he said it. I had not noticed it before right then. It made me strangely happy.

"I understand, Drenge. You can call me Nexus."

He nodded, stepping away to grab a Former coat from a hook near the door. He held it out for me, and I slipped my arms into it, surprised at the pride that swelled in my chest and the smile that played at the corners of my mouth.

"There," he said. "For the Fight."

I forgot, for just a second, that I was at the House Of Forms to design my own demise. The smile dripped off my face like melted ice cream from a cone on a hot Ending Day. I bowed to my new master.

"For the Fight."

Ep 9

Blind Bleeding The Blind

Life Tip: Nothing good ever comes in a vat.

"Formula, what is the most efficient way to extinguish an electrical fyre?" I had to scream so she could hear me over the sparks shooting in my face. After so many weeks of working in the House Of Forms, one would have thought Formula could decipher my voice. But no.

I balanced on the top of Stur, my Former-issued boots ingeniously equipped with gripping soles that proved rather useful for not sliding off the machine's slick surface and cracking my head open.

Formula's humanoid voice was hardly loud enough as she mumbled a response. The flaymes got sassy and kicked it up a notch, threatening to light the hem of my lab coat.

"Formula!" I used my best grown up voice, "Louder! Much louder!"

Her tone moved from matter-of-fact to know-it-all. "To extinguish an electrical fyre, first determine if the—" *Great. Even the tech is sassy today.*

"Stand back." Drenge, appearing out of nowhere, spoke to Formula on my behalf. "Formula, apply electrical fyre protocol to lab coordinate 36G."

"Right away," Formula responded, and an illuminated ceiling panel emitted a blast of icy air right over the baby bonfyre I'd started.

I flopped onto Stur's exterior with an exhale and stared at the ceiling, my hair now decently damp from being so close to the ice blast. "This is impossible, Drenge. Maybe if I had more training. Maybe if I weren't working on it alone—"

"Nothing is impossible. Statistically speaking. And no, you do not require additional training, Nexus. Trust me, you do not." Drenge examined my destruction, squatting near Stur and lowering his spectacles, a new addition to his wardrobe. "What caused the misfyre?"

"Hand me my notes." Once he obliged, I flipped through the pages of scribbles, remembering why I failed penmanship in training. "Misfyre on ignition eleven. No matter what I do. Every time."

My master circled the monster I was making, slapping my dangling foot out of the way to poke at the open panel on the machine's side. Drenge's mustache wiggled, maybe my favorite part of working at the House Of Forms. The Dance of the Stache.

"You figured out the obstacle avoidance sensors?" he said, surprised.

"Yes, but, if I can't stop the engine from misfiring, none of that matters. It won't need to avoid obstacles if it can't fly."

Always strangely optimistic, though starkly stoic, Drenge sighed, "I miss metal."

I almost fell off my throne. Scratch that. I sort of did fall, sliding off Stur and landing on my feet with grace I didn't know I could summon.

He held up a hand to me, no doubt to restrain my already runaway thoughts. "Do not misunderstand me, Nexus. I am not a sympathizer with the Meta breed. I only reminisce of a time when we had an abundance of metal with which to build. It is the most magnificent electrical conductor, metal. Sturdy and malleable. Not to mention beautiful. A bit of mercury must slip into our electronics from time to time. Trace amounts only. But this, of course, is a City secret."

"But isn't that dangerous?" A genuine question.

"Any metal in the City is present in far too small quantities for Meta to use. Most cannot even detect it. So, while it is not preferred, it is not dangerous."

I had never heard anyone speak about metal outside the iron in blood, much less romanticize it. I wanted to know more, but I was too afraid to ask. Then Drenge's words rattled into my brain. *If a question is pertinent, ask.* I was often scolded by my master for not speaking up when I should.

"Which metal did you use, Drenge? I mean, you mentioned mercury, but there is more than one type, yes? Which do you miss?"

"Good question. Yes, there are as many types of metal as there are people. Each with its own property, it's own purpose."

It's own personality, too.

He continued. "And alloys. Combinations of metals. Those are made by humans for special uses. They are more effective than synthetix. In fact, if you were forming with metal, you would have accomplished such a task as building Stur during your training. But with synthetix, the electrical conduction is tricky. The Metatoxin destabilizes the synthetix as well. It's all a mess without metal. And so only our best will work on Stur."

"Why did we stop using metal? When did it become dangerous?" *When did it become immoral?*

Drenge thought about this. Then slowly—carefully—he answered. "There are some who wield it differently than we could ever dream. They became a threat to us. And so we had no choice but to innovate a world around the absence of metal." He looked back at me. "Do you understand?"

No. "Yes, I understand." *No, no. I do not understand. I understand nothing. A threat how? What did the Meta do? And why is it wrong?* I had never seen a Meta actually do anything dangerous. I had never seen one do anything at all besides be a person. *How can it be so corrupt to be oneself?*

"I am petitioning for you to be the one to fly Stur on the day it launches. Our other departments are re-engineering the serum to be effective topically, via skin contact, so Stur will be able to drop the Metatoxin while airborne. It will take some time to adjust the serum. I am sure you will be finished with Stur's mechanical form before they are finished with the chemical one." He pushed his glasses back up the bridge of his nose. "You truly are a wonder, Nexus, though you may not think so quite yet. I must admit, I had my doubts when the House Of Houses arranged for you to work on this project. But you are gifted. You see things others cannot."

"That's one way of saying it."

"I know it makes life difficult. Seeing things differently. But it makes innovation possible. The truly brilliant are never truly blissful. Do you understand?"

"I do." I left my superior and ate a meal alone before meeting Onur on the curb outside the House Of Forms. He had not been his usual self since serving as a Fender Above. He was often late to get me even though he drove his own transport. Not only was his timing off, but he clenched his jaw tighter. He spoke less. He scowled more. And he certainly did not like that I could share nothing about my work.

"I only want to know how long until it's finished," he would say, smacking the steering wheel. But I could give him no answer.

When he dropped me off in the mornings, he kissed me like he might not stop. When he picked me up in the evenings, he hardly looked at me.

But the more I worked, the more I learned, and the less I leaned on Onur's demeanor for reassurance. It was like...my mind woke up. Shapes of machinery forms lifted themselves from the blueprints and rearranged themselves in my head. I could see Stur's rotors spinning in my imagination. I could smell the acidic burn of the motor's heat before I'd even assembled it. I could work for hours without stopping for a break. I could work for days without speaking to another person. Formula answered most of my questions, and Drenge knew not to bother me when I focused for long stretches. I had made it further than any Former who attempted to complete Stur, and I was doing it faster than anyone anticipated.

On day sixty seven of forming Stur, Drenge entered my lab and disabled Formula, something he had never done before.

"You are needed elsewhere today," he said, his voice solemn, though I detected a hint of excitement.

"Oh? Then why have you turned Formula off in my lab? I may need her."

"I turned Formula off in the entire building. This is an urgent matter, for your deepest discretion. Not even Formula can follow us where we are going. Do you understand, Nexus?"

"Of course."

"I will have to blindfold you. Do I have your consent?"

I paused before I spoke. "Yes."

So he wrapped my eyes with a cotton cloth and put my hand on his arm. My metal swirled within me, asking if I needed help to see. I comforted it, and it quieted back down into my arm. A few minutes and many steps and turns later, Drenge removed my blindfold.

The room was dimly lit, and a few Formers stood wearing goggles and frowns. A table, a tray with assorted tools. Normal scene for the House Of Forms. *So why the secrecy? Why the drama?*

"This is her? I thought you said she was a genius." The Former who spoke looked at me like he was a Fender and I was...well, me. "She is a child."

Drenge snorted. "She is more than that. Now tell her the problem. We have other work to do."

The snotty Former rolled his eyes behind his eyewear. "Other work? You mean the drone that will never fly? That hardly qualifies as work. This, on the other hand, is actually important. Too important for a primary rank to fiddle with."

When I spoke, my voice was clearer than I'd ever heard it. "How about you put the bickering aside and tell me why you dragged me down here?"

Drenge glanced at me, visibly surprised I'd said something. I was also surprised. *Where did that come from?*

The Former sneered. "Well at least she's rude. That's some sort of nuance, I suppose." He tapped a large vat of water in front of him, maybe two feet tall, that I had not noticed until right then.

"This is the problem. It is de-structuring at a faster rate than normal. And we cannot tell why, nor can we halt the process."

I stared at the water, then at Drenge. "I have no knowledge of chemistry. Why am I here?"

"You know more than you think," he replied, unshaken by my self-doubt. "Would you like samples to be drawn?"

"Of this water in particular? What is it used for? Is it unique?"

Drenge shook his head. "No, Nexus. Not water. This is where we store Meta blood."

I swallowed and stared. Stared and swallowed. Finally, I pointed my gloved finger at the vat. "What?" That was all I could come up with.

"So she *is* an idiot," the other Former scoffed.

"Shut up, Pharmon," Drenge growled.

Yeah, shut up, Pharmon.

Drenge directed his words to me. "It is Meta blood: harvested, stabilized, stored, and then manipulated for various uses. One of which is for the making of synthetix. The blood is mildly conductive and so extremely useful to us since we have no metal. None of our technology works without synthetix, as you must have gathered. De-structuralization of this blood puts the whole City at risk. Do you understand?"

"Yes." I wanted to ask a million questions, and also to cry, but I had to be careful. *Careful, Nex. Think first.*

I began by asking unnecessary questions that hopefully appeared pertinent. I already knew what to do with the blood. That part was easy. The answer clicked in place in my head the moment I heard the problem. The questions I needed to ask were to feed a different curiosity. One that could save my life. "Where does the blood come from?"

"Not pertinent," the Former grumbled.

"It is pertinent," I argued. "I need to know how it was stored and how long it traveled to get here. When it was harvested as well."

He sighed. "About twenty lengths from here. Stored at negative ten. Harvested from living participants, though perhaps while under duress."

Living participants. I'd thought for a second that the blood came from Ender Stream, collected underground somehow. But that could not be. Everyone died on that platform. Their blood was spilled, not harvested.

The House Of Certainty? Is that where the Fight harvests its Meta blood? Stored and transported here in something that regulates temperature?

"Have you checked the structural form of the blood cells?" I asked, realizing I was thinking and not talking.

"We are not stupid," said the Former. "Of course we checked. That is how we know there is a problem."

"How long were the hosts without metal interaction? Were they deprived of metal while you harvested?"

"Metal is *illegal* in high quantities."

"Illegal?" I lifted my chin in challenge. "Are we Fenders discussing policy or Formers discussing form?"

The Former went bright red, obvious even in the dim room. "Go on," he conceded.

"Have we considered that Meta do not exclusively manipulate metal, but that they might actually require it to survive? That eventually their blood de-structures if they do not acquire it? Why else would someone risk their life to wield metal? Unless they felt they had no choice."

"The theory is plausible."

"So test it. Add metal to this blood. See if the cells restructure and stabilize."

The Former lifted his empty hands. "Forgive me. I didn't bring any metal with me," he joked, eliciting chuckles from his henchmen.

"Incorrect," I said, my voice cool. I walked over to him, lifting the synthetix scalpel lying in a tray beside his table. I nicked his hand in one fluid move, before I really thought about what I was doing. His red blood squirted from his middle finger, but I pulled his arm over to the vat and let it drip into the Meta blood. "You bring your metal with you everywhere you go, Former."

And with that, I turned my back on the vat of human remains. "Will you blindfold me, Drenge? I'd like to get back to work. No need for me to stay while the blood is tested. Any idiot could do that."

Slit Throat Saga

As he led me back to my lab, I could hear Drenge chortling. I should have also been tickled to have shown that Former what was what. But I had something else to consume my thoughts: the scalpel I'd kept, jangling in my coat pocket, its narrow synthetix blade lined in a metal that called itself Titanium. I wondered if I'd lost my mind.

Or maybe I was finding it.

Ep 10

Ever Met A Feeler?

Life Tip: Remember to use the bathroom *before* the forced interrogation begins.

I leaned against Clay's door frame, still in my Former boots—it had been a long day with Stur. Clay was reading a book, but she glanced up when she saw me. The lantern light flickered across her almond-shaped face.

"Is that an actual lantern?" I asked, quite literally a mhoth to the flayme.

She smiled. "Do you want to touch it?"

No hesitation, I flopped down on her bed and touched the cool synthetix frame that held the dripping candle. "Where did you get it?"

"Refurbished from a distant era," she said. "It's actually really old. Maybe Negative Eighties, even. I had to do so much extra service to get it."

"Negative Eighties? So the Best Of The Best wasn't even born yet?"

Everyone knew we began counting with Year One when the current Best Of The Best took over the Fight. Everyone also knew that the mention of his name required a response of, "How wonderful." But Clay did not offer such a response. I definitely did not complain. It was a tiresome practice.

"No, he was not yet born," she said, setting her book down and taking in the fyre's light with a thoughtful gaze. "It feels as though it's from a different time. Fyre, I mean. Not the lantern. A time before...before this."

I did not often think of how things used to be before my time. I was too busy trying to plan a future that didn't include my head flopping forward on Ender Stream.

"Did you come all the way to my house to admire my lantern with me?" Clay asked. "There must be something else?"

Her wide blue eyes sparkled at me. Sometimes I wondered if she were hiding a whole Aarde in there. *How can a twelve-year-old be so wise?*

"I was looking for Onur, actually. I thought maybe you'd seen him. Have you?"

She shook her head, soft brown hair swishing softly around her cheeks. "He has been gone most evenings. At the House Of Houses. Did he not tell you he would be unavailable?"

I sighed. "No. We have been so busy. And he's been...." I let my voice trail off. No need to criticize Clay's brother right in front of her.

"He has been different," she finished for me. "So have you, Nex."

I tried not to snap off the piece of her lantern I was playing with. "Me? Different?" Could she tell that I kept my lead humming in my left arm? Could she tell that my titanium liked to sleep nestled under my ribs?

"You seem happier," she explained. "More confident, albeit more preoccupied. You must like your work? Or perhaps"—she broke eye contact—"you've met someone new?"

A short laugh exploded from within me. "Genuinely no, Clay. I have no time to meet anyone. And who would go out of their way to talk to me besides Onur?"

She shrugged. "You never know. Strange things happen." She snuggled against her pillows. "I am very glad that you enjoy forming, Nex. I always thought you were beyond brilliant."

Of all the people to say what they thought of me, including those who pretended they thought I was talented when truly they thought I was dense, I believed Clay. She was always brimming with life and truthfulness. Though it was strange to see her bundled in her blanket before sunset.

"Are you unwell, Clay? Why are you in bed so early?"

She reached for her book. "In a reading mood, is all."

A loud conversation from outside the room broke into our discussion along with the stomping of boots and the slamming of doors. Clay sighed. "Onur is home." And when I looked puzzled, she added, "He and Dahn do not get along these days."

Strange. The Vanes house had served as a haven for me since I was a child. Edwidge was less intense than my mother, and Richter often seemed to manage a good mood. Uneventful. That's how I would have described the Vanes' home. Even with Dahn's dramatics, it all seemed so harmonious.

But I sensed discord. More stomping down the hall, and then Clay's door flew open. "Clay, you need to"—Onur froze, his blonde eyebrows raised as he spotted me. "Oh. Nexus. I did not know you would be here."

I stood up, leaving the lantern and my chat with Clay behind. "I was looking for you, actually."

"Well, I suppose this is just as well. I would have had to inform you anyway since you are rarely paying attention. You are to report to the House Of Certainty."

I hoped my overabundance of freckles and red skin hid the drainage of blood from my face, though I was not even sure if Meta could go pale. "Me? The House Of Certainty?"

"Everyone. With immediacy."

"Everyone? Everyone in the City?"

Onur grimaced. "You ask too many questions. You are beginning to sound like a Former."

"I am a Former."

"So you are." He stood straighter than he used to, still in his Fender outfit, the black fabric pulled in unbending lines across his chest. "Let's not keep the House Of Certainty waiting. They have much work to do." He glanced at his sister. "Are you well enough to come, Clay? I can request an extension until you are stronger."

Clay removed her blankets and scooted out of bed. "I will come now," she said. "I don't want to go alone later."

With that, Onur about-faced and left the room. I realized then that we had not even greeted each other. No kiss on the temple. No intrigue into how our days had gone. Just Onur's boots thudding on their wooden floor and Dahn complaining about not having enough time to properly straighten her hair.

I walked elbow to elbow with Clay down the street. Dahn was busy primping under the streetlights as they buzzed on—our moment at Hab's Ending as buried as his corpse—

and Onur was far ahead of us, instructing neighbors as they joined us on the way.

"What do you think is happening?" Clay asked. "An Ending? Perhaps someone ingested something telling?"

"No, I don't think so." I did not tell her that, at that point, I could detect the Metatoxin in most foods. It had a distinct smell and taste. After one encounter, I could identify it five lengths away. "Onur would have just said if it were an Ending. That would have been normal enough. This is something else."

Clay's brow creased. It was strange to see a frown on her pleasant face. "It cannot be good."

"I'm sure it will be alright," I said, hoping I wasn't lying to the girl.

The titanium within me gathered closer to my heart, steadying the beating on my behalf, echoing my words back to me. *It will be alright.* The closer we got to our destination, the less I believed it.

I tried to find my sister among the crowds, everyone in line to enter the House Of Certainty. Priyaa would not want to go in alone, and I doubted our parents would be careful to consider her nerves. But I could not find her, and leaving the Vanes' to search for her would only ensure that I was alone as well. I wished that Onur would make his way to me like he used to. He could have put an arm over my shoulders and kept me safe. Made sure I wasn't tossed back and forth in the sea of people. But he had already entered the House.

Richter and Edwidge remained with us. Edwidge worked as a Wizen and, though scholarly knowledge was her strength, she probably knew as much as I did about what was happening since Fenders did not like to share information. I hoped Richter, a Fender like his son, though of lower rank, might have had an idea of what to expect. But his face was pinched, and he seemed to be holding his breath, as much blindsided as the rest of us.

I had only been inside the House Of Certainty a couple times. It was no one's favorite place to be and certainly not mine. Not only because of the stony, cold architecture, but because Feelers were irreparably creepy.

Greeters met us at the House doors, Feelers wearing soft fleece scarfs and woolen socks. Everything about their appearance was gentle and agreeable. Each one smiled, bowing as we entered. "You are well come," they said, voices like iced sap tea on a warm afternoon. "You are so, so well come."

I bowed in response, pretending their smiles didn't raise the hairs on the back of my neck.

"They're so...*nice*," Clay whispered, her eyes wider than usual, her pupils dilated.

"Is this your first time in the House Of Certainty?" I asked her.

"Is it so obvious?"

I rubbed her arm to comfort her. She was cold as snow on the longest day of wynter.

"They are much smarter than they appear," I warned her. "But they won't want to harm you. They only want to read you."

She nodded, leaning into me as we were jostled forward in line past the greeters. "I am learning about them in training. They will read my feelings. It doesn't hurt. But it can be a strange experience."

"Exactly. In fact, they have already begun." The lightest tickle along the base of my spine and around to my forehead. The feeling of being watched. Being noticed. Being determined. "You can feel it if you concentrate, but it is usually best if you try not to feel them feeling."

I did not take my own advice, of course. I had not survived this long with my secret intact by ignoring perilous situations. The opposite was required. I needed to gather as much information as I could. I knew exactly what it felt like to be read, to be analyzed. For my feelings to be interpreted and sorted and deemed harmless. How else would I have known what pages of myself to turn to?

I realized then, with her leaning against me that Clay was only breathing in, not out. Her cheeks and neck were covered in fine perspiration. "Breathe, Clay."

Her blue eyes filled with tears. "I'm afraid. I do not like this at all."

Up ahead of us, there were more Feelers, sorting us into new lines. It seemed purposefully randomized. It meant Clay and I would be separated. She must have noticed too, because she gripped my hand in hers.

"Nex," she said, her voice breaking. "Please don't leave me. I'm afraid."

I breathed loudly next to her, so she could hear me and perhaps emulate the rhythmic sound. I wished I could have sent titanium to her, so it could have encircled her heart and steadied her as it did for me. I wished I could have given her lead, to increase her vitality. But I could only give her well wishes and mediocre last minute advice.

"Listen, Clay. All will be well. Don't try to think thoughts that are too happy. You will be pulled aside for further reading. No one is ever happy here. They will know you are lying. And do not become irrationally anxious. It's suspicious as well. Just be yourself, and you'll be more than fine. I'll do the same, and I'll wait for you on the other side. When we are finished here, we can go back to your room and admire your lantern together. Which year was it made again?"

She exhaled. "Negative Eighties. Maybe Nineties."

She would be a Wizen, just like her mother. Her love for history was charmingly clear. "Yes. That's right. Now think of your lantern, and we'll be back together before you even miss me." *And I will see you more often*, I promised her in my heart. *I will not be so busy. I will not be so distant. I will be better.*

The Feelers sent me to the left and Clay to the right.

That was the last time I saw my friend alive.

Ep 11

From Navel To Throat

Life Tip: Say no to drugs, kids.

I was directed to a small white table with a chair on each side. A Feeler—a woman with dark, brown skin and plump lips, her hair in beautiful, twisting braids—sat in the chair opposite me. She smiled, her teeth so white they hurt my eyes.

"Hello there, friend. I bet you're feeling anxious," she said. "And probably a bit parched." She placed a glass of water on the table and slid it toward me. "So sorry about all this."

The drink in the glass was sickly scented with Metatoxin, though no longer blue in color. *She is going to watch me drink it. Help me*, I thought, and my metal stretched itself, preparing for what I was about to do. I lifted the glass to my lips and downed the concoction, preparing for the sharp pain to hit my stomach so that I could properly resist doubling over. I only hoped my stomach would not gurgle too loudly as my metal met the serum head on, curling around each molecule in an effort to neutralize the invader.

The Feeler studied me: my facial expression, posture, tone, the way I smoothed my dress over my knees. Looking for deception. Looking for signs of pain or discomfort. Looking for Meta.

I'm a better liar than you are, Feeler.

"Glory to the Best Of The Best, we have something new to try tonight," the Feeler cooed after observing me give my daintiest belch.

"How wonderful," I responded. "What is it?"

"It's a lovely little bit of technology, made from a special solution. Everyone in the City will get one, and it will remain with you all your days. A gift from the City to its people. For the Fight."

"For the Fight."

Stay with me? What on Aarde is this Feeler talking about? She did not stop smiling, not once. Not while she pulled out a small device with a long pointed tip. Not when she asked for my arm. Not when she held me still with her soft, perfectly moisturized hands.

"There will be an initial shock, a bit of discomfort. But it will fade in time. Do not worry. If the pain becomes unbearable, let The House Of Certainty know, and we will adjust it for you."

Adjust it? She means by stringing me up on the platform pole.

"Forgive me, but how does it work exactly? I am curious." I knew better than to think I could buy myself time. I was buying information.

She chuckled. "A Former. I can tell by the boots." The woman leaned in closer and winked. "And the questions." She rubbed her thumb against the exposed skin of my arm, the soft flesh of my inner elbow. Feeling for my pulse no doubt. To see if it quickened. "This device was developed by Formers of course. Such advanced technology. We are so thankful to your House."

I nodded, eyeing the device. "May I look if I promise not to touch?" I asked as politely as I could.

"I don't see why not," she smarmed. Feelers liked to say 'yes' whenever possible. Those they questioned put their guard down when they got their way. A tactic of theirs that I would use to my advantage.

She held out the device, and I peered as closely as I could without touching my nose to it. The forms came to life in my mind. I could twist and turn the pieces like a puzzle. A needle, a sealer, a liquid chamber, a trigger, and a stabilizer. *This is not a medical device. This is a weapon.*

"Beautiful design," I said with as much admiration as I could muster. That wasn't all a lie. I did admire the mechanics. And I was beginning to understand how the Fight organized itself. This gun was Fender-ordered, Feeler-inspired, and Former-designed. A synchronized extermination effort. Just like Stur. "I see that it does not merely eject a liquid. The shaft is too broad for that."

"Correct, Former. You are quite skilled, I see. We will do the honor of injecting you with something a bit more permanent than liquid. For your protection."

Right then, a scream split open the mumbling of voices in the large hall. Followed by another and another. Down a few tables, I saw a young girl, maybe ten years old, buckle to the floor, rolling herself up into a ball. Well...every part of herself except her arm, which she was insistent on detaching from her body. Morals stepped in and scooped her up. She must have been very light, very easy to carry. They did not struggle to take her away. The Feeler who had been reading her simply picked up her chair and said something silly like, "These things happen."

I turned back to my Feeler amidst the screams of others receiving whatever treatment I was about to get. "Thank you," I said. "For your protection."

She pressed the needle to my arm and pulled the trigger. A very narrow cylinder, much like a thin capsule, embedded into my left forearm. And my lead screamed. Not in a way that the Feeler could hear, but in a way that broke my heart.

My titanium rushed to help it, but it too began to cry out. I focused on one thing to keep from tearing my arm off. I imagined the sound of my cloth shoes being dragged across the wooden platform. The hum of my people wishing for my End. *Do not. Do not show them who you are. Hide. Hide. Hide it, Nexus. They will kill you. Hide.*

The Feeler seemed to be enjoying the part where she watched me try not to explode. I was sure it was one of the most exciting things she'd ever done in the House Of Certainty. She would probably be paid with praise if she caught one of us. But it would not be me. *Not that easily.*

After a few moments, she sighed a pleased sigh, tinted with disappointment. "Please enjoy the rest of your night, Former. The House Of Certainty is so happy to be of service to you."

She motioned toward the back of the building, and I commanded my legs to walk. *One, two, one, two. Look normal. For the love of god themself, if you cannot be normal, you must look normal, Nex.*

I did not turn my head to search for anyone once I exited the building. The warm, night air threatened to choke me as I marched through the streets, normalizing. I was not even sure if I was headed home. Just away. Away from the House Of Certainty and the Feeler's feeling and the weapon that had probably been created down the hall from where I was building Stur. Away from the truth that I was designing something more terrifying, more dreadful than what I was forced to endure at the hands of the smiling Feelers. Stur would rain this pain onto the heads of people. Meta would drop dead in the streets of the City. Lovers. Parents. Children. Because of me.

I made it as far as I could, to some alley I did not recognize, before I could no longer walk. My body grew stiff, each of my joints locking. Whatever was in my arm was stronger than any serum-laced ice cream cone. It would kill me this time. *I will die here.*

I leaned my head against a wall, noticing that I could not swallow. Something was choking me. Or rather I was merely choking. My muscles contorted, including those of my larynx and abdomen. Breathing shallowed. My brain itself began to burn. My metal was raging within me. A ringing pierced my mind. *I will die here.*

"On the count of three, I will cut you open."

The voice was oddly clear, though I could hardly make out a face. I wanted to know what delusional hel I was slipping into. I wanted to know what I had done to deserve to go there. *Why? Why? What have I done?* I managed a laugh as I realized my dying thoughts would be questions.

"One," the strange voice said.

A man. Young. Strange way of speaking. My mental notes. The last ones.

"Two."

My fingers were stiff as tree branches, my heart slamming out of control in my chest. I was aware, suddenly, of every cell in my body. Every mitochondria. Each one contained a living cyclone. The ringing. The hum. It came from rotors. Trillions of little blades spinning and spinning inside me. The difference between being dead and being alive. I was no more than a collection of microscopic engines. And they were spinning out of control. *This is how I die.* And I would have laughed if I could have. *I die wild.*

"Three."

And in a darkened alley, with the silky moon's light just above the horizon, a blade—not made of synthetix, I can assure you, and wielded by someone I had never met—ripped me open from navel to throat.

Ep 12

Of Shirtlessness And Strange Boys

Life Tip: Thoughts are for thinking, not saying.

I was nudged awake by something fuzzy. Well, not fuzzy, exactly. But it's tickle was like balls of cotton against my cheek.

"That's nice," I mumbled, my words slurring.

"Is it, now?"

I tried to jump out of bed—the voice was unfamiliar—but I quickly realized that I could do no such thing. My body was heavy, like an elefant the size of Stur were parked on top of me. "What the hel is going on?" I sounded drunk. "Who the...hel are you?"

I picked my head up, an excruciating feat, to witness some male person I did not know standing in my room. Smirking.

"I'll scream," I warned.

"If you were going to scream, you would have already done it."

So I screamed. Or at least I tried to. A real decent effort. But my throat threatened to close in on itself, and the muscles of my abdomen and chest seemed to unravel, my bones creaking as though near collapse. Whatever the Feelers shot into my arm pulsed like fyre. I almost blacked out.

The person cursed as he rushed forward, putting his hand on my chest. That was when I realized I wasn't wearing a dress or a shirt at all. I sucked in air, preparing to scream again, but he held a finger to my lips.

"You're going to kill yourself if you try that again. Good goddess, I'm not going to hurt you."

I bit my tongue. Literally. Bit my tongue. His hand remained on my chest, so of course, he'd come closer to me. I decided to memorize him. You know. In case I survived the serial killing attempt and needed to identify him. Tan skin, straight nose, dark hair kept in short, wide curls, the sides of his head shaved low. Honey brown eyes. Full lips.

He's beautiful.

"What was that?" he asked.

Oh god, I said that out loud. At least my speech was partly incoherent. There was no way he knew what I said.

But when he looked at me, his eyes glittered. *Perfect. He's laughing. Now he's going to kill me and be cocky about it.*

His hand remained, and I felt my body relax again, which should not have happened since no one had seen me without a top since I was a toddler. *I should be overcome with embarrassment. I should...I should swoon.*

He tapped my cheek. No, not my cheek. The fuzzy thing near my cheek. It wiggled in response, stretching itself down my jaw and to the skin of my throat. The pain lessened.

"What is that?" I managed.

"Tin. For the skin." He pet the metal again. "It likes you more than me."

"I want my dress." I did my best to sound demanding.

He chuckled. "Soon. I'm not finished yet. Unless you want your rib cage to fall apart for the sake of decency, you'll have to wait to get dressed."

"I'll scream again."

"You'll only hurt yourself if you do that. No one can hear you but me."

No one can hear me? What has this monster done to my family? Where's Priyaa? My parents?

He reached out and tapped his knuckle against what I thought was the empty air around us. There was a thudding sound in response, as if we were in an invisible dome. "Aluminum, magnesium, titanium. Sound absorbers."

"You're...Meta."

His eyes danced. "Aren't you a quick one?"

My words were coming more smoothly. The tin was helping. His hand was helping. "You tried to kill me. In the alley."

"Is that so?" The corner of his mouth twitched with amusement. "And I'm such a good murderer that I brought you back to your room, laid you gently in your bed, and gave you some of my tin?"

I lay there for a moment, obviously still groggy. *What is happening? Nex. Slow down. Think. Strange man. Strange boy? Strange, yet handsome man-boy cuts you open in an alley. Why? What was happening then? You were dying. Why? Some injection. Why? The Feelers. Why? To find Meta. Why? To kill Meta. Why? Why? Why?*

"Why are you helping me?" I could speak almost normally.

"I thought you might die." He tapped the injection site on my left arm. "I can't get it out by the way. Impossible for me to get near it. It's emitting some kind of pulse. Hurts like hel-fyre."

A pulse. It's brilliant. "Metal conducts electricity," I said, thinking out loud yet again. "They are overcharging Meta who have metal actively in their bodies. It would be uncomfortable for normal people who still have iron blood, of course. But if you are Meta and hold greater quantities, it would electrocute you. And it would keep Meta from gathering more metal. From holding it. From hiding it. Meta will have to get rid of their metal if they don't want to be in pain. And eventually...." *They'll destabilize. Because Meta need metal.*

A new discovery. A new way to hunt Meta. Starvation. *And which dazzling Former came up with that notion? Who dripped iron blood into a vat of destabilized Meta blood?*

I shut my eyes. "This is my fault."

"Probably."

I glared at the guy. "I thought you were supposed to be helpful."

He grinned. But there was a way to it. It stuck to me, that grin. Like I knew I would see it again. Or maybe I'd seen it before. Like I knew that if I closed my eyes, I would remember its form exactly, no matter how much time or distance had passed. An odd feeling. Like a memory I'd forgotten.

"I didn't want to be this invasive," he explained." Cutting you open, I mean. I am certainly not the best healer. But I needed to pull out your metal and I did not have time to ask you to hand it over. I could have moved it out, without cutting, but your shield is far too strong."

"What shield?"

Genuine surprise. "Your shield. It's the strongest I've seen in a while. As tight as a newborn Meta. I couldn't even detect your metal. Thought maybe you had hundreds in there, but it was only two."

Something raged inside me the moment I realized they were gone. No hiss or hum in my forearm, no strength around my heart. "Give them back. Now."

He put both hands up in surrender. "I won't keep them. But I need to finish sewing your muscles and dampening the effect of this pulse."

He lifted his hand and ran a finger down my center, between my breasts and along what was becoming a dreadful scar. I could feel my muscles twitch and move under his direction. "How are you doing that?" I asked.

"Molybdenum. And silver. Small amounts because of this implant nonsense in your arm. Now shush. Let me concentrate."

He was finished after a few minutes, and he offered his hand. I took it and pulled so I was sitting up. I was sore, but much stronger. My arm, however, hurt more than if a Moral had smashed it with a synthetix club.

"Any ideas on how to stop this thing from frying you?" he asked. "The more metal I add, the more it activates."

I thought for a moment and almost asked Formula out of habit before realizing where I was. "I don't know enough about types of metals. But is there one that reduces energy consumption? It could absorb what the pulse gives off and release it elsewhere, maybe?"

He opened his palm, a cool gray sphere appearing, summoned from his pores. "Steel. But you owe me. It's hard to make."

"To make?" I asked, poking the ball of metal in his hand. It did not wiggle in response like tin or lead. It was steady. Its hum was more of a low ring, like a deep bell. "You can make metal?"

"It's an alloy. A creation, of sorts." He put the steel in my hand. "It's yours. But perhaps we won't put it inside you. Not if it's holding the current you need to get rid of."

"Where then?"

A shimmer, and his face changed. Or rather, his facial accessories became visible to me. They had been cloaked somehow until then, but the piercings he wore stood out stark against his tan skin. Piercings along his ears, his lips, his nose. After I stared for long enough, he stuck out his tongue, revealing three piercings down its center. All metal. So much metal.

"Good god. You walk around like that? How are you not Ended?"

"It's called cloaking, genius."

"I am an *actual* genius." My defensiveness shocked me. But it was true, so I didn't correct myself.

"I was only kidding," he replied. He pulled a sliver of steel from the ball in my hand. "Hold still."

He leaned in, kneeling on the bed beside me, and tugged on my bottom lip. I did wonder why I was not putting up a fight. He was still a stranger, and he was moving closer and closer to me. But when I saw his piercings, common sense vanished, and there was nothing I wanted more than to have at least one of my own.

He slid the steel through my lip, then, releasing the metal, twisted his fingers in the air, almost like a snap.

Without him touching it, the metal curled into a perfect circle in response.

I had a response of my own to the magic I had just witnessed. I grabbed his hand and examined it, the lust for knowledge a familiar burn in my brain. "How did you do that?"

He let me turn his hand this way and that, studying me as I studied him. "Do what?"

I snapped with my right hand, mimicking his motion, not releasing him with my left nor looking away from his hand.

"Metal moving?" he said. "It's not difficult. Even little kids can do it."

"If you're done belittling me, perhaps you can show me how."

He scoffed. "Maybe when you're not on your literal death bed."

I shrugged. "I will just try it as soon as you are gone. I don't need your permission."

He flashed a smile. "I like you," he said. And not in an alarming way, but in a sincere way, how someone says to a friend. "Your metals are on the desk," he said. "Move them to you."

I snapped. They did nothing. I snapped again. I had the sense they were laughing at me.

The guy who sliced me open in an alley the night before outstretched his arm and unfurled his fist, like his fingers were petals of a flower, opening at dawn. Titanium rushed to him.

I want it. I want to do it. I will do it. I must.

"Explain."

He sat, the bed bouncing under his weight. He was a decent size—not too thin, but not too heavy. Tall but not too tall.

"You are not really moving the metal," he replied. "It is already moving. Always moving. Even when it seems still. Just as you are always moving. Even when you sleep. You can feel the current, feel the spinning. It never stops. So when you move metal, you are a moving thing, pulling another moving thing toward you in your current. You are directing its movement." He paused, searching for words. "Or...not directing...."

"Requesting."

"Yes. Exactly. A magnet doesn't demand the metal, it *asks* for it to move one way or the other. It suggests."

"And I am a magnet?"

"Yes. You are a magnet."

Sometimes, someone says something, and you know it's a lie. But sometimes, someone speaks, and you know it's the truth. Real truth. Deep truth. Truth that changes you. And it's like you've heard that truth a thousand times before, but never once.

"I'm a magnet," I repeated. I had no idea what a magnet was, but I knew I was one. I outstretched my arm and unfurled my fingers. If I listened, I could hear the spinning of my cells. Not wild and out of control like in the alley, but gently whirring. Like the blades of a rotor on a hovering craft. Like a byrd gliding over the City. I could feel the lead, its own particles swaying and bumping one another. I could feel the space between us. The space itself was just a suggestion, its own current. The metal could cross the space if it so desired and if all three—me, the space, and the metal—agreed.

And so lead floated to me like a sultry cat crossing the room.

"Goddess, I love lead," he said with a sigh and a hint of jealousy. He turned his attention to me. "Are you being electrocuted?" he asked. "Any near fatal symptoms?"

The pain was still there, radiating from my arm, but it was endurable. I tapped my lip, swiping the blood I hadn't realized was leaking from my new piercing. "It's working."

"A cloak then, for the piercing, and we can call it done." He pulled two metals from himself and shaped them around my lip with another snap. "Aluminum and silver. Make a great mirror. You can move them to reflect your skin as well. I'll preset it for you." Then he stood to his feet. "I'm off then."

"No," I said and I almost reached out to grab him. "I have a hundred questions."

"Hopefully, you never see me again." He pulled his sound barrier into himself and reapplied his face cloak. "Careful, Nex." And with that, he backed up to my open window, leaned, and fell right out.

I realized, with utter awe, that I had forgotten all about my being half-naked. I had forgotten about the pain. I had forgotten about the vertical scar that trailed from the hollow of my throat to right between my hip bones. Forgotten about my blood-soaked sheets and the smiles of Feelers and the smooth surface of Stur.

For the first time, I thought...maybe one day I could feel alive. And fall out of windows. And grin. And stick out a tongue filled with piercings—one I didn't have to control or weigh down or bite to keep from speaking.

Maybe one day, I could be Nex the way he was him.

Ep 13

Not The Last Slap

Life Tip: Sisters are for braiding hair and lying to.

My sister's voice through the door. "Nex? Mother is calling for us."

I swung my legs over the bed and realized just how stiff and heavy I still was. I could not be quick. And quickness was required when it came to my mother. At least the blood on my sheets was clear and not scarlet. I winced as I pulled them off my mattress and put them in a pile on the floor for the wash.

It took more strength than expected to bend down and locate a dress from the pile of clean clothes on the floor. I struggled to get it over my head, my skin pulling and pinching around my scar, my bones groaning as I moved my torso.

My image in the mirror arrested me. *I look like actual, literal shit.*

When Priyaa knocked again, I shuffled over and unlocked the door. Her eyes widened at the sight of me. She came in and slipped the lock into place behind her.

She stepped into my room with her jaw agape. My floorboards were scraped, my dresser scuffed and leaning.

Dresses were scattered; cloth shoes and synthetix footwear littered the floor like grenades from one of the Old Wars.

I braced myself for Priyaa's usual ribbing. For a jab at my appearance or the state of my living quarters. She crossed the room toward me and put her hands on my shoulders.

"Sit," she said, leading me over to the edge of my bed and helping me down. She graced her hands over my hair and cheeks, searching my face. "You look like you might faint," she said. "I should call a Wizen."

I took her hands in mine. "No, Priyaa, I'm alright. Really."

She knelt in front of me. "No, Nexus, I don't think you are." She didn't bother to scan the room again. "This is too much. They are pushing you too hard, too fast. I never get to see you anymore. All you do is...is form. You need to tell them to slow down. You, Onur. Everyone from your training year. I don't know why they are pacing you like this, but you cannot keep doing it forever."

"I like forming, Priyaa. It is not the work."

"Then what is it? Are you...are you pregnant?"

"No. Definitely not." Though the time to partner and form a house would come too soon, if the Fight kept rushing us forward.

"Are you sick? Is someone hurting you?"

It was my turn to put my hands on her cheeks. "Little sister, listen to me. I am okay. I will be okay. Everything will be okay. Right now, our mother is calling us. And I need your help to appear presentable. Will you help me?"

I pretended that my sister's eyes did not fill with tears as she nodded and found my brush. She pulled my hair into a quick braid and wiped my face with a cool cloth.

"When was the last time you ate?" she asked, supporting my elbow as I stood.

"Yesterday, I think." Lies. I skipped my meal at the House Of Forms and had not eaten breakfast before reporting for work that day. "I'll eat a big breakfast after mother speaks to us. I promise."

I halted at the top of the stairs, preparing for how much the jostling descent would tilt my bones and wrack my frame.

Priyaa's face pinched as she noticed. No doubt she was used to me running—tripping—down the staircase at full speed. I was not being my usual self. "Nexus, they will notice," she whispered. It was no longer worry in my sister's eyes, but fear.

I smiled at her. I did not know where the resolve came from, but it always came. "Just watch. You'll see. Everything will be okay."

I masked each shot of pain, all the way down the stairs and to the place where my mother and father stood.

My mother was so cold, I felt a chill. "You have kept us waiting."

Before Priyaa could say anything, I bowed as deeply as I could. "It was my fault. I overslept. Priyaa woke me."

My mother's eyes were calculating, observant. "Much is being asked of you in the House Of Forms, I have heard, with details spared. And you are exceeding their expectations, though not close to reaching my own. And I am sure last night's festivities at the House Of Certainty have left everyone somewhat depleted. Are you experiencing pain, Nexus?"

"Slight discomfort. Mostly I need to mind my health while remaining focused on my work. I can adjust."

"These balances are important. Your increased maturity is notable." She turned to my sister. "And you, Priyaa? Is there pain?"

"I am well, though my arm is sore."

My mother nodded. "On to why I have called you. I have regrettable information regarding not our house, but a house close to us. Last night, the cycle of Clay Vanes ended."

Nothing happened next. That's the best way to describe it. I stood and did not move and did not think. I just existed there, in our living room.

My mother garbled something about Clay's waning health. About visits to Wizens and what a shame it was for a child to die of illness with a Wizen mother of such decent rank caretaking her, and that surely this would lower the Vanes rank yet again.

But nothing *happened*.

She said that we would go to the Vanes house and help them to eliminate their grief, so I dragged my body a few streets over. Priyaa cried and cried, and Dahn did not come out of her room. Edwidge and Richter were gray as pillars. A few neighbors came as well. Onur was not present.

After spending most of the day not-grieving on couches and settees, we moved into Clay's bedroom, as was the custom, to not grieve for her there. To her face.

She was not curled up reading a book. Her lantern was not casting shadows on the walls. She was not...Clay. Her skin was pale, her round eyes closed, her chest unmoving beneath her blanket. Dead. She was dead.

"I do not understand," I said, even though we were supposed to be silent. But I could not be silent, because I did not understand.

"Our daughter was not well for quite some time," Edwidge answered, her voice trembling.

Her partner nodded. "You did your best, Edwidge. You are a talented Wizen."

But Edwidge's eyes brimmed with tears until they slipped down her round face. "We will lose rank for this, Richter."

I could not understand it. "Is that why you did not tell us she was sick?" I said, an edge to my voice I did not care to hide. "Because you did not want your rank lowered?"

"Nexus." My father's voice boomed. "Silence, please. We are here to help eliminate grief, not to generate it."

I did not go silent. Because I could not understand. "But Clay is *dead*. If we had known she was sick, we could have helped. We could have saved her. You kept it a secret instead of asking for assistance. It's *stupid*."

"Nexus."

"She shouldn't be dead. It's not right. It's not fair." *I should have been there. I was too busy. I was too self-important. I promised I would meet her. I promised I would walk her home and I did not. What if she died alone? What if she died afraid?* "Someone should have *been there*."

My mother grabbed hold of my arm so firmly that I thought the pulse device would shoot right out of me. Outside the room, once the door was shut, she slapped me across the face. It was not the first time my mother had hit me. It was, however, the first time I thought about hitting her back.

Heat rose under my skin, and if I was not injured, I would have done something reckless. But, as always, I did nothing. Just stood there while she stood there. At least that time, my disdain matched hers.

"You will go home."

I bowed. "Matrix, yes." And I left the Vanes house, my mother, and the whole silent ritual. And I left Clay.

By the time I made it home, I was exhausted. I wanted no company, not even the strange boy who had either saved my life the night before or tried to end it. I still hadn't made up my mind on which it was.

Outside the door to my room, with my hand on the knob, my metal whispered to me. Tin blew a fine warning like dust telling that a sandstorm is coming. *Someone is here.*

I made a mistake: I opened the door.

Ep 14

A Night With My Love

Life Tip: Keep your doors locked when you leave the house.

Onur Vanes stood in my room, flipping through the books on my desk. He wore his Fender clothes. As presentable as ever.

"This place is a mess," he said. "You should clean up after yourself, Nex. Order is important."

I took a few deep breaths, trying not to lean against the wall for support. *This is the longest day of my life.* But as vulnerable as I felt, I was sure Onur's wounds went deeper.

"Onur, I am so sorry."

"Sorry?"

I blinked at him. *He must be in denial.* This, I was taught in training, could happen if grief was not eliminated quickly enough. "Yes. I'm sorry about Clay."

He tossed the book onto the desk. "The only thing I regret is my mother's incompetence."

I chewed my lip to keep from arguing. "What kind of sickness was it? I know nothing."

"Precisely."

I wanted him to leave. First, it was not allowed for him to be in my room without supervision. We were not partnered, and my house upheld City rules. Second, he was being unkind. Third, I was tired and hungry enough to throw up. But all my food was poison, and there was an electric pulse embedded in my body trying to kill me, and now I was hiding a piercing which, at that point, throbbed from lack of care and being slapped with my mother's firm hand. I had lost a large quantity of blood the night before. Oh, and one of my dearest friends was dead because of fear and ranks and societal idiocy.

But I did not ask Onur Vanes to leave. Why not? Because. Because he had been my very best friend for half my life. And my first and only love. And my protector. And my confidant. And his sister was dead, and even though he was wearing that ridiculous uniform, I loved him. Because sometimes love was just because. And that had to be good enough.

I crossed the room with well-placed steps and leaned into him—carefully—offering a hug. He had held me so many times when I needed it. I could hold him for once.

He leaned his forehead against mine, like he used to. I missed the way his blonde hair would tickle my nose when he did that. Instead, this Onur kept his hair slicked back behind his ears. I missed the way I used to slip my hands under the hem of his shirt when he kissed me—the feel of warm skin and the sloping curves of his back. Instead, this Onur was strapped into his Fender outfit.

And so I wasn't sure what to do with my hands when he kissed me. He kissed me anyway. More. And then more. Until I thought he would topple me. I wanted to tell him that I was not my usual self. That I was too tired. That I was too weak. That I was in pain and I couldn't explain why. But I said nothing, and he kept kissing.

That is the word I chose to describe what was happening. Kissing. We were kissing. That was all.

But that was not all.

He shoved his hand under my dress, no discussion, no permission, and I tried to dissuade him, but I suppose I was not so good at trying. I was afraid he would notice the still fresh scar above my belly button. But Onur was not in the noticing mood. He pushed past my efforts, reaching for more than he ever had before. Until I did not have my dress anymore or anything else, for that matter.

That is the way I decided to word it. I did not have anything else after that.

I was on my bed, on my back, and I was sure that I would be torn in half yet again if he did not stop. His mouth was too firm on mine, and so I said nothing. *Help me*, I thought. *Help me*. And then I knew to put my hands on his back. To move. And if I couldn't move Onur and I couldn't move myself, I would move metal.

I could feel the spinning of Onur's rotors, of the little cells in his body that flew so fast in their circles. I asked the metal, and it agreed, slowing down his cells until, mercifully, Onur drooped onto his elbows and then slumped on top of me.

For a blinding moment, I thought I had killed him. And I wondered what I would do and how I would lie and when I would be found out and become the first person in years to be Ended for something other than being Meta.

But I realized Onur was not dead. Only deeply sleeping. And simultaneously crushing me beneath him.

With great effort, I wiggled out from under him, falling to the floor to catch my breath. I wanted to cry, but I saw that he had not even bothered to close the door to my room. Anyone could have found us breaking the rules. Anyone could have found him breaking me.

I decided that naked was the last thing I wanted to be. I put my dress back on and left Onur snoring on my sheet-less mattress, his pants around his knees and his mouth open. I decided that I hated him. Easiest decision of my life, at that point. And that if I did not leave right then, I would kill him after all.

So I climbed—mostly slid—down the vines outside my window and half-walked, half-dragged myself down the street. *How many times in a row will I wander through this City in pain?*

I'd expected very simple things out of life. A partner who cared about me. Parents who gave even the slightest shit. A job I didn't hate. And to live. That was all.

But instead, I had a body full of metal.

Fine, I thought. *If fate wants to tempt me, I'll bite its face off.* So I made my way back to the Vanes house with every intention of slapping Viveka right in her conde-scending mouth.

Ep 15

By Lantern Light

Life Tip: Crazy is as crazy does.

I always liked the way Wizens smelled. Not everyone cared for it, but it reminded me of safe places and safe people, of the teachers in training who took their time with people like me, and of Edwidge, who had been kinder to me than my own mother in so many ways. The scent of old books, antiseptic, and latex. The fragrance of deep thought and informed interventions.

The Vanes house smelled more like Wizens than usual. Made sense, since there were many of them—maybe half a dozen—flowing in and out of the space. I snuck around the back of the house to what I knew from memory was Onur's room. Since I was sure he would not be there, I opened his window and crawled in, lucky that the Vanes loft was on ground level.

I wanted, for a split second, to collapse onto the empty bed and sleep, but it was Onur's bed, and I would have died before I went near it. So, I cracked his bedroom door and sat on the floor and watched, looking for my mother. Looking for something to hurt so I wouldn't have to.

"This is the way it must go," I heard someone say. Gray-headed and wearing one of the long gray frocks that showed him to be a Wizen. He sat on the couch next to Edwidge, holding her hand. She was clearly distraught, her face bearing deeper wrinkles than I remembered her having earlier that day. Her hair was loose around her shoulders. I had never seen her like that. Usually a Wizen wore their hair in two braids, one on either side of their faces. Edwidge should have looked beautiful and free with her blonde hair down, but she was bedraggled and forlorn.

"I cannot bear it," Edwidge said to the other Wizen. "This is too much."

He nodded knowingly. Around the two of them, Wizens entered and exited the home, carrying boxes and stacks of books away. When each one passed, Edwidge stared with sorrowful longing. "Please, Gamall, please," she said. "Please."

The old man touched her cheek. "You know how unhappy this makes me, Little Book, but I cannot stop this. We must be reasonable."

"I can rise again, Gamall, I can. I only require the opportunity. I did everything I was supposed to. Even took her to the House Of Reason, but no one could help. Not even you. The child was sick, yes, but—"

"The child is *dead*, Edwidge. We are the bearers of ancient knowledge, the keepers of medicine, the trainers of the future generations. If our people see our children dying, they will no longer deem us worthy of such honor."

"How could I achieve the impossible, Gamall? How could I heal what could not be healed? Must I be *punished*?" Her voice broke at the last word.

"It is we who are being punished, Little Book. To lose a Wizen as knowledgeable and dedicated as yourself. You will be sorely missed in the halls of the House Of Reason."

From the crack in the door, I did not see my mother anywhere. Only the Wizens packing Edwidge's things, and Edwidge following her master outside and pleading, tears and snot streaming down her face. Would I cry, if my life's work were ripped from my hands?

I wondered, then, if anyone was with Clay. Or if they were all busy packing books and damaging lives and begging for mercy. Perhaps Dahn was sitting with her sister, brushing her hair and weeping. Or Richter, recalling fond memories of Clay as a child. Perhaps we could not-grieve together.

I sort of crawl-hobbled across the hall to Clay's room. It was past the acceptable time to visit, and I had not let myself in the front door, so being spotted by half a dozen Wizen strangers would be unfortunate. The Vanes' would understand. Wizens were much too reasonable for shenanigans. I pulled the door in behind me and realized how strange I would look to the room's occupants, entering like a gremlin who'd come down with stomach cramps.

But there was no one in the room. No one besides Clay.

She lay where I had seen her last. On her bed, with her hands straight at her sides and a blanket up to her chin. She was just as pale. Just as still. Just as small.

With no one there to tell me 'no', I crossed the room and sat on the edge of her bed. She still did not move.

I cried then. As silently as I could. It made my ribs hurt and my head pound, but I cried. Because she deserved it.

She deserved for someone to be heartbroken on her behalf. To long for her. To need her.

I found her lantern and lit it, the light bouncing off the walls and illuminating her face. It made her look almost alive again.

"Everything is so bad," I confessed to her. "I know I keep saying that it is fine and I am fine, but it is not fine and I am not fine. And maybe that's selfish because you are dead, so you are having a much worse time. But me seeing you dead is worse, Clay. It's so much worse than anything so far. I don't want you to be dead. I want you to be here."

I leaned forward, planning to kiss her forehead and tell her, for the last time, that I loved her. That is when I heard it. Very soft, very faint.

A hum.

The slow, low spin of rotors in cells. The buzz of life deep, deep down. *I am crazy*, I thought to myself. Crazy. Delusional. Wishing I could change fate. Wishing fate could change Clay.

But when I leaned my ear close to her, it grew louder. So I crawled up onto the bed and placed my cheek to her chest. To see. To hear. There it was. *Not dead.* No. Not dead. *Sleeping.*

"What do I do? What do I *do*?"

I did not know. It was not in my understanding. It was not in my experience or in any of the teachings the Wizens imparted in training. There, I learned how to bow and nod, how to respect expectations, and how to make myself useful in the Fight. But I did not need bowing and nodding right then. I needed to break expectations, not respect them. I would have to use a different kind of knowing. One that did not come from books or from lectures or from laws.

It would have to come from metal. And it would have to come from me.

I closed my eyes, trying not to hyperventilate. I could not repress my anxiety, but I had to do it anyway, anxiety and all. I focused. Focus, Nex. When I was very still, so still that I thought maybe I also was dead, I spoke to my metal. "Show me how."

I cannot explain fully how anything happened after that. I was not even sure that things happened at all. I straddled Clay, my knees digging into her mattress on either side of her. And I put both my palms, one on top of the other, onto her chest. Sort of like the strange boy had done when he mended my bones and skin. I kept my hands there and did not move. I only waited. And listened.

I cannot say which metals moved. The closest answer is that all of them came, even ones I did not have in me. For those next moments, all metal were my metal, and all metal—perhaps metal itself—moved for me. Moved with me.

We agreed.

When it was time—when I felt the time had come from somewhere within me—that was when I thrust my hands downward, pushing as hard as I could into Clay's sternum. Seven times I did that. Seven times, with as much force as I could summon.

I stopped and slid off the bed, my ribs burning and splintered and sharp pains shooting through my muscles. Nothing changed, except that my arm was made of hel-fyre. *I am crazy after all.*

And I believed that even more so when Clay gave a tiny cough and gasped for air.

Ep 16

All Is Now Well, I Assume?

Life Tip: Know when to run.

Run.

I shuffled down the hall and out Onur's window. I could not go as fast as I needed to. My best attempt at a sprint was more of a shamble. I kept to the shadows as I made my way back to our flat. But I could not make it up the vines to my room. I collapsed outside, my back to the stucco of the exterior wall.

They will catch me. They will End me. They will catch me. They will End me.

I fell asleep there even though my heart was racing. My feverish dreams were laced with images of Clay's lifeless face flooding with color. I heard echoes of the sound of breath rushing into her lungs.

I woke to the sun inviting the morning. I made it up the vines, my legs trembling, to find Onur still asleep on my mattress.

I hated him. But I wanted to live more than I wanted him to sleep forever. I could not let anyone know that I had been to Clay's house, or that I used metal on her. So I was smart. Smarter than I was brave. I took my dress off and crawled into bed next to the one I used to love. I pulled his heavy arm over me and bit my tongue to keep from whimpering as I endured the physical contact.

I closed my eyes and found the slow spinning of his cells. I asked my metal to speed him up again, to let him awaken. And then I pretended to be asleep.

It was risky. I knew he might notice my scar. Or how filthy I was from limping around the City and breaking into houses. Or how my body shivered even though the morning was balmy.

When Onur sat up in bed, he leaned over, and kissed my shoulder. "We must keep this between us," he said in what he probably thought was a sexy, husky voice. "We cannot risk being reprimanded with fending going so well for me."

I didn't answer. I didn't need to. He took my silence as conversation. I wondered whether Onur ever listened to me, if at any point in our lives he considered my side of things. *I am an idiot.* A cold, tired, terrified idiot. Onur had always loved me for himself.

He buckled his pants and, since he had not bothered to remove his shoes before he climbed atop me the night before, smoothed his hair and left. I had been concerned about my scar for nothing; he did not look at me once.

I slept on the floor for an hour or two more. I could not imagine ever sleeping in my bed again. But then it was time to go to the House Of Forms. It would be unacceptable for me to miss my duties two days in a row, not to mention suspicious. So I gathered my things and visited the washroom. I sank to the bottom of the bathtub and let the water wash me clean. I was covered in blood, grateful for once that it was clear enough for no one to see. That is the nature of both blood and pain. Unseen but still felt. And difficult to wash away.

A fresh dress and the brushing out of the braids Priyaa had woven into my hair. If I were to be a ghost, at least I would be a presentable one.

I made sure to eat breakfast. My mother, already in the small kitchen, prepared hers as well. We shared the silence. She would not speak to me of slapping my face, and I would never speak to her of what happened with Onur while our houses were not-grieving. After all, my mother's high rank provided me with the comfort of my clothes and the fulfillment of my food. That was her version of speaking to me. That was the only way she could love.

I left before Priyaa awoke since my sister was already worried enough about me and would have known something was more wrong than usual with one look. I did not feel like faking smiles. Truly, at that point, I simply did not feel.

It was not tolerable for me to wait for Onur to drive me to the House Of Forms, so I walked. It gave me time to think, time to be on my own without being actively hunted. *Did I really do what I think I did? Can a person come back to life? Is metal that powerful?* I dragged my feet against the cobblestone. *Am I that powerful?*

No, I decided. *I'm having a mental break of some sort.* It was a more plausible explanation. *Maybe Priyaa was right. Maybe I should see a Wizen after all.*

Formula scanned me into the building, and I acknowledged no one as I progressed to my lab. One benefit of working on a classified project: no friends to ask how I was doing and why I looked like someone spat me out.

Stur gleamed as he always did. I touched his cool synthetix exterior and rested my forehead against him. *Giant machines can't ask questions.* He was pretty much my best friend—the only one I had left.

Before I could begin work, Drenge entered. He had freshly shaped his mustache, and it wiggled at me from across the lab table. "You missed a day of work," he said. It wasn't an accusation. Just a fact.

"I did."

"Is there an explanation either of us would benefit from you sharing?"

"There is not."

He paused. "Neurologically speaking, it might benefit you to share a burden, even if it is a psychological one."

If I shared, I would cry And if I cried, I would be crying. And that just wouldn't do. So I said nothing and chewed on the invisible ring on my bottom lip to keep everything from spilling out of me.

"I will not force you, Nexus," Drenge said. "But I will implore you once more to share."

"My friend died," I said, as plainly as I could manage.

He raised his eyebrows. "Did I somehow miss an Ending?"

I shook my head. "She was ill."

"My god," he said, setting down the clipboard he was holding. "Ill? That is rare."

I nodded. "As was she." One tear escaped—the traitor—and I swiped my lab coat sleeve to eliminate it. *A tiny little Ending.* My silver chuckled at that. It had a decent sense of humor.

"May the end of her cycle bring us all peace."

Only there would be no peace. Because I was very surely mad and didn't know what I could do about it.

"Drenge?"

"If there is a question, simply ask," he stated.

"What will happen if I am unfit to work? Psychologically?"

He did not miss a beat. "It is more common than you think, especially in these strained times. If you are unwell, I will request a visit to the House Of Reason. That is the protocol."

Before I could claim to be well-adjusted, Drenge asked Formula to schedule an appointment for that afternoon.

"It is not good to put these issues off," he explained. "Stur is important, but if you are not well, there will be no one to complete him. That makes you important as well."

Apparently, when someone of Drenge's rank called the House Of Reason—I had no idea what rank that was, as Formers thought it pointless to brag about such things— the Wizens sent a special transport.

It was cool inside that transport, and a young Wizen, probably primary rank as I was, welcomed me with a glass of water and a warm towel for my face. The water was clean, free of Metatoxin, and I drank it like a starved animal. We drove in quiet bliss, except for the few health questions the Wizen asked so she could record the answers in her journal. She was familiar, but I was too tired to care.

The House Of Reason was wider than it was tall, with many rooms for the sick and for storing books and relics. I knew this only from training. I had never ventured outside of the training facility there. The rest of the House seemed as uninteresting as it did mysterious.

Once I arrived, stoic healers in long gray robes massaged my shoulders, fed me a clean meal, and put me in a dim, empty room so I could rest. My metal relaxed, perceiving no danger, and so I relaxed as well. When I awoke, the Wizen who'd transported me bowed her braided head. I remembered her finally. From training.

"Var, right? Your name?"

She did not seem surprised I recognized her. "Yes, that's me."

"We trained together. I'm Nexus."

"I know who you are," she said, her voice gruff. And then she softened, resuming her gentle tone, void of emotion, as was the speaking habit of most Wizens. "All is now well, I assume?" More of a statement than a question.

"Um...okay." It did not seem well to me. My brain was still my brain. And my body still hurt. And my friend was still dead. And I still thought maybe she wasn't.

"And I must inquire," she said, "as to whether you are experiencing any pain or any weakness in your body?"

I made sure not to glance at my arm when she said it. "Not anything unusual, no. Just mentally—"

But she bowed again before I could finish. "Then all is well."

On my way out she handed me a useless book about maintaining strength and cultivating a positive mindset for the Fight against Meta called, "The Fight Within." Poor thing had no idea what was really within.

The halls of the House Of Reason were bland. Almost sterile. The lights were a gloomy gray-white, and the floors were carpeted in mauve to absorb sound and decrease morale. *At least I smell good*, I thought, inhaling the fragrance of books and mediocre healthcare.

I dropped the book on my toes when I saw Onur at the front desk of the House.

"There you are," he said, leaving the Wizen seater and angling toward me.

I picked up the book and clutched it to my chest. Shoddy defense, but it was all I had. "How did you know I was here?" My metal awakened, making little storms inside me. I tried to calm them all, but they hardly listened.

"It is not difficult to find those under my watch," he answered, annoyed that I asked.

What on Aarde does that *mean? Under his watch?*

He led me out by my arm and ignored my recoil at his touch. "Something has happened. I need you."

"Something...else?" *What could have happened? Is it Dahn?* My heart flipped, disregarding titanium's support. "Is it your mother?" *What if Edwidge is too disheartened? What if...?*

"It had better not have anything to do with my mother," Onur snapped.

He was going much too quickly for me, practically dragging me toward his idling transport, his fingernails digging into the skin of my upper arm.

"Onur, slow down," I told him.

He didn't. And once he was behind the wheel, he programmed his car to the edge of the allowed City speed limit.

"You're going to get us killed, Onur. What is going on?" I insisted, still clutching my book as we zoomed away from the House Of Reason.

His eyes red, his skin pale, and his lips tight, he made fists at his sides. "It's Clay," he said through gritted teeth. "She's alive."

Ep 17

Balancing The Balancing Acts

Life Tip: Practice being crazy so you can get better at it; be the best crazy you can be.

We took a left when it should have been a right. I gripped my seat belt to keep from smashing into the transport door, abandoning my Wizen book to the floor.

"I don't understand," I said, trying to remember to breathe. "Where are we going? And what do you mean alive?"

By the second sharp turn, my metal protested being tossed around inside me. I had never heard them be so bossy. *Balance me, balance me*, they demanded. I kindly informed them that I was a little busy and also did not know how. But they insisted. I attempted to move them around so they were evenly spread inside me. But lead did not like being on my right, and magnesium refused to be concentrated in one area. Titanium gripped my heart like a toddler holding onto a stuffed behr, and calcium jumped from bone to bone. I ended up with a rampaging stampede inside me. It took some soothing to calm them all and put them back in their places, all while pretending I was doing nothing of the sort while the pulse in my arm flared.

Finally, with a long exhale, I refocused my attention on Onur only to realize he had been talking for quite a while and that I'd missed most of the life-saving information I could have gleaned. I did not thrive in multiple conversation scenarios. I did not thrive in most scenarios.

Since I dared not ask Onur to repeat, I listened extra hard to whatever he had left to say. So many years I'd spent trying to listen, trying to focus, trying to balance. My lifetime could have been summed up simply. Every failure or every success was preceded and followed by one thing. Trying.

"...and this is the worst possible situation. Our house is being denigrated beyond repair. My mother—if she can even be called such at this point—is completely unraveling. They have already taken her in for questioning, but I assure you, they will deem her fit for a stay in the Hall Of Repair, who knows for how long."

The Hall Of Repair? I could not imagine Edwidge spending even one second there, unless it meant caring for the unwell. Those who were sent to that wing of the House Of Reason did not often return, and if they did, they were not nearly the same people as they were when they entered. It was a place not only for healers, but for Feelers. Just thinking of it made me shiver.

"Surely Edwidge will heal in time if left in her usual comfort?"

Onur looked at me as if I'd said the most repulsively idiotic thing. "It is her usual comfort that has brought on this behavior, Nexus." He shook his head, his neck and cheeks still flaming red. "And I am still not convinced she did not tamper with my youngest sister."

"Onur, what do you mean, 'tamper'? You don't really mean Clay is actually alive? I don't know if I can believe such a thing. I saw her. Forgive my bluntness, but she was very dead."

"As I said before, she is alive."

My heart swelled in my chest, and it took every bit of control to keep from screaming with relief. *She is alive. Alive! She was dead and now she is alive.* I cleared my throat to keep my voice measured. "I could not be happier, Onur, truly. When can we see her? Is she well enough now? I would give anything to wrap my arms around her."

"You will see her soon enough."

Another turn, and we pulled onto Ender Stream. The transport came to a stop outside the House Of Certainty, and Onur unbuckled.

"Onur...what is this? Why are we here?" I prayed the fear in my voice was hidden.

"You have proven to be brilliantly minded, Nexus. Your master in the House Of Forms believes this, at least. And I could use a brilliant mind on my side now. We must determine what has caused this. We must find who did this to my sister. And we must make it right."

"Who did...who did what?" I dug my fingernails into my palms. "Onur, Clay is alive. A miracle has happened. You must see it that way. This must be a miracle." I was begging. Which was pathetic. Onur would see whatever he wanted.

"This is no miracle," he said, his words filled with graveled hatred. "This is Meta."

We circumnavigated the building, heading toward the rear, me following just behind Onur. I'd never gone through any other entrance to the House Of Certainty than the front.

The rear lobby was lovely. Trees flourished in the indoor space, vines running along the floors and desks. Flowered shrubs adorned seating areas. It looked like they were serving hot cups of coffee. The smell of the bitter drink blended with the sweetness of the soil. Light filtered in through the glass ceiling, dancing on the glossy green leaves.

Just as the scenery began to soothe me, a Feeler bowed. I swore he snuck up on me. I did not even hear his footsteps as he approached. When I startled, the Feeler smiled. Rather young, maybe my age. He wore his fleece scarf draped over his head and around his neck. His pearl earrings shone in the sunlight.

I stared longer than I should have. Our people did not usually wear jewelry or flourish their scarves.

"You must be Former Nexus Aerixon," he said in a sweet, all-too-Feeler tone. He handed me a cup of steaming coffee. "So much gratitude for coming on such short notice. You are greatly appreciated."

I sniffed it, but the coffee appeared clean. *Perhaps they do not suspect me?* The Feeler did not even seem to be examining me. He chatted with others as they walked by, laughing and slapping his knees.

Onur put a hand on my back, making me jerk away involuntarily. "I must be off. I will check in with you shortly for your findings."

My findings? Before I could ask what he meant, he left me, his boots heavy on the floor as he rushed into another room.

The Feeler took my empty cup and handed it to another. "Feeling a little more settled, I'm sure?"

"I feel fine," I said.

"My name is Monny, and I'll be at your service for this little query. I've heard you're quite talented. How exciting." He smiled again, motioning toward double glass doors. "Follow me, my dear."

I followed Monny to a side room not far from the lobby entrance. It too was filled with plants, the vines twining up the legs of the table. The room contained a board and writing utensils, paper and pencils, and Drenge.

I almost hugged him. Maybe he almost hugged me.

"I take it the visit to the House Of Reason went well," he said.

"Do I detect a joke, Drenge?"

His mustache wiggled. "Jokes are inefficient."

The Feeler, Monny, slid onto the table and crossed his legs. "All right boys and girls, here is the problem that must be solved. And you are just the two to do it. Drumroll please!"

I blinked at him. "What's a drumroll?"

He waved it off. "Is there a type of form that can bring someone back from the dead? Just that simple! And who better to answer than the best Formers in the City?"

"Where is Clay?"

Monny's turn to be surprised. "I'm sorry?"

"My friend. Clay. Where is she?" I narrowed my eyes. "I was told just a few minutes ago that Clay, who was dead yesterday, is alive today. And I came here hoping to see her. Instead, you put me in this room to work. I am not working until I see Clay."

Monny chuckled. "What a day you must be having. I cannot even fathom it. Of course, I would want to see my friend as well, but first, questions must be answered. We need to be certain all is well. Do you understand?"

Oh, he was good. Using Former phrasing on me like that. But I was smart. Smart enough to know that Monny was not as harmless as he appeared, with his earrings and his smiles. I felt the subtlest tingle along my scalp. Monny was working harder than most. I wouldn't be surprised if he read better than any other Feeler I'd ever met.

"Do we know each other?" I asked him.

"You and me? Perhaps. What year did you train, Former Aerixon?"

"Year Four of the Best Of The Best."

"How wonderful," from both Drenge and Monny.

"I was Year Three," Monny said. "We might have crossed paths."

"Well," I said, clean, "we are certainly crossing paths now."

Monny smiled, and his eyes glinted. "We certainly are, aren't we."

Drenge cleared his throat to break the tension. "Let us begin, Nexus. There is a question to be answered."

I picked up a pencil and tried to ignore the lead at its center. I—somehow considered one of the greatest minds to ever Form—got to work on answering the question: how does the Meta who resurrected the dead prove that it cannot be done?

"For the Fight," I said.

And everyone responded, "For the Fight."

Ep 18

Coffee For Cowards

Life Tip: Pack a snack when consigning others to brutal Endings.

Drenge threw his glasses on the table and pressed his fingers into his eyes, massaging his sockets. "You are not listening, Nexus. I am asking *how* a Former could do such a thing. Perhaps biology? I do not know. I am not a biologist. Nor is my specialty chemistry. My specialty is forms."

I leaned over the table to return his glasses to him. We were tired. Well, except for Monny, who was addressing the state of his cuticles and pretending to ignore us while reading us intently. It had been hours. Maybe more than hours. There was no telling time in the room. Only when we used the washroom could we attempt to glimpse the cast of the sunlight.

The steady supply of black coffee was enough to keep Drenge and Monny wired. It settled me. Any more in my cup, and my sluggish mind would have fallen asleep. Yet, I kept drinking. Cup after cup. Anything to appear as normal as the rest.

"Drenge, it is you who are not listening. I *know* that we are not biologists. And not chemists. But I also know why forming is the best work in all the City. Because all things are forms. When you either break them down or add them up. Forms. What is biology made of, Drenge?"

A robust sigh. "Cells."

"And do cells have shape? Do they have form?"

"Of course they do. But I am saying that I know nothing about those shapes and forms."

"We do not need to know how a Former could resurrect a person, Drenge. We only need to know if it can be done."

He sat up a little straighter. "So...you think this resurrection occurred on a cellular level?"

"Well, dying happens on a cellular level. So bringing someone back to life must too."

Drenge chuckled. "How does one manipulate the form of a cell?"

I chewed on my bottom lip. A dangerous habit, seeing that a treacherous steel ring had taken up residence there, but one that could not be helped nonetheless. "It would have to be some force. A force exerted on the cells of the deceased."

"A massive force, great enough to affect change on a cellular level."

I interrupted the growling of my stomach by smacking my hands on the table top. "No! Not a massive force."

I rushed over to Monny and pulled him to his feet. It was my first time touching a Feeler. The dark brown skin of his arm was so smooth I thought I'd ripped it. And he smelled like chocolate.

"You smell so nice," I blurted out. *God, I am so tired and hungry.*

Monny smiled. A genuine one.

"What are you doing to me, Former?" he asked.

I positioned him to face me. Then with no warning, I reached out and slapped him in the face. Hard. He was taller than me, so I had to stretch, but it was a decent blow.

He gasped and, without hesitation, slapped me back. He was pretty strong. My jaw twisted and my teeth banged together. I stumbled backward, knocking over the wooden chair behind me.

"What is the meaning of this?" Drenge half-yelled, standing to his feet.

I put my hands up. "It was a demonstration," I tried to explain.

Monny's eyes flashed. "You hit me. I know Formers have crazy streaks, but good god, you hit me in the face."

I pointed at him. "And you hit me back."

"What is the point, Nexus?" Drenge insisted.

"Monny hit me back as a reaction. And then I stumbled and knocked over this chair. If you only looked at the chair in the reaction chain, it would seem like a miracle. How did it just fall over on its own like that? But it did not. It was part of a chain of events. Reactionary force. We do not need to locate a massive force. We are looking for a tiny one that caused a massive reaction."

Drenge began to pace, his hand to his chin, his glasses safely back at home on his nose. "A Former would have had to have created this small force, and they would have to have known it would revive the dead girl, and they would have to have done it from afar, since no Formers were present at the moment of the subject's revival."

Monny chimed in. "But why would a Former do it? What would they gain? Nexus is the only one who would care enough to plan something, but she did not even know the girl was ill and has an alibi for the time of her revival."

Can't believe I am thanking Onur right now, but his sweaty, deadweight body is the reason I'm going to survive this.

I took over where Monny left off. "A Former could not do this. Nor would they. Unless they had a device of some sort that has not been invented. And a motive that does not exist. Including knowledge of biology and chemistry. Knowledge of life and death. Knowledge of reactionary forces. Knowledge that Clay was ill. Knowledge of the time and location of her house's not-grieving." I had to take a breath after that mouthful.

Drenge snapped his fingers. "Not a Former," he said. He paused, and I wondered with amusement whether it was for dramatic effect. "A Wizen."

That hit my heart like titanium. "A Wizen?" I asked. But I could already see where he was going with it.

"A Wizen. Think about it. They have all the knowledge. Access to any knowledge they desire, really. Chemistry, biology, life, death. Including records of whether this sort of thing has been done before. Detailed records of the subject's declining health."

Monny frowned. "But how?"

"Meta," Drenge said. "A metallic reaction. Maybe in the blood? In the cells? A small one that rippled, causing a reaction."

Monny nodded as he processed. "So a Meta Wizen. But why? What motivation? The subject is not Meta, unless she is impossibly good at hiding it. Why revive her?"

Drenge exclaimed, "Because her death casts a shadow on the House Of Reason. She is the daughter of a high ranking Wizen, is she not? If they could reverse her death, they would reverse their shame. I'm sure they hoped it would be deemed a miracle."

Monny clapped his hands together, bouncing on his toes. "This is exciting," he giggled. "It could not be a Former, but must be a Wizen. Now we know one of those Wizens present at the residence in question must be the culprit, and we will find them by determining which one is Meta. It's only a matter of inquisition."

I could not be excited with them. My stomach hurt, and not just from being empty for so long. A handful of Wizens, including Edwidge, would be questioned. And if any of them were Meta, they would be Ended. It was my fault. And I was too much of a coward to do a thing about it.

I would stand in a stream of Meta blood and know in my heart it was I who spilled it.

Ep 19

When Did Drenge Get So Tall?

Life Tip: If your mother is suddenly nice, you're wrong; she isn't.

We reported our conclusion to the Feelers, yet we remained in the small room near the back lobby.

"We can't leave," Drenge muttered to himself for the four-teenth time, "because the door is locked. And the door is locked because we are not permitted to leave."

Monny, his legs still crossed and his nails, at that point, perfectly manicured, darted his eyes toward Drenge. "Nexus," he whispered, "I think he's broken."

I sighed, leaning back in my chair so that I balanced only on the back legs. "It's not Drenge who is broken, Monny; it's his logic. He can't think himself out of this room." I tapped my fingers on the table, tugged at the leaves on the vines. Anything to stay collected. "Do you know why we're still here?"

Monny shrugged. "My guess is they are investigating, and we are more useful here than at home. Even though it's been like...nineteen hours."

"At least you've stopped trying to read me."

He grinned. "You noticed, huh? I'm usually pretty good."

"No, don't get me wrong. You're very good. I'm just sensitive."

He raised his eyebrows. "Are you now?"

My turn to shrug. And change the subject. "What rank are you, Monny?"

"Feeler Second. But you are still primary rank? That's odd, given your skill set."

"Everything about how Fenders arrange this place is odd." I bit my lip. I was saying far too much. But it was hard to be so quiet when stuck in a small space with someone as charming as Monny.

"Don't worry," Monny said. "I'm definitely off duty at this point. I won't tattle. Besides, no one likes Fenders. They're so superior."

He stood, tugging on his sweater as if it were one of the straight-lined coats the Fenders wore. He snapped his heels together and scowled. "What is the meaning of this? Have you forgotten yourself? Be respectful. There is an order for a reason and a reason for the order. Sit straight, lest you shame the City. Everything for the Fight. No arguments. No thoughts. No, no, no."

I giggled. Standing, I bowed deeply. "But, Fender Master...."

He harumphed. "Excuse me?! Fender Master? I am Fender Of Fenders! I am the greatest Fender to ever fend! I am fending itself!" He stomped around, saluting to no one.

The door opened right then. I shrieked, and Monny knocked over the pot of stale coffee. Drenge, who had nodded off to sleep amid his crazed ramblings, snorted awake.

My mother stood in the doorway, and so I bowed. For real. "Matrix, hello."

"Hello, Data."

Did my mother just...respond to me? Like I am a living, functioning, valid human person? Like...I am her daughter?

She stood as straight as steel. "Thanks to your thinking, we have eliminated the likelihood that the House Of Forms might have designed the abomination that is the resurrection of the dead. A cycle ended must remain ended. We are all in agreement on this fact."

We are?

"An investigation of the House Of Reason has ensued, and we have found four culprits, one being Wizen Master Gamall Herres. All four Wizens are found to be Meta and must be set back on the right path. Not only are they guilty of being Meta, but they are responsible for the atrocity of the waking of Clay Vanes. Do not worry. We will make this right. This is why the Fight goes on."

"For the Fight," we all said.

Before my mother could say anything else, I interrupted. "What about Edwidge?"

Viveka's laser eyes scoured into me. "What about her?"

"Is she...I mean...is she...also guilty?"

My mother did not answer me. Instead she turned to Monny. "You have Fought well. You may leave." And then to Drenge and me, "The two of you remain."

Monny flipped his scarf over his broad shoulders and made for the door, offering an elegant bow to my mother. Once behind her back, he blew me a kiss. If my mother were not watching, I would have caught it and put it in my pocket. He would have liked that. I would have liked that. But it did not matter what people like Monny and I liked.

"There has been a proposal," my mother stated. She then paused.

Drenge and I both exchanged puzzled looks. I wiggled my toes in my shoes and my metal, which had been quite relaxed with Monny and Drenge over the long hours, shook awake inside me.

"Um...okay?" I offered.

Viveka almost growled. "A proposal from Onur Vanes."

I still did not know what she meant. "A proposal for?"

"For Housing. With you, Nexus."

I audibly gasped. *What? No. What? No.*

My mother crossed her arms behind her back. "I am aware that you and the Vanes boy have shown interest in one another for some time. Perhaps our houses hoped, at one point, that the two of you might make the Fight proud by housing together."

Oh god, oh god, oh god. This is it. The moment I die. What I had hoped for all my life was finally happening. I was being partnered with Onur Vanes. For the rest of my days.

"I need to know, Nexus," my mother said, speaking only slightly louder than my titanium, "how much you care to be with this boy. Are there...emotions involved? Are you determined?"

"You're asking me...what I want to do?"

"No. You are mistaken. I am asking what you are intending to do. You state your hopes, and I will state my expectations." She motioned with her hand. "You may go first."

"Okay." I took a deep breath. "Please don't be mad, but I hate him."

She was genuinely shocked. "You hate him?"

I nodded. "Yes, very much."

"That may prove to be unfortunate. I had hoped you had no emotions toward him. But hatred is a strong one."

"You want me to have no emotions toward Onur?"

"Of course. It will make partnering with him easier. You would be more objective."

"But I don't want to partner with Onur. At all. Ever."

"You will have him." Her words were final.

Drenge cleared his throat. "Why am I here? I would like to leave."

"You are a part of this," my mother snapped. "My daughter will partner with Onur Vanes, but they will not make House Vanes. They will make House Aerixon."

I turned my thinking up a notch. *Another House Aerixon.* To do that, I would have to outrank Onur at the time of our partnering.

"You are asking Drenge to raise my rank. And you will lower Onur's. So I lead Onur when we partner, and not the other way around."

Viveka straightened her shoulders even more. "I am not asking. My daughter will partner with Onur Vanes, and she will outrank him when she does." She angled to Drenge. "Do you agree, Former Master?"

He stood up, straightening his glasses. "If it is in the interest of Nexus Aerixon, I will agree to just about anything." He looked taller than I remembered. "I will begin the paperwork."

Viveka dismissed it with a wave. "Consider it approved."

Then they shook hands.

And the second House Aerixon was born.

Ep 20

Toast To Tomorrow's End

Life Tip: Spiked drinks go down better with a chaser of utter terror.

Onur Aerixon's fists shook at his sides. With great possibility, he would have killed me if our houses were not gathered.

"From great tribulation comes great triumph. To the Fight we welcome Former Above Nexus Aerixon. And to the Fight we welcome House Aerixon anew."

I bowed and made a smile appear on my face. Onur did not even try. I did my best to remember it was not too long ago that he would have swooped me into the air and kissed me at such an announcement. But in that scenario, I was becoming his. Instead, he was becoming mine.

Viveka held a Metatoxin-laced glass of fine brew in the air. "Welcome, Second Fender Onur. You will enjoy reaping the rewards of the Aerixon legacy."

He found his glass and lifted it to the air. It looked painful for him to swallow. But Viveka, as Fender Master, could have his rank lowered as she pleased.

It was quite literally painful for me to swallow. I forced the toxin down, and my lead swished to action, which made the pulse in my arm throb, which made my steel piercing activate to displace the charge.

Dahn Vanes slammed her glass down on our dining room table. "Are you all insane? We can't celebrate right now. We can't do *anything* right now. Our house is in shambles. I haven't seen my little sister since they took her away to the House Of Certainty. My mother is in the Hall Of Repair, and no one seems to care. It has been four days since Clay died. Remember that? She *died*. And now we're toasting to new houses like it's a Holy Day?"

"It is not the time, Dahn," Onur hissed at her.

"Oh? No? When is it the time, Onur? When are you *not* trying to impress Viveka? Let me see Clay, and you can do whatever you want with your partners and your ranks and your houses."

I knew Onur would hit her. Before I could stop myself, I moved forward and grabbed his wrist midswing. Gently, I lowered it back to his side.

"We are all tired," I said carefully. "And many things have demanded our attention." I released him and faced our houses. "We have time. Partnering, though official, does not have to be instant. Rushing ahead will make House Aerixon less stable." I looked to Onur. "I intend for us to be strong. Don't you?"

His jaw still clenched, he nodded and raised his glass again. "To strength."

We all drank, except for Dahn who chose to glower from her perch at the table.

Priyaa came to me once the toasting was over, her eyes red and swollen as if she had been crying. She squeezed my hand. "I can't believe this is happening. It's all so...fast."

I squeezed back. "It will be alright, Pri."

She smiled, but neither of us were convinced by her display. "I'll believe that when I can hug Clay again."

"Soon." I took a few deep breaths. "It has to be soon."

Priyaa moved closer to me, so no one overheard. "How long before you must...find a new flat? With Onur?"

I knew what she was implying. *When will we actually carry on with partnership duties? When will we begin contributing children to the Fight? When will we begin consummating our partnership?*

"I don't know of a transition period being shorter than a month. But—"

"But this is all unprecedented." Priyaa's eyes filled with tears. "I will miss you when you go."

I sighed. "I know. Who will constantly screw up so you look perfect all the time?"

She rolled her eyes. "You'll still screw up plenty. And with the Aerixon name on your front door. Mother will watch closer than ever."

I hardly noticed my mother and Onur speaking in hushed tones in the corner of the room. Onur left in a huff, and my mother took a moment. Her usually impossibly pale skin wore a hint of red. It made my stomach hurt. I had seen my mother angry. Indifferent. Unapologetic. Even mean. I had never seen my mother flustered.

She looked up, noticing me observing her, and motioned me to her side.

"Nexus," she said.

"What is it?" I asked, my heart racing. There was even a thin sheen of perspiration on her forehead.

"Onur attempts to outwit us. You may end up a Vanes after all, if he succeeds."

Like hel. "No. That cannot happen." I could not imagine being subject to Onur. To his rules. To his desires. If he outranked me, I would have no say. No power. Who would protect me from my protector then? "How, Mother? How is he outwitting us?"

"A last minute play for raising his rank."

"Can he...do that? It is already official, isn't it?"

"He will try to appease the Fender Of Fenders. And if he succeeds, he may be granted a reapplication for partnership. These things can happen if one is an especially talented Fender. And Onur is no fool."

"But you are a Fender *Master*. And he's just been lowered. How can Onur persuade the Fender Of Fenders if you can't?"

She twisted her head to crack her neck, releasing tension. "He will offer to pay the highest price."

That's when I understood. Onur would do anything to make me Nexus Vanes, to make me his, and to profit from anything I achieved. He would do anything for his rank. He would do anything for himself. Not just because he was a talented Fender, but because he loved himself and no one else.

Onur would offer to have his little sister Ended. And he would say it was for the Fight.

Ep 21

Monster In The Closet

Life Tip: Schedule naps around life-altering events, not during them.

My mother took me to her private study. It was sparse, only writing utensils and cold lighting. A desk with a single stool. She sat very still. This was the most severe case of the Thinky Grumps I had ever witnessed. I was not sure she was even breathing.

She snapped out of it only to ask a question. "How quickly can you finish the machine?"

"I am not allowed—"

"Good god, Nexus, now is not the time for trivial Former rules. Just give me a timeline."

"Former rules are not trivial," I said firmly. "They are set in place to protect the integrity of something I care very much about. I won't sacrifice the House Of Forms or my position there. How then will I outrank Onur? I will lose my rank by breaking the rules of discretion. We will be working against ourselves. That makes no sense."

My mother examined me for longer than usual. I couldn't tell whether she was impressed or dismayed. "What then do you propose, Former Above?"

In the pocket of my dress, I pulled powdered magnesium to my fingertips. The smooth texture coated my thumb and index fingers as I rolled it around. A distraction, so my thoughts could come clearly. "What if the City found out that Onur broke a rule? A violation that has been overlooked due to the search for the Meta who awakened Clay?"

"Go on."

"What if he...." And even though I wanted to, I did not say anything else.

"Did he truly?" My mother sat with her hands on her knees, unmoving as she thought, her face blank.

I considered her, her pale skin and straight, narrow nose, her fine hair in a tight bun at the nape of her neck. We could not have been more different.

I nodded. "He did."

"Did you consent?"

I took a deep breath. A few more. There was not enough air in the study. Not enough air in the City. In all the Aarde. *Calm, Nexus. Careful.* "I did not."

She sat even more still. "It will not work. I cannot ensure his demise for breaking celibacy without implicating you in the violation as well. It takes two, and two will be held accountable. The Fight will not consider consent a factor."

"They won't? That cannot be true. How can we know this unless we try?"

She cleared her throat. "They will not, Nexus. It is not something they have ever been concerned about." She turned toward me, and when her gray eyes met mine, I remembered we shared our hue. The same intense stare. It was not passion nor desire nor even curiosity. We shared the will to survive.

"Are you injured?" she asked.

"No, Mother."

"We should take you to a Wizen."

"God no. *No.* They will only give me water and waste my time."

Her lips twitched, as if she were holding in a laugh. But her sobriety returned. "Well then. We will have to choose another partner for you. Seeing that Vanes is as good as shit."

A short burst of laughter escaped me. "Really? I can have someone else?"

"Indeed. We must look elsewhere. There are better men, Nexus. If you choose a loyal man, he will be stupid. You'll carry him all your days, but he will not leave your arms. Choose an ambitious man, and you will bed your greatest rival. But choose shit, and shit is all you get."

"Which did you choose?" I asked her.

"Which do you suppose?"

I grinned. *Am I...enjoying a conversation with Viveka Aerixon? Is this real? Who even am I right now?* "My father? A rival."

"Mmm. Richter does hate me, quite vibrantly."

I shrugged. "That's his own doing. I would not choose to go up against you without acknowledging the possibility of losing. He chose to, and now he is losing. It's his fault he is so surprised."

"And this Vanes boy will be surprised as you soar past him. Ambition is blind. It does not see the enemies it makes as it climbs. He will make a fool of himself, Ending his sister with no house partnership as reward. He will do it for nothing."

I chewed my lip. That familiar pang in my chest that told me I was powerless and could, in the end, hardly save myself, much less anyone else. *Still. Try, I must.* "If we tell Onur I am not to be partnered with him, he will stay his hand. Why offer his sister then? Clay will live. We will win."

"You must let that notion go, Nexus. That girl will die. It must be done. The only thing up for debate is whose fending will benefit from her End." She stood, signaling that our talk was over. "You will do well to remember that he is not trying to win *you*. He is simply trying to win. He will offer her with or without you. It gains him favor. It is brilliant."

I wanted to say that there must be some way. *Who could I speak to without drawing suspicion? Which Fender would give me their ear?* No one. Fending was politics. And I was a pawn, not a player.

I went to my room, thinking briefly of Stur, who I evidently would never finish, and Priyaa, who I would never spend time with, and the friends I would never make, and the lovers' strolls I would never take.

I grunted and groaned while flipping my mattress, denying that anything had ever happened on it other than innocent drooling and lucid nightmares. Then, I recalled—and immediately ignored—the laundry I'd finally started in the bathroom basin that had never left the soaking stage. I fell into my pillows with abandon. Sleep, and then I would figure out how to save Clay's life. Again.

A rustling, and then a thump in my closet. "Get back here," I grumbled to whichever metal daring to make a run for it. "I'm too tired for this. Please just behave for once."

No response. I did a quick roll call to see which metal I was missing, making a mental note to ascribe that task to one of my more responsible inhabitants at a later date. But the whole circus was present.

Fantastic. Now I'm being haunted. Carefully, I slithered off my bed and crept to the closet. *Maybe it's someone new who wants to cut me open. Or my next lover come back from the future to torture me.* I yanked the door handle, bracing myself to meet the undead or whatever ridiculous monster represented my next turn of events.

Half-covered in a pile of my sweaters and shoes, and apparently decently unconscious, was Dahn Vanes. *She must have hit her head—ah, there was the source of the thump sound—on the side of the closet.* Trickling down her perfectly manicured brow?

Blood. Clear as water.

Ep 22

For Your Piercing Pleasure

Life Tip: If someone's dying in your closet, let them.

"What on Aarde am I supposed to do with this?" I stood outside my closet, taking in the complete mess that was my life.

I decided making sure Dahn wasn't dead was a reasonable first step. The whirring of her cells confirmed she was alive. That and the fact she was breathing. *Guess I should have checked for the obvious thing first.* I dragged her out of the closet with a grunt. She was much heavier than I expected. *Probably weighed down with all that charm.* Once she was laid out in the middle of my room, I poked her forehead. *Yep definitely bleeding.* I slapped her cheeks a little. *Definitely unconscious.*

I rocked back on my heels crouched beside Dahn. *Any of you want to volunteer your services here?*

My metal got really quiet. Lead pretended it was asleep.

Seriously? That's how we're going to play this?

Tin sighed and offered a reluctant wiggle.

So kind of you. I owe you one. Who am I kidding? I owe you a dozen at this point.

I held up my palm and let tin rise from my skin. I rubbed my hand on Dahn's forehead. Tin snickered and fluffed itself, caressing her wound with silvery softness.

It was nice to see tin. I hardly ever got a chance to look at my metals. There was so little time and so little opportunity to be alone without being in crisis.

Dahn smacked her lips as her eyelids fluttered open. Then, she sat up so fast I was afraid she'd pass out again. She startled tin, and it rushed back to me, sinking into the pores along my jawline.

"Oh my god, what did you do to me?" Dahn said, scooching away from where I knelt beside her.

"Me? Oh, I just stopped you from bleeding out in the closet. No big deal."

She squeaked, her hand rushing to what was left of the wound above her eyebrow. "I'm bleeding?"

"Sure are. Well, you were. We fixed it. Remember that part?"

Her almond eyes wide, she stared at me. Then after a moment or two, "I think I have to kill you now."

I blinked at her. "What?"

"I think I have to. Because you know my secret. You'll talk. You'll get me Ended. So, what other choice do I have?"

This should be fun. I had never really seen Dahn do anything, so watching her manage to kill me would make my day. I shrugged. "Okay, I understand."

"You...do?"

"Logical conclusion. Protect the secret. Kill Nexus. Do what you have to do." I looked around the room. "What will you use to do it? Your bare hands won't work. You'll ruin your nails."

She narrowed her eyes at me. "I will do it, you know. I'm not afraid."

"No, yeah, I believe in you, Dahn."

She actually looked around the room. "Maybe something stabby?"

I grinned. "Yeah?"

She grinned back like she couldn't help it. "You should clean your closet. I almost died slipping on one of those sweaters."

"Dahn, why were you in my closet in the first place?"

She sighed. "Not a lot of options. Because you were with your mother plotting my brother's demise or something, and your dad was using the washroom—like really using it—and Priyaa was doing whatever Priyaa does in her room—"

"Journaling?"

"Needlepoint?"

"Meditation?"

"Reapplying her flawless synthetix exterior?"

I chuckled. "She's great though."

Dahn rolled her eyes. "Yes, I know. That's why she's so annoying. And obviously I couldn't hide out in there."

"Dahn, *why* were you hiding out?"

"Did you...not see the blood? I thought we got past that part."

"No Dahn. I know you're Meta, but why were you hiding?"

She shushed me and shoved my arm hard enough to knock me over. "Don't call me that! And if you must know, I was hiding because"—she took a deep breath—"I know I'm not supposed to but I took some iron this morning. I was walking over here and I was so hungry because I can't eat anything anymore and I was so stressed with my sister dying and not dying and Onur trying to put it in you and my mom

being dragged away to a crazy house and I just needed
...something. So I took a little iron from this neighborhood
kid who was running around just filled with the stuff, all
normal with his blood and his iron, and I just took a tiny
bit. But then, I did and my *arm*"—she lifted her left arm
into the air and pointed to her inner elbow—"my arm caught
on literal fyre, Nexus. I mean, I can't lie and say I haven't
ciphoned a little iron here and there just to get by, but it
never hurt like this before. And it kept getting worse and
worse. I thought I would die. I thought the Morals were
coming for me. So I hid. I hid, and then you came in, and I
panicked and then slipped on your sweater and hit my head,
and this arm still hurts so goddamn much, God help me!"

As the pain escalated, she tugged at her arm like she wanted
to rip it off. I had to clamp my hand over her mouth to keep
her from howling.

"Dahn, you're going to get us killed. Shut up. Shut up!"

"It hurts. So much."

"It's the metal in you. It makes the pulse device in your
arm react. Let it go."

A couple tears slid down her high cheekbones. "But I need
iron, Nexus. I need something."

I knew the desperation. The desire to hold on to the metal
even though it hurt...because the metal was, in a way, life.
And letting go of life in order to live was hard to do.

"I have an idea," I said.

I pulled my metals out and set them on the ground. It
was a pretty good distraction for Dahn. For a minute, the
pain was clouded by intrigue. She had probably never seen
so much metal in one place, in so many forms. Still favoring

her arm, she poked lead, and it snapped at her. But silver was a flirt; it curled around her index finger.

The only metal remaining in me was steel. I twisted my fingers in the air, straightening the ring in my lip and pulling it out. I divided the steel piece into two and reattached my half. The other half was for Dahn. I was about to slide it into her lip, but I hesitated. I felt the steel pull to the right, as if saying, *No, not there.* I followed it until I felt it halt at her right ear and pushed the steel into the top of her ear and snapped my fingers. The steel curled into a ring.

Dahn, reacting to the sharp pain of the piercing, stopped mid-profanity. Her body visibly relaxed, her shoulders softening and her hands releasing their tension.

"How did you...." But her eyes filled with tears before she could finish. She threw her arms around me, collapsing against my chest, and wept. I ran my hand over her hair, perpetually unsure of what to do at such times.

"Thank you," she said, catching her breath and sitting back up. "I don't even know what to say. How to tell you...but just...thank you, Nex."

I nodded. I didn't tell her, as I took my metals back, that my own pain would double. Instead, I saved some aluminum and silver and taught her how to cloak her new ring. I was shocked at how long it took her to grasp the concept of moving. What I had learned in a matter of seconds, took Dahn almost an hour.

"How are you doing it so easily?" She was sweating. A slight tremor to her hands.

"We should stop," I said. "You lost a lot of blood earlier. No need to overdo it."

"But you don't look like you're struggling at all."

"I've had practice."

Dahn hugged her knees. "How long have you known?"

I'd never asked myself that before. Never really slowed down long enough to think about whens and hows. "I'm not sure. Maybe I've always known. It's like, there are two parts to it. Ever since I could form thoughts I knew I was...."

"Different," Dahn said.

I shook my head. "Powerful." I fiddled with my magnesium, rubbing it between my fingers. "But I also knew I should be afraid."

"I know exactly what you mean. Like...fear just comes along with who I am." She rested her chin on her knees. "I've never had a conversation with another one of us before."

"Is that why you started being such a bitch to me? Closed yourself off? You didn't want me to find out?"

"I guess I'm that way with everyone. Keep no one close. I guess except for Clay."

"Yes. Except for Clay."

Dahn touched her hidden earring. "How did you figure this out, Nex? Are you just that much of a genius."

How would the truth sound? A mysterious Meta sliced me open, saved my life, and then taught me how? Oh, and then he jumped out my window, and I never saw him again? I went with, "If I'm desperate enough, I can figure anything out."

"Well, where did you get so much metal, and how do I get some more?"

"I picked them up here and there. Sorry."

"Oh." But then she gasped. "I just realized. Onur's going to be so pissed."

I tilted my head. "What do you mean?"

"When I tell him that you know. He always gets so wound up about these things."

"Onur...knows you're Meta?"

"Don't use that word!"

"Dahn, explain what you mean right now." My titanium quivered. "He knows?" *About Dahn? About me?*

Dahn nodded. "Nex, Onur knows. He's always known."

Ep 23

Dinner Is, In Fact, Negotiable

Life Tip: The blander the food, the less you feel the poison.

Day thirty with no Clay. She was still in the House Of Certainty, her mother still in the Hall Of Repair.

I made progress at the House Of Forms, nearly completing Stur's circuitry and was preparing to weld the exterior pieces in place. Then on to testing. I still had no plan for how to prevent the subsequent genocide upon Stur's completion. *One death sentence at a time.*

My mother informed me that Onur's plan had worked. He had leveraged his sister's life for the restoration of his rank. When the House Of Certainty was done with Clay, they would do what must be done. I had until then, whenever 'then' was, to make a plan I couldn't pull off.

My mother began the work of finding me a suitable replacement for the bastard, Onur. This meant courting. Courting. *Me.* The whole process was something I had fatefully avoided until then, since Onur and I were childhood friends and quite literally fell into love. Not only were the nightly courtings mandatory—according to Viveka—but I had to endure them with half my steel gone and the knowledge that Onur could, at any moment, turn Dahn in for even more leverage. When I thought about whether he knew what I was or not, my brain began to shut down, so I avoided those sorts of contemplations. *He's always known.* That's what Dahn said the night I helped her. *Always known about her? About me?*

I scraped my fingernails against a sliver of titanium, hoping to rid myself of my nerves as I waited in the same diner Onur and I used to frequent. Nothing had changed, except for the sickly aroma of Metatoxin floating out of the kitchen with every dish. Courting was not my favorite. I'd even asked Formula for tips on how to end them swiftly. The previous night, for example, I had the great misfortune of dining with a First Wizen who smelled like damp socks and only spoke in riddles. A hard pass. But my mother was getting impatient with all my hard passes. She wanted a 'yes'. She wanted another house. She wanted to win.

Who will I be forced to eat stewed potatoes with tonight?

The glass door flew open. Straight past the seater walked a boy who wore his fleece scarf like a crown around his head, the fabric folded and twisted precisely to make a statement. His pearl earrings glowed in the dim diner lighting. His broad shoulders cast shadows as he moved. He glided into the seat across from me.

"Don't look so surprised," said Monny.

I felt myself light up. A strange reaction for being face to face with a Feeler. "It's actually really nice to see you." I was, in fact, delighted. My lead purred, making my arm ache, but still. At least it liked him too. As soon as it dawned on me that he was in my future partner's chair, I frowned. "I am supposed to be meeting someone here."

He smiled as he gestured to himself. "Ta da."

I laughed. A good long loud one. I even wiped a tear from my eye.

"Rude," he chided. "Monny Felagi will not be denied."

"No, no. Forgive me. It's just...you can't be here for me. Clearly, you're completely wonderful. And also ranked too highly. And also...." I didn't know how to word that last one. Not Meta, no. But something just as dangerous to be in the City. Monny was definitely not there for a 'me' type.

He sighed and slid my water his way, taking a smooth sip. "I am indeed highly ranked. Same as you. But I don't mind becoming an Aerixon. I hereby relinquish my right to head up our house. It's all yours. As long as you don't mind that other 'also' you mentioned. The fact that I am an 'also' needs to stay between us."

I leaned in so I could whisper. "Are you crazy?"

He leaned in too, so we were only inches apart, nose to nose. He really was very pretty. Thick, full lips and a creamy, dark-brown complexion. His large eyes were golden and brimming with life.

"You have great skin," he whispered.

I grinned. "Thank you."

"Nexus? Why are we whispering?"

"Because you are clearly unhinged. You're saying that you will partner with me and simply give me the name of our house? And in exchange, you only ask that our partnership remain...platonic?"

He wagged his eyebrows. "Always the clever one, Nexus."

"Did my mother come up with this?" I could not fathom her being so unconventional.

We sat back in our seats. "Viveka is not the only thinker in the City, as you well know being one of them yourself. When I heard of your predicament and how you ditched the handsome narcissist, I figured maybe you and I could work. Came here without Viv knowing, of course. We're both being pressured to partner, and I cannot end up trapped with some clingy female who needs access to my body for her to feel her own self-worth."

I arched my eyebrow. Monny made me do things like that—eyebrow-arching and whatnot. "What makes you think *I* won't need access to your body? What if I need to be madly in love with my partner? How would you know?"

"Because, Nex, you're obviously already in love."

What now? "I am not. With who?"

"With being alive. With being yourself. And I am too. I love being Monny. Perfect partnership if you ask me."

"But what if I want to fall in love with an actual human? Other than myself? If you're off the table, what then?"

Monny shrugged. "Fly your flag, darling."

I laughed again. The whole discussion left me feeling a little giddy. Albeit nonsensical, this was the most fun I had had in a very long while. "I could court other people? Consummate with other people? Complete freedom to do this? This is what you're proposing?"

"Freedom to do what you want? License? Encouragement? There's only one way to say tomato."

"And you would do the same? With other people?"

"Oh, I surely will."

"And we—you and I—would be...friends?"

"And allies. Confidants. We would be partners. No competition. No one-upping. No rivalry. No snitching. Keep your secrets, I keep mine. Have your lovers, I'll have mine. And, at the end of the day...we'd have each other. We'd have a house." He looked around for the seater who'd yet to come take our orders. "What do you say, Nex?"

"Well...my mother is not easy to get along with. I will have to pitch this idea, with some key details redacted of course."

"She'll say yes."

"How do you know?"

He tapped his forehead with his index finger. "She's an easy one to read most days. She knows what she wants and goes for it. And what she wants is a House Aerixon that increases her power and acclaim. She wants that Fender Of Fender rank. Our arrangement would help her get it. She'll say 'yes'." He looked me right in the eye then. "You, on the other hand, have a mental wall so thick it's almost impenetrable. So many hats, this Nexus. So many masks. But I have a feeling, underneath all that...."

The suspense was too much. "What? What's underneath?" *Don't say Meta. Oh god.*

"I see a hawke pretending she's a bumble bhee. A lyon dressed like a fyeld mouse. You're a legend waiting to happen. And I love a good story."

Oh sweet Monny. He has no idea how much laundry I never do and how much metal I need just to hold me together. Trying to change the topic, what with the heat growing under my skin from all his reading me, I tried to hand Monny a menu. But he denied it.

"Nex, let me explain something. I am a badarse. And badarses don't order off the menu."

I am learning so much today. "How do you order, then, Master Badarse?"

"I say whatever comes to mind and see what happens. It's usually quite the show."

Wait a second. Wait a hot second. I realized something was missing. "Monny, do you know what happened to the person my mother planned for me to meet here? Did he just never show? Chalk it up to serendipity?"

"He...tripped."

"He *tripped* out of courting me? What does that even mean?" I narrowed my eyes but couldn't help my smile. "What did you do, Feeler?"

He shrugged one shoulder. "For you, my Nex, partner of my dreams? I'd trip a fool or two."

So I ordered stewed potatoes, and Monny ordered 'whatever is purplest,' and we made each other laugh for an hour straight.

That marked the first uncoerced meal I ever shared with the greatest—yet rather platonic—love of my young life.

Ep 24

Oh Wow. A Party.

Life Tip: Install a peephole.

A knock on our door when the moon was mid-sky and the City fast asleep.

Monny stuck his head out of his room right when I stuck my head out of mine. In nothing but his underwear, he whispered across the narrow hallway of our new flat.

"Did you invite someone over?"

"No, Monny, I don't have any secret lovers banging on my door in the middle of the night. Did *you* invite someone over?"

"Yes, but he already left. My secret lovers are punctual."

Monny never fell asleep alone. As for me, I enjoyed my long nights sprawled out in my own bed, no longer pretending to read to look busy. No longer under my mother's watchful eye.

Another knock on the door.

"Maybe he forgot something?" I asked. "Are secret lovers forgetful?"

"He better not have. I keep a tight sleep schedule."

I wrinkled my nose at him. "You never sleep."

"Yes, and my insomnia relies heavily on that routine."

This time, the knock threatened to buckle the door in.

"I'll go," I said, pretending to be brave in my bare feet, not even a bra to support me.

"I believe in you," Monny whispered, retreating a little further into his room, where he watched with his door cracked. "House Aerixon forever."

I didn't need Monny to be a warrior. He was better than anything like that. The talk with my mother went just as Monny said it would. She said yes to our partnership almost instantly. Apparently, he had a decent reputation as a Feeler. He was going places. I was going places. Made sense we go there together. The paperwork went through the House Of Houses with great speed. I imagined my mother looming over the Fenders in charge of processing, her hands behind her back and her lips clamped, judging their inefficiency. But by the next evening, we were Nexus and Monny Aerixon. The luckiest plotters to ever have plotted.

I met Monny's family briefly. They were kind and astonishingly boring. Happy he was settling down, and with a Former no less, because I would be good for him. Whatever that meant.

It was great, though. Monny had his love life and I had ...well, none. Just as we planned.

Not long after our news was public, Onur made a partnership offer to a Wizen. The same one who treated me in the House Of Reason after I awakened Clay. Var Vanes. That would be her new name. The rank of their house was to be paid with Clay's blood. But it had been weeks. No Clay. No blood. Nothing.

The knocking on the door was incessant. My sleeping robe wrapped around me, I took three deep breaths and opened it up. Dahn stood before me, also in her sleeping robe, but soaking wet from the downpour of rain. In her arms, a child.

I let her in immediately, locking the door behind her. Our flat was much smaller than my mother and father's, so I had to push our couches out of the way to lay the boy on the floor.

"What is going on?" I asked Dahn, breathless.

She looked frazzled. Scared. Her eyes were wide, her pupils fully dilated. "I don't know."

"You don't know? Dahn, who is this child?" A young boy, maybe six in age. His orange hair sopping wet, his skin almost gray. Eyes closed. He looked dead.

"I don't know who he is," Dahn said, her teeth chattering. She needed time to calm down but couldn't afford it. "I found him like this."

"And you brought him here? Not to a Wizen? Dahn, we need to call for help."

She shook her head, water droplets flying across the living room. "Nexus, he's Meta." She pointed to his left arm. It was covered in claw marks, as if the boy had been trying to remove the pulse device with his own fingernails. "He doesn't need help, Nex, he needs you."

I stared at the boy for far too long. Not thinking. Not praying. Just understanding. That if I was going to help him, I would have to get brave. Quick. *Now.*

"Wait here," I said to Dahn. "And take some deep breaths. I need you to calm yourself."

I marched over to Monny's room and yanked the door out of his hands. He jumped and straightened, no longer needing to peek through the crack.

"Monny," I said as calmly as I could, "I'm Meta."

I waited for his reaction. For him to panic and call the Morals. For him to treat me like I was a monster.

"Is this supposed to be news to me?"

I reeled. "You...know?"

"Oh honey. I mean...yes. No one has a mental wall that strong unless they're hiding a bomb."

"And you still...picked me?"

He shrugged. "You have great skin."

I shook my head to clear it, promising myself I would kiss him on the cheek later. "I need your help." I dragged him by the hand into the living room.

He took in the scene. "Oh wow. A party." He paused. "With a dead child as a special guest."

"He's not dead," I said, kneeling beside the boy. "But he is dying. Sort of dying." *More like going to sleep.* His cells slowed to a gentle hum. Like Clay the night I awakened her.

Dahn pointed to his arm again, showing Monny. "He has one of those torture devices."

"I didn't think they were putting them in children this young." I looked to Monny, who knelt beside me.

"I did not think so either. The decision to do so must be above my rank." He frowned. "But you cannot take it out, Nex. It will electrocute anyone who tries."

"Hurts like hel," Dahn said. "Just leaving it alone is bad enough. Add a little metal, and it's like fyre."

"It certainly is intolerable," I added.

Monny's frown deepened. "I thought maybe the pain wasn't so bad. You seemed alright, Nex."

Dahn scoffed. "Oh it's bad, Feeler. I'd be dead if not for Nexus. That's how I knew to bring him here." She looked to me. "You do know what to do, don't you?"

"I'll do my best." I put my hands out, calling to the metal the boy must have been holding on to. Nothing. I tried again. Nothing. Then it came to me. "He's got a shield up."

"A shield?" Monny asked.

"The wall you sense around me. A shield. He has one, and it's too strong for me to pull the metal through. And if the metal stays in him, the device will not stop pulsing. He's not conscious. I can't exactly ask him to let the shield down."

"So...what then? We cut his arm off?" Dahn asked.

"Monny, go get me the sharpest knife in our kitchen."

Dahn shrieked. "Himmin and hel, Nexus, I was just joking!"

Monny returned with a synthetix blade. I examined it. Turned its form in my mind. Touched it to my finger. *Not sharp enough.* It didn't even draw blood. So I pulled platinum from my rib cage and asked it to line the blade, to add its sharpness and durability to what I needed to do. *Help me.*

Ready or not, it had to be time. "Hold his arms in case he wakes up," I told my friends.

"Nexus, wait," Dahn started, but Monny interrupted her. "Do what she asks," he said.

"And if she asked me to stab you in the heart? What would you say to that?" Dahn asked.

Monny didn't miss a beat. "I'd say she probably has a really good reason. And I'd lend her a hand."

I made a mental note to have a good cry about his comment later. *No time for that now.* If I cried, I'd be crying. Unacceptable. I lifted the blade, asked my metal to steady my hand, and lowered it to the boy's abdomen. *You can do this, Nexus.*

And so I did it. From navel to throat.

Ep 25

The Goddess And The Dead Boy

Life Tip: Practice major surgery at least once before attempting to perform it on a live patient.

Where is that magical, metal-wielding, thoracic surgeon boy when I need him?

I had already stabbed my knife into the chest of the small child. Know what happened next? Blood. That's what happened. So, so much. Fountains of it. And do you know what color it was?

Red.

I killed him. The knife trembled so hard in my hand that I dropped it. *He'll die here. For real. I'm a murderer. I'm a child murderer. He's not Meta. He's perfectly normal, and I put a knife to him. Oh god, oh god.*

But after a moment, the red blood diluted and began to flow clear. *He must have pulled iron from someone at some point.*

Working on instinct alone, I twisted my left hand and pulled the microscopic bits of iron from the pooling blood. I clenched my fist, forming the iron into a small ball.

"Catch," I said to Dahn, tossing it her way. "Collect them for me."

"Do I get to keep them?" she asked, still soaking wet, but amused by the tiny bit of metal.

"No, Dahn, we have to give it back. They're his."

She frowned but didn't argue.

"I'm here," Monny said from right beside me, kneeling in the mess. "What do you need?"

I shook my head. "Just you. Here."

"Well, you're in luck. I'm not going anywhere."

I owed Monny more than thanks. I had the feeling I would never settle my tab when it came to him.

I hovered my hands over the boy's chest. His shield couldn't stop me from feeling the metal anymore. He had quite a bit in him. Strontium. More calcium than I had ever seen. Titanium locked around his heart. Some that I did not have time to identify. I pulled them out as quickly as I could and tossed them to Dahn.

Think, Nexus, think. Now what?

"Now what?" Dahn asked, echoing my thoughts. Her voice came out in a series of squeaks.

"I don't know."

"You *don't know?*"

"No, Dahn, I don't know. I've never done anything like this. I've never even seen anything like this. I was unconscious for mine. I don't know how he sewed me back up."

Dahn and Monny spoke in tandem. "How *who* sewed you back up?"

"The boy from my window."

"Who?"

I yelled. "The boy from my window with the piercings and the dreamy smile. He cut me open, but I don't know

163

how and I don't know where he is, so he's of no use right
now! End of story!"

The blood ran and ran. I stared and stared.

"I thought the little guy was already dead," Monny said.
"But there's still so much blood."

"He's not dead," I said. "Not really."

"How do you know?" Monny asked.

*The same way I knew I could still help Clay. Listening.
Listening, and asking. Help me, I thought as hard as I could.
Begged, really. Help me save him.*

His metal began to vibrate from within Dahn's grasp.

"Oh god," she said. After a moment, she could barely hold
onto them. "What the hel is happening?"

The metal not only vibrated, it began to hum. No, it began
to ring. They clanged into each other, rolling around in her
open palms until she dropped them on the wooden floor.

"Ah! They're burning hot!" She shook her hands to cool
her singed skin.

The metal lifted off the ground and then, as one, they flew
toward me, colliding with my chest and knocking me backward onto the floor. Never had I experienced so many things
happening to me at once. They clung to my bones, cemented
my throat, entangled with my eyes. I coughed and I felt
powdered magnesium billow like a cloud within my lungs.

Knowing what to do was much simpler then. I sat up
and took the steel from my lip, shaving it in half yet again.
My body lurched as the pulse flaymed in my arm. But I was
determined. I returned my sliver of steel, inserting the rest
into the boy's lip.

Then I put my hand to his chest. *Iron,* I called in my mind, *go in and hold his blood still.* Iron went. *Molybdenum, stitch his muscles.* And it did. I continued this with each of his metals—and some of my own—until he was whole again. I spun his cells faster and watched as the color returned to his cheeks. He sneezed, and beautiful hazel eyes flickered to life again.

Once I finished with the boy, I pulled Dahn's hands to me. I lined my palms up to hers and let tin do its work, soothing her inflammation and repairing her burned skin cells. I pulled tin back into myself and felt it go cold and still. Exhausted. But I was so thankful for its help. *For all of your help.*

The next thing my memory found was me waking up, just before morning, to Dahn on all fours scrubbing our living room floor. I was on one couch, and the boy was on the smaller one, a blanket over him. He snored lightly. Such a pleasant sound.

Dahn noticed I was awake and inched closer, still on her knees.

"You're awake," she said, leaning her forearm on the couch.

"I suppose I am."

"We're going to sneak him back home, Don't worry." She fell silent. Her almond eyes danced with some unexpressed sentiment. Finally, she said something. "Thank you."

"For what?"

"For healing my hands." She paused, as if something caught in her throat, and then turned her hands over, examining them. "Why did you do that, Nex?"

"What do you mean?" I suddenly realized that the blanket over me was very soft. I snuggled in deeper.

"You already did so much. Saved a whole life. You should have seen yourself, Nexus. First you just sat there, staring. And I thought...'she is going to kill this little boy. What have we done?' But then," she made a swishing noise and zoomed her hands through the air. "Metal was flying everywhere and it smashed into you, and then you went flying. And when you got back up, you looked like...you looked like...I don't know what you looked like. You were...*alive*. You were magnificent. And you saved him. And you gave up almost all your steel. And then...." She swallowed, and her voice clouded over. "You remembered me."

I smiled at her. "You are nothing if not memorable, Dahn Vanes."

And then the girl who used to be my worst enemy kissed my forehead and went to see if Monny was ever going to start the breakfast.

She didn't notice that my body shuddered underneath the blanket. My left arm was too heavy and stiff to lift. My head was foggy, my mind sluggish. My heart skipped every other beat. My blood ran thin and slippery through my veins. A groan left me without my permission, and I hoped no one else heard. A thought came to me. One that I knew I couldn't shake. Primal. Fierce. Impossible to ignore.

I need. More. Metal.

Ep 26

Henceforth Known As Edwidge The Selfless

Life Tip: Before collapsing, set all breakables down.

Third time in one day. That's how many times my knees buckled before Monny sat me down. He put a cup of coffee into my hands without me saying I needed it.

"Drink," he said, reclining on the couch beside me and crossing his long legs.

Not in the habit of arguing with gods, I did as Monny said. The steaming liquid soothed my nerves but not the pain. That wasn't going anywhere.

"Nexus. Talk. And don't play coy. Not with me." He sipped his own cup of brew. "You've not been yourself ever since the night with that boy."

I sighed. Lying was like a reflex at that point, but it didn't make sense to lie to Monny. "I think I used too much Metal, Mo. Or maybe I just need more now? I'm not sure. I just know I need it."

"Well you did turn into some kind of metallic cyclone thing, Nexie. If I went all wild like that, I would have to eat an extra fifty weights of food." He paused, reading me briefly. "But it's more than being hungry. You're in pain."

I nodded. Saying it out loud, acknowledging the pain, made it so much worse. So I just didn't say it.

"Well, we have to get more," he said, as if it were that easy. He gestured to me. "This just won't do. I'm worried, and worry is no good for my complexion."

I smirked. "You are worried about me?"

He rolled his eyes. "It is so annoying that you haven't accepted this, Nexus."

I took another sip. "I appreciate you, Monny. But there's nothing we can do."

"Hmmm...what about that window boy? He had metal, right?"

"I am starting to think I imagined him. I have no idea how he found me or who he is or why he came in the first place."

"Well, reverse engineer it, Former. What circumstances surrounded your first encounter?"

I grinned. "You kind of sound like a Former, Mo. I'm impressed."

"I read enough of them. Besides, mirroring is part of being a Feeler. We study speech patterns, ways of thinking, even ways of moving. It's all psychology. All for reading into people. Finding their secrets. That being said, we find that guy, and I can read the hel out of him for you. Figure out what he wanted, what he wants." He settled in. "So out with it. What happened?"

I thought back. "I had just left the House Of Certainty. Onur brought us all in to get our pulses put in our arms."

"I'm still really sorry about that," Monny said, grimacing. "I wish I had another option. I wish I knew what it would cost you."

"I don't blame you at all. We do what we must," I said with a shrug. "So I get the injection. After that, I knew I needed to get out of there. I was in too much pain to hide it anymore." I left out the part where I was supposed to wait for Clay, where I promised I would hold her hand and walk her home. If I had been there, done what I swore, maybe I could have healed her before it was noticeable. *And she would be here now, meeting Monny and reading in the corner.* Not in the House Of Certainty being questioned for what seemed like eternity.

"Okay, so enormous amounts of pain. Go on."

"Right. I remember being confused. Meaning, I could not figure out exactly where the pain was coming from or how to get it to stop. It was like my logic turned off. That was the scariest part. Without understanding, I'm blind. I'm helpless. And I guess that's what happened. I was helpless." Recalling the feeling made my stomach roil. I closed my eyes and took a few breaths to get past it. "I stopped in an alley. I was pretty sure I would die. Pretty sure. I could feel my cells spinning out of control—"

"You felt this?" Monny's eyes widened. "That's not something people can usually feel, Nexus. I would know. I'm a Feeler."

"It's more like...listening...than feeling. I can hear them in a way that's very deep. It's hard to explain."

"And this is when you met the boy?"

"He showed up out of nowhere. He had me count to three. I don't remember anything else until the next morning."

Monny tapped his fingers on his mug. "So...near death experiences? Does that mean he's watching you?" He shivered. "That's so creepy."

I shook my head. "I have had lots of terrifying experiences, and he's never showed up. I don't think he's watching me. If he is, he is doing a really bad job."

"Then how did he know exactly when to show up?"

"How did he know?" If I had had enough strength in my muscles, I would have gotten up and started pacing to help me think. My own version of the Thinky Grumps. But a full day at the House Of Forms left me drained. "How did he know?" I snapped my fingers. "I didn't know! That's how!"

"Yes, we went over that," Monny said, puzzled.

"I mean something else. Something more. When I didn't know...he knew."

"Ooooh, that sounds magical," Monny said. He giggled. "This is getting good. So all you have to do is almost die and not know what to do about that? And then he'll show up?"

"I have no idea, Monny. Maybe? How would I even test a hypothesis like that?"

"Hmmm...I could beat you up. You wouldn't know what to do for sure."

I held my hand up. "You sweet, sweet boy. No thank you."

A knock on the door. Monny sprung up, pouring the rest of his coffee into my cup. "And that would be for me," he said with a little shoulder wiggle. "He's a hair early, but I salute his eagerness."

He opened the door and cursed. "Get in here."

Dahn came in, her long dress sweeping the ground, her usually pin straight hair woven into two braids. She held a child's hand in each of hers.

Monny pulled them inside and closed the door behind them. "This is a habit now, Master Vanes? We are not a training facility."

She stood silent for a minute. I had never seen her like that. No callous jokes. No sass. She just stood. Finally, she spoke. "The Wizens."

"Sit down, all of you." I motioned to the couches.

Monny sighed. "I'll get waters."

Dahn, still stunned, sat down, her hands clasped tightly around the childrens'. One boy and one girl. Both around age six. They snuggled closer to her.

"Dahn, what do you want to tell me about the Wizens?" I studied her strange apparel. "Wait. Did you get your primary rank?"

She nodded.

"And you're...a Wizen?" That didn't make any sense. Now Clay as a Wizen? I could see that. She had her mother's temperament. Kind and graceful. Helpful and patient. All the things teachers and healers needed. But Dahn? She was vain and brash and energetic and sultry. Almost any other House would have made more sense for her.

"The Wizens," she said. She held up the children's hands. "They...."

"They what, Dahn? Is that where you found these children?"

"My mother," she said, and then she gasped. Tears rolled down her cheeks. "She was trying to help, Nex. The *Wizens*."

A lump formed in my throat. "Help how?"

"They feed them food with no Metatoxin. They give them little bits of trace metal. Anything to keep them alive.

Before, they managed to keep them hidden until age twelve or so. But now...."

Everything clicked into place. I stood up to pace, weakness be damned. "The Wizens are making sure the children have shields. They keep them cloaked. Protect for as long as they can. It makes sense. The babies are all born in the House Of Reason. They are keeping the children safe. But now, with the pulses...." I chewed on my lip, thinking, thinking. "With the pulses, the metal the Wizens are giving the children only makes it worse." I looked at Dahn. "I don't remember Wizens giving me metal as a child. Do you?"

"They do it sneaky. Little doses. So you learn how to shield a little at a time. Though some never learn."

A hundred Endings flashed through my mind. Younger and younger Meta. Those who could not adapt quickly enough, thoroughly enough. Those who let their guard down too many times. Children the Wizens could no longer protect.

"All the Wizens do this, Dahn?"

"No. Not all. A few."

"Edwidge."

She cried even harder. "She saved me. She's always been saving me."

I remembered how safe I always felt at the Vanes house. How Edwidge was always so kind to me. So affirming compared to my own mother. But I did not cry. Instead, resolve grabbed onto my heart.

"We'll get her back," I said. "We will."

Dahn sniffled. "The Wizens don't know what to do. How to save them," Dahn said. "But you do, Nex. So I had to bring them here. Before it gets too bad. Before they need"—she glanced at the children, choosing her words—"an intervention."

"I understand, Dahn. But...." My knees lost their strength right in time to demonstrate my point for me. I caught myself on the couch, dropping the rest of my coffee, my cup shattering once it hit the floor. "I'm fine, I'm fine," I said before anyone could rush over.

Monny stomped his foot, setting down the waters he had been preparing in the kitchen. "You are not fine, Aerixon. And guess what? You do not have the metal to help these tiny people right now. You simply do not. And now you are going to listen to me. You are going to downgrade from goddess, just for a few hours, and you're going to *rest.*"

"But—"

"Dahn will fill me in, and we'll manage. You. Bed. Rest. Now."

"I thought you had a date, Mo?"

"This is by far more drama than my love life can generate. I'll reschedule." He pointed to my bedroom door again. "Go."

I shuffled into my room and clicked my door's lock into place. Then I readied myself.

Alright guys. My metal perked up inside me. *I need two things. To get as close to death as you can get me and to be really, really confused about it.*

Ep 27

A Pair Of Small, Smooth Stones

Life Tip: Remember to put on a bra before you summon company.

Turns out dying is pretty simple.

They left me.

All at once, my metal vacated my body, and there was no more pain from my pulse. No more fear in my heart. There was nothing. I was empty. Clear. But not like air. That was still something. And not like space. That was still something. I couldn't even say I felt like a vacuum. There was force to one of those—momentum, movement.

I was nothing. A shell that once contained so much. A husk. How had I ever existed without metal? Without myself? Who was I pretending to be then?

I stumbled, sensing my awareness narrowing, my mind clamoring, clutching for metal. But I was helpless. The sensation of intellect slipping through fingers.

A question came to me I'd never before considered as I crumpled to the floor. *Where will I go?* I would slip through my own fingers and then what? Nothing? Something?

In stories I'd heard at not-grievings as a child, my people met the ends of their cycles with grace and reverence. No more Fighting, no more striving. Peace and serenity.

Maybe I thought dying would feel like that. But I should have known. I was me, not them.

The worst part began when I changed my mind. The experiment quickly became unfun. I had no strength with which to tell my metal I had changed my mind, that they should come back to me and fill my body with strength and life again. That I needed them and wanted them as much as I needed and wanted to be alive. To be me. To be.

Face down on the floor at that point, I willed my arms to move, to request the metal to come home, but I could not. I called to them with my mind, but they could not hear me. My cells spun slower and slower, the silence in between each rotation increasing.

My last thoughts before my awareness folded in on itself and vanished for good were those of rage. I was angry that I was not careful in the end, but was so careless with myself. That I thought the best way to care for other people was to sacrifice my one chance to live. That I thought I could always reason myself out of dying. Rage. Rage because I did not get to do hardly anything at all. I did not get to scream at my mother. I did not stomp in the rain with Priyaa. I did not build a masterpiece with Drenge. I did not dance on the wooden platform of Ender Stream.

I had only ever succeeded at a series of mistakes. I had only tried. I never lived.

I tried to scream into the floorboards. I tried to bring them back. I tried. I tried. I tried.

Darkness.

Darkness.

Darkness.

My ears began working first. They were tickled by a dazzling string of profanities. Mutterings and the slamming of objects. Footsteps on the floorboards, though they were muted.

"I know you can hear me, goddessdamn it. What on Aarde, Nexus? What in himmin and hel? What were you thinking?" More slamming of objects. "It is not a rhetorical question. I want an answer. What were you thinking?"

I mumbled an unintelligible answer that the boy from my window obviously did not accept.

"You almost died, woman. You almost died *again*. And this one seems all your own doing. You had better be trying to tell me that this was due to negligence, Nexus, and not on purpose."

I peeled my eyes open. My vision was blurry, but I could make him out well enough. His dark curls had grown a couple inches so they hung in his eyes, the sides of his hair shaved low. He sported even more piercings than last time, some in his eyebrow, his nose, his lips. He glared at me with honey-brown eyes.

"Well?" he demanded.

"On purpose."

"What? Explain."

Not possible. I still felt too frail. Like my mind was slipping and my body was turning to dust. "My metal."

"Oh I tried to send them back to your body, but your metal doesn't listen to anyone but you. They are ridiculous. Stubbornly loyal. Stubbornly stubborn. I wonder who they belong to." He crossed his arms. "You're borrowing mine. Hurry up."

His metal. Hard to explain, but it moved like him. Sounded like him. Tasted like him. It was like having an eerily familiar stranger crawling around inside me.

Can you hear me? I used the strength from his metal to call out to mine. They rattled in response. *Come home.*

They raced toward me, a little offended to find uninvited guests in their places. I pulled out the boy's metal and sent it back toward him. He absorbed them into his skin without moving a muscle.

I felt instantly better. Even though I was still short on metal, it was better than how it felt to have none at all.

I sat up in bed and stretched, testing out my limbs. *Thank you,* I told my metal.

"Nexus, explain."

"I need your help."

He scoffed. "That is very obvious. You tried to kill yourself."

"No." I shook my head. "I didn't want to die."

He smacked one hand into the other. "Then why on Aarde did you send your metal away? How could you not sense what would happen? You are not stupid. You must have known."

"I did it so I could talk to you."

He frowned. "What do you mean?"

"I figured out that you show up if I am unable to save my own life. I still don't know why but I believe that's how it works between us."

His eyes held a hundred thoughts. He did not reply. Just stared like that with his arms crossed.

"Aren't you going to say anything?" I asked.

His tone changed when he spoke, but his eyes did not. "It's not a call button, Nexus. Never do that again."

I swallowed. "You didn't leave me a way to reach you."

"I don't *want* you to reach me. Ever thought of that?"

I pulled magnesium to my fingertips for calming. "Then ...why do you show up? And if you don't want me to try to figure things out, you should explain more thoroughly."

He sighed, dropping his arms. "What do you want, Nexus? Why am I here?"

"I need steel."

His eyes widened. "You did all this...for steel?"

"No. I did all this because if I don't get some steel fast, children will drop dead in alleys. And I can't help them if I don't have steel."

"Why didn't you find it yourself? I'm not your errand boy."

"I..."—I cleared my throat. I did not enjoy being vulnerable in front of him. If it were a ploy, there was no problem. But if it was genuine? "...did not mean to offend you in that way. I know you don't owe me anything. I...would love to find it myself. I just needed help."

"I thought the help you needed was steel?"

"Metal. I need metal, okay? I'm hardly functioning without it. And if I need it, how am I supposed to summon the strength to go get it? And if I can't get myself metal, I definitely can't find anyone more steel. I don't have time to take naps and disassemble old pencils until I feel better. I just need to know how to help myself so I can help everyone else. Please."

He considered me, examining my whole person from afar. He shook his head. "Your shield is magnificent. Luckily, I a lready saw that you have enough metal for everyday usage. Unless...you are performing more than everyday tasks?"

I blushed, yet again thankful that my red skin and abundance of freckles hid it for me.

"I can tell, you know."

I blinked at him. "Tell what?"

"When you blush. I can tell. I don't even have to look at you. It won't be as easy to hide from me, Aerixon."

I blushed even harder. *Fantastic. That's exactly what I need.*

I felt my nose wrinkle on instinct. "Are you a Feeler?"

"A what?"

"A Feeler? Do you work in the House Of Certainty?"

"Stop trying to change the subject. Out with it. What have you been doing that would drain your metal so quickly?"

"Now I don't know what *you* mean."

"Tell me or I leave. And if you do shit like this again, I won't come."

I groaned. "Fine." I averted my eyes for the confession. Telling the truth did not come as easy as hiding it. "My friend died."

"That's too bad. Now *tell me*."

"Well I kind of...maybe...woke her up?"

He went pale. "You did what?"

I shrugged. "I woke her up."

"How? Tell me in detail."

He crossed his arms again, and I noticed he had black writing scrawled along his skin. I had never seen anything like it. I wanted to touch it. I wanted it for myself. I had to snap out of it, refocusing on the story. "She wasn't really dead. My friend. She was just sleeping. Her cells were spinning super slowly." I twirled my index finger to demonstrate. So I just...asked metal to speed them up."

"And your metal did this for you? Impossible. You have a child's assortment."

"Hey! My metal is superb."

He rolled his eyes. "Everyone thinks their metal is the shit. But I know you didn't use yours. Whose?"

"Kind of...no one's. Everyone's. Like, all metal. Just"—I made a big circle with my hands—"the whole thing. Metal."

He ran his fingers through his hair and closed his eyes. "Oh goddess."

"Is it that bad? I was just trying to help."

He pointed a finger at me. "Don't do that again, Nexus. Not here. No one can know you did this. No one can know you're even capable of this. No one can know you can even conceive of this. And, I repeat, never ever ever do it again. Understand?"

"Ummm...."

"Ummm?" He bit his lip. "Why are you umming? Nexus?"

"There was this little boy—"

"Oh goddess!"

"You asked me to tell you! Why are you reacting like this?"

He extended an arm to me. "Come on. We're leaving."

I smacked his hand out of the way. "I'm not going any-where with you. I have no idea who you are or what you want from me."

"You trusted me enough to call me here. And it's clear you have no idea what you're doing," he said. "Come on."

"I agree. I don't know what I'm doing. You should tell me. And then I will make my own decisions from wherever the hel I want."

"Nexus!"

"Whoever You Are!"

"More stubborn than your metal."

"One to talk." I clenched my jaw. "I am not leaving. People need help. Children will die."

"*You* will die," he said. Piercing eyes held my gaze. "Do you not understand this?"

"If I die, it's because *I* decided it's worth it. Now, tell me how to get metal. How to get steel. And I won't have to call you ever again."

"This is what you want? You're sure?"

"Sure enough to almost kill myself in pursuit of it. Sure enough to implicate you and my dearest friends."

"Fine," he said, obviously livid but no longer willing to argue. "You're the boss."

He tossed me a pair of small, smooth stones.

"Walk through when you're ready. And come alone."

And then he leaned out my bedroom window and disappeared.

Ep 28

Behr

Life Tip: Pack a light lunch when traveling through portals.

What am I supposed to do with these?

I rolled the gray, smooth stones in my hands. They looked like metal but they felt different. They were not unpleasant. In fact, I liked the way they moved. I took one in each hand and tried to pull them apart. The stones resisted.

I twisted and turned them, holding them up close, looking for some sort of interlocking system that would explain their attraction. Nothing. There was no obvious reason why they fought being pulled apart. *Maybe I should take them in and ask Drenge.* No. Too much risk. They were definitely something only a Meta would have, whatever they were.

I strained to separate them and just like that, they gave way. Whatever force held them together only worked when they were in close proximity to one another. I could feel that force still pulling on the stones, trying to reunite them. When I brought them too close, they collided into each other so fiercely, it frightened me.

After pulling them apart once more, I turned the stone in my left hand over and then pushed them both together.

They refused, repelling one another. *What on Aarde?* I repeated the experiment many times. Same results.

I did notice that the stones made my metal react. They were pulled to the stones. It made me want to keep the stones in my pocket while I slept. *But no time for comfort.*

What do I do with you, stones? The boy said to walk through when I was ready. Walk through what? Well, think through it, Nex. What are things I could walk through? Windows. Hallways. Doors.

Doors. But how would two stones make a door?

I made myself get out of bed, realizing I had a decent headache upon standing. I set one stone down on the ground. Moved the other a few lengths away and set it down. I drew a rectangle with my finger so I could imagine the form of a doorway. Then, with full knowledge that my efforts were silly and I was grasping at nothing, I walked through the space in between both stones.

I was in a house. No. Not a house. Something like a house. More...subaardean. Under the ground. The walls were carved from the stone of the Aarde itself; I had the feeling I was sitting in her belly.

Fyrelight threw itself against the rough-hewn walls, bending itself into shadows. Wood crackled as it burned in some furnace I could not see from where I stood.

I realized I was standing out in the open of the strange place, my bare feet pressing into a dirt floor, and my intuition screamed at me to hide. So I scrambled to one of the walls and ducked under a table adorned with an old linen cloth. Pulling my feet in so they were hidden, I caught my breath before peeking past the table cloth.

I did not bother to wonder how I'd gotten to such a mysterious place. I knew I would be wasting my time with such contemplations. I only wanted to know where the smooth stones had gone and how I could find them and get back home.

That's when I smelled it. Floating on the air like a fresh baked cake. It sang to me. It seduced me.

Metal.

I had never sensed anything so alluring, so powerful. Its scent filled my whole body. I knew I was trembling without even experiencing it. I lurched forward in my hiding place. No way to tell for sure, but I might have been drooling.

My mind frenzied. I was at once aware of how weak I was and how strong I could be if I found the source of the fragrance. My eyes darting to ensure the way was clear, I moved forward on hands and knees, scurrying toward the epicenter of the smell.

The room was cluttered with strange items I had never seen before along with many lanterns, books, maps, and scrolls. With no one in sight and no sound but the growing crackle of flaymes, I made my way deeper into the mysterious home.

A room, separated by a tattered, hanging curtain. In the center of the room, I found the source of the crackling: a raging, iron furnace. I had never seen such a sight. An entire furnace made purely of metal, not a trace of synthetix. The fyres were so lively that the heat overwhelmed me, even from many lengths away. But it was the source of the smell, and so I could not leave, nor evade my gaze.

"I hope you brought decent pay," someone said.

I was so startled that I shrieked. I could not see who spoke, but I realized I must have looked deranged, on all fours in my now filthy, cloth dress, likely drooling and definitely trembling, my wild curls springing into the air.

I said nothing, debating whether I should run and try to find those stones. The debating was useless. I was tied to the spot. I wanted the metal that bad.

I sat down on the dirt floor with a strained huff, giving up on any semblance of decency. I was too tired to stand up. Clearing my throat, I asked, "What is pay? I don't know what that means."

The woman stepped out from behind the blaze of the furnace to get a good look at me. She was like nothing I had ever beheld. Her tan skin glistened in the light. Her body was more muscular than any Moral's I had ever seen, and she was no Moral, that much I knew. Her veins rippled down her neck and arms. Her eyes were sharp and deep set, but a blazing blue, even when the shadows crossed her face. Blonde hair, almost white, was woven into a long braid down her back, the sides of her head shaved clean.

"Your mouth is hanging open, child," she said. "Pay. You must give me something valuable if you want metal."

I snapped my mouth shut. My eyes flew around, my hands patting my dress. *Surely I have something. Surely. Please. Something of value.* But I had never needed pay before, never had to carry valuable things for exchanging.

"Do you not know of money?" the woman asked.

I shook my head, wishing my mouth were not so dry. The furnace was so hot, perspiration poured from my skin.

My dress was already half-soaked, clinging to arms I then realized were quite thin and spindly.

"Money is a token. Represents something of value. You can use it as pay. But I assume this is not so in your homeland? Where are you coming from, child?"

I avoided the question, as I did most inquiries that could get me into trouble. "I have never heard of money. We trade our service for what we need."

The woman grunted and pointed an enormous hammer at me. "You are too weak and sickly to offer me any service of worth."

My eyes filled with tears. She was, of course, correct. I did not know what she needed the hammer to do, but if I tried to hold that thing, my arms would fall off my torso. "I may be weak, but I am very smart. I could...think for you."

The woman scoffed. "I do not need to think to do my work."

I looked her in the eye. "Untrue. You have so many books and maps and scrolls. If you did not need to think, you would not need to read."

The woman chuckled. "Not bad, child." She crossed the room and knelt before me, setting her hammer in the dirt. "Now tell me. Who sent you?"

"I don't know."

"Then I will kill you." And she meant it.

"I don't know his name. He never told me."

"Goddess." She spit on the ground. "What does this idiot look like?"

"He has lots of piercings."

"We all have lots of piercings. Be more specific."

I noticed she had rows of hoops and studs on both of her ears and black drawings along the sides of her head and neck.

"He has dark, curly hair. And eyes like a bhee's honey."

"Is he generally an arsehole? In your opinion?"

"Well...he gave me some smooth stones and did not explain how to work them, and then I ended up here with no explanation. So. Yes. A general arsehole."

The woman stood and pointed her hammer to me in one fluid motion. At first I thought she was going to smash me to bits, but then it clicked that she wanted me to grab on to it. I did so, and she hoisted me to my feet.

"I am Yrsa. Yrsa Wolent. Behr Of The Blacksmiths."

Ep 29

Hold The Hammer Like This

Life Tip: Royalty knows royalty.

"That's a long name," I gulped. "Yrsa...Wolent...uh...Black-smith Behr."

"No, fool. Yrsa Wolent *means* Behr Of The Blacksmiths." She stoked the furnace, keeping a close on me, her biceps—coated in ash and grime—bulging. "What are you called?"

"Me? Oh." I chewed my bottom lip.

"Did you not receive a name, child?"

"Oh, no. I have one, Master Yrsa Smith Wolent...Behr. It's just...I don't know what it means. I never knew names were supposed to mean something."

"You may call me Behr. Now, tell me the name."

I bowed as best I could. "Nexus Aerixon."

"Hmm."

Sparks shot up as Behr forced an iron rod into the flaymes. I almost reached out and bit a piece of the rod, but iron was not emitting the smell I desired. It was something else. And so I was patient.

"Nexus," Behr said. "It means connector. And Aerixon. It means Daughter Of The Ruler Forever." She frowned, leaning on her hammer for a moment. "Nexus Aerixon. Daughter Who Connects The Rulers Of Forever."

I snorted.

She glared at me. "It is a very important name. And my interpretation is sound. You should accept its meaning."

I swallowed my sarcasm and bowed again. "Thank you for interpreting, Behr. I am honored."

"Why did you laugh, Ruler?"

Her calling me Ruler made me want to laugh again, but I refrained. It was obvious Behr did not think it amusing. "Where I come from, my name should mean something more like, 'Girl Who Hides And Constantly Falls Short'."

"But that is not your name, is it? So why do you hold so tightly to a meaning like that, when it is not who you are?"

I wanted to swallow that truth, but my throat was far too parched. "Forgive me, Behr. Do you have water?"

"It's not water you came here for, Ruler. Come. See."

I circled around to see what she was doing. Deep in the fyre pit was something that glowed a brilliant white and yellow. She pulled it toward her and banged her hammer into it, sending sparks soaring. Then she plunged it into a bucket of icy water. It sizzled, sending up a plume of steam that made me cough.

She returned to the furnace. "This next one will be yours," she said. "Now, hold the hammer like this."

I wanted to argue, to say there was no way I could handle an instrument of that size. I was used to the delicate machinery of Stur. I did not have the definition needed to wield a beast. But when I placed my hands on the hammer's handle, Behr curled her fingers over mine and squeezed tight.

"Up," she shouted. And we lifted our arms as one, bringing the hammer down onto the glowing orb. "Up," she shouted once more. And we swung again. "Now to the depths with it. Go on. Do it yourself."

With forceps, I lifted and then sunk the orb into an ice-water bucket. It steamed to the ceiling, filling the room.

"Now see what you have done," Behr said.

I pulled out what was once a glowing orb. It had become a glistening, glorious piece of metal. Silvery and rough in texture. The source of the delicious fragrance.

"Iridium," I whispered. As if it were holy.

Behr raised her blonde eyebrows. "It tells you its name so easily? This is a powerful metal. Usually, it withholds."

"What must I do? To keep it?" I asked her, my voice crackling like the fyre.

"You have labored, Ruler. It is yours."

"I...no, I cannot accept." I tried to hand back the large ball of metal, even though my hands shook. "You said I needed to pay. I will do that first. And then—"

"Come again sometime, and I will put you to work as you desire. For now, take it, before you vomit on my floor."

I held iridium to my forehead. It was different from my other metals. So much denser. It should have been too heavy to lift. But still, I held it.

Please come, I asked it.

The metal considered me, and after a moment, it bowed and entered through my eyes, finding its place in the elaborate wiring of my brain. It was then I understood that iridium was not simply different. It was royalty.

I inhaled and exhaled. The breath in my lungs came out of me like a dragon's. At least that's how it felt. A noise proceeded from my mouth without my consent. A shout of my own. My body was surprised by how alive it felt. It would take some getting used to.

I bowed again. "Behr, I do not know how to thank you, truly."

"I am the one who is glad to have met you, Ruler."

"If I may, I have three questions." No idea why three seemed like the right number.

"Go on. And then I must work."

"First, do you have any steel?"

Behr grunted. "Steel is hard to come by these days. An alloy. I have none. I could acquire some for you with time."

"I see. The second question: how do I get home?"

"That depends," she said. "Where is home? People come from many places to my smithy. Travel is unique."

I hesitated. I didn't know why, but I did. But Behr gave me no reason to distrust her. She had not even questioned if I was Meta or not. She seemed beyond the trivial nature of the Fight. And so I told her.

"I am from the City."

She did pause. "The City, you say?"

I nodded.

"How can that be? What has that idiot boy been up to?" She sighed. "You will need magnet stones to get home. A portal door. Is that how you got here?"

Magnets. That's what they are. I nodded again. "I don't know where they went."

"They will be waiting for you wherever you used them last. Ask them to take you back. They will be missing you by now."

"All of this would have been nice to know before journeying here."

"I told you. The boy is an idiot."

I smirked. "That brings me to my third question, Behr. What is his name? The idiot boy?"

She shook her head. "A name must be shared by its holder. I cannot tell you his name. He must offer it himself, when he feels it is right to do so. It is a sign of trust to share names."

So that was the issue. *The boy does not trust me.*

"Ask me another, Ruler, since I could not answer your third."

"Thank you, Behr, for sharing your name with me. I am so honored. And I will ask...what is this place?"

Yrsa Wolent smiled, revealing teeth of platinum and gold. "Heim," she said. And then *she* bowed to *me.* "Welcome Home, Nexus Aerixon."

Ep 30

You Met A Behr In The Mystical Not-City?

Life Tip: Lemon poppy is not a good look.

My room seemed small and stupid. Cold, straight, gray walls with no texture. Smooth floors of identical wooden planks. Lighting that didn't dance on the ceiling. Nothing like the place I'd just been. No alluring scent of metal. No roaring furnace calling to me.

I picked up the magnet stones off the floor and stuffed them under my pillow. Then I threw my door open and headed into the living room in time for Monny to come through the front door.

"Oh you're up," he said. "I had Dahn take those kids back to where they came from. No use having them wait here when we can't help them." He stopped when he got a good look at me. "Oh my god, how hard did you sleep? You look positively bedraggled."

"I didn't sleep at all, actually."

"Okay, one insomniac respects another but you're covered in dirt. Like...*covered* in it. Is it some new skin regimen? Why do I not know about this? You know you're supposed to tell me these things."

"No, Monny. It is not."

He inched closer. "Is that soot all over your face?"

I grinned. "Probably."

"Nexus, what is that look in your eye? What is going on? Something is always going on with you, honey, so out with it."

"I...went somewhere."

"Just now? While I was gone? I wasn't out for long. Where did you go?"

My grin widened. "Home."

"To Viveka and Joacin's flat?"

"No, Monny. *Home.*"

"Mmmhmm." Monny kept a wide berth as he moved to the kitchen. "Maybe a visit to the Hall Of Repair for you? You sound a little crazy, Nex."

"This isn't a joke." Each time I took a step, my body felt different. Moved in a new way. I felt more lithe, more agile. "I went to another place. Not like this place at all."

"What do you mean 'this place,' Nex?"

"Not the City."

Monny laughed. "There isn't any other place besides the City, Nexus. This is the whole thing. The City."

I crossed my arms. "Then why do we use the name Aarde? Where did it come from?"

Monny sputtered. "Aarde is the name for the place where the City is." He stomped to make his point. "The ground part. The...the air part." He drew a circle with his hands. "The whole place. Aarde."

"So we made a name for the place where the only place is? That's nonsensical."

"You're nonsensical," he snapped, obviously flustered. "If it even existed, how would you have gotten someplace like that and back, Nex?"

"I went through the portal door in my bedroom."

"The who?"

I sighed. "The one I formed with the magnet stones."

"The what?"

"The stones the boy gave me."

Monny perked up, eyes sparkling. "You saw him again? When? How? Is he handsome? He is, isn't he? So mysterious."

"Yes, Monny, I saw him a while ago. He gave me the stones. I went to Heim. I met Behr. I got iridium. But there's no steel. And then I came back and walked out here and immediately told it all to you."

Monny abandoned the notion of making it to the kitchen and sat down on the couch. "So...you met a behr in this mystical not-City place where there conveniently is no steel?"

"The lack of steel would be classified as an inconvenience. And no, I did not meet an animal. I met a woman named Behr. Behr Of The Blacksmiths. And she showed me how to wield her hammer, and I love her."

"*You're in love with her?*" Monny basically screamed.

"No, god, Monny. No. She is just amazing, that's all. So strong and scary." I motioned with my arms, trying to make myself big and intimidating like she was. Admittedly, I looked quite like a behr in my attempt. "She has huge, rippling muscles. And the sides of her head are shaved. And there is black writing on her neck and scalp. And her teeth! Her teeth are made of metals. Shiny ones. Gold, one is called, and platinum."

"Ohhh, I want to meet her. Can I meet her?" He nodded his head toward me. "You look much better by the way. Less sickly."

"Thank you," I beamed. "I feel wonderful. But I don't know, actually, if I can take you or not. The boy said to go alone." I bit my lip. "In fact, I don't even know if I can go back."

"You went alone? He didn't offer to go with you? That sounds reckless of both of you."

"Oh. I forgot the boy had offered to take me somewhere. Held out his hand and everything, until I slapped it. But how could I be expected to accept what I don't understand, Monny? He should practice explaining himself better."

"Maybe you should practice accepting help." Monny stuck out his tongue after he said it, and I threw a couch pillow at him.

A knock on the door, and Monny and I both jumped.

"God help us, what now? I swear if this Dahn character has more children for us," Monny said heading to the source of the knocking. He flapped a hand at me. "Go and bathe yourself before someone actually believes your story about stones and behrs. I'll get the door."

I bathed, the sorrow surprisingly deep as I washed away little bits of Heim dirt that clung to my skin. There were too many things to think about. *What is this land, this not-City, where a Meta is not questioned and strong women wield hammers? Who is the idiot boy who comes when I need him most? And if my name really means what Behr says it means, what am I supposed to do with it?*

Finally clean, I pulled a dress on. Behr didn't wear white cotton dresses. No hem tickled her knee caps. She wore dark, thick clothes with metal chains hanging from them. She wore sweat and grime. She dressed like herself.

I tortured my wild, silver curls with a long-needed brushing, patted my freckled cheeks, and then went out to find some food, crossing my fingers that Monny had spared some leftovers. *Maybe muffins.*

The kitchen honored my wishes, and I crammed half a lemon poppy pastry into my mouth.

"Hello, Nexus."

Onur Vanes stood just inside our front door in his Former attire, his hands folded behind his back, his blonde hair slicked just so.

"Oh god," I mumbled, a bit of muffin crumbling from my mouth. "Um...wow. Hello. What—"

Monny turned to me with his most Feeler-y smile, all charm, no real emotions. "Former Above Vanes is here to invite House Aerixon to a lovely dinner at his flat. Tonight."

"I await your response," Onur said.

But he stood there, unmoving, his eyes on me. After too many moments, it occurred to me that I was head of our household, and as such it was up to me whether we accepted or declined the invitation.

"Yes, of course," I said. "I have to report to the House Of Forms now, but afterward, at dinner time. Sure."

"Var and I will receive you both warmly." He nodded, about faced, and left.

"Not too much warmth, I hope. Might start a fyre, that one."

Monny snorted a laugh. "You fell for all that, Nexie? He gives me the shivers."

"He was different once," I explained.

"No, I don't think so," Monny replied. "You were too busy hiding to notice you didn't like him."

"I'm still hiding."

Monny grabbed the last muffin and kissed my forehead as he went to his room. "Sure you are."

I glanced down at my hands and realized they were in tight fists. Without meaning to, I imagined Behr's fingers over mine, us swinging the hammer, sparks flying at my eyes.

Careful, Nex. But the truth? I wasn't.

Ep 31

New Life. Same Fight.

Life Tip: Next time just say 'no'.

Var Vanes slid the roast onto my plate. It reeked of Meta-toxin. She focused on her task like the fork and meat were bombs ready to detonate.

"It looks lovely, Var," Monny said in his sweetest voice. "And you don't look so bad yourself. Partnership suits you."

Var blushed scarlet and darted into the kitchen, while Onur wiggled in his chair, uncomfortable with Monny complimenting his partner.

Onur, his back erect in his chair, folded his hands in front of him. "We'll wait for Var to tidy the kitchen and join us," he informed.

I stuffed my hands in my pockets and surveyed the room. They kept their house different than we did. Less decor. Even more clean lines and empty space. Sterile, almost.

Var returned from the kitchen and finished plating the roast. She slid into her seat, her hair still in two braids from work at the House Of Reason. I wondered if she was one of those Wizens Dahn spoke of, the kind who risked their lives to help Meta. Then she sipped her water with the tightest lips possible, and I decided there was no way she was anything like Dahn or Edwidge.

"You have been doing well at the House Of Certainty, Monny? Or at least so I've heard," Onur began, taking the tiniest, most polite bite of roast he could.

"Ah yes. There are always readings to be done, questions to be answered. Thank you for your interest in my work, Onur." Monny smiled, but I knew he was pissed. Feelers did not appreciate the nosiness of Fenders.

I cleared my throat to break the tension. "And you, Var? How is the House Of Reason? In which capacity do you work? Still healing?"

"I am floating around as of late," Var said. "We have had some tumult in our House. We seem to be short-staffed."

"It is to be expected from a House as ill-managed as Reason," Onur said. "It's a miracle you have accomplished anything at all."

Var said nothing in response. Just chewed her food and bored her gaze into her plate.

Onur turned his attention to me. "You look as if you've gotten some sun, Nexus. Have you been enjoying the outdoors?"

Had the blaze of Behr's furnace been that hot? "I like to walk to the House Of Forms these days. Helps my mood."

"It's beautiful," Onur said. And then he added, "The change in your complexion. It's beautiful."

We all stared at Onur. He didn't seem to care.

"I used to drive you," he continued. "To the House Of Forms. That's why you never walked before."

I chomped on the much-too-dry meat. "Uhhh, yes?"

"I...*enjoyed*...those rides in the transport."

Var stood up suddenly, causing her chair to scrape against the floor. "I will refill the waters," she said before disappearing into the kitchen.

Onur didn't seem to notice that she'd left. "Do you remember those? The rides?"

"I guess."

"Hmm." He sat back in his chair and looked from me to Monny and back again. "The Aerixons," he said, his tone a bit glib. "What a pair."

"Nexus is a delightful partner," Monny said.

"Same," I chimed in. "Monny is a dream."

Onur fixated on Monny. "Do you have a transport, Feeler? Do you take Nexus on...rides?"

Monny grinned and winked. "We prefer staying in."

Onur did not like that answer. He left the table to follow after Var.

Monny and I pivoted to face each other the second he left.

"What the hel?" Monny said in a hushed tone.

"He's never been *that* creepy."

"How do we get out of here, Nex? There's only so much of the subtle, dominatrix interrogation routine I can take."

"Me? I don't know, Monny. If I knew how to get out of things like this I wouldn't have come in the first place."

The Vanes' returned to the table, and Monny and I straightened back up, trying to eat more quickly so our plates were empty faster.

"We should do this more often," Onur said casually. "Houses such as ours will be important to the Fight in the future. We must not isolate ourselves. And speaking of the Fight," he directed his next question to Monny, "I am not permitted access to the status of Clay Vanes, who is being held in your House Of Certainty. I am hoping you could be of assistance in that regard, Monny?"

"Perhaps," Monny said, using his business voice. "What do you need to know, Former Above?"

"The schedule of her Ending is classified. But I would like to have some influence in setting the date."

I'll hurt him. My fist came out of my pocket, but Monny's smooth hand grabbed my wrist under the table. Gently, he held onto me, still facing Onur as if all were well.

"I may be able to help you with that," Monny said. "But we have a question for you as well, if that's alright?"

Onur nodded.

"Nex has been complaining about needing some special parts for whatever it is she's doing over at the House Of Forms. I really don't know the details. But I thought you might know where very special parts are kept in the City?"

I had no idea what he was talking about. I never mentioned any special parts to Monny. And I definitely didn't need him asking any favors of Onur on my behalf. *What is Monny getting at?*

Onur's lips twitched. "The House Of Morality. Your search will lead you there."

Monny's turn to nod. "Name the date."

"I would like her Ended three days from now. Precisely."

Monny raised his eyebrows, still holding my hand under the table as it shook. "So soon? What's the occasion?"

Onur gave a full-on gleam of a smile. "It's rumored," he said, "that's when the Fenders Of Fenders will die. The leader of our House. Really, the leader of us all. And I want his rank." He tilted his head. "For the Fight, of course."

And we said, "For The Fight."

That's when Var put her hand on her partner's arm. "Onur, I thought we called them here to tell them the news?"

"What news?" he said.

She frowned, her voice soft, cautious, each word carefully placed. "The child, Onur."

"Oh," he waved his hand flippantly. "Yes. We will have a child. You are right, Var, that was to be announced as well. I suppose now it has been."

Monny had to let go of me so we could clap our hands in celebration, the appropriate response to such an announcement.

We said what we were supposed to say to the happy couple. "New life, same Fight."

And then we left. Quickly. Without dessert.

Ep 32

The Plan Of Plans

Life Tip: If someone can make cinnamon scones, befriend them at once, at any cost.

"So let me get this right. Your plan is for us to infiltrate the most protected House in the City, get past hundreds of highly trained Morlas, discover the location of large quantities of metal which could be nonexistent, including steel, which is not even available in The Mystical Not-City you hallucinated, remove that steel from the House Of Morality, and then secretly insert rings into the lips of every Meta we can find. All without being caught and Ended. Is that right?"

Dahn was perched on our kitchen table, her long legs crossed, her sarcasm smarmy. She looked ridiculous in her Wizen robes, like an elegant swann wearing a bulky sweater. She'd undone her braids, so her deep red hair hung in gentle waves past her waist. She nibbled on one of Monny's cinnamon scones as she summarized our plan.

"Oh, and parts for Nexus' Former work too? We're multitasking a heist?"

Monny frowned. "No, that ploy during dinner about her Former work was just me trying to get your sweet, sweet brother to tell us where specialty items are held. Our bet is that's where they keep the steel."

Dahn thought about it. "And you're sure the sexy Meta boy doesn't have any steel to spare?" she said. "Maybe if you ask him really, really nicely?"

"Asking him is absolutely out of the question," I said with a stern tone.

She put a hand up. "Alright, alright. Touchy subject," with a little emphasis on the 'touchy.'

"Nothing happened between us," I snapped. Then I collected myself. "He is not my biggest fan. Besides, I'm hopelessly in love with Monny."

Monny pretended to swoon. "And I could never be without you, Nexie."

I grinned, preparing to catch him before he could hit the ground. But he was heavy enough to squish me under his weight. We ended up in a pile on the floor.

"Oh yes. Clearly you two are the masterminds destined to save all the Meta in the City." Dahn rolled her eyes, reaching for another scone. "It's not fair. You two get to have fun all day, and I get to bandage oozing sores and busted toes. I hate the House Of Reason. Hate it."

"I know it's not your style, Dahn, but you are in a position where you get to help people. You're amazing for what you do."

She accepted the ego stroking with a smug shrug. "It won't last long, seeing that your plan is going to get us all killed."

"It's not a plan yet. It's more of an agenda. A basic outline of what needs to get done. Now we have to figure out how to do it." I turned to Monny. "And what about Clay? There's no way we're going to let Onur leverage her Ending for the highest position. He's already leveraged her once for the rank he has now. How many times is that going to work?"

Monny frowned. "Politics, Nexus. Basic fending. Timing matters more than the act of sacrifice itself. Act when no one is watching, you gain nothing. But do it when people are looking, and you win. He really is a brilliant Fender."

"Then we have to get Clay out of the House Of Certainty," I said.

"That, my darling, is impossible." Monny wasn't joking around anymore. His voice even lowered half an octave.

"You'd rather entertain the idea of breaking into the House Of Morality than the House Of Certainty, Mo?"

"House Of Morality is the most guarded of all the Houses in the City. That means they won't expect anyone to ever try. But Certainty? It is impenetrable. You would die even trying."

I raised my eyebrows, curious. Iridium loved when I was curious. Crackled behind my eyes like a tiny fyre. "Really? I would die? Why? What would happen if I tried, Monny?"

"No, Nexus. No. I won't tell you because if I do, you'll try to figure it out, and you cannot figure your way into and out of that place. You'll have to listen to someone for once. Just trust me. I love you and there's no way I'm going to let you die for nothing."

I bit my lip to keep from arguing. I had no idea Monny was so protective.

Monny sighed, releasing the tension in his broad shoulders and sharp jaw. "House Of Morality. Risking our lives." He snapped his fingers. "Let's refocus."

A funny feeling. Tingling down my neck and spine. Iridium sizzling in my occipital nerve. All indicative of the birth of an idea.

"I know what to do."

Everyone got quiet.

I set three scones on the table and gestured to them dramatically. "These things are not isolated; they are interconnected."

Monny and Dahn stared at my illustration with blank faces. Finally, Dahn wrinkled her nose. "Is this about pastries, Nexus? Like...a scone is a scone is a scone?"

An exasperated sigh. "No, no, no. Okay, I'll start over. I didn't explain." I tried to run my hand through my hair, but it got stuck halfway in and I had to give up. *Pull yourself together, Aerixon. You're losing it.* And like that, I felt iridium sharpen my focus.

I pointed to the first scone. "Exhibit A: The Fender Of Fenders." The second scone. "Exhibit B: Clay's Ending." The third scone. "Exhibit C: The House Of Morality. These three things are not isolated. We are going to use them all to get what we want."

Monny gasped. "You're a genius. A *genius*. The Morals will be busy with the Ending. If Onur has his way, that Ending will occur around the same time as the death of the Fender Of Fenders. It will be a huge event. A gigantic distraction. We use that distraction to break into the House Of Morality, get the steel we need and get out." He paused. "Wait, no. You're also leveraging Clay's death if we do it this way, just like Onur. We'd be no better. And she'd be no less dead."

I shook my head, my cells spinning faster as my idea solidified. "There will be an Ending, but like hel am I going to let Clay die again."

Confusion on the faces of my friends, but certainty in my own chest as titanium curled around my heart.

"You two will go to the House Of Morality to get the steel. I'm going to the Ending. I won't let Clay bleed out on that platform. I won't let her cells stop spinning. I don't care if it takes a hundred days. The Fight will eventually order her back to the House Of Certainty for questioning. And the last time something like that happened at an Ending, Richter Vanes lost his rank. This time, it's Onur who will lose.

"So in one move, we will get the steel, we will crush Onur's ambition, and we will save our friend." I brought my hand down on the table, and for a moment, I felt like I was wielding Behr's hammer. "I will stand in that crowd on Ender Stream, just like always. But this time, I'll be doing a different kind of humming."

"I think she's crazy," Dahn said as she beheld me, scone crumbs still in her gaping mouth.

"I think she's wonderful," said Monny, his eyes wide.

I put my hands on my hips and stood with my feet planted on the wooden floor, imagining dirt between my toes and the roar of a furnace at my back. "I'm going to make Clay Vanes immortal."

Ep 33

One Thought

Life Tip: People like to say, "There are worse things that could happen," but there never are.

Ender Stream. Alone. The sun nearly below the City skyline and the people pressing in to bear witness.

I stood a few lengths away from the platform, closer than I ever dared before. I stayed off to the side, though, so as not to appear too suspicious and in case I needed a quick escape. It was hard work to keep from being forced into the center. Much like swimming against the current.

News of the Fender Of Fenders' sudden illness had spread. It seemed everyone in the City, young or old, sick or well, was present for the Ending. I hoped that Priyaa would not find me and try to keep me company. Even more so, I wished my mother would not join me. She would ask where Monny had gotten off to, and I would have to lie. Monny was busy breaking into the House Of Morality with Dahn. Not exactly information I wanted my mother to have.

My job was to focus on what needed to be done.

The humming began, and I saved my breath, not wanting to waste my energy. I knew I would have to hold onto Clay

for a long time if my plan was going to work. Maybe hours.
I had to be ready.

As the platform raised, the Morals dragged a flailing body
from the House Of Certainty's balcony onto the wooden
planks. I kept my eyes trained, hoping to catch a glimpse of
Clay before they slit her throat.

But it wasn't her.

They dragged another out. And then another. And another.
Out came more Morals with more wooden poles to be
mounted on the platform. I recognized one of the people who
had vines tied around their wrists. Gamall. The bearded
Wizen who spoke with Edwidge on the night I awakened Clay.

All four of those Wizens, accused of bringing Clay back to
life with metal, when really it was me. My doing. They would
die because I acted. They would die because I kept quiet.

The faces of the Wizens were swollen and bruised. All
that remained of their hair was tufts and knots. They still
wore their Wizen robes, ripped and stained.

Only a couple resisted being tied to the poles. The others
looked half dead already. Gamall said nothing, only hung
his gray head. I thought, maybe, I could hear him weeping.
But I tried to focus. To wait for Clay.

Yet despite my efforts to stay calm, my heart raced. *This
is my fault. This is because of me.* Those people had friends
and family watching, just as I waited for Clay, and they were
no doubt begging, pleading, their own mouths clamped shut
out of fear.

The Best Of Us came out of the House Of Certainty.
A new one this time. A younger man with a sharper white
robe and slicked blonde hair that reminded me of Onur's.

He clapped his hands and waved his arms with enthusiasm, the wide sleeves of his white robes flapping in the dusk breeze.

"Welcome, welcome, and aren't we all glad to be here?" He had to shout to be heard, even though the crowd fell silent when he appeared. "This is the moment when things are made right! And what a Fight this will be."

He did a twirl and scooted over to where the four Wizens were tied to their poles. He gestured to them with open palms, his fingers, each adorned with a glittering ring, wiggling for extra emphasis. "Here we have those who thought they could challenge what God set in motion. To undermine the Fight, they stole from a *child*"—he screamed the word 'child' in his highest pitched voice—"her right to a peaceful cycle's end."

A few people gasped. He continued.

"Though, as you have heard, our Fender Of Fenders has met the end of his cycle, we will not grieve. We will make him proud today by defending our City. Our Fight remains," he went on, "to resist such inhuman attempts. To demolish those who Fight against us. To persist. To prevail. To perfect."

People nodded, their eyes fixed on the Best Of Us as he gave another twirl and slapped his hands together as hard as he could manage.

"And now we do what we must." He clapped again, creating his own applause, and stood aside as they carried out a small person, her bare feet dangling, her head bobbing as she rested in the Moral's arms.

Clay.

They erected a fifth pole, this one taller than the others, and tied the twelve-year-old to it, coiling vines around her entire body so she could not wiggle away from the pole. Her head lolled forward, her brown hair in ratty strings over her face, her white dress—the same one she wore when she showed me her lantern—soiled.

It's time. I listened. I needed to find the hum of her cells fast, before the Moral ripped her throat open. I listened and reached and tried.

But there was nothing.

I listened again, pushing myself harder than I ever had before. Trying to locate even the faintest hum of her cells.

I was only vaguely aware that I was weeping. There was only one thing that filled my head as I stood there on Ender Stream with metal buzzing inside me, ready to do what had never been done before. One thought that sat on my shoulders like a heavy stone, dragging me under.

Clay is already dead.

Ep 34

The Moon Above Ender Stream

Life Tip: There is such a thing as too much blood.

The Best Of Us stomped with glistening red shoes, shaking himself so that his robe shimmered. He rambled on and on about the fate the child was about to meet, how the Wizen traitors had created this reality for the child, and that Clay would have ended her cycle peacefully if they had not intervened, that now she would meet the edge of a knife.

But Clay was not sleeping. Clay was not unconscious. Clay was all the way dead. She must have been for some time, based on how her gray skin was starting to swell. *They killed her in the House Of Certainty and they will fake her Ending in front of the whole City.* And I knew in my soul there was nothing I could do to change it.

That's when I decided that no one else was ever going to die on Ender Stream. And certainly not because of me.

Three quick breaths. Then I locked my attention on the tiny cells of the four Wizens and waited.

The crowd began to hum, and the Morals lifted their synthetix blades, spilling blood down the chests of the prisoners. I paid no attention to the colors of the blood or the sounds of the people. I thought nothing of Monny and Dahn and whether they would find the steel and make it out alive. I did not even think of Clay, whose lifeless corpse hung in the center of the display, false blood spilling down to the Stream.

For a brief moment, I thought I saw Onur Vanes standing beside his partner, unmoving, watching his fending come to its fruition. But I didn't care. I could only hear the spinning of those four, of trillions of cells at once. I could only feel metal—all metal everywhere—responding to my request with a resounding 'yes'. I could only taste the perspiration that slipped into my mouth when my breathing became ragged and my lips parted.

The people stood. The people watched. The people hummed. But the Wizens did not die. They bled and bled and did not slump. Their hearts kept pumping. Their brains kept thinking. Their eyes kept seeing.

Clay's false blood ran dry. She hung as still and cold as she did before they slit her throat. There was nothing I could do to reverse the actions of the Fight. But I could not think about how she died, afraid and alone, being questioned in the House Of Certainty for something she did not do. I couldn't bring her back again. But I would make sure no more cells stopped.

I had no idea how long we stood like that, but the sun was long gone and the moon was high overhead. The blood of the Wizens filled the street. It flowed and flowed and flowed. Some on the street below grew faint and began to lose their footing, slipping in the Stream. Others reached to steady them. Murmurs replaced the humming. Then the murmurs turned to clamor.

Finally, someone—maybe a Fender—shouted that every-one needed to get face down on the ground with their hands on their heads. That everyone needed to lie there and not get up. No more clamor. Instead, the people began to cry out. They were afraid. Nothing like that had ever been asked of them during an Ending. Children wailed, belly down in blood.

I, of course, would not lie down. I had work to do. My focus would not be lost, not for Fenders, not for The Best Of Us, not for the Fight, not for one moment. I would never let them End those four Wizens. I owed Clay that much. I owed the Wizens that much. I owed myself that much.

I would be the last one standing on Ender Stream. And that would be that.

A firm hand around my ankle. A swift tug and I hit the ground hard. An arm over my shoulders, pressing me down, keeping me from getting back up. I kicked my legs to get free, but resisting was breaking my concentration. And I was exhausted. I could feel the Wizens slipping.

I turned my head to see who was pinning me to the ground. Honey-brown eyes met mine. All his piercings hidden, he looked almost like a different person.

"Let me up," I told him, choking on blood and the grime of the Stream.

"Nexus," he whispered, his arm still over my shoulders, his eyes trying to say something for which there were no words, "please."

A trilling siren I didn't even know the City had blared to life. Morals began stomping through the crowd, swinging at those who were not yet face down.

I slammed my fists into the ground, pushing against his heavy arm, denying how tired I had become, rejecting the need to close my eyes and rest. "Let me," I said, gagging. "Let me."

He removed his arm from my shoulders, instead gripping my hand, his own face half-submerged in the muck. "Nexus...." He squeezed my hand, and I felt metal move through my skin. It was hard to hear him over the sirens and screams. "Please. Let them go."

"No," I shouted at him, at everyone. At the whole City. I cried but it didn't matter. "*No more.*"

He moved so close that I could feel his breath on my ear. "They'll kill you. And it will all be for nothing. They will die anyway if you die, Nexus. Please."

I could hear the stomping Morals moving closer through the crowd. My mind started losing its grip, and the Wizens' cells began to slow. Their hearts slowed pace. I could not see them but I could feel what they felt as if it were happening to me.

I choked back a sob as I lost control, as my weariness overpowered the resolve. I wasn't sure what made me say what I said next. But I was angry and tired, and my words came from someplace that had only ever come to the light when I was that broken. "You're just going to leave me again."

The boy recoiled like I drove a knife into his chest. I regretted it immediately. If there were a way for a person to regret themselves, their own existence, it would still not describe how badly I wanted to change it all.

He let go of my hand, reaching over and resting his palm on my cheek, his thumb rubbing my temple, his fingertips gently pressing into the back of my neck.

"I know," he said, his voice cracking. "But I will always come when you call."

I wanted to ask him his name, but he lifted his head, sharp eyes assessing our surroundings. "Can you run?"

I gurgled a yes, even though I wasn't sure it was true.

"Good. When I get up, you get up. Don't stop until you're home." And then he kissed my forehead, and lightning shot through my spinal cord. That's what it felt like. His lips touching me. Like pain and pleasure. Himmin and hel. Like life.

He sprang up, whipping something in the air that exploded like gunpowder from the Old Wars. I was not the only one who took to running after that. People shoved and hollered, trampling others as they stampeded away from Ender Stream. The Morals swung, and the Fenders ordered, but the people ran anyway. Back to their homes. Back to their pretending.

I only looked back once. The floundering of people trying to escape. The moon above it all, judging what we'd done. Five heads hanging forward on the wooden platform—one a child's, guilty only of living the life handed to her.

This time, when I turned toward home, I decided I would never look back again.

Ep 35

Voice In My Head

Life Tip: When called, go.

I almost ripped our front door off its hinges. Dahn shrieked in response to my dramatic entrance. Or maybe it was because I looked like I had narrowly escaped being buried alive.

Monny raced to the door to close it behind me. "Tell me that's not all your blood."

I yanked at the cotton dress, soaked through with scarlet, and screamed, "No, Monny, my blood is not *red*."

He didn't seem offended, but I didn't really care either way. I screamed again and threw our lamp at the fyreplace. The glass and synthetix shattering into a thousand fragments made me feel worse, so I sat down on the floor and cried. No one touched me or tried to make me feel better. I really appreciated that. After some time, my tears ran out, and I felt my stomach churn as anxiety took the place of rage.

"I'm sorry," I said, sniffling. "I'm acting like an insane person."

Dahn and Monny didn't disagree.

"Everything is so bad," I told them.

They scooted onto the floor next to me. Monny pushed my hair out of my face for me, and Dahn put a hand on my knee, though the act seemed to repulse her, what with me coated in filth.

"Hey Nex?" Dahn said. "Is it like 'we should run right now' bad? Or 'this is going to scar us for life, but we should just go to bed' bad?"

"She was already dead."

Dahn took her hand back. "What?"

"Clay. Already dead. They brought her onto the platform that way."

Dahn stood up and left the house, slamming the door behind her.

"Where is she going?" I asked Monny.

"Give her time," he said, still stroking my hair. "But for you? We need to get you cleaned up."

I pushed him away. "Monny, they killed everyone. Five people. Because of me."

"Nexus, I *know* you did everything you could—"

"No. I did not. Doing everything I could would have meant climbing up on that platform and telling the truth."

"That wouldn't have changed anything, Nex, except that there would have been six bodies up there, not five." He reached into his pocket and handed me a large item wrapped in cloth. "But we did get this."

I could sense it through the fabric. "Steel."

Monny smiled. "You were right. Very few Morals were there. But still, it wasn't easy. The House Of Morals has very high windows. Dahn made a sort of ladder with her metal and she scaled a wall. *Dahn.* Scaled a *wall.* She listened for the steel until she found it, then dropped it out the window to me. She said there was a lot more in there, but it was too much to carry."

"Why did she carry it?" I asked.

"How else would we have gotten it to you?"

I smoothed my hands over the cold steel, then broke a piece off. Squeezed that piece until it crumbled and absorbed it into my palms. I didn't expect my pulse to quadruple its energy output and I had to pull the steel back out before my arm exploded.

"Oh," I said. "I'm not that smart after all."

"You're just tired, Nexus. But you should probably add more steel to your ring before you get some rest."

Instead of increasing the size of my ring, I formed a second thin strip and added a new ring to my bottom lip, right beside the first.

"You didn't even wince," Monny said with a smirk. "Badarse."

"Too angry for wincing. Too tired for badarsery."

Monny frowned. "She's really dead? Your friend?"

"Is that normal? Do the Feelers kill people during questioning and then pretend they're alive?"

Monny shook his head. "That's not at all allowed. Live Endings are a requirement. I've never even heard of such a thing."

I sighed—more like a groan really—and laid my disgusting head in Monny's lap. "You missed the worst Ending in Fight history, Monny. I kept it going for a long, long time. There was screaming and sirens, blood enough to fill a river. Explosions."

"Explosions?"

"Explosions, Mo."

"You did all that?"

"I had a little help."

"Sexy boy? He was there?"

"He was. Created a diversion so I could get home."

"Nexus, you are stunningly amazing. I know it doesn't feel like that right now, but you are. So you're going to take a bath, give me that dress so I can burn it, and go to sleep. Tomorrow, we figure out how to get that steel into people, okay?"

I blinked at Monny. "Did you just say into 'people'?"

"Um...yes?"

"I don't think I've heard someone refer to Meta as 'people' before."

Monny grinned. "Go take a bath, person."

I had to close my eyes while I scrubbed the blood off me. It made my skin crawl as I washed it away, like tiny microscopic insects were invading my skin. The water stung my face and arms and legs, even though I ran it lukewarm. It all calmed down after a bit, and I cleaned and brushed my hair without incident.

I need you.

The voice was so clear that I jumped, sloshing water out of the tub. Frantically, I looked around the room. No one was there. I wondered if I was losing it and my metal was actually speaking to me.

I need you. I need you now.

I stood up, searching the room again. Still no one.

"Monny?" I yelled, wrapping a towel around me. "*Monny?!*"

He hurried to the washroom. "Nexus, what? Are you okay?"

"Did you hear something?"

"I heard you calling my name?"

"No, did you hear something else. Another voice. Not yours or mine."

His eyes widened. "Oh god. Look, Nex, I love adventure, but I don't do so well with spooky."

"No, no, it's nothing. Nothing. I must be tired, that's all—" *I need you.* "There! That? Did you hear that?"

Monny shook his head. "No, honey bhee, I most certainly did not."

My heart picked up its pace. I was familiar with the feeling. The rush and the squeeze. Like drowning and falling at the same time. It was becoming a close friend, that feeling. Danger.

I need you.

"I have to go," I said before I knew what I was talking about.

"Go? Nexus, go where? To do what?"

"Don't know. Have to go."

I ran past Monny, dropping my towel and tugging my dress over my head. Monny caught up to me and grabbed my shoulders, turning me to face him. "Nexus, listen. You need to *sleep.* It's the middle of the night. And if the Ending went anything like what you described, the streets and alleys will be crawling with Morals and Fenders. I am not losing you because you think you hear a mysterious voice. I am not losing you ever, Nexus, for any reason. We've risked enough."

I put my hands on his cheeks. I had to stretch to do it, he was so tall. "I know you love me, Monny. And I am so thankful. But if I tell you I am going to my room to sleep, I will be lying to you. And as soon as you are in bed, I will leave. And you won't know I've gone. But if I can be honest, if I can tell you I'm going, no matter where I am, I'll be able to think that back in our flat, Monny Aerixon is waiting for me to come home. And it will give me so much courage."

I need you. I need you.

Monny sighed. He put his long, brown arms around me. "Okay. I know you're going to go no matter what. But can you just pretend for me? So I can get to sleep?"

I grinned as I pulled away. Then I yawned and stretched. "Oh wow." I used the most theatrical voice I could muster. "It is getting late, and I am beat."

He put his hands on his hips. "Of course you are silly. You should get to bed. And stay there."

"Yes, you're right. As usual." I wrapped my arms around him. "Good night, Monny."

"You wake me up if you have bad dreams, okay, Nexie?"

"I will."

He kissed my forehead and went to his room. I went to mine. Then, I reached under my pillow and pulled out my magnet stones. I knew the voice by then. The one in my head. I didn't know where and I wasn't quite sure how, but I knew who.

I pulled my Former boots on and spread the stones out on the floor.

I need you.

"I know," I said, even though I knew he couldn't hear me. Not yet. "I'm coming."

Ep 36

Sandstorms and Secrets

Life Tip: Monsters are real.

I stepped through the stones to a blast of sand and wind. It whipped my face, throwing my hair upward, the bits of dust and tiny stones flooding my nostrils. This was not the Heim I remembered. By instinct, I crouched down, pulling the skirt of my dress over my mouth and nose and burying my face in my arms as best I could. The air was hot. That hurt almost as much as having my skin grated off by the force of the wind. I stayed like that, in the tightest ball I could manage. *Nothing lasts forever*, I told myself. *Either the wind will die, or I will. But this won't last forever.*

My metal rattled inside me, knocking against my rib cage, reminding me of its existence and willingness to help. If Dahn could form a ladder to get into the House Of Morality with her metal, I could build something to keep from being buried alive in a sandstorm.

I released the Meta cloak that I used to hide my piercings and pulled the metals forward. Aluminum, calcium. Whatever I could. But it wasn't enough. *I wish I brought that big block of steel*, I thought. A whistling sound, and then steel, hurtling toward me, rammed into my left shoulder. *Did it come through the portal when I called it? Is that how portals work?* I asked steel to form an aerodynamic barrier around me, so the sand glided up and over my body instead of peeling me alive.

I could finally breathe behind my little shield and assess how badly I was injured. I already sported decent scrapes and bruises from being swept to the ground during the Ending. But now my shoulder ached from steel colliding with me. Tiny drops of transparent blood pooled on my skin from the sand's abrasion.

A while longer. Then the storm died down. I decided I would carry steel wrapped around my ankles since I couldn't hold it inside me. The rest of my metal, I pulled in, thanking them as they rested.

I looked around. Never had I seen anything like the place where I stood. The ground was every shade of brown, from almost white to nearly black. There were rocks and crags, caves and canyons. But no trees. No rivers. The sun blazed like it hated me. Even clouds were nonexistent. Just an orange sky that stretched a thousand lengths. A wasteland.

I spun in a circle, shielding my eyes from the light. *Why am I here?*

But the voice did not answer. So I decided to walk. I headed to the tallest of the canyon crags, hoping a higher vantage point would give me a clue as to where I needed to be. My boots were not built for sand dunes and they sank and skidded, filling with bits of everything as I went.

By the time I made it to the canyon, I was sweating. The saltiness stung my tiny wounds and burned my eyes. But I was thankful for my boots then. The rocks were jagged, the angles slicing into the soles of my shoes. If I had worn my cotton slippers, I would have been torn to shreds.

I froze when I heard voices murmuring a short distance away and snuck behind a wall of rock before anyone could see me. No idea why I thought to hide instead of walking up to whomever it was and asking for help. But no. I hid. *Classic Nexus.*

I waited, straining my ears for the words they were saying. Finally, I realized they spoke in a language I could not decipher. Two men argued, their words mostly guttural and sharp, but lilting and hollow in some moments. I couldn't get a good look at them from where I crouched, but they were not happy with one another. That was clear from the shouting. Eventually, the disagreement crescendoed, and I heard the smack that could only be one human hitting another. A short scuffle with much grunting. And then a string of what I guessed were curse words as one man lay defeated and the other lorded it over him.

I dared to inch to the edge of the wall, to peek around it to see what might be seen. I was right. One man walked away, haughty in gait, his tan shoulders bare and glistening with sweat in the sunlight. The other was sprawled on the ground in a sandy clearing, nursing a busted nose. I did not see any red. *If he's bleeding, and it's not red, maybe he's Meta.*

I stretched my neck out a little further, trying to get a more complete picture of the camp. I had no intention of asking the quarreling idiots for assistance. Clearly they had some emotional maturity to develop. But maybe there was someone else more sensible with them. A leader of some sort.

Underneath an overhang of yellow-gray rock, hands tied behind his back and lying on his side, was the boy with the piercings.

His back was to me, but I knew it was him. Didn't need to see his face to confirm. I knew the curve of his spine and the bend of his ears. I knew the shape of his waist and the rhythm of his breathing. It was him.

I felt for his cells first, to make sure he was not near death. He was alright in that sense. Quite literally sleeping. But he was incarcerated in some way by the buffoons. No wonder he needed my help.

A distraction. Then I could run in and wake him and free him. We would escape together before the men could stop us.

I called mercury to my fingers. *Go far until I call you back.* I sent it whistling through the clearing and away from the camp. One of the idiots cried out as it nicked his ear and ran off to find what had assaulted him.

The other fool remained, arms crossed, not willing to leave the boy unguarded.

Fine, be stubborn then. I focused and found his rather loud cells. Then, like I'd done to Onur, I turned them down until he crumpled to the ground, snoring.

I hurried out of my hiding place and dropped to my knees beside the boy, shaking his shoulder to wake him. He was also soaked in sweat, but he seemed peaceful. He blinked, his eyes focusing, and gasped when he saw me.

"Nexus?" he hissed. "What the hel? *What the hel?*"

I tugged at the restraints around his wrists. They weren't vines, like what Morals used at Endings. They were metal, maybe even simple iron, but they didn't respond to any of my requests. "Are these made of metal?"

"Get out of here," he said, yanking his arms away. He turned around, sitting up the best he could, leaning his back on the rocks for support. "Go. Now."

I reached down to his ankles. They were also bound. Same iron shackles. That meant no running to safety for us. And there was no way I could carry him. "Shut up and tell me how to get these off," I said.

"We can't," he snapped. "How did you find me?"

"That is not important. What is important is getting you away from here."

He sighed, exasperated. "These restraints are magnetically contracted. Only the person who put them on can make them listen. You'd have to saw my arms and legs off to get me out of them."

"Then what do I do?"

"You go home."

"Being glib is not helpful. It's inefficient."

"Being a stubborn tight arse is even less helpful in this case, wouldn't you say?"

I felt my neck get warmer. He was infuriating. "Why don't you just tell me why you're here. Maybe I can convince them to let you go."

"If you must know, they are going to feed me."

I glared at him. "You called me all the way out here because they want to make you dinner?"

He blinked, genuinely surprised. "I didn't call you."

"Yes. You did."

He blushed. "No. I didn't."

"Why are you really here? Just answer me."

"I already said. They are going to use me as food."

I almost gagged. "They want to eat you?"

"No Nexus, goddess! They want to feed me to something that lives at the bottom of that very deep cave over there." He tossed his head over his shoulder to one of the distant caves.

"Something like...a monster?"

"Yes. Like a monster."

"Because they just hate you so much? That's elaborate."

"Not everyone is as petty as you. They don't have any *opinion* of me. They want to feed me to the monster so he shits out copper. It's the metal they want."

I snorted in my effort to stifle my laugh. "They want to turn you into poop?"

"They'll force you to join me if you don't go."

"Me? So just anyone will do?"

"No, Nexus. Don't be stupid. You're not just anyone."

"Wow, I'm honored." My ears perked up. "That one guy is coming back."

"So go."

"I refuse. You called me."

"I wasn't calling you. Would you just listen to me for once?"

"I am listening to you, dammit. You called me. I heard you."

He blushed again, deeper that time. "I was dreaming, okay. I didn't actually call you. It was a dream. I'm fine. I've gotten out of worse situations before. Now please just go. Way too much time has passed."

I had too many questions to pick just one. So I scrambled to select the inquiry that would get me the most answers.

"Nex, *go*."

"Too much time has passed?" I asked at last.

He literally tried to push me away with his shoes, his ankles still tied together. "Yes, too much time. We...we can't. Now *go*."

"Can't what?" I asked. The man was almost back to the clearing, but I wanted an answer. At least one answer.

"We can't be near each other, alright? Not for this long. Now, trust me. Go home."

I chewed my bottom lip. "Fine. I will go. *If* you tell me your name."

He stopped, his deep eyes studying mine, calculating. "Not a good idea," he said.

I shrugged and sat down, prepared to stay put.

"You're extremely annoying," he grumbled. "Fine, but promise you'll leave immediately. Your magnet stones will take you where you want to go. Just think of home, where you left them, and they will pull you back."

I bit back my grin. "I promise. Straight home."

"Kallórr Vaettr-Tigerrinn. Friends call me Lórr."

I had no idea if I was a friend or not, but there was no way I would remember a name that complicated. "What does it mean? Your name?"

"Goddess, Nexus, seriously?"

"You are the one wasting time."

"It means He Who Roars At The Beast."

It gave me goosebumps all over my arms and down the back of my neck. I had to tell myself to take a couple deep breaths. *How could a name do that? Make someone feel something?*

"Do you really hate me, He Who Roars At The Beast?" I was being more vulnerable than usual. But I truly wanted to know.

He smirked, with no intention of answering a question like that. "I like the double lip ring. That's new, right?"

I narrowed my eyes. "You'll make the shittiest shit when that monster eats you."

He chuckled before he pushed me away with his legs again. For a moment, his voice sounded sad, his eyes clouded. "Go."

I called my mercury back to me and hid, watching from a distance. It didn't take long for the boy to lure the returning idiot to come close to him. He spoke in that strange language, and the man, enraged, walked right over. The boy swiveled, grappling and squeezing the man's head between his knees. The man released the locks in exchange for his ability to breathe, it seemed. Rendering the fool unconscious, the boy grabbed something from the man's pocket before disappearing into thin air.

Guess he didn't need me after all. I held out my hands, pulling whatever metal the idiots were hoarding into me. Then I called to my magnet stones, leaving Lórr and the desert behind.

But the questions? Those I took with me.

Ep 37

What Comes Beyond

Life Tip: Just because they are in charge does not mean they are in power.

A light jog was required for me to make it to the House Of Forms on time. Formula knew the weight and curve of my footsteps by then and she beamed a welcome to me, each square of the sidewalk lighting beneath my steps as I rushed to and through the front doors.

Many Formers knew my name, though I spent very little time with them. They watched as I hurried past. A few said hello, but most found greetings to be superficial and time-wasting. I took the stairs two at a time and burst into my lab, causing Drenge to drop whatever he was holding.

His tools clattered to the floor, and I apologized, scooping them up for him and sticking my arms into the sleeves of my white coat.

"You're late," he said.

"I am," I answered.

He sighed. "Are you alright? I assume you were at the Ending like the rest of us. I know that girl was a friend—"

"I'm fine," I said, much too quickly.

"Nexus, if you need—"

"No, Drenge, I do not need." I grabbed the clipboard, blowing my hair out of my face so I could see what was to be done that day. "Goodness, we are so close to being finished," I said.

"Yes." Drenge flipped his tool around, offering it to me. "We will test today. You only need to close up the panels."

"Really?" I reviewed all the data, all the forms, all the specifications. "Wow. Really."

"It has been a lot of hard work, Nexus. Work that most minds could not fathom. Your ability to see the forms, to imagine what they could be. It is remarkable. You should be proud."

I set down the clipboard. "Yes, I should be."

Drenge would have frowned if that weren't already his usual expression. "I can see clearly that you are injured. Abrasions on your arms, bruises on your legs. And I know you are not alright, psychologically speaking. None of us are after last night's events. You should see a Wizen."

I shook my head, glad my teacher could not see the large bruise on my shoulder from steel knocking into me or the marks around my ankles from carrying steel across the desert. Or my heart, from seeing my friend dead, despite my efforts.

"Please, Drenge, I do not want to go to the House Of Reason. They will just give me water and tell me I ought to feel well. Today, I only want to quietly work on Stur and...and think in my head to myself."

"I understand," he said. "But we must test today. And that will not necessarily be quiet work."

"We must?"

"We must."

"So say the Fenders?"

"So they say."

Drenge and I fastened the panels onto Stur, and I let my mind drift to the boy, Lórr, and what he could have meant when he said we could not be together for too long. I remembered the sadness in his eyes when he pushed me away. And I wondered why exactly I was inhabiting his dreams so intensely that he called out to me for help. *How does that even work? Is that why he comes when I need him? Does he hear me calling?*

"Nexus."

That startled me so badly I gasped and slipped my tool across my finger. Shoving the tip of my index finger into my mouth to hide the blood, I contemplated pulling some iron from Drenge before I realized I had taken iron from the idiots in the desert. I pulled it to my blood and then checked my finger. The drops were scarlet, nearly blending in with my complexion.

"Are you hurt?" Drenge asked, concerned.

"A small scrape. I'm fine."

"May I see?"

I tried not to hesitate as I extended my hand to him. He held my finger up to the light, examining. "You are correct. A minor incision." Then he looked me in the eye. "Are you ready for this?"

"Umm...yes?"

But he still did not release his gentle hold on my hand, did not alter his gaze. His eyes were steady through his glasses lenses. "Nexus. Are you sure you're ready for what comes next?"

I swallowed, suddenly nervous. "You mean...testing Stur?"

"Beyond that."

"I...have no idea what comes beyond that."

"Exactly my point."

I took a deep breath, ready to ask a more pointed, more yielding question, but Formula beamed, lighting the ceiling. "Proceed to the testing area," she said in her friendly but sterile voice.

Drenge patted the back of my hand before he let it go. Then he grabbed the clipboard and motioned for me to follow him. "Come on, Former Above Aerixon. It's time." He paused, glancing over his shoulder to observe the room, then moved through the lab door. "And bring your wits, my dear. You'll need them."

Ep 38

Power

Life Tip: If you got 'em, lace 'em up tight.

I did not know the House Of Forms had a rooftop testing area until I stood among a few dozen Formers, all with their own clipboards and intellectual scowls.

Drenge told me to stay put, then crossed the space to speak to someone—man or woman, it was too difficult to tell—who scowled particularly well. They listened to Drenge, leaning in ever so slightly as he shared information.

Drenge came back to me and, a bit flustered, perhaps because of the wind exposure, said, "Come with me, Nexus. They want to meet you."

I followed him over to the person and fought the urge to bow. Drenge introduced us.

"Former Above Nexus Aerixon, this is Former Of Formers, L Volva." Then he drifted away, abandoning me to a conversation with my boss's boss—one for which I was ill prepared. I had never met someone of so high a rank. I didn't know what to expect, how to act, what to say.

"What factors enhanced your expedient completion of the machine?" L asked. Their voice was flat, colorless. No greetings shared. No hellos or well dones.

"Drenge was instrumental," I explained. "A good teacher who allowed me to experiment and make my own mistakes. Formula was also very useful. It was easy to ask for help from something with no capacity to judge me for it. And...."

"And?"

"And the boots."

I wiggled my toes into the synthetix surface of the rooftop, the sole of my boot squeaking from the movement.

"The boots, Former?"

"Yes, the boots."

L Volva turned to look at me. Their eyes were hidden behind black lenses, their hair in extremely tiny braids, pulled away from their face. They were rather short, much shorter than me, and extremely slight. I would guess only one hundred weights. Their skin was a blend of many complexions...so that it was basically colorless. But most interestingly, they had no eyebrows whatsoever. Not one strand was present.

"Are the boots very comfortable?" Their voice was all gravel, despite their waif-like physique.

"No, not at all."

"Then why the boots?"

I couldn't help but smile a little. "They're better than cotton shoes. They make me feel...capable. And strong."

L Volva bent to study my shoes. I realized, my heart thudding, that I had not cleaned them from my trip to the desert. They were covered in dust and grit. Straightening back up, L Volva did not seem to care about sand.

"They make you feel powerful. The boots."

I swallowed, even more nervous than before. "That is not the word I would choose."

"No? Are you not powerful, Former Above?"

I could read no emotion from the person before me. And I knew what my mother would want me to say to such a question, if she knew I was speaking with the person who determined my entire role in the House Of Forms. But I was not my mother and I did not care about fending or positions or roles. Something about L made me unconcerned about anything I didn't want to be concerned with.

"I am powerful," I said, my metal swirling within me, but my words still measured. "But it is not always wise to admit to it."

Former Of Formers L Volva cracked a smile, white teeth almost blinding in the sunlight. "Well then. With that bit of wisdom, let's see if this storm can fly."

They snapped their fingers, moving to a more advantageous vantage point away from the crowd. They were the only one with no clipboard. All the other Formers clutched theirs to keep the wind from taking it.

Drenge approached me. "That went well?"

"I think so."

"I have never seen them smile. Ever. And I have known L a long, long time," he said. "What did you say?"

"I can hardly remember now," I lied.

Then I jumped back. The roof began to spin and open, twisting and spiraling like the House Of Forms' doors.

I observed the mechanics, basically drooling as Stur elevated on a platform, glistening in the sunlight. He was bigger than I thought he would be. I had never seen him outside of the lab.

I almost felt protective as the other Formers saw him for the first time, taking notes and muttering. A few let out noises of admiration. Others seemed almost jealous, their jaws clenched and nostrils flared.

"Alright, Nexus," Drenge said. "Get it going."

"Me? Really?"

"Hurry now. Everyone is waiting."

I scooted past the other Formers and moved toward the machine that had been my friend for many months. I pulled the remote panel from his exterior and stepped back. A click of a button, and he came to life. His engine buzzed and then roared. Like thunder.

Another click, and his rotors began to turn. There were more murmurs from my colleagues. Once the rotors were at full speed, I pushed another button, and then pulled his levers downward. He hovered, first half a length, then a few lengths above the rooftop.

Formers stopped their scribbling to either gawk or applaud.

"That's enough," Drenge said, patting my shoulder.

But I wasn't finished. I hadn't spent all that time so Stur could hover like a mhoth on its last day. I pulled his levers further down, so he rose many lengths into the air, then to the left, so he tipped and spun. To the right and higher still, so he circled around us like a fahlcon searching for prey.

I only landed him when enough breath was taken from my lungs, when the excitement made my arms and legs tingle. When I had had enough.

Drenge very quickly took the remote from my hands, and I let him without argument. I knew I had not listened well, and on a day that was very important for both of us. But obedience be damned and submission too. I just needed to see what I could do.

And I had done it. Truly. With no metal at all. And limited time. And the world closing in around me. I had formed a machine that could fly.

"This way," Drenge said, the remote still firmly in his grasp. "With greater speed, Nexus. Come along." Drenge led me over to the Former Of Formers once again.

Still, L held no discernable emotion on their face. The white Former coat they wore seemed to swallow them. They didn't seem to mind.

"We will need to move with precision," L said when only Drenge and I could hear. "Her mother will be here soon to witness the machine as scheduled. By then it will be too late."

Drenge adjusted his glasses. "The arrangements have been made?"

"Of course. We will move both her and the machine. And we will do it now."

"Excuse me," I said, my blood going cold. "What on Aarde are you talking about?"

"We will explain once you are safe," Drenge said.

I dug my heels in. "I go nowhere," I said, with what might have been interpreted as a growl, "until you explain."

Drenge was about to argue, but L Volva held up their small hand. "Your mother expressed to us the desire to keep you safe until the machine was completed. After that, we have been led to believe that your services will no longer be useful to the Fight. Because of this information and your incredible value to us as a Former, and to Drenge as a friend, we will act to keep you safe."

"I don't understand," I said, my throat closing as I spoke.

"Yes, you do."

"My mother? My mother harming me would make no sense." It would mean she knew I was Meta. It would mean she wanted me dead for it. "My mother made sure to secure the highest rank she could for me. Why would she do that if she wanted me gone? It would have been a waste of effort. My mother wastes nothing."

"It was not always her intention to harm you, Nexus. But with the Fender Of Fender rank open, her hand is forced. If she wants it, she must position herself for it. You must move from trophy to leverage."

"I don't believe you," I said too loudly, so a few Formers turned their heads.

L Volva removed their dark glasses, so I could see their eyes, which held no color. They were covered by a thick white film of sorts, and they did not move nor focus on anything when they spoke. "We will ensure that your mother cannot harm you, Nexus. That is our only intention. If you will come with me, my protection will suffice. I cannot ensure it will be effective if Viveka becomes Fender Of Fenders, but I can offer it to you now." They replaced their glasses. "I am not asking you to trust me, Former. Only for you to *think*."

If my mother knew I was Meta, there were only a few possibilities. She would study me. Learn my weakness. Or she would hide me, to keep our house's prestige. Or...my mother would do what Onur had done, would give up her family for the Fight, for a rank. I wished I did not believe it. I wished. But if my mother knew I was Meta, she would use me. There was no other possibility.

"I will not go without my partner," I said, trying to sound unshaken.

"We will do our best to secure him as well. And the machine, of course, cannot be abandoned either." L Volva turned away, toward the doors. "Shall we?"

I followed after L and Drenge, my boots squeaking and my metal screaming inside me. "We shall."

Ep 39

All Walls Are Jagged

Life Tip: You're never as clever as you think you are.

Monny squeezed me into a hug as soon as he entered L's flat. He was warm and he smelled like something he called sap trees.

When he let me out of the hug, he kept his hands on my shoulders. "You okay, Nexie?"

"I'm fine. Are you fine?"

He nodded, but his eyes were clouded. "Formers showed up at the House Of Certainty. Told me you were in some danger and to come quickly."

"Apparently, my mother has decided it's time to kill me."

It was a relief that Monny did not look surprised. "And what's so safe about this place, exactly?"

"Sort of took a leap of faith coming here. The Former Of Formers is offering us protection."

"Wow," he smirked. "I'm partnered with a real hotshot, then."

I leaned in so only he could hear me. "It's only because of my machine, I think. It worked."

His eyebrows shot up. "It did? What is it for? Can you finally tell me? Can I see it? What does it do?"

"So many questions, Feeler. Aren't you just supposed to read it all out of me?"

He rolled his eyes. "Answers. I am dying here."

"I'll try to show you if I figure out where they put him. But...his name is Stur. He's a humongous flying machine. Technically, he is designed to aerially administer Metatoxin."

"Oh," Monny grimaced. "That last part isn't so fun."

"No. But that's not Stur's fault. We're doing that to him. He's innocent in all this."

"The...machine? You know it's not alive, right Nex?"

I swallowed. "Oh, yes. I know that. Of course."

Monny looked around at the plainest flat either of us had ever been inside. The walls were gray, the wood plank flooring was gray, the ceiling was gray, the seating was gray. No paintings or pictures, no flowers or even windows.

"So the idea is that if Viveka sends Morals to pick you up, they'll be bored to death, and you'll be saved."

I chuckled. "L must have some sort of security system, I'm guessing."

"L?"

"The Former Of Formers."

"First name basis?" He draped his arm over my shoulders. "I'm sticking with you, Nexus. We're going places."

"You stick too close and you'll end up on a wooden platform."

He paused at that. Not easy to make a joke when we'd witnessed so many Endings. "You think your mother knows? About you?"

I sighed. "It seems like everyone knows, Monny. I mean, you figured it out. Who's to say the whole City isn't aware I'm Meta."

L and Drenge approached us. "Now that your partner is with us, we may speak frankly," L said.

"I would love that," I answered. "Go on."

"The City is not what it seems. And the Fight is not what it says. There are disagreements in logic, in function, in practice, in ideology. For example, there are some, like the previous Fender Of Fenders, who believed in isolation as a means to salvation. But others, like myself, believe in emancipation as salvation."

"I don't understand. Isolation from whom? Emancipation from what?"

L snapped their fingers and the room went dark. The floor twisted open and a diorama of sorts raised up. It was illuminated, detailed. Pieces of it moved and twirled. Houses, roads, large and small buildings. Trees, rivers, mountains. In one corner of the diorama was a large wall, like a jagged scar separating a corner of the land from the rest.

"What is this?" I asked. I had never seen anything like it, not in any training class or lecture. Not in any book.

"This is Aarde," L said. "At least all that we have charted so far. There is more, I'm sure, that remains unseen. And it is difficult to keep our records updated from in here."

Monny couldn't keep quiet anymore. "This is *Aarde*? I've never seen anything like this. Ever. What is this thing even supposed to be?" He tapped a snowy summit.

"That's a mountain," I blurted out. "They're magnificent."

Monny turned to me, eyes wide. "How do you know what it is, Nexus? You've seen one?"

I shook my head, my heart fluttering, my titanium trying to calm me. "I don't know how I know sometimes. I just do." But I had seen the subaardean furnace of Heim and the sandstorming desert with its colors and blazing heat. This, however, I did not mention.

"Well, you are correct," L said. "A mountain. Though we have none in the City." L pointed to the jagged wall and the land that lay on the corner of the map. "This is where we are."

"Why are we separate?" Monny asked. "And why have I never heard of any of this before? I thought...I thought the City was all that existed. I thought..." his voice trailed off, his eyes darting around the map, trying to make sense of anything at all.

"What did we *do*?" I asked calmly. "What did we do to be kept apart like this?"

L paused. When it was clear they would not say more, Drenge spoke instead. "We did many things, Nexus. We still do many things. And when the rest of Aarde could not convince us to stop, they banded together and decided to put us here, where we could do no more harm."

"What did we do? You haven't answered me."

L spoke again, their voice still gravelly, but almost tired, like a cliffside beaten by the wind. "We took metal. Not all of it, but most of it. We made forms with it. We used it however we saw fit. And you. Meta. We used you as well, to help us form it. We used it until Aarde trembled beneath us, until it begged. But even then we could not stop. We lost the knowledge of how to stop, how to be patient, how to listen."

"So there are other places? And they...locked us in the City?" Monny asked. His hands began to shake, so I held one of them in mine.

"Yes," L said. "Some believe it is a blessing. Here we can build as we please. No interference. No judgment. The Fight, in their minds, is to keep us pure, to purge us of everything—and everyone—who got us into this mess. But others see it as a prison. And for us, the Fight is to get out, to regain our freedom."

"If there is a world out there, I want to see it. I *hate* it here." I had never heard Monny speak so passionately. His whole body shook. "I didn't take anything, didn't take anyone's metal. I didn't do anything wrong. Why am *I* here? Tell whoever it is that it's not fair to punish everyone."

"I think that is what L is trying to do, Monny. That's why I haven't been turned in to the Morals. To my mother."

Drenge sighed. "We can't speak to anyone outside of the City. It's not possible. They left us with no way to reach out. And in here, things are getting worse. The people...we can't survive this way. Without metal. Without hope. Without Meta. Viveka would not agree. Most in the Fight would even say the City is thriving. But the truth is that our way of life is unsustainable. If we could tell the other realms this...if we could tell them we need some way to get out...."

"Why are you saying all this to us?" Monny shook his head. "You want us to join your Fight? You want Nexus to join your Fight? She drinks your poison. She wears your torture devices. She built your death machine. What else do you want?"

I put my hand on Monny's arm to calm him. Then I faced Drenge and L. "You're partly right, Monny. The Formers protected me. Gave me a place to work where I could be safe. And gave me what I needed to keep my mother pleased." I lifted my chin. "But it was not out of kindness. Or affection. Or good will. It was still manipulation." I took a deep breath. "You think I can find the people who locked us all in the City. Isn't that right?"

L was about to speak, but Drenge cut them off. "You are right. It was manipulation. It still is. We are offering you protection now in hopes that you will help us Fight. The question remains...will you?"

Ep 40

Ready. Aim.

Life Tip: Keep records of rights, not wrongs.

"I need to think it over," I told L. But there was little time for thinking.

A gentle alarm filled the room, the lighting changing from soft white to a subtle orange.

"Uninvited guests, L," a familiar voice said.

"Is that...Formula?" I asked, observing the changes in the room.

"What's Formula?" Monny asked, clearly uneasy, his pupils dilated. I hadn't realized how little others knew about Former practices. It must have been overwhelming for someone who spent most of his days in the gardens of the House Of Certainty.

L scrunched their lips. "Formula is an algorithmic presence, generated through circuitry. And yes, it operates here at my compound as well as in the House Of Forms." They snapped their fingers. "Formula, describe the guests to me in efficient detail."

"Of course," Formula replied. "It appears to be Former Master Viveka Aerixon with an accompaniment of Fenders and Morals. I sense aggressive intentions. Do you request my intervention, L?"

"Not necessary," L said, their voice still cool.

Drenge met my eyes from where he stood. "Nexus, we need to know if you will help us. There is no time for you to think about this."

"What will you do if I say no, Drenge? If I won't help you cross outside of the wall? Hand me over to my mother?"

L interjected. "We cannot justify the cost of protecting you if you will not help us, Former. This must be obvious."

I tried to remember to keep my head up while simultaneously making an effort to forget that I was speaking to the Former Of Formers, one who answered only to the Best Of The Best.

"Then this is more than manipulation," I said boldly. "You are threatening me. If I don't help you with your agenda, you will let my mother kill me for hers."

Drenge tried to speak, but L put up their hand. "If you choose to think of it this way, you will only cause yourself pain."

"How should I think of it, L?"

"Basic cause and effect. If you help, you are helped. If you do not help, you will not be helped."

Formula beamed. "The uninvited guests are demanding entrance."

L tilted their head as if they were considering me, but I was pretty sure their eyes could not see anything at all.

"Let them in," L said.

"What the hel?" Monny cried out, grabbing my arm as if he wanted us to run.

But I kept my ground. "If I run, I'm dead," I told him. "I'll need to use my wits for this one." I sent a look to Drenge, but we said nothing to one another.

A few moments later, my mother stood before us, in all her Fenderliness. The model of Aarde was still lit in the center of the room, and Formula still alarmed around us.

"Matrix, hello," I said, bowing to her.

"Hello, data," she answered. She looked as she always had. Her hair perfect, her clothes perfect, and her eyes perfect, sharp, keen. I reminded myself that in most ways, she and I were very different, which I would need, and that we had the same eyes, which I would also need.

My metal, which usually would have been roaring and roiling inside of me, remained at attention, each waiting, each focused. I had iridium to thank for that. It sparked just behind my eyes, giving orders to the rest. If I ever saw Behr again, I owed her a thousand thanks for giving me such a metal.

"Why are you here, mother?" I began the discussion, as no Morals came forward to haul me off.

"I am here to take you in for brief questioning, Nexus. It would be best if you cooperated."

"She will not be going—" L began, but I interrupted.

Oh my god, I cut off the Former Of Formers. While standing in their home. Me. I am doing this. Oh god. But there was no going back. "I am speaking to my mother," I said sharply.

L fell silent.

"Mother," I said, "I would prefer more honesty from you. It will save time and help us to avoid misunderstandings. So I'll ask again. Why are you here?"

My mother's eyes flashed and the corner of her lips twitched. A little different than amusement. Perhaps excitement. I had the feeling she did not think I would want to play.

"I have a suspicion that you are Meta, Nexus. I will have you questioned in the House Of Certainty, and if you are guilty, I will pay the highest price, and you will be Ended."

Pay the highest price. I remembered, suddenly, Behr asking me to pay for metal. The word seemed foreign to me in that context. *Is this what she meant? Something for another? A trade of worths?*

"What are you hoping to gain for turning me in, Mother?"

"I will become Fender Of Fenders, of course. The position is still open."

I shook my head. "Onur has already done this. Already paid the highest price with Clay. You are, at best, an imitator."

"No. I am much more."

"Oh?"

My mother crossed the room, examining the diorama of Aarde, running her fingers along the wall of the City. "Vanes succeeded in Ending some Meta and one poor girl who everyone could see was innocent. These things have been done before. Anyone could accomplish this. But you? You are not some ordinary Meta, Nexus. No starving child or sloppy old Wizen. You are...important."

She smiled at L, probably with full knowledge that the Former Of Formers could not see her do it. "You are important to those who wish to leave this place, this realm of purity, those who warp the efforts of the Fight for their own purpose. Sacrificing you would be the ultimate victory for us. For the True Fight. If Vanes had known this about you, he would have tried it. But he was too interested in what mysteries lie beneath your skirt to notice what you were really worth. Fending is not about making plays. Fending is about finding and keeping secrets. And you, Nexus"— she swiveled to face me, her hands behind her back, her skin glowing with her own pleasure—"are my most favorite secret."

I wanted to cry, but I did not. If I cried, I would be crying, and there was no time for things like that. "You are offering me nothing, Mother. And L is offering me a chance to live and to get out of the City and away from you. Why not side with L? Why would I just come with you now?"

My mother approached me, so that I could see myself mirrored in her eyes. "Former Of Formers is offering you nothing but a prolonged death at the hands of Realm Rulers. You are ignorant of this. I am not. L is not your friend. You are a tool to the Formers, same as you are to me. But I will make an offer to you as well, Nexus, if you insist on being wooed."

"Go on."

"I will offer you a swift End. And a safe and comfortable life for your sister."

I bit my lip accidentally, and then tried to hide the blood it brought forward. It took me a moment to realize there was no point in hiding anymore. There was never any point in hiding.

"Priyaa is not Meta. You can't just hurt whomever you want. That's not how life works."

"No," Viveka said, matter of factly. "She is not Meta. But she is a sympathizer. If you paid any attention to the secrets of others, you would know this. She has been smuggling metal since she was eleven years of age."

"She will kill your sister anyways. You would be smart not to listen, Nexus," L said.

Monny stepped forward and slipped his hand into mine. "Listen," he said. With everyone watching, he kissed my forehead like he was saying goodbye. "You are worth more than leverage. More than any of these people understand." His eyes locked on to mine. "You are worth the whole goddamn thing, Nexie. You'd better act like it."

I dared not argue with an actual god. So I pulled titanium to my fingertips and told it to aim for major blood vessels.

Ep 41

When L Doesn't Mind

Life Tip: Duck.

There are lots of things to remember about titanium. It's sturdy, nurturing, protective. You can depend on it, always. Loyal. Oh, and it's very, very sharp when it wants to be.

I was sure, though, that titanium only knew where major blood vessels might reside because iridium told it. The queenly metal heated to life behind my eyes, somehow directing titanium as it slid through the necks of Morals. The hooded figures stumbled and fell in mere moments, red blood spurting from between their black, gloved fingers.

Enough, I told titanium. It hung midair, awaiting my instructions. I tried not to let my thoughts have any room in my head. Because I had just taken lives. *Me. Nexus. I killed. I am a killer.* But I told myself not to panic, not to scream or run or cry.

"Move, and I'll do it again," I said. No idea why I sounded so calm. Didn't matter how calm I was, though. No one listened.

The Fenders ran forward, one going high and one going low. I ducked, shooting pellets of iron from my palms and into one of their faces. He screamed, reeling backward onto the ground. Meanwhile, Monny handled the guy careening toward me, smashing his chin with a sharp uppercut.

Of course, we had all learned basic self-defense in training. But the gentle Wizens with their long robes were not the most ambitious combat instructors. I mostly knew how to shove and call for help. Couldn't even manage that when Onur had snuck into my room.

I gaped at Monny, wondering how on Aarde he knew how to crack a jaw like that. But he just rolled his neck and turned to face L and Drenge, his fists balled and raised. I stood beside him, facing my mother, my hands at the ready.

"Fighting is a lesser evolutionary response," she said in her most condescending voice.

"I could say the same to you, Fender Master," I replied.

"We will not engage," L said plainly. "No need to slice any more jugulars here. But we will need to make a call."

Viveka rolled her eyes. "He does not need to be involved, L."

"I can smell the blood of Fighters on my floors, Viveka. If you try to take this daughter of yours by force, we will all be nothing but puddles on my floors. We must call him. He will settle this."

"He will side with you," my mother shouted. I had never seen her riled like that before, never seen spittle fly from her mouth or the whites of her eyes go red. "He will side with you and tear down the wall, and we will be doomed to repeat the same mistakes over and over and over. L, think about this. Think about more than your precious forms."

L did not move when they spoke. "The world is made of forms, Viveka. Not fending. Not lines of politics and imaginary rules of governance. Not handshakes and secrets and lies. It is made of forms. And if we have no forms, no way to sustain forming, in this City...we will all die. We must get out." L jabbed a finger in my direction, though they could not see me. "This girl will save us all. We will call the Best Of The Best, and he will see my way because I am the only one seeing straight in this whole Fight."

My mother took a step toward me, and L raised a hand. Something darted through the air, and my mother flew back and into the wall, making the whole compound rattle. She groaned from where she lay on the ground but did not get back up. I froze. Not in terror. Not in relief. Simply froze because there was nothing else I could think to do.

L had some device in their petite hand and passed it to Drenge as if they no longer wanted to touch it. He wiped it off with his lab coat and handed it back.

"It would be simpler if she were dead," L said. "But also more complicated. Don't you agree, Drenge?"

"It would be, yes," Drenge said, but he sounded nervous, beads of sweat on his forehead, his mustache noticeably devoid of wiggles. "Both more and less complicated."

"What is your vote, Aerixon?" L asked, their voice low and flat.

"My...my vote?"

"More or less complicated?"

I swallowed. "What? What do you mean?"

"If your mother were dead. More or less?"

I wished I could answer, but the question was unexpected and pointless. That was when I realized. I was talking to the Former Of Formers. Formers don't ask pointless questions.

Before I could move, L aimed the device at my mother's wounded body and fyred three times. My mother's body jerked with each hit, but otherwise she still lay where she'd fallen. L handed the device to Drenge once more, and he cleaned and returned it. The color was drained from his face, but he did not argue.

He said nothing.

I said nothing.

"Monny, is it? Your name?" L asked. Then they fyred once, striking Monny in the shoulder, making him drop to his knees with a cry.

I sent titanium. But Formula beamed, and something I could not see repelled my metal, sending it flying.

"Magnetic shield," L said evenly. "Doesn't stop my device, though." L took aim at Monny again. "I do not enjoy violence, Nexus. But I also do not mind it. Do you understand?"

My mouth was dry, my head pounding. Red blood ran down Monny's arm, and I realized I needed to help him, not fight.

"Step away from him," L said. "He stays with me, and you will go with Drenge. He will prepare you from what comes next. Accomplish the task we have for you, and your partner will be returned to you breathing. Do you understand?"

"If you hurt him—"

"I have already hurt him, Former. Please try to pay attention. There are others I would not enjoy but would not mind hurting as well. Friends, Family. Elderly. Children. I do not care what I must do. I will do it. I am no Fender, but I am desperate. You will go. Now."

"Nexus," Monny said, reaching out for my hand.

But I pulled away, as L had ordered. "You are worth more than leverage, too, Monny. But I'm not going to let you die here."

I looked to L before I left with Drenge. "If you hurt Monny again, ever again, I'll tear you apart. I'm smart. Believe me. I'll figure out a way."

"I believe you," L said.

"Good."

"No, Nexus," L replied. "Nothing about this is good."

Ep 42

This Time In the Alley

Life Tip: If you ask, they may answer.

Down the hallway of L's compound, I followed Drenge at a distance.

"Quickly, Nexus. Quickly," he said.

But I needed to slow down. I needed to breathe, to wrap my head around what was happening, what had happened. I braced myself against the stark white wall when the room started spinning. My metal tried to keep me upright, shifting to balance my weight.

"I have to stop," I said, my words squeezing out through my inhales. "Stop. For a moment."

Drenge took my elbows in his hands. "Nexus, I'm sorry. I'm sorry. I know what you must be feeling, but—"

I yanked away from him. "You don't know, Drenge. There's no way you know because I don't even know. How am I supposed to feel now? My mother is dead, and if it were reversed, if I were in a bloody heap on the ground, my mother wouldn't have felt a thing. She wouldn't have cared. All she would think about is losing a pawn, not a daughter. So how do *I* know what to feel? How would *you* know?"

Tears slid down my cheeks without my permission. "I don't even have the energy to hate you," I told him.

"Right now, I have one goal. And it is to make sure you survive this."

"Liar. Your only reason for knowing me at all is to get what you want from me."

"We need to move quickly, Nexus."

"*You* told me to come with L. To come here and be safe. I trusted you. And there's nothing safe about the Former Of Formers. Nothing safe about you. And don't you dare tell me you didn't know L was unhinged." I gasped out a sob. "And now that lunatic has Monny. I don't even know what you want me to *do*."

"You need to travel to the other realms. Meet with the rulers. Tell them the City needs rescue. That we will perish without help. Without freedom."

"Listen to yourself, Drenge. What realms? What rulers? What are you even saying? I don't know how to accomplish any of that. I can barely accomplish daily life in the City."

"You are the only one of us who can go, Nexus. The only one who can find answers. Not even the Best Of The Best can do what you can do. You must."

"If you want me to go anywhere, I need my stones. I have to get out of here and get them."

Drenge shook his head. "Are you aware of what crimes have been committed here today? You killed Morals and Fenders, Nexus. Killed them."

"Stop saying 'killed' please, for the love of Aarde."

"We cannot go walking around the City. You in the House Of Certainty will help no one at all. You must leave now. Go to the realms now."

"You can be as pushy as you want, Drenge, but it is impossible to go anywhere without my stones."

He exhaled. "Fine. I will retrieve them."

"No," I said. "You don't know where they are or what they look like. And then I'll have to wait for you to return. That's twice the risk and more than twice the time. I'm not risking Monny for your peace of mind. I will go. And leave from there. Now, where is the exit?"

"I cannot let you go alone—"

I locked on to his cells and slowed down their spinning so that he fell asleep on the ground. The act exhausted me, but I couldn't stop to rest. If only I had the strength or speed to do that to the room of Morals. Or maybe I should have had the resolve to slice the veins of my mentor. But unlike L, I did not enjoy killing, and I minded it very much. I fumbled through the back of the house until I found a door.

I hit the street running, my boots kicking up fine bits of gravel. It would have been much more convenient to drive and much less taxing on my exhausted body, but I owned no transport. So running was it. I stuck to back alleys, twisting and turning until I collided into someone. The crash sent me to the ground. I instantly knew I'd lost skin on my legs and palms.

"God, why!" The person, also thrown to the ground, stood up quickly, dusting off Wizen robes, nursing a scraped elbow. "Nexus? *Why* are you running?"

I stayed where I was on the ground, just long enough for my head to stop pounding and my heart to start aching again.

Dahn offered me a hand and hoisted me up. "You almost killed me," she complained. "Again."

But I just leaned forward into her and let the crying happen all the way. One person who wasn't trying to kill me was all I needed. Sometimes, the little things were what mattered.

Dahn put reluctant arms around me, probably worried about me snotting on her clothes.

"Nexus, what is going on? Talk to me."

"Can't," I said. "Have to go."

"But...what about the steel? I thought we were supposed to be doing a thing with that."

I forgot all about needing steel and helping Meta children. I forgot about everything except getting Monny back. "You're going to have to handle that, Dahn. I...I can't. I just—oh, you can talk to Priyaa, maybe? Apparently, she...." *I killed her mother.* Maybe I didn't fyre that device, but it was my fault. This was all my fault.

"Priyaa? What—"

I shook my head. "I have to go."

Dahn stepped forward. "I'll come with you. Wherever you're going."

"No," I said loudly, turning to leave. "You can't."

"Then you have to tell me where you're going."

I paused, my blood going cold, my metal going still. I turned back to Dahn. "Why?"

She blinked perfect eyes. "Why? Why what?"

"Why do you either need to come with me or know where I am going, Dahn? Why?" I stepped backward and inched away from her. "And why did I run into you in a random alley? More than once? What are you doing here? We're nowhere near the House Of Reason or your house or even any shops. So what are you doing here?"

"I was...."

And it made sense. Made sense and made me sick. "You were, weren't you? Oh my god, you have been this whole time. Why are you following me? Why are you questioning me?"

Dahn's eyes pricked with tears. "You don't understand."

"Then tell me, Dahn."

"It's fine to act all self-righteous, Nexus. It's easy to pretend you've never done anything you didn't want to do. Like you've never lied to save your own life. Like you've never hurt anyone so no one hurt you."

"Who are you spying for?"

She wiped her nose with the back of her hand. "Who do you think?"

"How long have you been keeping tabs on me?"

Dahn's tears spilled all the way out, but at least she didn't look away. She shrugged, her robe slipping off one of her shoulders. "The whole time."

"The...whole time? Since we were *kids*?"

"Since before we even officially met, Nexus."

I wanted to shove her, to hit her, but I could do nothing until I was finished asking important questions.

"And Clay? Did she...was she...just watching me, too?"

"I'm really sorry, Nexus. I'm so, so, so, so—"

"Stop!" I heaved. "Don't say that. Don't say sorry." I could feel energy course through me again. Hot, cold. Hot, cold. "Monny? What about Monny?"

Dahn shook her head. "I don't know. You'd have to ask him. And he'd have to tell the truth."

I jabbed my finger at her. "What did you do to me that day in the alley? The last time I ran into you? Tell me now."

"Tracker. To see where you...could go."

"To see if I could get out," I said, my thoughts racing but somehow sluggish. "How do I remove it?"

Dahn's eyes widened. "I don't know, Nexus! How would I know something like that?"

"Never again," I said. "Never talk to me or look at me ever again. I'm not your friend. I'm not your acquaintance. I'm not yours. Do you understand?"

I didn't wait for an answer. I shoved past the person who lied about loving me, about hating me, about wanting me, about knowing me, and ran toward the home that was probably built on lies and disrespected expectations.

Ep 43

Who, What, Where, When, But Never Why

Life Tip: When overwhelmed, try pulverizing molten metal; it helps.

I shoved my hands under my pillow and clutched the stones. I sat there for a while, on the edge of my bed, and just...did nothing. It was nice. No thoughts. No movement. Just sat there.

It wasn't until lead nuzzled me from inside my arm that I snapped out of it. Then, the thoughts came flooding. What would my sister say? My father? I was implicated in something convoluted, twisted, heinous. And I had been so naive about it. So busy trying to save my own skin, I didn't realize the puppet strings had been tied to me all along.

Sulking and drowning myself in overthinking won't get me to Heim.

I spread the stones on the floor, then stepped through.

The heat of the furnace nearly knocked me over. I had come through much closer to the blaze than the time before. I should have felt small standing next to such enormous energy, but it only enraptured me. True power was never condescending.

"Back already, Ruler?" Behr was stoking the fyre with a long iron rod, her thick blonde hair braided down her back, the sides of her head still shaved. She wore what looked like the skins of animals over her sculpted shoulders. Her cheekbones and nose were covered in soot.

"I'm sorry I stayed away so long. But so, so many things have happened." I had no idea why I was sorry. I didn't owe Behr my time, and Heim wasn't even *my* home.

"Just glad to have you back with all your appendages still intact and your head sitting upright on that neck of yours."

She took a longer look at me. "Not all the way intact, though, are you?"

"I...." I wanted to explain everything that had happened. The steel, Clay, Lórr, Stur, L, my mother, Dahn. The list seemed ridiculous. It overwhelmed me, and I thought with great terror that I would break down in front of the most magnificent woman I had ever met.

"Come," Behr said. She stepped back and had me squeeze in between her and the furnace. She handed me the long rod. "Stoke it like so." She showed me once, twice, then left me to it. We worked like that for a time, not speaking, just managing the flaymes. She even showed me how to make silver rings to adorn hands.

It was the most calming thing I had ever experienced, even more so than working on Stur. The fyre was more unpredictable than Formula, but it was so much more enchanting. It sang to me if I listened close enough, with surprising pops and sparks and soothing crackles. And the metal had more meaning to it than the synthetix of Stur. It moved and turned as we heated and cooled it. I had the sense it enjoyed being transformed.

"Enough of this now," Behr said. "You'll be staying a while this time, I gather. You'll need a place to sleep and some food to eat."

"I...you'll let me stay here?"

She hacked a laugh. "Will I *let* you stay here? Oh, you are a delight. I would go with you and set you up myself, but I'm not one for leaving my smithy." She plunged a hot piece of metal into ice water, sending a plume of steam raging into the air.

"This is a cave," I said looking around. "I didn't know the word for it before."

"No? That far gone, were you? Don't worry, it will all come back to you."

"Behr? I have a question...about realms. And rulers."

"No, no." Behr shook her head. "I'm not the one to be asking for that sort of advice. You should not discuss those things with just anyone, if you catch my meaning."

I nodded. "Then...who?"

"Someone you trust."

"But I trust you." I blurted it out too quickly and then felt the heat of embarrassment on my neck.

"And right you should. But these matters are not for my ears. Whomever you speak to must be trusted and qualified."

I chewed on my lip. "Do you remember the arsehole? Kallórr?"

She grinned, showing her golden teeth. "Told you his name, did he?"

"Well...I sort of made him. But that's not the point."

Behr laughed again. "You're an innocent one, aren't you? If I know that scoundrel, and I do, he does not do anything he doesn't want to. You may think you forced his hand, but that is only what he wanted you to think."

"Scoundrel as he is, could I talk to him? Would he be an option?"

Behr got serious, her eyes sharply focused on her work. "If there were one person, in all of Aarde, I could tell you to put your trust in, it would be The One Who Roars At The Beast. Remember that, Ruler." She lightened up, rolling her shoulders. "But he'll not be eager to see you, I'm sure. Regardless, he's one you could tell all those problems to."

"Problems?"

"The ones weighing you down with each step, the ones cracking your rib cage every time you breathe. All those." Behr waved behind her. "Take that way there, and someone will be waiting to show you around. But come back if ever you need to pound something, Ruler. I'll be here."

"Thank you, Behr."

I followed the way she pointed out and went through a tunnel of sorts. On the other side, I met a girl. Her skin was so white it glowed, even in the dim light of the cave. Her hair was white too. But her curls were just as wild as mine, going every which way on her head. A few locks of hair were braided and hung long down her back, with bits of metal tied to the ends. A closer look revealed that she wore white paint down the bridge of her nose. Difficult to detect against the brilliance of her complexion.

Her arms were crossed, and she was nowhere near as bulky as Behr, but still muscular. My age, it seemed. Her eyes were also gray like mine.

"Hello," I said with a bow.

"What was that?"

I straightened up. "What was what?"

Her eyes were like fahlcons. She spoke as if it were a bother. "What was that bendy thing you just did with your top half?"

"Oh. Um...it's called bowing."

"Bows are for boats. Or arrows."

"What are arrows?"

"Oh goddess. Why me?" She turned and gestured for me to follow. "Come on, before you slip and twist an ankle or something. Then they'll be blaming me for it."

I hurried behind her. She walked quickly, though she was just as short as I was. When she noticed me falling behind, she stopped. I, however, could not stop quickly enough. I rammed into her back, but she did not stumble forward. It was like hitting a wall.

"Ow, good god. Are you made of iron?" I said, rubbing my sore nose.

"Pretty much. And you are made of...paper? And naivete?"

"Jerk," I said without meaning to.

She scoffed. "You don't even hurl insults like you know who you are. It's pathetic."

I stuck my chin out. "The easiest way to remedy ignorance is information. Stop wasting time and tell me what I obviously don't know about what's going on here."

She smirked at that. "There you are. Much better."

"To be rude?"

"To be honest."

I shrugged. "That's not allowed where I'm from."

She frowned. "Where you're from?"

"Yes. The City."

"I don't know what that is. But I know where you're from, Ruler. And you're looking at it."

"I...wait, what?"

The girl thumped her fist into her chest and stood erect, her chin, though whiter than snow, jutting out to match mine. "Stjarna. Your sister. Good to finally meet you."

Ep 44

Taller Than The Trees

Life Tip: Don't confuse knowing with understanding.

"You're not my sister."

Stjarna frowned. "Are you stupid? Of course I'm your sister."

"I would be stupid to believe you. I know who my sister is. Her name is Priyaa, and she's nothing like you."

"If she's nothing like me, then she's nothing like you."

I stood face to face with the stranger who claimed to be family. We had similar builds. Nothing like the slender, curving waist of Priyaa. Stjarna's eyes held a dozen challenges, unlike the soft, fearful gaze of my sister. But if my mother was telling the truth, Priyaa was not as gentle and cautious as I had always assumed. She was smuggling metal for the Wizens, and even I had no idea about it. *So how do I know what's what?*

"Are we going to make eyes at each other all day, or are you going to come eat?" Stjarna said. She spoke with a different lilt than I did. It was more like Behr's, as if they were throwing the words around and catching them again.

My stomach growled, betraying my hunger.

"This way," Starjna said, motioning for me to follow.

Once I cleared the tunnel, I could only gasp. A network of caves and houses made of stone as far as I could see. Trees supported the houses, even growing inside and through them. Veins of metal ran through the hillsides and cliffs that decorated the town. A brilliant blue sky broke over the tops of mountains. People bustled through the roads and paths, some riding on contraptions or large animals, others swinging from treetops.

I stopped, my feet steady on the dirt and gravel path. "What is this?"

Stjarna paused so I could take it in. Then she chuckled. "I cry whenever I come home too."

I quickly scrubbed my tears away, unaware that they were even present. "It's beautiful. How...how?"

"Not like your City?" Stajrna asked.

It was my turn to laugh. "No. Not like the City." *If only Monny could see it. Or Priyaa. Or Clay.* "You *live* here?"

Stjarna grinned. "You do too, oh mighty Ruler." She started down a winding path, skipping over the large rocks and roots that jutted out of the roads. The place itself was like a puzzle. Children screeched and zigzagged through us chasing one another, covered in filth but cackling with pleasure. Old people—much older than anyone I'd ever seen in the City—sat outside of their homes and played games with little cards or chips of wood, cursing and teasing, drinking from large vessels.

We made our way up for quite a while until we reached one of the larger caves. "In here," Starjna said.

Inside, fyreplaces roared, torches blazed on rough stone walls, and lanterns lit the tables. I touched one of them, fighting down the lump in my throat when I imagined how excited Clay would have been to see so many in one place.

There were many wooden tables, with groups of people sitting and eating, some even wrestling on the ground while others cheered and laughed. It seemed like they were hurting each other, but no one else was concerned, so I walked by in awe. The food smelled incredible. There was no hint of Metatoxin in the air. Just smoke and charred meat.

We went into a back room where it was much quieter, then up a series of ladders until we were out of the cave and in a house built on top of a tree. There was a large deck with a railing lining it. From there, I could see much more of the whole place. Red clouds of dust rose from the ground, creating a thick haze that eventually joined the sky. The entire thing was a masterpiece.

I wanted to ask where we were and what this place was for and how come it was so beautiful and why it made me cry, but I couldn't say much of anything.

"Heim," said Starjna, almost as if she could hear me. "I can't imagine living a whole life without having seen it. Without having known where you're from." She leaned her arms on the railing, the wind catching her white curls and playing with them, her eyes drinking in the light. "Don't get me wrong. I don't pity you. Nothing like that. But it's strange to meet you now. To feel this way about someone I don't know."

"What way are you feeling?"

She put a fist to her chest. "When I look out over Heim, and it soaks in my bones and moves my metal in me. That's what I feel when I see you. It's just natural. I don't mean for it. Just comes." She angled her head to me. "You don't feel that?"

I didn't know what to say. I felt...everything. Too much. I couldn't sort it.

"He'll want to see you. Talk to you," she said. "I better leave you to it. But come down after, and I'll see to it you're fed." Starjna smacked me on the back as she left...so hard that I almost fell off the tree to my death.

I stood there, watching. Trying to understand. *From here? How? Sisters?* There was no way. No possible way. I wished suddenly that I'd stayed longer with Behr—asked more questions, found more answers in the comfort of the smithy—before throwing myself into this wild chaos.

"Well, now, what have we here?"

A deep voice. Shook the leaves of the tree. I gripped the railing and turned to see who could ever sound like that when they spoke, like thunder at night.

A man. He wore the skin of animals on his shoulders. His hair was many shades, dark as obsidian, gray like slate, and white like starlight. Big curls that did whatever they wanted. His beard was braided, hanging down his chest, with bits of metal tied to the ends. His skin was deep red. Deeper even than mine. White freckles exploded over his nose and cheeks. He stood taller than the tree that held us. Wider than a canyon.

I only stared. And stared. And when I didn't know what else I could possibly do, I ran forward and pressed my face to his chest.

He put the strongest arms, riddled with pulsing veins and black writing, around me and laughed. He kept a hand on my head to steady me and to bring me closer.

I let my eyes close and, for once, didn't have to think about anything at all. My metal did not move, did not speak. My heart did not race. No questions. No hiding. Nothing. Except for stillness and the full, overwhelming awareness that I was with my father. At last.

Ep 45

Never Come To Me Uncertain

Life Tip: Not all gifts bless the givers; not all givers bless the gifts.

"Come now, what's all this?" he asked.

When he spoke with me leaning on him, his voice echoed through me. It sounded like the beginning of time.

The man, my father, pulled me away to look at my face. "Half-starved, aren't you? We'll have to fix that."

"I'm rather hungry, yes, but not *that* hungry," I said. "I'm okay."

"You only say that because you have never felt what it is to be full." He lifted my arms, which felt like loose threads in his strong grip, and examined each one. "Are you otherwise injured? It seems your journey has been arduous."

"Injured?" If he was asking if everything hurt always and if I had bruises on bruises because there was never enough down time for me to heal, then yes, very much so. But in a world like Heim, I had a feeling 'injury' meant losing a limb or an eye. "I'm alright," I said.

"We'll see about that as well." He smiled, but his eyes grew far away. "You lie like your mother."

I shook my head and stepped away. "You have to understand how difficult this all is for me. I don't know you. I don't know any of you. And my life, my family, my world... they are all so different than any of this. *I* am so different. I don't think I can just accept what you're trying to tell me. That you are my father. That Stjarna is my sister. That this is where I'm from."

His eyes twinkled. "I never said I was your father."

I blushed and stammered. "I...I assumed...."

"No. You did not assume. You knew." The large man nodded, leaning on the railing as Stjarna had done, looking over Heim, his hair wild in the wind. "I am sure there are many things you know without understanding how. A gift from Heim. The ability to know."

"I thought that was just because I was Meta."

"Meta? The way of Meta spreads over many realms. Some gifts are Meta, but some are from your realm. Some are from your family. Some are only yours."

"But you are my father? My...family?"

He touched my cheek with a calloused palm. "I am." He paused, removing his hand. "Does this not please you? To be touched with affection?"

"It's just...my parents never did anything like that. It's new."

"Or very, very old."

I nodded. "Hard to tell the difference. But I don't dislike it." I cleared my throat to quell the emotions that were rising up from my chest. Titanium spurred to life, steadying my heart. Lead comforted me. "So Joacin...is not my father?"

My father's face grew dark. "I do not know who that is. But no, he is not your father."

"And my mother? Not...not Viveka?" I could almost see her. Her eyes, gray like mine, but nothing else the same. Nothing at all.

Just as quickly, his face changed. A deep sadness mingling with fondness. "Of course she is your mother. You are so much like her."

"Nostalgia clouds minds. I am not at all like her."

He grinned. "Exactly how she would say that. Same voice. Same gift of logic. Same keen insight." He gestured with his hands to everything around us. "I see wide. Viveka sees sharp, detailed. She's brilliant. Rarely did we get along, but always, I treasure our disparities." He sighed. "Does she know you have come?"

I didn't know what to say. So I said nothing.

After a few moments, he interpreted my silence and broke it, his voice so heavy it almost cracked me in two. "How long ago did she die?"

It would be the first time I admitted out loud what had happened. My metal raced to life, trying to support me, to keep me upright. "Technically...today."

"Technically today." He sighed. "Goddess, child. You are *not* alright."

I wanted to say that I was indeed fine. That I was not even sure I was sad. That being unsure made me more sad than anything else.

"Go with Stjarna," he said. "You should not be alone quite yet. Eat. Fill yourself up. Then sleep. We will speak again after that."

"Wait," I said, grabbing his hand before he turned to leave and then dropping it, deeply embarrassed that I could be so forward. I had not even bowed to him once. Joacin would never have accepted such wild behavior. "I...forgive me. But I do not know your name." And then I remembered Behr explaining how names worked in Heim, that they were offered as a symbol of trust and friendship, not formality and respect. "You don't have to tell me if you—"

"Woden Aerixon Skapa. My name. Ruler Who Always Makes Things Right." He came to me, put a hand on my curls, and kissed my forehead as if he had been waiting to do it for a hundred years. "I trust you with my life, daughter. Never come to me uncertain again."

Ep 46

Penny For Your Thoughts

Life Tip: Never bring a Ruler to a pub fight.

Back down in the caves, I met Stjarna. Every time I looked at her, it was like I could see more, almost as if she were revealing herself to me with each encounter. She had piercings in her eyebrows and nose and black writing on the side of her neck going all the way down to her fingertips.

When she saw me, she hooked her arm around the back of my neck and led me forward. "You met him, I see?"

"I did."

"Good, good. You'll need to eat even more after that. It is always great to see him, but it is exhausting." She took me to a counter and abandoned me for a moment, jumping over it and disappearing into a back room that I guessed was a kitchen. I sat down in an empty seat and tried to be invisible to those eating and drinking and wrestling near me.

A couple strangers, both boys, eyed me from across the cave. Eventually, they got up and sauntered over. One of them held a significantly sized axe, which he twirled when he realized I noticed.

"From which realm do you hail?" Axe boy asked. He had a small, scruffy, brown beard and a deep tan.

"Don't be stupid." The other boy, who had orange skin and a flat nose, shoved his friend. The rings of metal on his wrists and ankles jangled when he did so. "She's from Heim. Look at her skin. Look at her hair."

"We have lots of skins in Heim, fool."

"But not many red ones outside of Heim. And that hair." He tilted his head, staring at me. "Could look like Ruler hair, almost. Regal. And so pretty. Like platinum."

He reached his hand out to touch my hair, and I smacked it away.

"Ow," he said. Then he smirked. "Never mind. Too weak to be from Heim, much less a Ruler."

I stood up, and without thinking it through, pushed the boy back with both my hands.

He stumbled, just slightly. He was heavy, like he was filled with metal. But not nearly as sturdy as Stjarna had been when I bumped into her. The orange boy's eyes flashed, and an impish grin spread over his face. "Oh? It's a fight you want?"

No. It was not a fight I wanted. But the boy lunged, unraveling the metal bands he wore on his arms and legs. The metal came flying to me—or rather at me—and I remembered slicing open the Morals and Fenders in L's compound. How they slumped over and gurgled to death. I quickly decided I did not want to kill the stupid boys.

Instead, I focused on the metal, not the Meta. I lifted my hands, fingers tensed, palms facing out. The metal bands stopped their momentum, hovering in the air. I asked the metal who it was. A dusty orange. A golden brown. Green patina. It told me it's name was copper.

Would you like to come to me, Copper?

It raced toward me, coiling itself around my fingers and arms, acquainting itself with my other metal.

"Hey," the boy shouted, his voice cracking. "Give those back!"

"Enough, Api," Stjarna said, carrying a plate of food and a big wooden cup and hopping over the counter without spilling a drop of anything. "Are you this foolish?"

"She stole my bronze bracelets!"

"Copper," I said. "Not bronze. It's copper."

Stjarna paused, her eyes twinkling. "A classificist, are you?"

"A what?"

"You know her, Stjar?" Api asked, exasperated. "I should have guessed any troubling presence would be well acquainted with you."

"And I should have known you'd pick a fight with a Ruler on her first day home."

Api's small eyes widened. "I knew she was a Ruler! See Klok! I told you! I knew she was a Ruler."

Stjarna set down the food at a table and pointed her finger at him. "Then why would you pick a fight you knew you'd lose, idiot?"

Api stuttered until Klok guided him away by poking the butt of his axe at him. "I am sorry he is the way he is, Stjar." Then he saluted me with his weapon. "Keep the copper, Ruler. A gift. Welcome home."

Stjarna sat down at the table with a huff. "That's more like it."

I sat beside her. "What do they mean when they say 'Ruler'? How do they all know what my name means?"

Stjarna stuffed fried fish into her mouth and motioned for me to do the same. "It's not just your name, Nexus. It's a role as well."

My mouth filled, and I laughed. "Wait, you think I'm an actual in-charge type person?"

Stjarna did not find it funny. "You are. Doesn't matter what any of us thinks about it or not." She took a sip of the drink and handed it to me. "Did they teach you classification in the other realm? And how to move your metal so well? I saw how the copper came to you."

The drink tasted like warm milk but settled into my stomach like lava. "No, no. In the City, being Meta warrants a death sentence."

Stjarna frowned. "Being Meta?"

"Yes. Being born with no metal in your body. Having the ability to control metal. That's not allowed in the City. I had to hide so they wouldn't kill me. There were no teachers or things like that. Anyone who knows how to do anything with metal sort of had to stumble into it."

Stjarna wiped her mouth with the back of her hand after a big gulp. "Except for your mother, of course? She must have instructed you."

"No, Stjarna. My mother hunted people like me."

Stjarna shook her head. "That makes no sense. In Heim, we have no Meta or not Meta. There is just...Heim. Some people do things, and others do different things. Your mother knew this way of thinking. And she knew her daughter would have some sort of affinity with metal. You are a Ruler, and she could not have forgotten that. If she truly believed your 'Meta' *should* be hunted in your City, she would have killed you at birth."

"She wanted to use me. To hunt others. To find out more. To sacrifice me for her own advancement."

Stjarna thought about this. "Our father would not choose this type of person to marry."

"Perhaps that's why she left Heim. Maybe they had a disagreement."

Stjarna studied the rest of her fish before inhaling it. "Is your belly full?"

"It is. The food is very good and also not poisoned."

"You eat...poison food in your City?"

"It's meant to weaken Meta. So we eventually starve."

Stjarna grinned. "Yet here you are, Ruler. Very much alive."

I thought about that. About where I sat and the copper on my hands and the metal in my body. About my mother who couldn't love me and my father who didn't know me. My friends who betrayed me. Then I thought of Monny, who was with L somewhere wondering if I would ever come back and save him. There was no time for slow meals and long chats.

"Stjarna?" I asked. "Maybe you can help me with something. Do you know someone named Kallórr?"

She spit out her drink all over the table. When she spoke again, it was in a whisper. "How do you know that name?"

I leaned in to match her posture. "So you know him?"

Her eyes met mine. "I know *of* him. But there is no way in himmin or hel that his name should come out of your mouth, Nexus."

I tried to read what her pink-gray eyes held, but there was only a shimmer of fear, and the rest cloaked in secrecy. "Why?" I asked.

"Because the two of you are not allowed to know one another. Not ever."

Ep 47

Wild And Big

Life Tip: You knew who you were before you became it.

I had to run to keep up with Stjarna as she walked away, pushing past rowdy Heimsman in the tavern.

"Won't you at least tell me why I can't see—"

"Shh." She said, whirling around and covering my mouth with her hand. "Shut up. You're more stupid than Api, you know that?"

I pushed her hand away. "Fine. Don't tell me. I'll find out on my own. I always do. But I do need your help."

She raised an eyebrow. "Something that does not break every Aarde law, I hope?"

Breaking Aarde law? So she is serious about not mentioning Lórr's name. I made a mental note. "I need help to turn this"—I gestured to myself—"into that." I motioned to her.

"Ha."

I crossed my arms. "Don't 'ha' me. You know what I mean. You're...you're...."

"Strong, Resilient. Quick. Confident."

"Well...yes. And I am—"

"Weak. Unconfident. Tired. Sad."

"God, you don't have to be an arsehole about it, Stjarna."

She grinned. "What else are sisters for?"

"My sister would help me."

She dropped her smile. "You have another sister?"

"Oh." I cleared my throat. "Yes. Younger than me."

She nodded. "So your half sister. No relation to me. But if you love her, I love her. Don't worry." She shrugged. "I mean, I hate her. But I will love her for you. You're welcome."

"Thank you?" I shook my head to clear it. "Will you help me, Stjarna?"

"Of course. I must. No Ruler can walk around Heim like a just-born baby ghoat. Sleep, and then we will fix you."

She showed me to her room and offered me a space on her bed, which was animal skins on the dirt floor. I could not complain once I got in. I slept sweet and deep, like a river was washing over me. When I woke, new clothes were laid out for me.

White dress, with leggings and leather boots to go underneath it. A brown animal skin vest as well. I felt a little ridiculous until I tried it on. Then I thought all my City clothes must have been preposterous. *If only Monny could see me now.*

"You've slept almost two days," Stjarna said once I peeked my head past the linen that served as a door. She tossed me bread and meat. "Eat as we go. Steina is waiting."

I chewed with vigor as we walked from one cave to another. Stjarna's stride was easy but bold beside me. She reached over and took a bite out of my sandwich, then winked at me and wiped her mouth with the back of her hand. I would have been upset about her intrusion, but I was in awe of her. She shone like the sun when we stepped into the sunlight, her hair like diamonds and her skin like pearls.

"What does your name mean, Stjarna?"

She dodged a rearing animal—a hørs, I realized it was called—and hopped over a stone without even thinking. "Stjarna Aerixon. She Rules Like The Stars."

"You do." I didn't even know what I meant by that. But I knew it was true.

She smiled sideways at me. "It is. Now, I warn you. Do not flinch with Steina. And be honest about what you want. It is always best to go as far as you can. If you can bear the pain, go for it."

"Wait," I said as she grabbed my forearm and pulled me into a cave. "What do you mean pain?"

Inside were many places to sit and a few mirrors. It was well lit with lanterns of many sizes. A square, stocky woman snorted and thumped Starjna in the back, sending her stumbling. "You are late," she grunted. If a human could be a boulder, Steina was that. Her short body was almost all covered in black markings.

"This is the new Ruler?" she asked with a scoff. "Good goddess, we have some work to do. Some metal will do wonders to start."

"I can't," I explained. "Not unless you have more steel." I held up my arm.

Stjarna gasped. "What the hel is that?"

Steina took my arm and squinted already tiny eyes. "Who did this to you, Ruler?"

"It's to keep us from holding our metal. None of us know how to remove it."

"You weren't kidding." Stjarna said. "They really are trying to kill you."

I nodded. "It sends out electrical pulses. Basically, if you hold tiny amounts of metal, it's painful. If you try to hold more, it tries to electrocute you."

"How did you know to use steel?" Steina asked. "That is a brilliant move."

"Uhhh...." I glanced at Stjarna and decided to avoid Lórr's name. "I got lucky."

Steina nodded. "Drop your guards, then," she said. "Shield down."

I took my arm back. "I don't mind dropping the guards. Shield stays. No one touches my metal."

Steina rolled her eyes. "Damn Rulers."

But Stjarna chuckled. "Stubbornness is a family trait, I guess."

Steina observed me. Both she and Stjarna stared but made no comment when they saw the vertical scar running down my neck and disappearing into my dress. Steina fumbled in her cabinets and came back with buckets of metals.

"I'll pierce you and mark you. Balance by adding metals, not taking away. Think you can handle all that?"

I could feel my own eyes light up. "I get those black writings on me? Today?"

"If that's what you want, yes. They are painful—"

"I don't care. Yes. Please. I am so excited. Yes." I paused. "Wait, what are they for?"

Stjarna held out her arms. "Balance. Speed. Strength. Intelligence. They enhance what you already have. Balance you out. Help you feel as whole as you already are."

A shiver went down my spine. "Do you think my mother had these?"

"Who's your mother, young one? If she's from Heim, chances are I'm the one who marked her. And I don't forget so easy."

I hesitated. "Viveka Aerixon."

Steina froze in place. "Your mother? Viveka?"

"Yes."

She nodded, obviously swallowing her emotions. "We will do right by you, then."

I had never heard anyone speak of my mother with fondness before coming here. "What was she like?" I blurted out. "When you knew her?"

Steina smiled, a faraway look in her eyes. "Wild. And-...big. But still narrow. Focused. No other words for it. She took up the whole room. The whole of Heim. That's how I felt when I was near her. Like she took it all up, and then she'd make you feel like you did too. Like you were just as big. Just as wild. Just as good." She sniffled, breaking her memory trip. "Well now. I should have known. You are so much like her."

She sat me in her chair and lifted a narrow metal that flaymed red-hot. "No flinching," she warned. And then she dug in.

Ep 48

Wanna Play?

Life Tip: Learn the rules before you jump into the game.

"Am I dead?"

Stjarna's face floated above mine. "You look awful."

"I *do*?"

"Nah." She grinned. "You look like a Ruler."

"Did some of my finest work on her," Steina said before spitting into a clay jug that I realized only existed to collect her saliva. "Just wait until Woden sees her."

"I want to see me," I said, pulling myself up from the seat that had held me for what felt like the whole day. "Can I look now?"

"No," Stjarna and Steina shouted in unison.

Stjarna explained. "You can't look until you get the feel of it. That way you believe who you are before you see what you look like."

"What? I can't just peek?"

Stjarna groaned and started to push me out the door until I yelped from the contact with my raw back.

"Sorry," she said, cringing. "Forgot Steina put her claws into you. The writings will be sore for a while. But don't cheat and look in the mirrors."

She led me to another cave. This one was massive, with many smaller caverns inside. The sounds of grunts and the cries of pain and effort filled my ears.

I wrinkled my nose. "God, it smells like sweat in here. Sweat and...."

"Blood. I know, right?" But Stjarna inhaled like she was sniffing a sap tree in bloom. "Okay, let's see if you have any obvious affinities."

The first cavern she took me to was cluttered with boys, some wrestling and swinging weapons at each other and others hurling axes through the air. "Move," she cried. "Get outta the way."

They muttered and complained but obeyed.

Before us were wooden targets, all scuffed and chipped. Stjarna grabbed one of the many axes strewn about, hoisted it above her head, and flung. She knocked the target right over without even trying. Then she pushed an axe toward me.

"Me? Throw this?"

She nodded and stepped aside.

"I don't know how."

"Yes you do."

I took a single moment to acquaint myself with the metal on the head of the axe. Iron. Reliable. Eager to please. Strong. But malleable. *Go straight for me*, I told it. It was not the most intelligent of metals, but it so wanted to get things right. I flung the axe, and it hit the target dead on, but not with nearly the strength Stjarna had exhibited.

"Eh." She shrugged. "You're more balanced now. But not much power there. Let's move on."

We went from cavern to cavern, gathering a following as people heard the new Ruler was trying out her skills. I threw things, caught things, bent things, smashed things, balanced things. All eliciting an 'eh' from Stjarna.

"Well, that's all we have here," she said after a while. "Maybe we can try the cliffs or something tomorrow."

"Stjarna? Do you have anything more...more...thinky?"

She scratched her head with one of the knives she was holding. "More thinky, you say?"

Klok, one of the boys who I'd met in the tavern earlier, spoke up. "Try her with the machina, Stjar."

Stjarna perked up. "A decent idea, Klok. A classifist would enjoy it. And at least we know she has an affinity there."

"A classificist?" I inquired.

"You know which metals are which without having to study them. You identify them without any outside influence."

I nodded. "I see. Are you a classifist too?"

Stjarna winked. "Not as good as you, Nexus. But I have my own strengths."

"What are yours?"

"A long list. But one of my most useful is increasing the magnetics of metal when I move it. Gives a little extra power. Makes me a lot stronger than I look."

"Can you decrease the magnetics as well, Stjarna?"

She studied me as we walked. "No one's ever asked me that. What use would it be? Why would I want to decrease magnetism?"

I shrugged. "Maybe you could...I don't know...fly?"

Stjarna stopped. "You think so?" She grew wistful, studying her hands. "Like the Rulers of old?"

"I mean...I know nothing about the Rulers of old. But if you can decrease the magnetism of your metals, or rather reverse their polarity, you could probably at least hover, if not fly."

"Well, I will be trying that," Stjarna said. "But now, we will try you with the machina."

I was about to ask what the machina was, but we arrived, and all questions left me.

In the center of the large cave was a gigantic metal construct. Like a monster. But beautiful. Many types of metal all clustered around an enormous magnet. I could feel the strength of it pulling me on.

Suddenly, I didn't care who else was present. In fact, there was no one else. Nothing existed at all. I put my hands out and got the intense urge...to *play*.

So I played. I sorted through the metal, pushing and pulling, rearranging, lifting and dropping. Some I twisted. Some I straightened. I had never felt more at home in my entire life than when I stepped into that pile of metal and touched the magnetic core with my steady hands.

Whatever Steina had done by adding metal and piercings and writings to me made me feel capable and sure, like for once I did not have to second-guess myself. There was no wondering if I was doing the right thing or if anyone would see me. There was only play.

Finally, someone called out to me.

"Nexus! Nexus, you have to stop!"

Stjarna locked her arms around me and dragged me away from the metal structure. This was necessary, as my legs would not listen to me anymore and my hands would not stop moving metal. When I was far away enough, my concentration broke. And I could see what I had done.

The metal structure, the machina, had changed shape entirely. It stood so tall that it busted out of the cave altogether, letting in light and debris from the surface. It was so wide that most of the caverns were crushed, their contents scattered.

Everyone who had come to watch me stood in awe, mouths open. I could feel their hearts racing, their cells whirring. Mine began to pick up its pace as well once I realized what it was I had built.

"It's...a *drakon*." Stjarna's eyes were wide, her arms still around me.

The beast shone in the light. One of its talons was the size of my leg. Its wings were larger than an entire City flat.

When metal moved, it hummed. But apparently, when hundreds of weights of metal moved, they screamed to life. The drakon, with the magnet as its core, turned its head toward us and roared.

Ep 49

Like A Real Monster

Life Tip: You can't stay small forever.

I didn't truly understand what was happening until the drakon lifted one leg, cracking the side of the cave wall open and bringing it down, nearly crushing Api under its paw. Heimsmen yelled and dodged, some clearing the cave altogether, but most locating a weapon of some sort.

"Make it stop," Stjarna yelled at me over the sound of crashing rubble. "Nexus, Make it stop."

My whole body went limp. "I...I don't know what to do. I have no idea what—"

"You did this," Stjarna said, shoving me toward the metallic beast. "Turn it off!"

I could only stand there, watching it move and turn and... think. Like a real monster. Like it was alive.

The drakon spread its wings, destroying what was left of the cave. Three flaps, the metal groaning and adjusting, all pivoting and interlocking in the most beautiful forming I'd ever witnessed. *How can I have done this?* No person could accomplish something so detailed, so...miraculous.

The drakon lifted itself from the ground and overlooked Heim. The screams of the people lifted from the ground too. Every time the drakon landed, it crushed cave homes. Every time it flew, it destroyed tree houses.

"Come on," Stjarna yelled, grabbing my wrist and racing forward. "We can't let it destroy the whole realm."

Api and Klok followed us, and while we ran, Steina appeared, her chunky frame hurtling over fallen hørses and clusters of debris.

"We need Woden," Steina said, wheezing from exertion. "We do not know how to quell such a beast. But he will remember."

"He'll come," Stjarna said. "For now, we make sure no one is crushed."

And so Steina, Api, Klok, Stjar, and I herded people away from wherever the drakon decided to be. Some Heimsman could not help but try to fight the drakon. But no arrows, no spears, no swords could stall it. Finally, Woden appeared, so heavy with metal that his steps dented the ground when he walked.

"Where did it come from?" That was his first question.

"It was me," I said. "It was an accident."

He frowned. "You accidentally made a metal drakon?" He pointed an enormous hammer-axe at the creation. "When did you even have time to do something like this?"

Stjarna touched his arm. "The machina. I thought she would make a ball or an ax. This took her...maybe ten minutes, Father."

He examined me and, amid the chaos, put a hand on my shoulder. "Are you unwell? This was a great feat."

Am I? I hadn't noticed how my arms were numb and my metal groaned within me. *I could fall asleep right now, right here.* "I'm tired, but fine," I said.

He nodded. "How did you make this, Nexus? If it was not made with brute force, chances are it cannot be destroyed by brute force."

I thought back, trying to remember...anything. But it was all a blur. I couldn't remember what I was thinking or if I was thinking at all. I just...moved.

"I don't know how I did this, Woden."

Stjarna interjected. "She did not speak or respond when she was making it. It was like her ears turned off. Her face changed. She was so focused, it was like she was someone else."

Woden nodded. "Nexus, how do you move your metal? What is your process?"

"I don't know...."

"Did you imagine the metal in your mind? Do you regard its characteristics? How do you make it move for you?"

"Oh. If that's what you mean...I ask it."

"You...ask it?"

I nodded. "I speak to it. But not out loud. In my mind. But not in my mind, either. In my...me. And then it...honors me?"

Stjarna stared as if I were levitating. "Goddess," she said. "I thought those were just stories."

I looked from Woden to Stjarna. "Is that not how everyone does it?"

Stjarna stumbled into her words. "Nexus, when you classify metals...how do you know what they are?"

"They tell me. How else would someone know such a thing?"

Stjarna covered her face with her hands. "Oh, goddess." She looked to her father. "I should have asked better questions, Father," she said. "I had no idea...."

Woden's face did not change as he regarded me. Serious, stoic, a deep understanding in his eyes.

"We will keep this between us. Until it is no longer possible to do so."

"Keep what between us?"

"Nexus," he said, carefully, quietly, "you are an Old Ruler."

I blinked. "Now you think I'm...old?"

Stjarna's eyes were wide, like she was seeing me for the first time. "You're a *goddess*, Nex."

I imagined my eyes were just as wide as my sisters because her words did not register in my brain.

Woden snapped his fingers to get my attention. "If you spoke to make the drakon, you can speak to calm it." He gestured that I should lead the way. "We will follow you."

Follow me? Follow me where? Why? I went forward, trying to envision how on Aarde I would communicate with that much metal at once. After dodging a good deal of debris, I made it to the drakon.

"Let me try. Alone," I told my father.

He nodded and commanded that everyone move away from the drakon at once.

The creature was raging, obviously overwhelmed and, I could tell somehow, rather confused about why people were trying to break it.

Come now, it's alright. It's alright.

The drakon stilled and turned its attention to me. It seemed silly—a small girl beside a gigantic beast. But there I was. I held my hands out, and the drakon lowered its magnificent head to me.

I could sense what it was most afraid of then. That people would make it go back to disorganized darkness, that its purpose would be stripped away. It was afraid to die. Which meant...*It is alive.*

I touched its nose—cold, beautiful silver with traces of bronze. Its metal purred to me, glad to be admired rather than feared. It was not the drakon's fault people were always so scared. The drakon could not be blamed for its size or its power. It could not help that the houses and caves were not made with the drakon in mind. That an entire civilization was formed based on its absence, rather than its inclusion.

So I made it a promise. *I will protect you with my life.*

It was thankful for this and glad not to feel alone.

And then I closed my eyes and gave my creation a gift. I pulled on the space between the particles of metal, reducing its magnetic forces and collapsing the structure. *Be small now,* I said. And the drakon honored me. *Only for a while,* I explained. *And then one day, you will be yourself again.*

Nothing agrees to become small without knowing how big it truly is.

Once I was done, all that remained was one round, smooth stone. It was so heavy, I had to move its metal just to pick it up off the ground. I could not put it in my pocket. The density would have ripped any seam in an instant. So I made a nest for it at the base of my spine, where my blood could keep it warm. I turned to face the bewildered crowd.

If anyone wanted to hurt my drakon, they'd have to tear me in half first.

Ep 50

Truly, And Very Deeply

Life Tip: Don't knock it until you understand it.

"Quickly," Stjarna said, leading me through a network of treehouse terraces.

But Woden put his hand on her shoulder. "A Ruler never rushes, Stjarna. We hasten. We don't hurry."

She paused, taking a calming breath and recentering herself. "You are right, of course, Father. I cannot help but be worried."

He smiled, though his eyes remained clouded. "Rushing does not ease worry. It feeds it."

"These are very wise lessons," I interjected. "But rushing and worrying aside, what's going to happen? Where are you taking me?"

Stjarna turned toward me, her emotions immediately heightened again. "You crushed half the village, Nexus. You don't think you'll be expected to answer for that?"

"I never said nor implied that I should not answer for it, Stjarna. I am inquiring as to your customs. I know what would be done with me in the City, but I am a stranger to Heim. I would like to prepare myself for what's in store."

Stjarna shoved my shoulder. "Well, I'm not going to let anyone hurt you, if that's what you mean. I don't care what you have done or didn't do."

"The laws—"

She interrupted me. "The laws are not my family. The laws are not my blood. I will never choose laws over you, Nexus."

"But...but we just met. These are bold claims coming from a stranger."

And then my sister slapped my cheek. Her eyes were like burning stars in a dark sky. "You are mine. I am yours. I do not need to have known you a long time. Time is nothing but a law. I know you now. I knew you then. I will always know you. And it is *hurtful* that you are too stupid to understand this." And then she left.

I stood with my hand to my stinging cheek. "Why is she so angry?"

Woden sighed. "You must try to understand. It is clear to me that in your City, they teach you that family is a means to an end. An organization with some agenda. A strategy. In Heim, family is life itself. Without it, you would float off into the sky, disconnected. And so we build the connections strong. Stjarna feels for you now what you would feel for her after fifty years of embrace. It offends her that you do not see her that way, for she cannot unsee you."

I nodded, fighting down the lump in my throat. "She loves me."

"Yes, Nexus. Truly. And very deeply."

I didn't know what to do. I stood very still. Thinking. And Woden let me process. Finally, I spoke. "I don't know what to do with it. With that kind of love."

"That I cannot answer for you. But I will answer your other questions." He ran a hand over his curls. "Here is what will happen next. The council will convene. They will question you in front of any who wish to attend. And they will make a judgment. It will be as fair as possible. You may choose to obey it or not. If you choose not to, you would have to fight. And any who join you in thinking the judgment is unjust may share your response to it, as well as your fate."

"And what sort of rulings would you consider fair, here in Heim?"

"Common ones are detention, imprisonment, service to other realms, and banishment."

I studied him. "What about death?"

"A life for a life has been ruled, yes. But not often."

"Do they slit throats here?"

He seemed surprised, his eyebrows raised. "No. This is common practice in your City?"

"Very common. Yes."

He shook his head. "It is peacefully done in Heim. Like drifting to sleep."

"But it's still death."

He sighed. "It is still death."

"And you are on this council, Woden?"

He nodded. "I am. But I will be asked not to speak, since you are my family and I cannot be expected to rule against you."

I straightened my shoulders. "Alright then. Let's go. I'm ready."

He chuckled. "No, you are not." He put a gentle hand on my hair, brushing off rubble and dust. "You must present yourself as a Ruler. As an Aerixon. As you. Go and wash and prepare. I will send Steina to you. She will help. And then, daughter, I will see you in the council tree."

Ep 51

In Her Eyes

Life Tip: Not everything said has words.

Steina remained wordless as she prepared me in a room
near the council tree. She had me choose a dress. I picked a
white one with a black leather bodice on the front and
leather straps on the sides. I picked long black boots and
gloves that left my fingers free in case I needed to move any
metal. Steina braided my hair, twisting my growing curls
into a masterpiece that ran down my spine.

Before she was finished, Stjarna came. She was clearly
still upset with me, her jaw clenched and her eyes sharp.
She sat on the ground, pounding a large rock with a stone.
After a few blows, I realized she was pulverizing something
in between the hard surfaces. When she was finished, she
scooped a fine white powder into a wooden bowl and added
water. It formed a thick paste.

She sat me down and knelt beside me. With careful hands,
she applied the paint to the tops of my shoulders, my fingertips, and my chest, tracing along the vertical scar. Then she
put some down the bridge of my nose.

"This is my fault," she said after a long time of silence. She worked slowly, intently.

"It is not, Stjarna."

"It is. I should have been more careful with you."

"You could not have expected what I would do. Even I didn't expect it."

"I knew you were powerful. More powerful than me. Maybe even more than Woden."

"If that were true, then *I* should have been protecting *you*."

She shook her head. "You only say that because you don't understand power. Those who have a great deal of it need more help. Imagine a stream flowing through each person. Those with small streams have strong trunks supporting them. But those with mighty rushing streams flowing through them have no space for strong trunks to allow such might to pass through. They are all water, so the vessel is thin. These people with great streams of power...they need help. They need support or they will break and the water will rush out and destroy things."

Stjarna's eyes pricked with tears. "I should have supported you, Nexus. You have a great stream of power. I knew this, but I wanted to show you off rather than keep you supported." She took a rattled breath. "It is my fault."

I took her hands in mind and came to my knees so we were eye to eye. "Stjarna...did you choose to put a big stream in me?"

"No, but—"

"You did not put it there. And you are not responsible for what I do with it. I am fortunate to know someone like you who desires to support someone like me. But you have no responsibility to do that. Even if we are connected, you are still you, and I am still me."

She leaned forward and wrapped her arms around me. "I missed you," she said.

I squeezed her back, though I didn't know how to respond to her depth of feeling toward me or how someone could love me outside of time. "I feel like I should be more afraid of what comes next," I confessed.

She grinned, releasing me and wiping at the tear that slipped from her eye. "Maybe that drakon you are hiding inside you is giving you some extra courage."

I grinned too. "Maybe so."

She pulled me to my feet. "Time to see yourself, Ruler." And she took me to a mirror, where Steina was waiting impatiently.

I looked...taller. Bigger but shaplier. My skin was adorned with black writings, some carved down my forearms and more across my collarbone and neck. There were even some behind my ears and down my thighs.

I had piercings—rods, loops, and studs—on my nose and lips, many on my ears. Steina put rings on my fingers and bracelets on my wrists and ankles. She clipped metal beads to the ends of my hair and wove wire through my braids. On my cheeks and shoulders, she dusted shimmering, silver powder. The white paint on my face made my eyes stand out like diamonds in a sea of black.

"What do you think, Ruler?" Steina asked.

"I...." I tried to remember what I used to look like before. What I used to feel like on Onur's arm. A small girl in a white cotton dress with cloth shoes and hands trembling in my pockets. I could not recall the last time I'd shoved my hands into any pockets. Or the last time I'd felt gravel under cotton shoes. Or cowered under someone's gaze.

"I look like...me."

Steina smiled. I didn't know her face could do that, but she smiled. "Most would have wailed at the pain of my needles. You did not even wince."

I put my arms around the wide, short woman. "Thank you, Steina. You are a true master. I must pay you, somehow, for all this work. I must...thank you."

She shook me off, trying not to get emotional. "Your mother was my dearest friend. I loved her. And so I love you." She pushed my chin up. "Call me Na. It was her name for me."

"Was she really...good, Na? I feel like I'll never know what she was really like. She hid everything from me."

Na chortled. She took me back to the mirror. Closer, so I was almost nose to nose with my reflection. "You see those eyes, Ruler? Cunning. Brilliant. Searching. But protective. A defender above all else. At any cost. Against any risk. Always." My gray eyes looked like they would crack the mirror with their gaze. "Those," Na said, "are your mother's eyes. And when those eyes look at someone, and you *see* that someone, that person is loved like no other. No matter the cost, be it death or hel or heartbreak."

I stepped back and looked at Na. Looked at Stjarna. And I began to understand what Woden meant about family. *It happens all at once.* That you can see someone, and every-thing changes, because they were always there.

I could not see my mother before she died. But I knew a truth right then, readying for my judgment. Something I could not have known before that moment. I knew that despite every one of her actions—every lie, every manipulation, every icy moment of ill regard and neglect—when Viveka looked at me with those eyes, she saw me.

My mother *loved* me. And I would tear apart whomever it was who forced her to lie about it.

Ep 52

For Only A Moment

Life Tip: Those who mean well don't always do it well.

The tree was bigger than a City flat. It rose from the center of the village, its bark twisted and braided, its branches shading one half of the town in the morning, the other half in the evening.

The council members sat on the ground cross-legged. They varied in age and appearance—women as old as the tree in which they sat and men not much older than me. One girl looked to be twelve. One man, I was sure, was so ancient he was already dead. Though they differed from one another, they all shared the same stillness, the same gravity.

"Come and sit," they said.

I stepped into the filtered, late afternoon light. The tree leaves rustled as if saying 'hello'. I sat down in the center of the tree and crossed my legs. Others from Heim had come. Some scowled in my direction, but others, like Na and Api and Klok, looked worried as they watched with the others.

The very young girl stood up and held her arms out. Her blond hair was shaved rather low, and her body was spindly. But she had the confidence of a dozen drakons.

"Daughter Who Connects The Rulers Of Forever." She lifted her chin, meeting my eyes. "Here you are, to be judged by the Council Of Heim. Are you ready?"

"I am." My voice was louder than I expected.

"It is said that you destroyed much of this village. Is it true?"

I swallowed. "The drakon I created did so."

"Are you to blame?"

"Yes."

A slight murmur from those who watched, but the girl raised her hand and brought them to silence again.

"Did you mean harm to Heim?"

"No. Of course not. I don't mean harm to anyone."

"Do you mean to help Heim?"

I thought about that. "Help? I suppose...not. How would I help Heim?"

"Are you not a Ruler of Heim, Aerixon?"

"So you all say. I am not entirely sure what responsibilities that entails."

"You define the terms, Ruler."

"Alright."

"Why are you here?"

And here is where I had to start lying. I remembered Behr telling me to keep my reason for coming to the realm to myself unless there was someone I trusted. And I hadn't found that person yet.

"I am here because I had nowhere else to go." Not exactly a lie. I couldn't stay in the City. I would have been killed because of the deaths of those Morals and Fenders. And saving Monny was a non-option; I had to go.

"How did you make it here?"

Oh no. How can I word this without saying that Lórr helped me? "I found magnet stones."

"These were given to you?"

"They were acquired. I found them among my mother's things after she died."

More murmurs. A few gasps. Apparently people didn't know my mother was gone.

"How did you know where they would take you? These acquired stones?"

"I did not know."

"Then how are you here?"

"I don't know."

"You don't know how you left the City Wall and traveled across realms to your place of birth?"

"I was born here?"

The girl paused. I had the sense I was not cooperating with her questioning the way people usually did. She did not intend to supply me with information, but to gather it for herself.

"Why did you come?"

"I already said. I had nowhere else to go."

"But you did not know where you were going?"

"No."

"Then how did you know this was someplace you could go."

"I don't know."

"Then why did you come? If you did not know?"

"It just...happened."

"Do things often 'just happen' to you?"

I took a breath. "Yes."

"And do these happenings often result in chaos or destruction?"

I thought about that. About my house and my work and my friends. "Sometimes there is destruction, but I do not cause it. It's caused by people who don't like what I create."

"Explain."

"I make things. And people try to destroy them. That's not my fault. And it's not the fault of the things I make."

"You have made something alive before?"

I chewed on the ring in my bottom lip. Lead came to my fingers. It didn't usually leave its bed in my arm unless I really needed stability. I felt iridium awaken behind my eyes, enhancing the speed of my thinking.

"I have."

"Another drakon?"

"You could call her that." I tried not to smirk. "Her name was Clay. She was just a girl and magnificent and kind. And she died because...." It clicked into place, thanks to iridium. "Because everyone in the City is ill. She died, and it wasn't right. I gave her life again. And they destroyed many because of it. Because instead of honoring her, they attacked. And when I made my drakon, it was also magnificent and also kind. But you—Heim—attacked it instead of honoring it. And here we are."

The girl seemed to be staring into my soul. "Here we are."

She turned and walked away toward the other council members. They huddled, speaking in the hushiest of tones. The girl did not stand after that. She sat back down. And the ancient man—the dead-ish one—was helped to his feet.

When he spoke, his voice creaked and groaned, like a bough about to break. "Daughter Who Connects The Rulers

Of Forever. Born here, in this tree, given life by Viveka and Woden and all those who came before you and all those who will come once you are gone. You are many things. We see in you the furnace—who makes things, creates things, destroys things. We see in you the Magna—who pushes and pulls, who forms the world in the spaces between. We see in you the mother—the protector and defender, the one who takes care. And we see in you the drakon—a wild and untameable force, to be unchained and unstopped.

"We judge now, that you are welcome to remain among us all your days. This would honor us. But the wildness in you cannot stay, Ruler. It must be quieted. It must be watched and guarded. To remain, you must swear to no longer move metal in this way that makes life where there was darkness. And those creations may not enter Heim. This part of you must go. But you may stay. Is this acceptable to you, Ruler?"

I stood up. That's when I realized my hands were shaking. Not with fear, but with anger.

"You are saying to me...I can stay here. Here where I was born. Here where I belong. But I cannot be myself here?"

"It is for the safety of this realm. Many will seek to destroy what you make. We can protect you, Ruler. But if you continue to bring life, you will bring death."

Hot tears slid down my cheeks. "And you want me to give up my drakon." The egg sat still and warm against my spine.

The old man sighed. "It must be so."

"No," I said. I had never heard my voice filled with so much spite. "No, it does not have to be so. You want it to be so."

"The choice is yours."

I took a deep breath. "I will never. Never. Go back to the way I was before I knew what I could do. You...you want me to be small. And careful. And afraid. But I won't do that again. And if you won't protect me...if you won't be home for me, for all of me...I'll just have to make one myself."

"It is only a drakon, child."

"It's not only a drakon." I pounded my chest. "It's my drakon. And I don't abandon the things I make, no matter how much power they hold." Even though my words were strong, my breath shook. "I accept your judgment, Council Of Heim. I will go, as you wish."

I bowed, out of habit, and turned to leave.

"Wait, Ruler," the old man said.

I turned back around, unable to hold myself together for much longer.

The council stood and stepped toward me. At first I was afraid, but then I realized that many of them wore tears on their cheeks that matched mine. They pressed in tight, so their arms were on my shoulders and head. I felt a heavy hand on the back of my head and knew it was my father's.

The old man spoke. "This is the answer we hoped you would have, Daughter. For you have far to go. And to make it, you must leave us behind you. But this choice we could not make. It was only yours."

And then...and then...they hummed. All together. Many melodies intertwining, going down beneath the caves and up above the treetops. I felt every Ending lift off of me, though my heart broke into many pieces.

There, among the people who loved me for only a moment, I lost my story...and Began.

Ep 53

To Get Through The Day

Life Tip: Always ugly cry alone.

I was told I could collect my things before I left.

What things? I asked myself. *Before I leave to go where?*

I asked Stjarna to use her room for a few moments. She understood I needed space and said it was fine but that she would not be far if I needed her.

As soon as the door was closed, everything flooded me at once. Every emotion I held back during the judgment. Every fear. Every sorrow.

There was no telling myself not to cry. Crying was the only possible response. Either that or unleashing an entire drakon, and that did not go well the last time I tried it.

My metal attempted to calm me, but that was not possible either. My heart was a black hole. There was something worse than having no home. It was having no home, finding one, and then losing it. Finding a father who smiled when he saw me, and then knowing I could not see him again. Being myself for the first time, and having it outlawed.

The sob lurched me forward. I fell to my knees without meaning to. I tried to keep myself quiet, but I didn't have control over how my body reacted anymore. I cried that way until I thought maybe I would die. Maybe I would never catch my breath. Maybe the pain of losing something I had never known would destroy me.

Lórr put his arms around me and pulled me to him.

Realizing he was there only made me cry harder.

"Nexus," he said, his voice cracking. "Breathe."

I shook my head, trying to tell him that I, in fact, could not breathe and that I would probably perish right there in Stjarna's room. "So sad," the people would say at my funeral. "She died of a bleeding soul."

He slipped his fingers into my curls and leaned me against his chest. Kneeling beside me on the ground, he stayed that way and breathed deeply. He had a soothing heartbeat, this boy. Listening to it calmed me.

"What happened?" he asked.

"I...can't stay," I replied, hiccuping.

"Are you hurt?"

I didn't know how to answer that. But the tears just kept coming and coming. I had never experienced this kind of pain before. I didn't know what to call it.

"Nexus," he said. "What happened?"

"I made a drakon. It was an *accident*."

I could tell he was smiling without looking. It was like his body warmed. I smacked his arm. "Are you laughing at me right now?"

"No," he said, obviously suppressing a snort.

I shoved him so I could glare at him. "You are laughing at me. God, you're such an *arsehole*."

He grinned and held up his thumb and index finger, squinching them together. "A teeny tiny little drakon has you crying like this? Did someone step on it?"

"It is not tiny," I snapped. "It's enormous. It destroyed half the village."

"Did I not tell you to stop animating lifeless things, Aerixon. And why did you destroy Heim? I thought you'd like it here."

"*It was an accident!*"

But he only grinned. "Careful, Nex. You had better calm down. Don't want another 'accident'. Then I'll have to throw away yet another shirt. You already snotted all over this one."

"I did not snot on your stupid shirt."

"Whatever you have to tell yourself to get through the day."

"What do you want from me, Lórr? Do you show up just to torment me?"

"*You* called *me*."

It was my turn to smirk. "I am beginning to think you come just because you want to see me."

His face grew solemn. "Why would you think that?"

I shrugged, taken aback by his change in demeanor. "I don't know. We seem like friends."

"We're not."

I narrowed my eyes at him. "Why do you pretend? You try to be mean to me. But we both know it's not how you feel. So why?"

He blushed. "I'm not...I don't...."

"Why shouldn't I know you. Stjarna says it's not allowed. Is that why you act this way? Are you not allowed to be nice to me?"

"Technically, I'm not allowed to be nice at all."

"You're not? *Why?*"

"I have to go, Nexus." He tried to get up.

But I grabbed his shirt. "No," I said, and I meant it. "Please don't go yet."

He didn't leave. It was like I'd chained him to the spot. "You should let go of my shirt." His voice was all gravel and ash. I had the feeling he didn't have the heart to pry my fingers off him.

"I have a real question. I can't stay here. Do you know where I can go? I am trying to meet with the Rulers of the realms. The City...they killed my mother and they have Monny and they won't let him go unless I meet with the Rulers. I can't go back to the City until I do this. I'm kind of...lost."

"This is a dangerous notion, Nexus. Convening the Rulers rarely goes well for anyone involved."

"I don't have any other choice."

He nodded, thinking. "Do you know where Shuĭ is?"

"Of course not. This is a place you're talking about?"

"Yes. It sits on the Great Waters. If you can make it there, look for someone named Gege. A friend of mine. Tell him this if he doesn't believe I sent you: 'the sea may part for men to pass, but the fool wanders out to collect the fish.' He will help you with whatever you need. Trust no one but him."

"And you? Should I trust you?"

He smirked, lightening back up again. "We all have risks we must take."

"Behr said I should."

"You met Behr?" He smiled. A big genuine one. It made my heart glow back to life. "That beast. How is she?"

"Magnanimous."

"That she is. You know, most people do not know Behr exists. Not even here in the realms. Quite enigmatic."

"She does seem rather private. But is she...*here*?"

He shook his head. "No. And yes."

Oh good. Unintelligible answers. My favorite. "So...why are you always rushing off?"

He touched my cheek. "I'm glad you are feeling better. And I'm sorry you lost this home. But you have another. Don't worry too much about that."

He's going now. I knew this. It made my stomach hurt. I didn't know how I knew or why I wanted it to be untrue. "Lórr." I took his hand before he could stand up and walk away. "Tell me who you are."

"Best not to," he said. Then he winked. "Trust me, Nex."

And he vanished. Just like that. Gone.

In my hand, he left a tiny pair of stones.

Ep 54

Like Fleas

Life Tip: Leaving before you're left is a terrible strategy.

When I opened the door, Stjarna was approaching.

"Oh good," she said. "I was thinking since you came with nothing, you should take some of my clothes."

"You don't have to do th—"

"Shut up," she said. She held up some bags. "Behrskin. They will hold up in any terrain. Let's take only what we need."

"What do you mean 'we'?" I took the bag, mainly because she hurled it at me.

"Don't be stupid, Nexus. I am coming."

"No. No, no, no." I snatched at the bag she had in her hands. "You are the one being stupid. You're not coming with me, Stjarna. I don't even know where I am going."

"Liar." She yanked the bag, almost tearing my fingertips off. "You are on a mission. You may not want to tell me what it is. But I know there is one. And I am coming. You will have to kill me to stop me." She started stuffing clothes into the bag.

"You might be killed if I don't stop you. I can't let that happen."

"Not your choice. Where I go is my choice. I'm coming."

"No."

"Don't be selfish!" She stopped packing so she could look directly at my face. "You are not the only one who has a stream in her, Nexus. Have you ever thought, even once, that maybe people need you? That maybe I need you? I am coming!"

I inhaled. "I just...don't want to lose you."

"So you leave me?"

I stared at my empty bag, trying to hold myself together.

Stjarna sighed. "You think you protect people by doing things alone, by keeping yourself a secret. But what you are doing...is leaving people, Nexus. And then what? Those people have to do all the things without you. And they can't even tell you that everything—even the hardest things—are better when you are there."

I remembered Clay. How scared she was the night they put the pulses in our arms. The last time I'd seen her alive. I'd promised I would wait for her, walk her home, and hold her hand. But I didn't. I was in too much pain. I thought I was too dangerous. I was afraid I would get her hurt and so I left her alone. And she died without me. Leaving her did not make her more safe.

"Alright," I said. "I won't leave you, Stjar."

She punched my shoulder. "Good. Now what kind of weather are we packing for?"

"Umm...Shuï?"

"Really?" She lit up. "I've never been. But it is windy there I heard. We will need sealed coats. And warming metals." But that last bit she did not say to me. She yelled it out the door.

Klok stuck his head in. "My guess is we need buoyant metals as well. Lots of water in that realm."

Api popped his head in as well. "I should bring my fingerless gloves. I heard that Shuï girls can't resist a bad boy."

Stjarna scoffed. "Maybe bring maglocks, Api. Full restraint is the only way you'll get a Shuï girl to spend time with you."

"You can't all come," I said. "You...can't."

Klok grinned. "I've always wanted to be banished," he said, sticking his pierced tongue out. "Looks good on my resume."

Stjarna looped her arm around my neck and pulled me into a kiss. "Give up, Nexus. These fools go wherever I go. Can't get rid of them."

"We're faithful," Api said.

Stjarna rolled her eyes. "Like fleas."

"Nexus, you know...you should pack more fingerless gloves too. I like a girl who—"

Klok elbowed his brother's ribs, and Stjarna yelled for him to go pack his own bags or she would drown him in the Great Waters.

I gathered some things while they bickered, my heart lighter than it had ever been. I thought I would be alone. Turned out, love had a way of following me.

Ep 55

Hardly An Hour

Life Tip: If you forget to pack snacks, pack muzzles.

Api groaned so loudly that a flock of krows scattered into the air. He kicked the toe of his boot into the ground and flailed his arms. "No one told me we were walking all the way to the coast! I'll die of starvation by then!"

"Walking like a gohrilla will only expend more energy, Api," his brother said. He took deliberate steps, every one planned. "And talking so much will make you sweat."

"But I'm hungry," Api whined, still flopping his legs.

Klok looked back at the village. "We are not even ten lengths away. Why didn't you eat before we set out?"

"I know," Stjarna said, adjusting the behrskin bag on her back. "Once we get a few lengths out of Heim, we could eat the most annoying member of our party."

Klok chuckled. "I make amazing smoked meat. The trick is to seal in the juices."

"Actually," I interjected. "I wasn't planning on walking to Shuǐ. I thought we could use these." I held the magnet stones out in my hands for them to see.

All three peered in awe.

"Where did you get those?" Stjarna asked.

"They were a gift."

Klok scoffed. "From a sultan?"

"Oh...are they rare?"

Api straightened up. "Normal people don't carry around items like this, Nex. This is next level shit."

Stjarna shrugged. "Nexus is next level shit. So I guess we shouldn't be surprised."

Klok examined the stones in my palm. "May I?" he asked.

I tossed them to him. He played with them, moving them closer together and then further apart. Then he shivered and handed them back. "They make me feel weird."

"Like you want to keep them in your pocket forever?" I asked. That's how I felt the first time I held magnet stones.

"No." He wiped his hands on his pants. "Like...scared. Like I shouldn't play with them." He settled for sticking his hands in his armpits to calm himself down. "What are they for?"

"You don't know? I thought...maybe this is how people in all the realms traveled."

They all shook their heads.

"The council knew about them. They asked how I got to Heim." I swirled the stones. "This is how. They make a door. A portal, you could say. I think about where to go and then walk through. When I want to return, I ask the stones, and they bring me back."

"Can I try?" Api asked, his orange skin glowing as he hopped up and down. "Please, please, please?"

"Maybe Klok should go first," I replied.

"Why not me?" Api groaned.

"Because you are a bit of an idiot, Api," Klok said. Then to me, "I would be honored to give it a try...as long as I don't have to touch them again. Perhaps I will travel to some place close. Like right over there to that tree." He pointed to a small sap tree.

I set the stones how I always did and carved an imaginary door frame. Then told him to step through. He did. Nothing happened.

"Let me try," Stjarna said. "Maybe it's a Ruler thing."

"Oh, yes. Of course. The glorious Rulers get to have all the fun," Klok grumbled, stepping aside and plopping down on a rock like a tired tertle.

Stjarna followed all the steps. Nothing. She crossed her arms. "Maybe these are broken. You try, Nex. Let's see if it works."

I set the stones down once more and asked them to take me to the sap tree. I stepped through and put my hand on the rough bark. Then asked for the stones to take me back.

All three sets of jaws dropped.

"Well, they definitely work," Stjarna said. "But not for us. Which means...you would be much faster without us tagging along."

I frowned. "You've changed your mind about coming?"

"No," she said. "But I don't want to make this worse for you. Walking to Shuï will take some time."

"I know nothing about this world. And you all do. You're worth slowing down for. Trust me."

Stjarna's grin was cut short by a metal-tipped arrow. It lodged into her shoulder, sending her down hard.

Slit Throat Saga

Another nicked my right arm, releasing a quick spurt of clear blood.

Hardly an hour into our journey, and someone wanted us dead.

Ep 56

The Babysitters Are Here

Life Tip: Nameless gifts are the best kind.

Turned out, Klok actually knew how to use that axe of his.
He threw it in the direction the arrow came from, and we
heard a thud and a cry of pain. But then, the axe was gone.

"Get down," he called out.

We dropped and moved behind a cluster of rocks. Stjarna
hissed as she positioned herself to examine her shoulder,
where the arrow was firmly planted.

"Who would be trying to hurt us?" I asked, as arrows
pinged against the rocks.

"Anyone," Klok answered.

"Everyone," Api echoed.

"What? Why on Aarde?"

"We're Rulers, Nexus," Stjarna said through clenched teeth.

"For the thousandth time, I do not know what that means."

"We set the rules of Aarde. Of the realms. People want to
change the rules, they need Rulers. And there are a lot of
people who hate the rules, Nexus."

Api tried to peek past the rocks and almost lost his scalp.
"No time for self-discovery. I think they're poachers."

"What are they poaching?" I asked.

"Rulers," they all said in unison.

"So you only *look* smart," Api said.

I punched his arm. "I am smart. I just don't have enough information to make quick decisions." I took a deep breath and felt iridium spinning faster behind my eyes. "I can make one or two of them fall asleep," I offered. "And I can send metal after a couple more, but it might kill them."

"Killing them is fine with me," Api said. "They want to feed us to a monster for copper. And I am too charming to be monster food."

"You wouldn't turn into copper, Api; only the Rulers would. And you don't know that these poachers plan to bait them," Klok argued. "They could take Stjar and Nex to the fault lines instead. Crush them deep in the earth. Get some iridium out of that."

"Shut up, shut up." Stjar slapped at them. "There are countless horrific deaths we could face at the hands of poachers. Let's focus on how to avoid them altogether." She nodded to me. "Nex, send out that metal first. I'll push the magnetics on them to make sure we pulverize the targets. Klok, you focus on moving your axe back to you. And Api, gather some of these arrows. If Nexus can classify the metal in the arrowheads, we might be able to move them away from us."

So we started on the plan. I pulled out titanium and platinum, with copper for flexibility around corners. *Find the targets*, I asked the metal, *and let Stjarna push you.* They complied, and I felt a jolt when Stjarna changed the magnetic field around us, propelling the metals with greater force.

After a while of concentrating, Klok brought his axe back to himself, along with an entire pair of trousers belonging to whomever pocketed his weapon.

"Here, Nexus," Api said, shoving a bouquet of arrows into my face.

A quick look, and they started to shimmer before me as if they were showing off. "Brass," I said.

"Wow." Api shook his head. "I've never seen anyone classify that quickly."

"They will listen to me, I think, if we want to send them back at the poachers."

"So quickly?" Api asked. "They just...listen?"

"She built a drakon in just a few moments, Api. I think she can command some brass arrowheads," Klok said.

But there was no time to do anything of the sort.

Something extremely dense zoomed overhead and crashed into the ground, fracturing the surface with a large, thunderous crack. It was so intense that we lost our positions, falling over onto each other.

Our clumsiness didn't matter either because a literal metal shield materialized around us, deflecting any arrows that were still coming our way.

I thought it was miraculous, but Stjarna scowled, and Klok and Api sulked.

"What's wrong? Is this bad? What's happening?"

Klok heaved. "The babysitters are here."

"Babysitters?"

Stjarna sighed. "Our father. Here to save the day. Already. Again."

"At least he cares," I said. "If this were my parents, they would be orchestrating the attack."

Stjarna sobered. "I suppose I am being a child about it."

I nodded. "It's nice to have help."

The raid was obviously over. The shield came down, and Na pulled the metal back to herself.

"Are you young ones alright?" she asked. "We heard reports of poachers and thought you might need some help."

"We're fine," Stjarna said but then glanced at me and added, "thank you for being so kind."

"You are not fine," Woden said, approaching us with a collection of various weapons he had obviously taken from the very dead poachers. "There is an arrow sticking out of you, Stjarna."

"Oh yeah," she said. "I forgot." She went to pull it out.

"Wait, Stjar," Klok said. "Let me."

And carefully, he twisted his fingers in the air and contracted the arrow so it slid out clean. Blood like water gushed out of Stjarna's shoulder.

I pulled out some of my iron and disintegrated it into a powder, bound it to her blood, and asked it to stop flowing. The blood, made scarlet by the iron, obeyed.

"Well then," Woden said. "It seems you do not need the old ones like us to keep you safe. You are clearly capable of taking care of one another."

"See, Ma," Api said, jutting his chin out at Na and puffing his chest. "Woden said 'clearly capable'."

"Oh?" Na revealed a bundle of cloth. "I suppose you won't need this extra food I brought for you. Seeing as you're so 'capable' and all."

Api snatched the bundle and bent to kiss his mother's cheek. "Thank you, Ma."

She grunted and pointed at both boys. "Protect one another. The Rulers are counting on you."

Both boys nodded, already sorting through the snacks.

Woden offered Stjarna a hand, which she reluctantly took. But instead of pulling her to her feet, he hoisted her up into the air, making her squeal. She fell back into his embrace. Then she slapped his chest.

"I'm too old for that, Father. Put me down."

"In a moment," he said, still holding her. Then, he set her on her feet. "Be patient with yourself on this journey, Stjarna."

She sighed. "Yes. I will. As long as you don't follow us the whole time and try to save us whenever poachers want to drop us into Aarde."

He drew an 'X' on his chest. "Promise. I will not do that the whole time. Only most of the time."

She stomped off, and he chuckled.

Then he turned to me. He motioned for me to come closer. I hesitated.

"Nexus," he said. "You are still my daughter."

"I know."

"Then why do you not come, so I can embrace you?"

I dug the toes of my boots into the dirt. "I suppose...now that I know I can't stay in Heim, I don't want to get used to that sort of thing."

"Affection?"

"Fathers."

He sighed. "Well, used to me or not, I have something for you. I give gifts to all my children. And I am sure your mother already gave you hers."

"I doubt it."

He grinned. "Oh? Care to explain how you can classify metal faster than anyone alive?"

I chewed my lip rings. *That came from Viveka?*

"Hold out your hands," Woden said. "And look into my eyes."

And when he took my hands in his, I felt a pain rip through my arms and threaten to tear my chest apart. I tried to pull my hands away, but his grip only tightened. When he was finally finished, my hands were so hot that my skin steamed.

"What did you do to me?" I asked, my eyes stinging with tears I refused to let fall.

"I gave you a gift only I could give. One only you could receive." Then, he approached me and, cautiously, kissed my forehead. "Do not be afraid of yourself, Nexus."

We said our goodbyes, and the four of us turned toward the coasts of the Great Waters.

"What do you think he gave you," Stjarna asked as we walked.

"I don't know," I replied.

But with every step I took, I felt Aarde tremble beneath me.

Ep 57

What The Sun Brings

Life Tip: Earplugs are essential to travel.

"I think she's part bhadger."

Klok propped his head up with this arm so he could see Stjarna. The fading fyrelight flickered across her face. She looked like the moon fell to Aarde, her pale skin and white hair glowing. Then, she inhaled with a sharp snort and exhaled strong enough to kick up dirt.

"More like an elefant," I said, lying on the other side of my sister. "It's the exhale."

"Mmm, you might be right," Klok sighed, falling back into the dirt and looking up at the stars. "What's it like where you're from, Nexus?"

"I am not sure how to answer. It's...very different than Heim."

I plopped to my back as well so I could see the stars. They swept across the sky like magnesium powder, with tiny pinpricks of silver and platinum. I wondered if Priyaa ever looked at the stars lying on her back.

We were not far from Shuï. The sound of the waters lapping the land almost overwhelmed the crackle of the fyre, the hum of the crickets, and the roaring of my slumbering sister. At daybreak, we would cross the water bridges and enter a new realm.

"Why don't you tell me the best and worst parts of your home, and I'll tell you the best and worst of mine," Klok offered. "Since neither of us can sleep, we might as well share."

He was understating. It was the fifth night of sleeplessness. Talking through it was the only way to survive.

"Alright," I replied. "The best part of the City...." *There has to be something I love about the place where I lived my entire life.* "It is difficult to make friends there."

"And that's the best part?" Klok asked with exasperation.

"It is difficult to make friends there, so the friends I did make were priceless. Like parts of my soul."

"That's beautiful," Klok said, sitting with it for a while. We both startled when Api rolled over in his sleep, but he was dead to the world, probably drowning in his own drool. Even Stjarna's snoring could not wake him.

"My turn, then, Klok offered. "The best part of Heim? The stillness of the morning. It's maybe my favorite thing about being alive, actually."

"*You?* Like stillness?"

I could almost hear him smile from where he lay. "With a brother like Api, a mother like Steina, and a friend like Stjar, stillness is hard to come by. But the morning never fails to bring it to me."

"Wow." His words gave me shivers. "You're quite the poet, Klok."

"What's a poet?"

I chuckled. "Someone who is gifted with words. They can make a person cry with one sentence."

"Did I make you cry, Nex?"

"Almost." I followed a shooting star across the sky, wondering where it was headed and what it was running from. "My turn again. The worst part of the City? The fear."

I heard Klok roll over to look at me. "The fear? What were you afraid of?"

"How do I explain this? In Heim, lots of people move metal. But in the City, it's rare. And we are hunted for it. If they find out you can do it, they kill you. In a public execution, with all your friends and family watching. They slit your throat. I was always afraid. Even before I really knew I was Meta. Something told me to be quiet. To be small. To be careful. I was terrified every single day. And that fear...it lives in me still. It's always ready to come back to life, to take over, to make my decisions for me."

"Why though? Why did they hunt metal movers?"

Because. So much time spent trying to figure that out. And finally, it clicked. *Because we can take the wall down. Because the Fight is not to kill Meta; it's to keep the City intact. But why? Why did my mother want to keep us trapped in that horrid place? Especially when she knew how welcome we would be in Heim?* "Maybe because...we are dangerous. Something to be contained. Eliminated."

"Dangerous doesn't mean bad."

"But it rarely means good." I sighed, ready to move on. "What's the worst part of Heim?"

"Being the same. Everyone knows everyone in Heim. They've known me my whole life. And whatever they think of me...they will never change their minds. When they are mistaken about who I am or who I want to be, the mistake sticks. Forever. I'll always be the same in Heim."

"Who do they think you are, Klok?"

"An idiot."

I grinned in the dark. "And who are you really? Who do you want to be? The you that Heim can't see?"

"I'm...a poet."

"A poet with an axe."

He laughed. "Who are you, Ruler? The you that your City could not see?"

I let the stars fill up my eyes. Let the dirt of Aarde press against my spine. Let the warmth of the embers heat my skin. "I want to be...good. But it seems like no one will let me. Not in the City. Not in Heim, either."

"It does seem like that, doesn't it?" Klok let the silence soak in between us. "Let's make a deal," he said at last. "I won't let you give up until you're you...if you don't let me give up either."

"Deal."

"Deal."

And we stayed quiet until the sun cracked open the sky with grays and purples, oranges and pinks, set against a bursting blue. Klok was right. *The morning always brings the stillness.*

Ep 58

Walking On Water

Life Tip: Do not be wary of what seems odd, but of what seems perfectly innocent.

Someone should have warned me.

Once we passed the cliffs that separated Heim from Shuǐ, there was...water. The Great Waters stretched out to eternity. That's how it seemed. I had never seen anything like it. The blue was bigger than my mind could understand. While the others in our party went on toward the first water bridge, I stood on the final cliff.

A deep sadness. That's what I felt. Not because there was anything wrong with the water, but because a few days before I stood on that cliff, I did not know such things existed. My whole life was Fenders and Formers, small alleys and tiny flats. It was cotton shoes and linen dresses. It was Ender Stream and hollow hums. But here, before my eyes, was the truth. That there was a whole world. And the City, for some reason, had none of it.

"Come on, Nex," Stjarna called from the ground below me.

I made my way down the cliff, and we met up with the flow of people hoping to enter the realm. What they called a 'bridge' was made of water itself. It stood as tall as any cliff, somehow sculpted out of liquid, both moving and sturdy.

"What on Aarde?" I would have given ten years of service to figure out how it was done. "How is this possible?"

"Beats me," said Api. "Looks mystical as hel."

"It is one of my favorite things to see," Stjarna said. "Feels even cooler to cross."

But I wasn't listening. I wandered off to the bridge, searching for someone who knew how fluid water could be organized into a structure.

"Excuse me," I said, bowing to a person who looked like they operated the entrance to the bridge. "Are you affiliated with the operation of this structure?"

The person, a slender young woman with short black hair and a scar on her lip, smiled at me. "I am. Who are you?"

"My name is Nexus. I am very curious as to how this mechanism works. Please, is there a way to learn more about it?"

The woman repeated a motion with her hands, as if she were reeling and then releasing some invisible coil of rope. "You are not interested in gaining passage into Shuï? You only want to know about the bridge?"

"First things first," I replied. "I *must* know how it works. It is too magnificent to ignore."

"Come," the woman said. "Open your hand."

I approached her and spread my fingers wide. She pulled a bit of water from the tributary that flowed beneath the bridge and deposited it into my hand.

"Did you just...move the *water*?"

She grinned. "Feel for yourself. I can tell you are gifted at moving. You nearly knocked me over when you came down the hill."

"I'm sorry," I said. "I didn't mean to."

She shrugged. "It was not intentional. I can tell that sort of thing too. Now, feel the water."

It was...squishy. Like clay. Though it looked exactly like ordinary water, it did not run out of my hand. I held the blob of water up to eye level. "Sodium," I said out loud, amazed. "There's metal in it!"

"There is. We learn to structure the water by moving its metals."

"This is a marvel," I said, staring up at the massive bridge. "Perhaps one of my favorite days ever."

"Wait until you get into Shuï itself," the woman said, still smiling. "Many more marvels await."

"We may enter? Really? I thought we would have to apply? Or...pay?"

She shrugged. "You can keep that bit of water too, if you want."

I sucked it into my skin, just in case she changed her mind. "Thank you so much."

"You're welcome, Ruler."

I blinked. "How...did you know—"

"Your power. It radiates. Some may fear it, but I enjoy its presence. You'll be quite welcome in Shuï."

"You're very kind. Thank you." And then I paused. "Oh. We are looking for someone. Do you happen to know a person named Gege?"

The woman laughed in a short burst. "Center of town. A red tent." Her eyes twinkled. "Good luck, Ruler. And if anyone asks on the bridge, tell them the Nŭrén sent you through."

I rejoined my group, and Stjarna nodded over toward my new friend. "Who was that? Did you know her?"

"I suppose I do now. She taught me how the bridge works."

Klok sighed. "That's nice. But she did tell you how to get on it? It seems they are not letting anyone through without approval."

"Actually, she said we may go. She was very helpful."

Klok gaped. "Just like that? Just...go ahead?"

"Yes?"

He scoffed. "Rulers. Always with the special treatment."

Stjarna poked his ribs. "You don't seem to mind being the beneficiary of Ruler treatment, Klok. If you don't like it, why don't you stay behind?"

"No, no. I will bear it."

We crossed the bridge using Nŭrén's name. Each step was uncertain, as if the water would cave under our feet. But it held, even though it moved and ebbed and flowed.

"What now?" Api asked.

"To the center of town. We're looking for a red tent."

Shuĭ. The whole place bustled. More people than I had ever seen in one area. The hørses and carriages even collided with one another. People shouted and cursed, laughed and danced. It was like a thousand parties being held at once. It reminded me of Ender Stream during a popular Ending, but there was life to be celebrated, not destroyed.

In the center of the town was a cluster of large tents. From that center flowed many streams of water, cutting through the buildings and trees. Boats zigzagged along the streams, zipping by those who walked or rode on the paved streets.

In the tents, people seemed to be waving objects in the air and screaming at anyone who walked by. Scarves, hats, axes, swords. Breads and cakes. Even live animals were being passed around and admired by those who walked by.

"What are they doing?" I asked.

"They're selling wares," Stjarna explained. "Trading goods for money. It's called a market."

"Himmin. There are so many goods."

"Because there are so many people."

In the middle of the ruckus was a large red tent. It stood apart from the rest, with gold embroidery that made it shine in the sun.

Before I approached the tent, I felt a thud in my chest and a twisting in my stomach. A feeling I hadn't felt in a while, since the City. It nearly made me sick.

I stopped in my tracks. Stjarna did the same.

"What is it?" Api asked, looking from me to Stjarna and back. "Why did you stop so suddenly?"

"Nerves I guess," I answered, still afraid to move forward.

"These aren't nerves," Stjarna said, her hand on her belly. "It's a warning."

Klok's eyes widened. "A warning? What kind this time, Stjar?"

She sighed, almost more annoyed than alarmed. "Death is close."

Slit Throat Saga

When she said it, iridium sparked to life behind my eyes. *Pay attention*, it seemed to say. *Look. See. And be careful, Nexus.*

Careful.

Ep 59

Again So Soon

Life Tip: Never go in alone.

"Death warnings are no joke. What should we do?" Klok asked, his hand moving to the axe he kept strapped to his back.

"We fight," Api said, pulling metal to his hands to form weaponized knuckles.

"No," Stjarna said. "We don't even know what we would be fighting. If it were obvious, we wouldn't need a warning."

"It's just a feeling," I said. "No need to be alarmed."

Stjarna shook her head. "It's not just a feeling, Nexus. It's real. That dread, the sense to be careful or to be prepared to fight. Those aren't imaginary. Rulers have such survival mechanisms from birth. They're as concrete as Api being able to smell a meat pie from two streets over. Or Klok seeing better than the rest of us in the dark."

All this time—living in the City, hiding—I had thought I was simply paranoid. But could I really have been sensing the danger all around me? Impossible. "I felt like this almost every day in the City," I explained. "There's no way I was warned that often."

Stjarna put a hand on my shoulder. "Nex, one of these days, we're going to have to sit down, and you can tell me exactly what sort of helscape your mother brought you to. But all it means now is that you are very attuned to warnings. So...what are you sensing we should do? I prefer not to die."

"I think...proceed. With great caution. And with the *least* amount of violence possible." I emphasized the last bit to Api, who still had not put his knuckles away.

And so we walked to the mouth of the large, red tent. This tent had no sellers coercing passersby. No jewelry or pastries for auction. Only guards who stood stone-faced at the entrance.

"Hello," I said, tentatively bowing, forgetting that people in other realms did not seem to care for that custom. "I am here to see someone."

"Who?" The first guard asked with a huff.

"Gege."

The guard's expression didn't change. "No one here by that name."

I peeked over his shoulder. There was nothing to see but the flaps of the tent. "Are you sure? I was told this is where I could find Gege."

"Who told you that?"

I almost said the name of the woman I met at the bridge, but the warning made my stomach lurch so hard that I stumbled forward.

"I don't know who," I lied.

"Then get lost."

Stjarna interjected. "Let us in, or we will have to tell Huangdi that you are not at all accommodating."

The guard's nose twitched. "You don't know Huangdi."

"Of course not." She shrugged. "Everyone in Shuǐ just throws the emperor's name around like this."

A grunt. "Wait here," the guard said, disappearing inside the tent. Not a moment later, we were invited in.

We followed the guard through the strangest tent in existence. People lined the walkways, but they didn't dance or sing or move at all. They knelt on the ground, their heads down and eyes closed.

"What are they doing?" I asked Stjarna.

"I have no idea," she said. She seemed as nervous as I was.

Finally, we arrived at a small enclosure within the tent.

"Just her," the guard said, pointing to me.

"Never," Stjarna replied, grabbing my hand. "We all go in."

"I have my instructions," he said, reaching for a weapon.

"Stjar, I'll be fine. Trust me. I'm more capable than people think. Remember?"

She clenched her jaw, her eyes stern. "I will stand right here. And listen."

I squeezed her hand before I let go.

Within the enclosure stood a man with a long, thin beard and a completely bald head. He sat on top of a table, his legs crossed.

"Are you Gege?" I asked, trying to look confident even though my stomach ached.

"Where did you hear that name?"

I didn't answer.

The man looked me over. "You are Heimsman? I know no Heimsman who would speak the name Gege."

"I was told to find you."

"By whom?"

I inhaled. *Might as well go for it.* "Someone named Kallórr."

The solemn man cracked a smile. "That arsehole."

"So you do know him?"

"Very few people would dare to call me Gege. He is one of them."

I felt a little breathless, my nerves toying with me. "Is it...an offensive name? I apologize for my ignorance. Lórr never explains anything fully."

He smirked. "It means 'brother.' Lórr is one of the few who can claim me as such."

"You're...his family?" They looked absolutely nothing alike. "Is Lórr from Shuĭ?"

He laughed at that, sliding off the table and onto his feet. "He is closer than a brother to me. And no, he is not from here. Though I'm sure he wishes he were from Shuĭ. Any other realm would do, I'd imagine." He calmed himself. "If he gave you this name for me, it's because you need some serious help. What is the matter, Ruler?"

"I need to meet with all the Rulers at once."

Gege stared at me. "Are you trying to get yourself killed then?"

"No. The opposite. I'm trying to save someone. Someone who is closer than a brother to me."

"I see. So it is valor that drives you. Not stupidity. Those two are easily confused."

"Can you help me?"

He nodded. "Indeed. But it is dangerous to summon all the Rulers. That is how rules change. And it is almost never favorable for the one who did the summoning. Nevertheless, it will be arranged."

"How will I know when and where to meet?"

"You will know."

"I owe you so much thanks, Gege. Can I...pay you? Is that appropriate for something like this? Payment?"

He tilted his head at me. "Where are you really from, Ruler? Must not be Heim, though you have the look. From Vuur? They have no payment systems there."

Lórr said I could trust him, so I did not hesitate. "Technically, I am from the City."

He gasped. "No. Truly?"

"Yes, truly. Why? You know of it?"

He looked at me as if I were made of rare metal. "So you are the one they sent?"

My heart began to gallop inside my chest. "What do you mean?"

"And you do not *know*?" He stroked his beard. "Who are your parents?"

"Aerixon."

"The plot thickens." More beard stroking. "Woden and Heili?"

"No." I could not have been more anxious. I even brought magnesium to my fingertips to calm me. Titanium held onto my heart. "Woden and Viveka."

At that, he sort of shrieked. "*Viveka*? Gods. You certainly are the one they sent."

"Please tell me what that means. You're making me very uncomfortable."

"Don't be," he said, shaking his head. "I mean you no harm. It is only...you are so interesting. And I love to meddle.

I will set the meeting, as you wish. And I will expedite it as best I can for you. You have my word."

I sighed with relief. "Thank you."

"When you see Lórr next, will you tell him I said hello?"

I nodded. "Of course."

Gege clapped his hands. "Aha! So you are seeing one another? You and Lórr?"

I blushed. "What? No!"

"Then how did you know to find me?"

"Oh. If that's what you mean, then, yes, I have seen him. Only for short moments."

"More than once, Ruler?" Gege ran a hand over his bald head and sighed. "He is going to get us all killed."

"Why?" I stepped forward. "Tell me why people keep saying this? And do not say I'm not supposed to know."

Before he could answer, Gege put his hands in the air, glaring behind me.

"Don't try anything, old friend." The voice, a woman's, sounded quite pleased. "I would hate to take your life this fine morning."

"Nŭrén, you cannot possibly be this foolish," Gege said, his hands still raised.

I swiveled to find the woman from the water bridge. She was smiling at me. But in her hand was a crossbow, trained at my heart.

"Nice to see you again so soon, Ruler," she said. "If I were you, I would stay very, very still."

Ep 60

Privileged

Life Tip: If you have it good, make sure no one has it worse.

"You will not harm her," Gege warned.

Nǚrén chuckled. "I am the one raiding your tent, Shān-grén. I give the orders." A few more men came in after her, all with crossbows of their own. "I will take these fine guests," Nǚrén continued. Oh, and twenty Devoted will do as well."

"You are wasting your time," Gege, who apparently was named Shāngrén, asserted. "You will find no worth for these in the Dark Markets."

Nǚrén waggled her eyebrows. "A Ruler who can hold water on her first try. Who calls the great Shāngrén 'brother.' And another who throws around the name Huangdi like a child with a ball. I think my time will be well-spent taking these lot off your hands. What fortune to find them all in one place."

She turned to her minions. "Load the Devoted into our carriages. And the Rulers will ride with me." Then, she looked at me again. "I already have your lovely friends. Move your metal, I slit their throats. Now. Hold out your arms."

I did so. A minion clapped metal handcuffs on me. They reminded me of the ones Lórr wore when I met him in the desert. Magcuffs, they were called. Locked by the one who put them in place.

True enough, speaking to the iron around my wrists did not work. It wanted to listen to me but could not. Almost as if the metal itself was enslaved to its owner.

As I was led out of the room, I called out to Gege. "This changes nothing. Please do what we discussed."

I hoped he heard me. I hoped he would listen better than the iron on my arms. If I could not gather all the Rulers together and ask for the City wall to be taken down, I would not get Monny back.

Outside the room, those who had been kneeling on the ground were being rounded up, causing quite the stir as they were shoved and hoisted.

"Where are you taking those people?" I asked. "What are you going to do to them?"

"My plans for the Devoted are none of your business," Nŭrén answered.

"I agree. None of this is any of our business. You should let us go. Now."

"No, I don't think so." She led me outside and stopped me in front of a small carriage. The market bustled on around us as if mass abductions were no big news.

"Do you want to know what I *do* think?" she continued. "You are foreign Rulers with connections. I will ransom you to Emperor Huangdi, and he will pay quite the price for you. How do I know this? Because it will not look good to let foreign Rulers be killed in his realm. Such things start wars. He will want to avoid this. And so he will pay."

"Pay? You are doing all this for money? That's so...*stupid*."

She struck my face. Not like Stjarna did that one time she was cross with me. No. Nŭrén hit me hard enough to draw blood from my nose.

"Keep your privilege to yourself," she sneered. "I don't need all four of you alive to make this work for us."

Her people shoved me into the carriage, and I landed right on top of Klok and Api.

"Ugh," Api said. "Get off, Nexus! You're so heavy. Goddess!"

"Stop flailing, Api!" Stjarna commanded. "She could be injured. You'll hurt her!"

"I'm fine," I said, struggling to sit up in the cramped space with my hands still bound. My face throbbed, but it was nothing compared to having my chest sliced open in an alley. "What are the Devoted? Do any of you know what that means?"

"Wow," Stjarna said, frowning. "Hello to you too. How are you? Everyone alright? So glad you're alive, beautiful sister."

"Yes, yes, I am happy you're not dead, Stjar. Cheers all around. Now, do you know what the Devoted are?"

Stjar shook her head. Api mumbled something about missing lunch.

"I read about them once," Klok said. "'The Devoted kneel when the light comes, and they rise up when it sets.' It was in a Shuĭ scroll."

Stjarna wrinkled her nose. "Where did you find a Shuĭ scroll?"

Klok shrugged, his hands cuffed in front of him. "I read."

"Sure you do," Api said. "Me too. I read so many scrolls. A regular scholar."

Klok blushed and went silent.

"So the Devoted serve some ritualistic purpose?" I tried to bring magnesium to my fingers, to calm me and help me think, but realized I couldn't move metal with the magcuffs on. *This will be the worst case of thinky grumps ever.* "That means it's likely Nǔrén is planning to perform a ritual of some sort. But what kind? And how can we use it to get the hel out of this?"

"Oh," Stjarna said, perking up. "Rising and setting. What about the moon? It's full tonight."

Klok nodded. "Moon phases affect the tides on Aarde. And there is so much water here. Maybe whoever is taking all those kneeling people needs something out of the moon."

"Nǔrén said she wants payment. That's why she took us. To bribe the emperor for our release. But what does payment have to do with the moon? With the Great Waters? With the Devoted? We are just an added bonus, but she *planned* to take them."

Stjar paled. "*That's* this woman's plan? To ransom us to Huangdi? The emperor will never bend to it. He isn't exactly...understanding. There isn't a sense of diplomacy or family in Shuǐ like there is in Heim. If there were, Woden would have just asked him for help."

"So...he won't pay Nǔrén for our release?"

For the first time, Stjar looked afraid. "I was just bluffing to get us in the tent. Huangdi won't give a shit about us."

I chewed on my lip for a moment, thinking. "Stjar, do the people like their emperor? He sounds harsh."

"He's a Ruler, just like we are. But he holds all the power in Shui. They have no council. The people really have no say regarding affairs. As far as I know, he is not their favorite."

I began clicking the pieces into place, like a drakon coming together. "What does it mean to call someone 'privileged'?"

"It means you have more money or status or power than others," Klok answered for me. "You and Stjar are privileged, depending on who you ask."

"And if you're not privileged? Specifically in Shui? What would happen to you? What would life be like?"

Stjar thought for a second. "There are whole sections of the realm where poor people live. It is very disheartening. If it were me, I would be angry to live there. It doesn't seem fair. In Heim, we share. But in this place, that is not how it goes."

So close to understanding. The carriages began to jostle as we rode away from the market. We could not see, but I knew we needed to think quickly.

"If I wanted payment, more than anything, I disliked the emperor for keeping it from me. I would want to get payment and hurt him at the same time. Change the system, maybe. And somehow...I could do this by using the moon. What am I planning? What?"

Klok grinned. "I know what Nŭrén is trying to do."

Ep 61

Unless He Loves You

Life Tip: Shadows illuminate just as often as light.

After hours of travel, we lurched to a stop, and one of the armed minions whipped open the carriage and dragged me out.

"She wants you," he said, all gruff.

Sure enough, we were tucked behind a hill, but I could smell the sodium in the air. We had to be very near the Great Waters. And the sun gave its last moments of light to the land. The moon would rise soon. And Klok's prediction, if he was right, would begin.

"Nǚrén, it would be best if you uncuffed me," I said.

She walked away from the discussion she was having with one of her minions. They were already taking the Devoted out of the other carriage and having them kneel facing the direction of the Waters.

"And why would I do that, Ruler?"

"Because...you and I both know that Emperor Huangdi will not pay anything for ransoming Rulers. You bluffed on our bluff."

She grinned, an evening breeze ruffling her short black hair. "Still doesn't explain why I would release you."

"Because you want my help. And I can't offer it without being able to move metal." I tossed my head over to the carriage. "You may as well release my friends, too. You think you need to hold them for leverage. So I comply. But I am very tired of people kidnapping my friends and forcing me to do their bidding in exchange for their release."

She stepped closer to me. "If I release them, you will not help me."

"If you explain your reasons, I may help you without coercion."

She chuckled. "Out of the goodness of your heart?"

"Out of the goodness of yours."

"Ah yes. We all know the trope of the benevolent kidnapper."

"Why are you opening the bridges to Shuǐ, Nǚrén?"

She sighed. "I have enough Devoted to accomplish it. I don't need your help."

"Then you will not have it." I shrugged. "I know you don't plan on harming us. Not really." I glared. "You did hit me though, which wasn't very nice."

"I had to make it look convincing."

"Well done."

She chewed on her fingernails. "Fine. Fine." Then she motioned to the hill, which we climbed together. From the top, I could see a sprawling island kingdom, connected to the rest of Aarde by multiple enormous liquid bridges. The rest was water. So much water.

"My father hates me," she explained. "He hates everyone. And he exploits the poor to please the rich. I refuse to do so. And so...well, I cannot be his daughter if I'm not like him. And since I'm not a Ruler...let's say the odds are stacked against me. I'll never be able to lead Shui. Nothing will ever change."

"You're his *daughter*? The emperor is your father?"

She grinned. "You made it seem like you had it all figured out, Ruler."

"I knew you were trying to open the bridges. I assumed you would receive payment from enemy realms who wished to cross into Shui."

"No," she said. "I would never do that to my people. But I do have another plan." She studied the sky as the moon began to rise over the horizon. "I am allowing those in the poor districts to leave the realm of their own free will. When there are no poor to exploit, the rich will flounder. They will panic and turn on my father. When he is deposed, I will take his place. Once I am in power, I will ask the people to return to Shui. And things will be different."

"Because you are not privileged?"

"Because I acknowledge that I am."

I nodded. "You will use that privilege to make things right."

"Precisely."

Behind us, the Devoted began to hum. The toning call lifted over the hills and rolled down to the waves.

"Won't Huangdi try to stop you?"

She smirked. "He has been trying to kill me for some time, yes." She looked down to the Devoted. "Why do you think Gege tried to stop me?"

"He doesn't want you to get hurt."

She nodded. "He's not one to be crossed. Unless he loves you." She paused. "That is why he tried to keep the Devoted from me. He did not think I would be bold enough to come and get them. He hoped I would abandon this plan of mine."

I studied the serene posture of the people who knelt, keeping perfectly still, eyes closed. I listened to the vibration of their voices, lifting and falling in unison.

"They're moving the waters?"

"No," she said. She pointed upward. "They're moving the moon."

Even the moon contains metals. I remembered how it shone over Ender Stream the night Clay died. "Moving the moon will open the bridges?"

She nodded. "If they have the strength, yes. The bridge guards will fight us. And we must accomplish it before the moon rises too high."

"The sea may part for men to pass...." I waited.

She smiled. "...but the fool wanders out to collect the fish." She turned to me. "Who taught you that?"

I shrugged. "A friend."

She laughed, her arms crossed. "An arsehole."

"Well," I said, lifting my arms, "you had better take these cuffs off if you want help overthrowing an empire. We're running out of time."

Ep 62

The Weight Of A Ruler

Life Tip: Never underrate the need for proper stationary.

"I think it's a genius plan," Api said, springing to his feet.

Klok grabbed his brother by the back of the shirt and yanked him down. "You just love fighting, Api. That's not a good reason to pick one with an emperor."

The four of us sat on the ground—uncuffed—outside the carriage we'd been carried in discussing what to do with Nŭrén and her invasion plan. The Devoted were doing their thing a few lengths away, swaying and humming and bowing before the moon as it rose.

Klok frowned. "I did not think your business in Shuĭ involved destroying it. This is too much for us, Nexus."

I sighed, running a hand through my combination of curls and brains and jangling the metal clasps strewn throughout. I had to admit, Na was a miracle worker. The metal not only gave me balance but it calmed my hair down. Or maybe it just made me like its wildness more.

"I will be completely honest with you now. All of you. About everything. And then you can decide what you want to do. If you want to go back to Heim, I understand." A big breath. "In the City, Meta are hunted and killed by a governing body called The Fight. I remained in hiding there. Lived in terror but also did a few things while in hiding. I resurrected a dead friend by moving metal. She was later killed because of what I did, along with four others. I designed mechanisms that will eventually be used to hurt people like me, maybe even including me. And all the while, my mother made it seem like she was trying to destroy me. I am still trying to convince myself that it is not true. And finally, right before leaving, I discovered the Fight is divided into two factions: one which seeks to keep us within the safety of an Aarde-imposed wall, and one that thinks we will die if we do not get Aarde to break the wall down. The second faction murdered my mother and kidnapped my life partner to force me to come here and petition for the wall to be removed and the City to be free. So here I am."

Klok pressed his fingers to his eyes. "Oh, goddess. Okay, that's...so much."

"I left quite a bit out. We don't have that kind of time."

He shook his head. "What does this have to do with Nǔrén? Why help her? You have enough to focus on, enough to recover from. I don't understand how making enemies with a Ruler like Huangdi, one who could help you take down your wall...will help you?"

I chewed the rings on my lip. "It...doesn't."

Stjarna stood up suddenly. She had been silent and brooding during our discussion. And she remained so, but also stretched out her arm.

"I am with you, Nexus."

"You...are?" I put my arm in hers, my eyes wide. "Why?"

"I've heard bits and pieces of your story, Nexus Aerixon, and now, what I know has taken more shape. I know that you are resilient. That you survived hel over and over. That you brought life where there was death. That you designed your own demise to keep yourself and others safe for as long as possible. That you believe in family even when yours disowned you. I've seen you bring life to metal when it cried out to you. I've seen you protect that life when others sought to destroy it. I've seen you lose your true home to be true to those you love." She smacked my chest. "True power is in giving it away. And so, I will follow you. If you think Nŭrén's cause needs our protection, I will give it. Not because I love you. But because you honor others."

I wanted to be noble and salute or turn and walk away as if I were not affected. But instead, I leaned in and wrapped my arms around the warrior who I got to call sister.

"Thank you, Stjar."

She hugged me back. And I could feel in my chest what she claimed to feel the moment she saw me. A moving of more than just metal. Like her heart was integrated into mine. As if she were precious, and my very being told the story of her.

Klok stood up next. He offered his arm. "I am in on one condition."

"Oh? What's that?"

"I require pen and paper during these exploits. So I can write down our story. This is no longer a little visit to the water realm. This is a saga."

I nodded. "I'll ask Nŭrén. A poet needs his weapons."

Api hopped up and scooped me into a hug that almost crushed me, my legs dangling. "Goddess, you are as heavy as Stjarna now, Nex," he said with a grunt. "No worries. I'm the strongest of us all by far. I can carry any of you Rulers. No problem."

He kissed my cheek and ruffled my hair when he put me down. I wondered if this was what it was like to have brothers.

A hørs whinnied as it approached, pulling me out of my fantasy. On its back, moonlight shining on his bald head, his back straighter than a Synthetix blade, was Gege.

Ep 63

My Father Is My Father

Life Tip: There is a fine line between reckless and brave.

"What are you doing here?" Nǔrén asked, stomping across the hill to where Gege was riding up.

Our little party of Heimsman was right in the middle of what was shaping up to be an epic shouting match.

Gege, still on his hørs, threw his hand in the air. "Nǔrén, you cannot go starting wars on a whim!"

"And you cannot keep the Devoted from me. I do not have to do what you say, Gege. You are not my father."

"No. Your father is your father. And he will have you killed for this. It is treason, Nǔrén. We must put the Devoted back. Leave the bridges. Leave the moon. Leave Shuǐ."

Still many lengths away, and still screaming to be heard, Nǔrén pounded her chest with her fist. "'My father is my father' is not an acceptable excuse for me, Gege! He is hurting people. And I have the power to stop him. I will not leave the bridges. I will not leave the moon. I will not leave Shuǐ. I do not need to be a Ruler to love something to death. Watch me!"

Gege dismounted and began walking. Nǔrén did the same until they met in the middle, where we stood.

Gege sighed. "I wish you were not so reckless," he said to Nǔrén. "But I am proud that you are. And if I cannot stop you, I will protect you."

She smiled. "I knew you would. Once you finished scolding me." Then she turned to us. "And you? I suppose I cannot force you to lend your power. It was a mistake to think I could."

"It was a mistake," said Stjarna. "But Nexus thinks you deserve our support. And so we'll give it."

Nǔrén looked at me. "Thank you, Nexus."

I nodded. "What do you need us to do?"

"The moon is ready. The Devoted are loyal to our cause and they will move the metal, open the bridges all at once. Shuǐ will expect an invasion then. They will look as if enemies are trying to force their way in. They will have no plan for people forcing their way out. Once they realize this is what is happening, they will try to close the bridges. We must hold them open without destroying them so the people can cross. We also must protect the people as they make it out."

Klok shook his head. "You think the Shuǐ bridge guards would honestly hurt their own people?"

"Yes," Nǔrén and I answered in unison.

Klok nodded, his frown growing. "Goddess. We are not in Heim anymore, are we?"

"What's the best way to fight your guards, Nǔrén?" I asked.

"Good question. They have magnetic shields. They deflect metal, so it's difficult to move at them. But it can be done if you disable the shields." She tapped her left forearm. "The shields project from the arm. Small magnetic bracelets."

"Nexus is good with magnets," Api said.

Nǔrén looked to me, startled. "What?"

I shrugged. "Lórr taught me. But I only know how to travel through the stones. Not how to disable them."

"He...did *what?*" Nǔrén shook her head, refocusing. "Okay, if Nexus can figure out the shields, we will have a great advantage. If not, weapons are our best bet against the guards, not moving metal."

"My crew will help," Gege offered. "I am sure they were all hoping they would get to fight."

"Positions then," Nǔrén said. "Nexus, with me. The rest, spread out on the hilltop and prepare for incoming metal from Shuǐ. Gege, your men can protect the Devoted, or we lose the bridge. The Heimsman crew and mine will protect those evacuating."

We crept through the hills toward the bridges. The night grew peaceful, the moon bathing the water in milky light.

The commotion happened all at once. Many lengths away, the sound of water striking water as the bridges opened their liquid gates all at once. As Nǔrén predicted, the guards roared to life, facing away from Shuǐ to whomever might have been invading the realm.

And, also as Nǔrén predicted, hundreds, maybe thousands, of people rushed the guards from behind, pushing themselves onto the bridge. They ran with abandon, dragging the fallen along so they were not trampled.

All the while, we inched closer and closer. Once the guards understood that Shuǐtes were fleeing, they turned on the people, forcing them away from the bridge. When the first

Shuite—a woman in rags with desperate eyes—fell dead
from the blow of a guard, I knew what would happen.

We would have to fight.

And I would have to kill.

Ep 64

And The Storm?

Life Tip: If you want something, you must be willing to lose everything.

"Protect the people," Nŭrén said, "at all costs."

Stjarna, Klok, and Api, along with those Nŭrén brought from the hills, began to work, crouched in the dark near the edge of the water. Rather than attack the guards, which was useless at that distance, especially without being able to get past their shields, they moved metals to the ground. Doing so made the guards lose their footing, giving the Shuĭtes the upper hand.

"Come with me, Nexus" Nŭrén said, leading me away from the others. "What can you do with those shields?"

"The only way I've ever taken down a shield is to cut the person open with a blade. I don't know how to *move* shields down."

Nŭrén stared at me in the moonlight, her expression difficult to read. "You...have cut people open before, Ruler?"

"Only once. A little boy. But I've had it done to me before." I focused on the fight across the sea. "We can't use that tactic here."

If we can't deactivate the shields ourselves—and doing so might require severing a lot of arms, which is not expedient—how can we get the guards to lower their shields on their own? With less bloodshed. Maybe still some. But less.

My iridium sparked inside my brain. "I have an idea." I showed Nŭrén my left arm. "This is why I was cut open. An electrical shock device was implanted in my arm to keep me from collecting metal. It's so painful, anyone with metal would want to lower their shields and lose the metal immediately. And with the amount of metal those guards are carrying, if they don't remove it all...."

"They die." Nŭrén nodded. "But what do you mean, though, by an electric shock?"

"Like...lightning."

"Your people had you put lightning...*in your body?*"

"Yes. Yes they did." It was hard to focus when the memories of that night came back to me. It was the last time I saw Clay alive. And the first time I met Lórr. "I will need two things if I am to pull this off. One, enough metal to reach the guards all at once. And two, something very tall and pointy, very high up." I chewed my lip to think. "Oh and three, a massive storm."

"Copper could work," Nŭrén said. "I may not be a Ruler, but I can move metal better than most. I studied under the best metal scholars of nearly all realms. Copper and lightning. Boom." She observed the fight across the water. The guards were beginning to notice that the real attack was coming from the hills across the sea where we hid. "Seems like we might be able to slide the copper under their feet. That area is unprotected. No one shields their soles."

"Brilliant." A brief flash of standing on Ender Stream. The watery blood running down, soaking through my linen shoes. I shook my head and fought the lump in my throat. "And the storm?"

Nǔrén grinned. "That's a Shuǐ skill if ever there was one. And, lucky for us, one of Gege's specialties."

"You can move storms into existence?"

"Gege likes to say there's always a storm somewhere just waiting to be moved. The clouds hold iron and sodium in traces. We can form clouds and we can add water to them. Swirl that up with enough fury...and we have lightning." She got to her feet just as a blast erupted from the Shuǐ shore and soared through the air, colliding with the hills. "I had better go tell him before he gets clobbered to death."

"Tell the others that any copper we have needs to line the shoes of those guards. I will work on something tall enough to pull the lightning you make from the clouds and to the copper."

Nǔrén ran, dodging the fiery rain that the guards were unleashing on our group. I saw Stjarna and the others redirect their efforts, sending glowing copper across the water.

The Devoted, still humming, still kneeling, worked to keep the bridges open, with just a few Shuǐtes able to make it past the guards and across to safety.

And then the clouds rolled in. Dark, thick, heavy clouds that threatened to block the moonlight and interfere with the labor of the Devoted. We had to act quickly. Around me, metal bombs cracked and shook Aarde. My own metal vibrated within, urging me forward.

And I knew, then, what I could put in the sky to pull the lightning down to Aarde.

I waited for the first crack of electricity in the burgeoning clouds to fill my ears. And then I closed my eyes and breathed.

Will you help me?

The nudge at the back of my spine told me my drakon was more than happy to stretch its wings.

Ep 65

Driving Rain On Stony Docks

Life Tip: To save life, you must take it; all debts must be paid.

I moved the drakon stone out of me, pulling it through the pores of my skin and reassembling it in the time it took to exhale. The stone itself was no bigger than my hand. A swirl of metals in different shades, iridescent in the growing haze.

"Stjarna," I shouted. "Send it far!"

My sister nodded from where she stood on the beach. I understood the white paint she wore on her face then. It was easy to see her, even at a distance. Where some warriors preferred camouflage, the people of Heim fought for valor. To be seen, never hidden. I recalled, in an instant, the way she concentrated when she ran her paint-covered fingers down the bridge of my nose. I was glad she was with me then, and now. To show me how.

I hurled the stone into the sky and she pushed its magnetic field so it rocketed farther than possible. Halfway across the water to Shuï. The moment it reached the air, it began to unfurl, its many metals screeched and scraped, the shrieks echoing over the land and sea. A hundred lengths above me,

it reached its full width, grander than the hills themselves.
A true nightmare.

Guards and Shuïtes alike stopped to witness my monster
rise high above the Great Waters. Thunderclouds gathered
behind and above it, casting shadows and light against its
exterior in flashes.

I need to speak to it, I told iridium. *We must be precise.
It must understand me. Can you help?*

And iridium, that royal metal, spun so brilliantly behind
my eyes that my head became violently hot. Deep breaths did
little to cool me. I desired to plunge head first into the water,
but I had other work to do. The pain would have to wait.

I sprinted to the top of the highest hill as the drakon flew
to the shores of Shuï. *Listen,* I told it. *Listen.* And I asked
it to call the lightning to itself.

At first, I thought the drakon could not hear me. Or did
not want to. But then, in a blaze of crackling white, a column
of lightning shot from the clouds, engulfing the drakon.

"Now," I screamed to anything that could hear me—to the
drakon and all the metal everywhere, to the sky and those
still slinging copper at the feet of the guards. To the people
running to the bridges for a desperate chance at new life.

A thousand beams of lightning shot from the drakon to
the guards who blocked the bridges. From the ground up,
their shielded bodies convulsed. Some were lucky and let
down their shields in time. But most were not. They shook
and screamed and fell like driving rain to the stony docks.

The people of Shuï saw their chance and took it. They
clambered over the fallen guards and raced over the open

bridges—bridges which trembled to remain open with the light of the moon hidden behind the storm clouds.

My ears rang. My brain burned. My lungs tightened. Nŭrén shouted, waving for me to come down off the hilltop. But she seemed so far away, and I could not move. I could only witness what I had done. My drakon circled over the land, and hundreds of Shuĭ guards lay dead. The few who survived writhed in agony as they voided themselves of metal. Some were trampled to death as the poverty-enslaved ran for their freedom.

The dread in my stomach returned, wrapping me in cold. A warning. To get down. Get off the hill and run. *Run, Nexus.* But I remained. *Not without my drakon.*

Come back to me, I told my monster. And it did, soaring through the skies until it was small enough to fit in my palm. I returned the stone to its home along my spine with only seconds to spare.

A flaming ball of metal struck the hill, and I dropped into the crack it created in Aarde.

Ep 66

Woden's Gift

Life Tip: Good things aren't always nice.

Turns out Aarde was not the friendliest place.

Living on its surface was fine enough, but inside it was a scorching, jagged helhole. The rocks crushed my body, and my ribs creaked under the pressure. Dirt stuffed my nose and eyes, and I kept my lips squeezed tight so I could sip the air.

My metal slithered from my pores and pressed against the walls of Aarde so I had just enough room to exhale.

A brief self-examination. I was, indeed, injured. The skin along my collarbone was torn clean off, and the ankle and knee of my right leg throbbed like they required immediate scaffolding.

From above, through the crack that remained on the surface of the hill, I could hear my friends calling to me. They wanted to get me out. To save me. I couldn't answer them to let them know I was alive unless I wanted that to become untrue. A mouth full of dirt would ruin any good pair of lungs.

Nexus.

That voice did not come from my friends. Not from Nǔrén or Gege either. I wiggled, trying to make more room, but nothing could be done on that front. Not unless I forfeited breathing space.

Nexus. I need you.

I shivered. The kind that wracked my entire body. Even though my head still burned from the iridium and my back throbbed from the drakon stone.

Nexus. Help me. Help me. Nexus, Help.

I had never heard him like that. His voice, as it rang through my head, cracked just like the hilltop. His words were ragged. Wherever he was, I could somehow hear that he was alone.

But how to get there? How? I stretched my fingers, trying to reach the magnet stones in my pocket. But I couldn't do it without cascading dirt from above.

Nexus. Nex, please.

So I took a deep breath. *Silver? Bring the magnet stones to my hands.* Silver listened, and the dirt packed in around me just as my fingers gripped the stones. But they were not far enough apart. The stones both sat in one of my hands.

Suddenly, as if it were meant to be so, I remembered my father, Woden, putting his hands on mine and giving me a gift. *God, let it be something I can use now.*

Washing over me, like a hundred waterfalls. Like the waves of the Great Waters. I felt Woden's gift to me.

Peace.

Everything that did not matter faded in that moment. My mother's body limp on L's wooden floor. The dead guards on the Shui shore. My friends screaming my name on the hill above me. Even Lórr, calling for me, begging for me.

I used silver to carve a path through the Aardean rock so that the magnet stones were on either side of me. And then, while still holding my breath, I moved the stones so they passed by me instead of me through them.

In an instant, I went from the sweltering heat of the sub-aaredean crevice to the icy forest of some unknown realm.

I landed with a snap on what was surely a very broken leg and careened down a steep hill, rolling myself into a ball until I came to a stop against the trunk of an enormous tree.

I stayed there. I needed to stay there. As the peace slipped away, it was replaced with shuddering, mind-bending pain. Though the ice and snow cooled my head, my soul was rent. Why I thought I could accomplish any feat, let alone great ones, was beyond me then.

Nex...please.

It was the boy who came to me in the City, in an alley, on the worst day of my life. On the day I should have died. And saved me. When I had done nothing to earn it. I called. And he answered.

So I pushed myself up, my palms in the slush. *I'm coming.*

Ep 67

The Collective Snarl

Life Tip: First things must come first.

I could go nowhere with a broken leg. And bleeding to
death wasn't helpful either. A fleeting wish that I had a
Wizen with me—someone who'd studied how to mend
a person without the use of metal. But I was all I had.

I moved titanium from its usual nest around my heart and
used it to prop up my aching bones. Copper formed a coil
and twisted around the titanium, helping to hold it tight.
Iron stopped the blood from flowing out of my collarbone.

I was tired. Exhausted to my core. Food would have done
wonders. And water. *Water....*

I scooped a handful of snow into my mouth and let it
melt down my throat as I pulled myself upright. Any weight
on my leg was pain beyond pain.

Iridium? I knew what I was about to ask was risky. Basic
training taught me that much about anatomy. But I needed
to be able to move. So iridium slipped further into the
bundle of nerves at the base of my brain and, with a sizzle,
clamped them shut.

I felt nothing. Not cold or hot. No pleasure or pain. Just a dull numbness.

I made a mental note to kiss Behr for giving me such a metal as iridium.

I hobbled forward as fast as I could, trying to make my way through the world of ice and shadows I'd landed in. I imagined that I was freezing, though I couldn't experience it. Patches of ice made the way slippery. That, paired with the fact that I had no idea where on Aarde I was going, made it a treacherous endeavor.

Nex....

I followed the voice in my head, which I admitted to myself made no sense. *How am I following a voice that exclusively lives in my mind?* But I kept going...until I heard a sound unlike any other.

Footsteps smashing through snow and the collective snarl of a tangle of beasts.

And then something crashed into me.

"Goddess!" Lórr gasped, half on top of me in the clutches of a snow bank. *A snow bank.* I realized, with a hint of mistimed giddiness, that I had never even heard of snow before, yet I knew exactly what it was.

Lórr, breathless, hoisted himself off me. But not for long. He collapsed onto his elbows, air rattling from his lungs.

"We...have to...move."

I planned to be snide about how impossible it was to move with Aarde's heaviest Meta crushing me, but I got a good look at his face and clamped my mouth shut.

He bled from his forehead, the watery mess flowing into his eye. His skin was pale, his face drawn. Whatever energy he had left in him was fading.

"The wolves..." he managed.

I glanced up to see them gathering around us. Bushy, wild-eyed animals. Very different from the hørses of Heim. They bared fangs that glistened in the moonlight.

"They smell blood, Nex."

He was bleeding eccentrically, and I was covered in the stuff.

"We run?" I asked, gathering the courage I would need.

"Use the stones. Go back."

"No."

"Nex—"

"Three."

"*Nexus.*"

"Two."

He reached out and put his hand on my cheek. If only I could have felt it.

"Run."

He leapt into the air, grabbing my arm and pulling me up with him in one motion. I forced my body to obey me, to push through its brokenness. My leg wobbled as it collided with the uneven terrain, but I could not stop, even when I feared it would snap.

Make me faster, I begged my metal. And they rearranged in my body, reducing my resilience while increasing my speed.

"Tree!" Lórr shouted, leading the way to a towering evergreen with low branches.

Climbing was harder than running. And that was truer for Lórr than it was for me. I made it halfway up the tree, while he stalled on the first branch, his torso bent over the bough and his legs dangling like a wolf snack.

Before they could pounce, I sent metal out like knives. Again and again. It slowed them, but they were relentless. They would catch him. They would devour him.

So I left my perch, threw myself from the tree and landed in the snow. The maneuver forced me to roll, my leg giving way. With no time to plan, or even to think, I asked all the metal that lived in the snow to help me. Mercury answered. The prince of metals.

It chilled for me, going completely solid when I moved it forward. It engulfed the wolves, encasing them in tombs of mercurial ice.

Lórr slipped from his precarious position, hitting the icy ground at the base of the tree. He lay unmoving, eyes shut. I only hoped he was still breathing.

Reviving the dead did not usually go my way.

Ep 68

Magnetic Fields Don't Grow Flowers

Life Tip: Boys are stupid.

My leg refused to let me walk on it. No matter. I dragged myself over to Lórr and tried to feel for his pulse. But I couldn't feel much of anything. So I grabbed his coat front and shook. He still did not wake up.

But he was breathing.

He was heavily shielded. I couldn't even help his cells to spin faster. So I ripped at the buttons of his coat to see what else could be done.

Beneath the layer of leather, his linen shirt was torn to shreds, his skin ripped, the gashes leaking. But with his shield as strong as it was, I couldn't even use iron to stop the bleeding.

I leaned over him, almost nose to nose. "Wake up," I said, my hand on his cheek. "Wake up."

After a while of my coaxing, his eyelashes fluttered open. He really was quite stunning, even when he was bleeding to death in a tundra.

"Take your shields down," I said. "I'll help you."

I felt the resistance dissipate, and then he closed his eyes again.

I took the iron from my wound and applied it to his, turning his transparent blood to a deep red. I used whichever of my metals I didn't need to prop me up like a dilapidated puppet to stitch him back together.

And then I spun his cells faster, warming him up and pumping energy back into his body. Once I accomplished that, he opened his eyes again. He took one look at me and sat up.

"Nexus, goddess of gods, what are you doing?"

"You called me," I said. It was only then that I realized my words were slurring.

Wincing, he shrugged off his coat and threw it over my shoulders. "You're freezing to death, you beautiful idiot. You're purple."

I sank down and leaned against the tree trunk. "I...turned off my nerves."

He grabbed my hands and breathed on them. Then he moved nickel to his hands and rubbed them together. Lórr pulled my boots off and placed them on the soles of my feet. "You'll lose your fingers and toes. Nexus, do you have any idea how cold it is here?"

"No. Where are we?"

"Auon."

I pointed at the frozen wolves, their faces mid-snarl, their bodies stuck in motion. "You almost died."

"Yes." He worked up more nickel, placing it on my hands. "I almost died."

"Why are you alone in the woods in the middle of the night?" I bit my tongue and lips when I talked. Apparently, my mouth was too cold for speech.

Lórr noticed my leg and swore. Then swore some more. "Woman, you are impossible." He shook his head. "Is titanium literally holding you together right now?"

"Lórr, answer my question."

"And...silver?"

"Lórr!"

"Alright!" He inhaled. "I am alone in the Ulfur Woods in the middle of the night because my people put me here."

I must be hearing wrong. "They...put you here?"

"Yes."

"Why, Lórr?"

"Because I am a Ruler of Auon."

"Is it...like...a test?"

"Sort of. Except I will be tested again and again. Forever. Until I am dead." He worked diligently on my leg. I could hear him snapping bones back into place. Luckily, iridium kept me from feeling any of it.

"Dead?"

"Everyone dies, Nexus."

"Why are they doing this to you?"

He glanced at me—for just a moment—and then went back to work. "It's a long story."

"Fine. Tell me a different story, then. Deal?"

He shook his head. "I can't tell you that one, Nex."

"Please? Lórr, please? No one will tell me. And don't say it's better that way. It is always better when I know the truth, the fullness of something."

He sighed, tugging at the metal strands he was wrapping around my leg. "What do you want to know?"

"Why shouldn't I know you?"

"Because. You and I are Rulers of a different sort."

"What sort?"

"We are called Magna Rulers. I am one end of a magnet, and you are the match. The inverse, yet the same. Magna Rulers are either drawn to one another, or repelled."

"And we...are drawn?"

He swallowed. "Yes."

"But that's...bad?"

He stopped working so he could look at me. "Aarde is held together by magnetism. Magnetic fields, to be exact. And these are created by lying magnets. By Magna Rulers. Not only do we set the rules for humans on Aarde, like other Rulers, but we set the physical rules as well."

"Physical...rules?"

"If I hold your hand, a stone might crumble. Or...a mountain might fall into the sea. It depends on how close we spin together. And every move we make is affected by the moves other Magna Rulers make. Some days, we could share a meal, and all would be well. Other days, if I think of you too long, a village could flood. Do you get it?"

I blinked at him. "You think...I could move a mountain?"

"The last time we spoke, you told me you stepped on Heim."

"That wasn't me—"

"Nex."

"Alright. Fine." I wiggled my fingers, wondering if they were warm yet or if I'd have to have them amputated. "So

the idea is we should never ever talk to one another or
even think about one another?"

He cleared his throat. "That would be...safest."

"But you came to me in the alley. In the City."

"Silver and gold for memory, huh?"

"Why would you risk that?"

"Why did you come here?"

"Ignorance."

He shook his head. "You did not understand the risk
to Aarde, but you saw the risk to your own life and still
you came."

"I...owed you."

His eyes flashed when I said that. "I see. Well, now we're
even. And you don't need to incur any more risk to settle
your perceived debt."

"I didn't mean to offend you," I said.

"Don't worry about it. I'm always offended." He took my
hand and pulled me to my feet. "Time to go, Aerixon."

"Wait. How do I know we didn't end a civilization just now."

He held up his hand to show me an intricate carving of
black symbols on his arm. I looked closely, and points on
the design moved about. "Magna tima. Measures how much
time we have before we rewrite any rules. It's helpful, but
sometimes a Magna Ruler makes a sudden change, and anything goes to hel anyways." He lowered his arm. "You'll need
one yourself, now that you know."

"Why haven't I had one all along? Why keep me in the dark?"

"You'll have to ask Woden about that one."

I began to take off his coat, but he pulled it tighter
around my shoulders. "Keep it. In case. And don't revive

your nerves until you're in a bed somewhere safe, or you won't be able to move."

I wrinkled my nose. "Are you being...*sweet* to me?"

"Me?" He brushed his lips against my cheek. "Never."

Then he disappeared.

I took one last look at the mercurian wolf pack, for that silver and gold memory of mine, and disappeared as well.

Ep 69

I'm Not Hiding, You're Hiding

Life Tip: Learn the rules, or they'll break you before you can break them.

I learned something about magnet stones that night.

They did not prefer to transport their owners into imminent death. In fact, they wouldn't. They'd take their wielders *near* death. Like to a frozen forest crawling with ravenous wolves to save a boy and probabilistically doom Aarde in the process. But, apparently, they didn't like belonging to definite dead persons, trapped in their pockets while they rotted.

And apparently, my odds of surviving being trapped in a crevice of Shuĭ while bleeding and busted were very low. So the magnet stones refused to do as I asked by returning me to my demise.

Instead, a different set of magnet stones answered my request. A set of stones I'd left in my bedroom. In a flat. In the City.

My entrance into my old realm wasn't at all graceful. I hit the wooden floor with a thud, my leg unable to support me in any way.

"Oh god," I grunted, trying to collect myself. I felt immediately out of place. The smells were foreign—much-too-old pine, synthetix fumes, and self-deprecation. The sound of electricity humming and transports driving by. *How could I have ever thought I belonged here?* Truth was, I never thought that. Even though I tried my very hardest to convince myself.

"Who's there?"

That made me shriek and snatch up my magnet stones. It wasn't Monny's voice, that was for sure. And it wasn't Morals. They weren't known for asking questions.

"'Who's there' to *me*?" I called out, readying myself for a fight. Or to run. "'Who's there' to *you*. This is my house."

The door to my bedroom swooshed open. And Onur Vanes leapt in with a yell, a Moral club raised in his hands, poised for a strike.

The club clattered to the floor when he saw me.

"*Nexus?*"

"*Onur?* What are you doing in my house?"

"I...what...how did you...?"

"If you don't answer me right now, I'll drop you where you stand. Why are you here?"

He scoffed. "Drop me? With your super strong Former muscles?"

I sent my copper coils out, wrapped them around his ankles, and pulled. His back hit the ground hard, knocking the wind out of him.

"Oh god in himmin!" he cried. He covered his eyes with his hands and lay there, unwilling to get up and certainly unwilling to fight me.

"You're fine, you know," I told him. "You can sit up. I didn't actually kill you."

He sat up, staring at me. His usually slicked blonde hair had flopped out of place. His Fender garb was askew, his jacket vest bunched up at his neck and a few of his buttons popped.

"You...you just...was that...*metal?*"

"Yes, Onur. It was metal. But you already know I'm Meta. So let's not pretend to be all surprised about it now." I dragged myself over to my bed. The second I touched the mattress, I felt my body start to fall asleep. *Not yet*, I told myself. *Rest is coming soon.* Just not yet.

"You can't have this much metal, Nexus. People will know."

"And?"

"And you'll be Ended."

The threat felt hollow. Months ago, I would have quivered at the thought. "Stop avoiding the question. What are you doing in my house?"

"Why are you dressed like...like that?"

I forgot. Onur was used to seeing me in white linen dresses and cloth flats, my hair the only part of me expressing my rebellion. And there I was in my Heim furs and boots, drenched in red, ironed blood, white paint on my face and black writing scribed into my skin. It was all quite a shock for his tiny mind. And Fenders didn't like what they couldn't predict. Or manipulate.

"Why are you in my house, Onur Vanes?"

He swallowed. "Hiding."

"Hiding? Hiding from what? What could Fender Above Onur Vanes be scared of?" Titanium tried to keep me calm, but the longer I looked at Onur, the more rage built up, calcifying my heart. I wanted to scream. I wanted to hurt him. And more than anything, I wanted to know why Onur was allowed to poison my life on the regular, when Lórr, an actual decent person, had a permanent writing put on his arm to help him avoid me.

"Fender Master," Onur corrected me.

He did not know how close I was to wrapping my copper coils around his manhood and asking them to do what must be done.

I inhaled. "You got...a promotion? My *mother's* rank? And you're hiding like some coward? Onur, what did you do, and how do I turn you in for it?"

"And I'm not hiding myself, Nexus." His shoulders crumpled. Lines of worry creased his forehead. "I'm hiding my baby."

Ep 70

See For Yourself

Life Tip: Even if you cover your eyes...they can all still see you.

"No," I said. "Nice try, Onur. But I know how *time* works. There is no way Var has hatched that baby. You may not think very much of me, but I'm not an idiot."

Onur rubbed his forehead. It had certainly not been several months since I was gone, but he did look many years older than the last time I saw him.

He pointed to me. "You look like death is breathing down your neck. Where have you been? So much has happened...."

"To be honest, I am probably not doing the greatest right now. So...I really need you to get out of my room. Out of my house actually. Now." *I want to mend my wounds and lie down. I want to sleep. I want to figure out why Woden never told me I was a Magna Ruler.* I wanted lots of things. None of them were Onur Vanes.

"I can't do that," Onur said, his voice cracking as if his whole body were under pressure. "There's nowhere else for us to go."

"Who? You and your imaginary baby? Why aren't you at *your* house?"

"My flat is the first place they'll look."

"Who's 'they'? Who is looking for a Fender Master so intently that he has to hide at his former lover's flat?"

"I'll show you."

I blinked because what he suggested was so ridiculous, there was no other response. "*Show me?*"

"Just come."

I held up a finger. "I am not going anywhere with you."

His lips tightened and his jaw clenched. "It's just to the next room, Nexus. Don't act like such a child."

I hopped up and across the room with just enough momentum to swing for his nose. He dodged my fist, but that didn't deter me. I kneed his crotch next. Then he lunged for me, sweeping off my feet—but not in the romantic way. And he attempted to choke me, his fingers tight around my neck. But it was so easy to wrap my copper coils around his.

I knew that if I asked them to tighten, the coils would crush his windpipe. And I would never have to look at his blue eyes ever again. Instead, I had them pin him to the wall.

I made my way to him, so I could scream into his face. *This*, I thought, *will feel better than murder.*

"I will never help you. Never. You have only ever used me. You have only ever hurt me. You always take! You never give! And I am done giving to you!"

Only it didn't make me feel any better. Because it didn't erase what had happened. That I once trusted this person, and he once acted like he loved me. I was wrong, and he took what I liked most about myself. He took it in one night, with just a few thrusts, and no apology.

"*Nexus?*"

Priyaa stood at the door, her arms laden with stuffed cloth bags. Her round eyes filled with tears.

"Nexus, you're not dead?"

She dropped the bags and crossed the room, throwing her arms around me and causing me to release the copper that held Onur.

I put my arms around her too. She smelled like she always did. Like childhood and sap tree tea in the spring. Her soft, straight hair against my cheek reminded me of being children together, of hiding in my room when our mother had the Thinky Grumps or our father felt upstaged at the House Of Houses.

"I thought you were dead! We looked everywhere for you, Nex, everywhere!"

"I'm sorry," I told her, rubbing her back, trying to soother her. "I'm so sorry."

"Mother...."

"I know," I told her. *God, do I sure know.*

"Were you...were you taken? Where have you been?" Priyaa asked, sniffling and taking a step back to get a look at me.

"I wasn't taken. I was forced to leave."

"And you didn't think to leave me a note? Or a message? Nexus, who thinks of everything? You just...left me? To make up stories in my head?"

I shook my curls. "There was no time, Pri."

"You've been hiding here all along? And...what are these clothes?"

"No. I was very far from here. And, believe it or not, I wasn't hiding. It's a long story, Priyaa. First, I need to lie down."

Her eyes widened. "You're bleeding. You're...*destroyed!* What have you been doing? Wrestling behrs?"

I grinned. "I can wrestle a lot bigger than a behr at this point."

Priyaa nodded, her eyes still bulging. "Dahn can help you with these wounds. She is a Wizen after all." She turned to Onur. "I'll help you with the baby. We should go quickly. It's already been too long."

"Stop," I said. "Priyaa, stop. There cannot seriously be an actual Vanes baby."

Priyaa sighed. Then she put my arm over her shoulder. "I'll help you to the other room," she said. "You have to see for yourself to understand."

Ep 71

Where Wailing Comes From

Life Tip: Carefully schedule all future hel unleashings.

Outside of Monny's room, I leaned heavily on Priyaa. I still couldn't feel the pain, but my body was too tired to support itself. There really wasn't anything to see with the door closed.

But boy was there something to hear.

A shallow grunting noise. Like a wild animal cornered by a hunter. It came in between gasps for air. And it was interrupted by a wailing that made my metal want to hide.

"What is that?" I asked. "No seriously, what is that? Some sort of experiment?"

Onur opened the door, and Priyaa helped me limp inside. Most of Monny's things had been moved—or maybe catapulted—aside. The walls themselves were splintered. It reminded me of the first time I slept with my metal outside of my body and it tore apart my old room.

I was much more terrified at that moment than I'd been with lead on the loose.

In the center of the room was Var Vanes. She sat in one of our kitchen chairs. Monny's linen sheets had been used to tie her arms and her round, pregnant belly to the back of that chair. Her mouth was gagged with a cloth. And sweat poured from her face and neck. Her hair was no longer in Wizen braids. It was flung around her face, slick with grease and perspiration.

The sounds—the groaning, grunting, panting, and wailing—they all came from Var.

"What...the hel...is going on here?"

"Nexus—" Onur started.

"Someone give me a straight answer right now!" I shouted. And Aarde itself shook beneath the floorboards of our flat.

Priyaa spoke. "She is trying to kill the baby. And herself. Nexus, we don't know what else can be done."

"What else? You take her to the House Of Reason! You don't tie her to a chair!"

"You don't understand—"

"I am releasing her. Let go of me, Priyaa."

Onur stepped between me and his partner. "I cannot let you do that, Nexus. You of all people will see the problem when I explain to you that the baby is Meta."

I took a sharp breath. And then I narrowed my eyes at him. "How would any of you know something like that?"

The next voice came from behind me. "All the mothers know."

Dahn stepped forward, dressed in her Wizen garb. And even though I was supposed to be angry with her still, she kissed my forehead, and I let her. Because I missed my friend, even though our friendship was an illusion all along. Funny how the heart could miss being broken.

Dahn continued. "The women...the mothers...they know when a baby is Meta. Before they're even born. It leeches metal from them. They crave foods high in iron and other required metals."

"If that's true," I said, "why wouldn't they turn their babies in to the Fight."

Dahn was different. More stoic, more measured. She reminded me of her mother as she dipped a cloth in water and began to soothe Var's slick skin.

"The mothers don't turn their babies in because they are mothers, Nexus. Most hide them. Even from their partners."

"And Var...?"

"Var is one of the few who cannot handle this reality. That her baby, who she loves, is her enemy. We could take her to the Hall Of Repair, but it is unlikely she'll ever return."

"...Edwidge—"

"It is unlikely." Dahn said this with a finality that made my stomach drop.

"Can't we give her metal?" I asked. "For the baby? Do we have to tie her up like an animal?"

"Look," Onur said, touching one of the walls where blood and splintered wood commingled. "When we left her resting here, she tried to kill herself by slamming her head into the wall. So we keep her over here, where at least she can't cause harm."

"But this is...."

"Wrong," Dahn said. "She should be in the House Of Reason. But the Fight watches it too closely now. The mothers can't come for help like they used to." She sighed. "They will starve them out of hiding."

"No," I said. "They won't."

Onur shook his head. "Listen, I sided with the Fight because I want advancement. But this? This advances no one. My house cannot flourish in these conditions. We cannot even survive them."

I scoffed. "You would turn that baby in for a promotion, Onur. You don't get to speak." Then I addressed Dahn and Priyaa. "I will not let pregnant mothers and innocent babies starve. And I won't let children die in alleys. I will make them listen to me."

Dahn took me from Priyaa, supporting me with her too-tall shoulder. "I'm sure you will, Nexus. I always figured you would. But right now, I'm going to make sure you don't lose that leg."

I sighed, my eyelids fluttering closed even as I walked. "But...I'm supposed to be unleashing hel."

"Give them hel, Nexus," she said. "Tomorrow."

Ep 72

Better Than Firsts

Life Tip: Hearts break easier and heal faster than bones.

"How are you not screaming in pain right now?" Dahn asked as she sliced the boot off my foot. "The bone is shattered."

It was weird, lying in my old bed with my old friend taking care of me. "One of my metals has been cinching my nerves. But it's getting tired. I need to turn the feelings back on."

"Let me set it first," she said. "If you let me, I can use metal to help. It'll heal faster, too."

"Go ahead," I said.

I watched as she snapped bones into place, my swollen purple and yellow skin bulging with each adjustment. "Okay," she said. "Turn it back on."

I thanked iridium, and it gladly released my nerves, as eager to rest as I was. My body didn't know how to process what had happened to it over the last few days. Immediate overload was the only response. I clutched the pillows and sheets in my fists and tried to instruct my limbs to relax, but they only tensed further, until my whole self was rigid.

"Try to breathe," Dahn said calmly.

I tried, but there was no use. My breath was the only thing holding me together. I couldn't release it.

"You'll pass out soon," Dahn warned, all matter-of-fact. "But that's okay. You'll be able to rest then. And I'll clean your other wounds while you sleep."

I pushed away the white-hot agony and tried to tell myself not to call out for Lórr's help. *I'm not in danger,* I attempted to convince whatever mechanism had the habit of informing him when I was in peril. *I'm not dying. I'm okay. I'm okay.* He had his wound to tend to. His own realm to fall victim to.

I tried to focus on Dahn's face. On the way her scarlet hair wove into perfect braids and her high cheekbones reflected the dim light. She seemed different. Her eyes were steelier, her brows slightly knit together. She reminded me more of her mother.

"I lost everything," she said, as if she read my mind. "My father's rank, and then Clay. My mother. And then Monny. And you." She exhaled as she folded the dressing on my leg. "And Var...we weren't close, but this hasn't been easy. Treating someone who's lost their mind...it's an actual nightmare." She shook her head. "It isn't until you lose everything that you realize how beautiful it all was. And how much you took it all for granted."

I could do little more than grip the sheets and try not to fade to blackness. There was no response I could give her.

"It was your mother," she continued, "who first asked me to make friends with you. 'I need you to watch Nexus,' she told me. And so I did. At first, it was because Viveka had the power to make things easier for our family. But then it was because...you were fun to watch." She shrugged, and the saddest little smile tugged at her lips. "I wish I had spent less time watching you and more time loving you. Clay was much better at that. But if you ever forgive me...I can learn, Nexus. I want to learn."

I squeezed the word from my mouth. "Forgiven." It wasn't a difficult decision to make. I'd seen Dahn risk her life to help children in need. I'd seen her fight for people who could give her nothing in return. Yes, she had spied on me, but she could have used everything she learned against me. She could have profited. Been a Fender—the best of them all. Risen in the ranks. Taken my mother out like Onur tried to do. She wasn't the best friend to me then, but she was worth forgiving. Sometimes, second chances could be better than firsts.

"Good," she said, with a genuine Dahn smile. "It won't take you long to heal. I'm actually pretty good." She jabbed her thumb toward the door. "They all thought you were dead, you know? But that didn't sound like you to me. I figured you were off coming together with that sexy boy who shows up in your window." She made kissy lips and then she winked. "Oh, and when you're all better, I'll show you where the Formers are keeping Monny." She clapped her perfect hands, though they were no longer manicured. "I love a good jailbreak."

Ep 73

Aren't You Righteous?

Life Tip: Beware leather coats; they'll make you weak.

I missed the moon over the Great Waters. It seemed darker
in the City, even with the buzzing street lights and the
zooming transports. In the next room, Var had finally
calmed down enough to sleep. I'd spent hours stuck in bed,
listening to her howl. When the others ungagged her to give
her food, her wild hatred took the shape of words—about
the abomination growing inside her, and how the Fight had
chosen her to End it, to End it all. Needless to say, I much
preferred the silence of the dead of night.

"Knock, knock."

Only he didn't use a door. Lórr appeared just inside my
window. He wore a long, leather coat; a loose white shirt
beneath it; and boots that looked like they were made of
the strongest metal. Traces of his latest injuries still marked
his face.

"What are you doing here?" I asked under my breath.
"I'm perfectly fine."

He crossed the room with long, playful steps. "I'll be the judge of that." He lifted my blanket, taking a look at my treated leg.

"Hmm," he said. "Someone knows what they're doing."

"My friend, Dahn. She's a Wizen. Like...a healer."

He nodded. "Is it still painful?"

"It's fine. I'm fine." I lifted my chin to him. "Why are you here?"

He hovered near my bed. "None of your business."

"*Lórr.*"

"To check on you." But he did not blush or redirect his gaze. "I left in a hurry, back in Auon. I had to be sure you were alright. And now that I see you are, I will go."

"Sit down," I said, calmly at first. But when he did not listen, I smashed my finger into the mattress. "*Sit.*"

He sighed and sat down, careful not to get too close. "Happy?"

"No."

Another sigh. "Then what do you want?"

"Why were you in those woods? Running from wolves? Alone?"

He looked down then, his boldness slipping. He played with the edges of my blanket to keep himself busy. "It's a long story."

"And let me guess...we don't have much time?" Without thinking, I reached out and grabbed his hand, holding tight. "The more information I have, the better I can help."

He shook his head. "You can't help with this. And it's not what I came here for."

I paused a moment, choosing my next words with care. "Who is hurting you?"

He tried to take his hand back, but I held, gently yet firmly. "It would be selfish to burden you, Nexus."

"It's selfish to keep it from me, to let me worry in the dark."

"Fine. But let go of my hand, before we raze a village."

I released him, bringing magnesium powder to my fingers instead.

"In my realm, in Auon...we have a history. Our Rulers were just and kind and noble. They dealt fairly with all. Fairness is one of our ideals. Until one day, the fairest of Rulers was challenged to war by another realm. This realm did not share the values of Auon. They did not fight fair. And many Auonians were lost.

"The council of Auon saw the kindness of the Ruler as weakness, for it cost the realm nearly everything it held precious. And so they demanded strength from Rulers and not fairness. Kindness was to be traded for ruthlessness. The council would make sure that every Ruler displayed these new ideals. And the people thought it wise, so it stands."

I nodded, wishing I could take his hand again, but resisting, as he wished. "That still doesn't explain why you were in that forest."

"I am a Ruler of Auon. And so I am to be tested. Tested until I have proven without a shadow of a doubt that I am cunning and ruthless and strong. That there is no kindness or justice or trust left in me."

It was like I saw him for the first time. His taunting, his reservations, his caution. How he second-guessed his own warmth whenever it showed.

"So your people really did put you in that forest?"

He nodded. "They ensured I bled first, of course. A decent amount. So it would be almost impossible to survive."

"They almost *killed* you."

He chuckled. "That's kind of the point, Nexus."

"When does this hateful testing end?"

He ran his hands through his dark curls. "It doesn't."

"What do you mean, 'it doesn't'?"

"It never ends. It keeps going as long as I live. Harder and harder each time. For the good of Auon."

I didn't care. I took his hand back and held tighter than before. "But you see that something like this is wrong. What they make you do is wrong. What they are doing to you is...evil. You see that, don't you?"

He half-smiled. "Aren't you righteous?"

"Goddamn it. It's not funny."

He laughed. "No it's not." Then, with his free hand, he traced a soft line from my forehead down my cheek and to my chin. "You're the one who's funny. You get so...vindictive."

"Someone has to vindicate people, Lórr."

"And you have taken on this responsibility for all of Aarde? That's too much for one person, Nex."

"No." And I made sure he was looking into my eyes so he understood my meaning and couldn't make light of it. "I take this responsibility for people I love. And I'm not one person. I'm your person."

His smile faded, but his hand remained, now resting on the back of my neck, as if it were the most comfortable place for it to be. "Well you can't fight all of Auon. That's three realms you'd be rivaling. How will I look after you then, huh? You'll outpace me."

My turn to half-smile. "You forgot about Shuï."

He blinked. "Wait, what?" Then he cursed. "*Nûrén*."

I shrugged. "What can I say? I get around."

He glanced at the markings on his arm as the points drifted. "Time to go."

I grabbed that arm. "Go where, exactly? Safely home to bed?"

"Ha."

"Don't let them do this to you, Lórr. We can think of some way—"

"I am going to break a rule. With your permission, of course."

"No, you're just trying to distract me."

"Yes. By breaking a rule. May I?"

I sighed. "Sure. I hate rules."

He grinned. "You don't even know what I mean, dummy."

"Don't care. I'm not scared of you."

With a soft chuckle, he leaned in and pressed his lips to mine.

Then, like the arsehole he insisted on being, he disappeared.

Ep 74

Must Be Getting Worse

Life Tip: Remember there's more under than there is above.

Two days. That's how long it took my leg to heal with Dahn's help. I had a peculiar limp, which she assured me would dissipate over time. But I was thankful, limp and all.

Priyaa chose to stay behind to help Onur with Var and the unborn baby, in large part to make sure Onur did not do anything selfish if the opportunity arose and in small part because she had a very successful metal smuggling organization to run, so Dahn and I set off together.

"I feel terrible," I complained as we headed toward Ender Stream under the cover of darkness. The moon was the only part of the journey that felt familiar. It made me shiver, imagining how many changes the silver orb witnessed over the centuries without the agency to speak out against them.

"You look great," Dahn replied. "Why do you feel terrible? Is it your leg?"

"No," I groaned. I tugged at my white linen dress, its seams threatening to snap. "It's too small now. It fits weird." I yanked the wild curls of my metallic hair. "And without the metal in it, my hair hates me." And then I dragged my feet against the cobblestone, as if I could ignite the cotton soles with the friction. "I walk so slow in these stupid things." And then I threw my arms in the air. "And I don't have my copper coils, so my limbs feel weird and gangly. And the paint on my face helped me know which direction the light is coming from at any given time, so now light is surprising, and my arms feel all gooey and tingly with the guards over my black writings. And I have to be quiet while we walk so I don't take up too much space. And keep my chin down like...like a child. I hate it."

Dahn smirked. "Well, Master World Traveler, most people don't know anything exists outside the City. No realms, no Rulers, no magnet stones, none of it. That's the first reason you need to keep it quiet and blend in. The second reason, which clearly you've forgotten since you're shouting in the street, is that L and their faction of the Fight can't know you're here and definitely can't know you're about to spring Monny from their little prison."

"Oh. Right."

"Besides, we both know all that Old-War-behrskin-metal shit increases your badarsery by a million. You'll be back to it soon. For now, we play the part."

I looked sideways at Dahn while we walked. She probably felt terrible too, in her Wizen braids and her long, gray cloak. "You like playing the part, Dahn?"

"Me? Oh helllll no. I'm divine, Nexus. Have you ever seen this body in a skin-tight, full-length dress? But this pretending won't last forever. We can fix this."

I nodded. "You know you are a very talented Wizen, though."

She grinned. "I can be beautiful *and* brilliant. Some of us are born with multiple doses of extreme talent."

I chuckled. "Power."

"Power?"

"That's what Stjarna likes to tell me. Those with great power need extra help."

"And that's your sister, right? Stjarna? You told me about so many strange people and things, it's hard to keep them all straight."

"Yes. My half sister. You would like her." I thought about that. "Well, you would either be great friends or fierce enemies. I'm not so sure. You're both...a lot."

"Ha," Dahn scoffed. "I'm not a lot. I'm the *most*."

"Exactly."

I stopped. My hand went to my stomach. "Uh oh."

"Don't tell me you're pregnant too. Nexus, I cannot handle another Var right now."

I grabbed her arm and ran into the nearest alley, forcing her to crouch next to me. "Shh, shut it," I whispered.

"You see something?"

"No," I said, keeping my voice hushed. "I felt a warning."

"What?"

"Shhh."

I peeked around the corner. Morals. They stood, in their black woolen hoods, at the entrances to the House Of Certainty and guarded the wooden Ending platform. The platform itself was chipped and scorched. Colors slashed into the stakes that lifted it off the ground.

"What happened to the platform? And why is it guarded?" The Fight was not the type to redecorate for fun. So some-

one had to have vandalized City property. It was the
only explanation.

"People have been rioting. Ever since the night Clay died.
The Endings are not like they used to be." She shook her head.
"The Morals guarding the Stream are new, though. Must be
getting worse."

"Does their presence make finding Monny more difficult?"
I asked.

"It makes it impossible." She pointed to the platform.
"He's there."

I squinted. There was no one on the platform. Either
Monny had gone invisible or Dahn was losing it. "No one
is up there, Dahn."

"Not up there," she said. "Under."

I let my vision slowly fall to the ground beneath the
platform. "Tell me you don't mean buried."

"No, Nex." Dahn took my hand and, since we were already
crouched, pushed it to the ground. Bits of gravel pierced the
skin of my palm, but I kept still anyway. "Look under."

"Look *under*? Dahn—"

"First of all, stop talking. Second, *you* taught me this trick."

"Me?"

"Yes you. You've knocked me over in so many alleys. All the
time I spent on the ground got me thinking. What if there
were things we couldn't see below us? It was like a sense,
I guess. So I...looked." She placed her own hand on the
ground and closed her eyes. "Metal knows metal. And if you
try, you can ask your metal to find what's under the ground."

I closed my eyes, pressing my hand down with more intention. *What can you show me?* My metal moved and twisted, calling out for whatever lay beneath my feet.

Slowly, like pieces of a puzzle, like the mechanics of a great machine, I could see images in my mind. Complex and looming, crisscrossing for many, many lengths.

"Tunnels," I said with a gasp.

Dahn and I opened our eyes and stared at one another. "Filled with metal-rich food," she said. "And steel. And iron."

My mouth went dry. "Filled with...people."

Dahn nodded. "Filled with Meta."

Ep 75

More Plotting, She Says

Life Tip: Making drakons is easier than making friends.

"We go down," I said, stretching my stiff shoulder muscles. "We go down now."

"What? No! Nexus, we can't just go down there."

I looked her right in the eyes. "My partner is down there because of me. And I am not leaving him in there one more minute. Not one more. I tried to do it the right way, Dahn. The way they wanted. I went to Heim. I did my best to set up their Ruler meeting, to play by the rules. But why are we the only ones with rules? Why does the City get to say who walks free and who gets their throats slit? Why does Heim get to decide who gets to be home and who's too dangerous to have one? Why does Shuĭ get to pick the ones with enough to eat and the ones who starve? And why does Auon get to choose the nature of another human's soul? They tell me I'm a Ruler, but I can't make any rules? Tell me, does that make any sense to you?"

She gaped.

"Dahn, that was not rhetorical. I was hoping for actual feedback."

"Oh," she said, "sorry. Um...yeah, that makes no sense."

"The Fight...they say Meta are too dangerous to let them live among the people. But they show themselves to be more dangerous every single day. Why do we listen to them?"

"Because...it's what we've been taught."

"And now, I'm the teacher. And I have had to reteach myself every single thing I've learned my whole life. And this is what I'm finding out. That I am the one who does something. I have to do something. Anything! Everything! And I have to do it *now*!"

Dahn sighed, staring down at the ground beneath our feet. "I do miss him. So much." She stomped, as if testing out the cobblestone. "How are we going to get in there? Is there a secret door or something?"

I reached into my pocket and pulled out two small stones. "I can get in."

"Alone? I'm not letting you go in there alone, Nexus."

"I'll go in, find a door or something, and let you in after me. Then we can find Monny together."

Dahn nodded. "Okay, that works. Also, this is the coolest thing I've ever done, and everything I do is pretty cool."

"Keep an eye on my stones until I get back, or they might get lost," I told her, placing them on the ground about two lengths apart.

I stepped through and appeared in a red clay cave, dust making its home on hundreds of books and scrolls and maps. Lanterns and compasses on shelves. I recognized the scent in the air as ancience. The sound of metal pounding metal rang through the air, reverberating on the rough walls.

I was not in the tunnels under the City. There was no secret door of coolness to open for Dahn, who no doubt still sat watching my stones in an alley on Ender Stream. No Monny to save from the clutches of the Fight. No L blocking my path, prepared to pay for the sins of murdering my mother.

I hated to admit, though, how relieved I was to walk into the next room, past the tattered cloth curtain, to find the monster of a woman plunging molten ore into a bath of ice water.

"Behr."

The feeling of belonging that welled up in me was unpredictable. A foreign invader. Not even when I gripped Stjarna's hand or leaned against Woden did I feel such realness of acceptance.

"You are weeping, Ruler," Behr said, her accent thick as her muscled arms. "Come here. Let's do some work."

I scrubbed my tears with the back of my hand and squeezed myself in between Behr and the flaymes. She was making small rings, maybe bracelets or some kind of disks for throwing, out of an alloy of many metals. The density impressed me even more than the shine of the finished products.

We worked in silence, and my shaky breaths became full and strong again. After what seemed like hours, Behr set the rings on a large cloth and sat down on the ground to polish them. I had never done this work before, but it pleased me greatly to scrub at the metal and see it come to itself again.

"You are weary," Behr said, her eyes on the movement of her hands. "And angry."

"Yes. To both."

"But no longer afraid."

The first time I went to Behr, I was the most terrified and small version of myself I could have been. I even hid under the table, though there was no threat to me present. It was my default mode of existence. And now....

"Things are only getting worse, Behr. I am trying to make them better, and I fail every time. I wonder if...I feel I have only two options. To give up or to break it all."

"Push with longer strokes," she instructed me, watching patiently as I adjusted my technique.

"Like this?" Instead of scraping the metal with brutish rubbing, I lengthened my strokes, pressing rather than tearing with the cross. "More pressure?" I asked her.

"Yes, Ruler. More pressure, less panic. More plotting, less planning. Power flows in many ways. In sudden bursts, which damage the metal. Or in steady motion that brings the metal to new life. Both ways will make you weary, but only one will bring beauty."

I held my breath. "But Behr...they won't listen to me. The realms, the Fight, the Rulers."

"You want them to listen, but you are not yet saying anything. You are only reacting. To be who you are, you must create."

"Like...my drakon."

She flashed her metal teeth at me. "Like your family."

She stood up and hoisted me to my feet. "Now, we must get you dressed. These childish clothes won't do."

"Dressed?" I tugged at my ill-fitting linen dress.

"A Meeting Of The Rulers has been called. And you have no choice but to attend."

Ep 76

No Buts

Life Tip: When stuck, enjoy.

The tan dress was a bit short, but there was room for my growing muscles to move, and so I did not mind. The leather boots were thick around my ankles but cushioned and warmed my feet. Rope twined around the length of my midsection. Not rope, I realized as I studied the woven pattern, tracing my finger across it. Vines.

"Come," Behr said. And I sat against her knees as she twisted strands of my hair into braids, clasping bits of metal to the ends. The fyre crackled and settled into a mild roar. "I braided her hair like this," she told me.

"My mother?" I tried to imagine Viveka with her arm draped over Behr's strong knee, the fyre heating the soles of her feet.

"And your grandmother. And her mother."

"How old are you?"

She chuckled. "Young."

"Behr...why did she choose the City for us?"

"Love. Love and power, Ruler."

Then she turned me around, dipping her hand into ground white paint. She coated my forehead and nose with the mixture, running a straight, thick line down the center of my lips, marking all the way to the scar on my throat.

"We do this to be seen," she explained, "and so that we may see."

I had to calm myself, to breathe slower on purpose, my metal helping to slow my heart rate. Shivers ran through me. "Who is we?"

Behr smiled that metal smile.

"I suppose I will figure it out," I sighed.

"We almost never do." Then she glanced at the door and stood to her feet. "Ah, here comes another."

"Another?"

But it only took a moment to figure out who she meant. Gege walked in, a blue and gold silken cloak billowing behind him, his bald head gleaming in the flickering light.

"Well, now, this is where you've been hiding, Yrsa?" He folded his arms across his chest, bands of gold shimmering.

"Do not feign ignorance. You knew exactly where I've been and still chose not to visit."

"So now I am in trouble?"

Behr laughed. "These things never change. It is also why yours is late."

Gege sighed and chose to turn his attention to me as I stood. "I'm glad you are not as dead as I had assumed, Ruler."

"Thank you for your concern," I teased. "And thank you for calling the meeting as I asked. But...I'm a little lost. You and Behr...know each other? You've known each other this whole—"

A clatter from outside the cavern. The sound of scrolls tumbling to the ground and a lantern smashing. A few curses to follow. Then, "I'm not late."

Lórr stepped into the room, dusting snow and ice from his shoulders. He wore the same leather coat as the last time I saw him, but the sides of his head had been shaved lower. He sported new piercings and writings as well.

His dark eyes sparkled when he saw me. "I thought for sure I'd beat you here," he said.

"You've never beat me a day in your life."

He grinned. "We'll see, won't we?"

And then he approached me, pulling me into an embrace. It surprised me. That's why my heart almost exploded in my chest. At least that's what I told myself. It didn't help that he lingered a few moments longer than he should have.

But this was not lost on Gege, who quite literally inserted his arm between us to pry us apart.

Another surprise, though. It was not so easy for me to step away from this person. This Kallórr. It was as if something deep in me was drawn to something deep in him. The power of it made my ears ring. I felt lightheaded. Immediately, fine perspiration sprang out of my pores. *God, what is happening right now.*

I knew my red skin made it difficult for anyone to see me blush, but there was no way Lórr failed to notice the literal heat coming from my face and neck.

Gege frowned. "Enough of this now, the both of you."

But Lórr put his hands up in surrender, his chest still pressed to mine. "I'm not doing it on purpose," he confessed.

Oh no, is he a little breathless? Shit, that makes me breathless. Oh hel. Oh no.

"I can't," I said. "I can't let him go." *Why did I say that? Why do I sound like this? I will never speak again. That's the solution. Yes. Silence forever.*

"Goddessdammit." Gege rubbed his bald head with both hands.

"Goddammit." Behr said, truly frowning for the first time.

I looked up at Lórr, trying to calm myself down and failing. "What should we do?"

He shrugged and smirked. "Enjoy it?"

"But...."

"But?"

Ep 77

Come On, Get Yours

Life Tip: Consider stopping stopping the stoppings.

"Absolutely not," Gege said, trying to make his voice come off as authoritarian as possible. "Lórr, do not you dare."

"Just a little longer," Lórr said. And I couldn't tell whether he was trying to convince Gege or me or himself. "My map says we have time."

"You have a few moments. And the closer you are, the less you have." Gege got behind Lórr and grabbed his arms. "Yrsa, come on, get yours."

Behr sighed. As she came up behind me and held on to my hips, she whispered in my ear, "He is always so dramatic."

I chuckled, all the while wondering what on Aarde it meant that I was Behr's. Behr's what? But I was also learning that my incessant questions would not be answered by the mystical Behr. Gege scowled at her comment, his eyebrows furrowing in disapproval. Then Lórr snorted, and I laughed even harder.

"Just pull," Gege grumbled.

He tugged, and Behr yanked, but there was nothing they could do to separate us. We were trapped, chest to chest.

He was taller than me, but I could feel his hip bone pressing just above mine. No amount of prying could decrease whatever force held us together.

"They'll miss the meeting," Gege said, exertion levels maxed as he let Lórr go, scrubbing sweat off his shining head.

"Tearing their limbs off their bodies only makes it more likely that they will miss the meeting. But come. We will devise a way. It is not like this hasn't happened before."

Gege's scowl softened to a frown. "No. It's not like it hasn't happened before." He pointed a finger at Lórr. "Do not bring this cave crashing down on us, Ruler. Behave yourself."

"Aren't you late for having us ready on time, Gege?" Lórr teased.

If there were a door he could have slammed as he followed Behr, Gege would have.

So Lórr and I stood together, alone, waiting for them to return with some way to separate us.

"What is this? Why do you think we are stuck?" I asked, trying to make conversation. He smelled like cedar and snow, which really distracted me from trying to distract myself.

"We're not," he replied.

"What?"

He sighed. "I'm tired, is all." He put his hands around my waist so they were not just dangling at the ends of his arms.

"Are you hurt?"

He shook his head. "No, I'm fine. It's just...this is how I feel with you all the time. It takes a lot of effort to maintain my distance. And I just...got tired of it. It's exhausting."

Oh good. Great. I am literally Aarde's most exhausting person.
Fun fact I suspected about myself, but I'd never been quite sure until then.

But Lórr traced his hand up my spine, gently, as if admiring the shape of it. "I'm not tired of you. I'm tired of staying *away* from you."

"How did you know what I was thinking just then?"
My tone was slightly accusatory, slightly amazed. *Is he a mind reader?*

"It was a guess. But you're not very difficult to read. You keep your emotions right in the open. And you don't try to manipulate people with them, so they're not something I feel like I need to avoid. When you become sad, it's both obvious and genuine. And just then, you got sad. I figured it might be because you misunderstood my comment about being tired."

"Oh good, so I'm not exhausting, I'm obvious."

He leaned his chin forward, resting it on my forehead. "Don't be mean to me," he said. He was partly joking, I knew, but there was some truth to it. Lórr spent a lot of his life having people who were supposed to care about him be really, really terrible to him.

I wrapped my arms around him, trying to pretend I didn't notice the muscles of his back slightly moving against my hands. And then I sighed too. Once I stopped trying to stop whatever was happening, I realized it was quite enjoyable and that stopping stoppings was the exhausting part, not me. It was like I'd been striving for a very long time. Like running in snow or moving against the wind. And finally, I could stay still. And belong somewhere.

"This is nice," I said after a few moments.

"Mmmhmm."

"Lórr?"

"Mmmhmm?"

"Why did you kiss me?"

His body tensed a little. I wondered if I had ruined our relaxing moment. *Am I stopping or starting something here?*

"Honesty required?"

"Yes please."

"I wanted to know how it felt. I know I shouldn't have. I just...wanted to know."

Acceptable answer. Curiosity sourced most of my calamities. "How did it feel?"

He stood up straighter, his hands on my waist. "I'm not confessing that to you!"

"Coward."

"You tell me first, if you're so brave. How did it feel to you?"

"It was quick. And unexpected. I mostly felt surprised."

He nodded. "I should have planned it. I forgot spontaneous things are much better when planned first."

"Shut up."

"I should have sent in a formal request."

I laughed. "Don't be mean to me."

Chuckling, he took one of his hands and traced a finger down the white line on my nose and lips. All the way down to the scar he made. Then he leaned his forehead against mine.

"Is this the formal request?" I asked.

"Yep."

"Permission granted."

"Really?" He seemed genuinely taken aback.

My heart was already pounding, and I knew he knew it because it was pressed close to his. But I was curious to know what he'd wanted to know. "Really."

"Oh thank goddess." He gripped the back of my neck, his other hand still on my waist, and met my lips with his.

Ep 78

But I Said Nothing

Life Tip: Set a timer.

This was not my first kiss. It wasn't even my first kiss with Lórr. But this was the first time I'd ever stood face to face with someone and felt like I *should* be kissed. Like I was worth the attention. Worth the affection.

Being with Onur made me feel...special. But not because of anything I offered. It was because I felt lucky to be with him. Lucky for myself, lucky that people would see us together. He was always superior, and that fact made me feel fortunate to have him near me. The problem wasn't that Onur failed to see me as something great. It was that he refused to let me see it.

But Lórr.

When he brushed his hand against my collarbone, tracing the line of it, I was convinced he knew my secret. That all along, even when Onur and the Fight tried their best to dissuade me, I knew. I knew I was great. I knew I was powerful. I knew I was Nexus. And not only did Lórr know this too...he *wanted* it for me.

And so I returned the kiss. I more than returned it. I lifted my chin, pulling his mouth to mine. My hand moved until I found a way to slip under his shirt, and I stroked my way across his midriff. This, naturally, made him inhale sharply.

"Goddess," he mumbled, stepping forward with me in his arms so I could lean my back against the curved cavern wall. "More."

I agreed. More was necessary. Luckily, he thought to flirt with the rough hem of my dress, his fingertips light on the skin of my thigh. It didn't matter that we already pressed so firmly together. I had the realization that closeness was still an issue. That there had to be a way to become even closer. And that I wanted it. Deeply. Like every bone in my body, even the mending ones, wanted to be with his.

And that's when it became more than kissing. More than two young idiots touching in an empty room. There was gravity to it. There was...history to it.

I didn't want Lórr. Something in me, something so old and so new that I couldn't name it, needed him. No... *demanded* him.

I had no more breath by then. It was all his. And there were firm hands in places I didn't know they could go.

Voices came through, muffled and ringing in my mind. Slowly, I remembered the night at Ender Stream, when Clay was dead and the Wizens were dying, and Lórr took me to the ground and begged me to let go of my madness. How he kissed my forehead then, our faces drenched in blood and the moon over us. I remembered explosions threatening to burst my ears, making me dizzy. That is how the voices sounded. Like they were tearing us apart.

Finally, my ears adjusted, and I could make out those voices clearly. *Gege. And Behr.* Shouting to us. They seemed so far away, like they were calling from across a magnet stone portal, from some distant realm a world away.

"Lórr," I said, squeezing my eyes shut, trying to figure out what the hel they were trying to say to us. "Lórr, do you hear that?"

He stopped, his lips still on my neck, and listened. Then he looked up, his eyes on mine. He held something in those honeyed eyes. A look that said it was time to go. Then he trailed his thumb across my eyebrow, down the side of my face.

"We have to stop?" I asked.

He half-smiled, one corner of his mouth tugging upward. "We should not have started."

I meant to tell him that I didn't want to end it. That I felt most like myself when he was very close, like he was right then. And when I could look over and he was standing there. And when I knew, at any moment, he could speak my name if he wanted to, and I would be there to hear it. But I said nothing.

With what looked like effort, Lórr tore himself away from me, stumbling backward and tripping over something on the ground.

It was like the world came back into focus all at once. The force of it slammed my head back into the wall. But then I could see. And as I looked around, my hands began to sweat, and my titanium worked double duty to keep my heart from detonating.

"Oh...*shit*," Lórr said from where he'd landed on the ground, his eyes just as wide as mine.

Oh shit, indeed.

Ep 79

All Cracks Are Jagged

Life Tip: Sometimes the worst things feel the best when you try them on.

The sparse, sturdy furniture in the cavern had been demolished, turned upside down, some even inside out. Anything wooden had been sliced to splinters. Anything metal lay panting, stuck into the walls and the floors at off angles. Maps were charred, the curling corners still smoking. Glass glittered on the ground, marking the graves of so many lanterns.

And from the floor to the ceiling, curving along with the sloping ceiling of the cave, was a long, jagged crack.

"Time to go," Gege said. "Now." And he hoisted Lórr up by the collar of his coat and shoved him toward the exit.

Lórr disappeared in an instant. Leaving me leaning against the wall, my ears still ringing.

"What...*what?*"

Gege pointed at me, his eyes firm. "This was not your fault," he said. "You have no idea what you're getting yourself into. But he does. And I will speak with him."

He motioned to the travesty of a room. "Yrsa, I will fix this. You have my word. Don't lift a finger."

"No need," she replied. "I am capable of cleaning up my own messes."

With that, Gege left through the exit in haste.

I slid to the floor, my arms resting on my knees, and pressed my hands to my eyes. I needed to think. I needed to wrap my head around what was happening. But first.... "Behr, what is happening?"

Behr put her large hands on her hips. "He's your match. Your opposing nature. You are drawn to him, Ruler."

"Yes, but why did that destroy half your cave?"

"Too close, too long, too...much. You began rewriting rules. What you really must worry about is not within this cave. Others will notice. And if you are found out, they will think you are irresponsible. Mostly because, Ruler, you are being irresponsible."

"I just wanted to be with a boy I like. How is that so bad? How is that"—I gestured to the wreckage—"this bad?"

"You are not a girl. And he is not a boy. There is no 'just wanting to be' with the two of you."

I groaned, hoping that if I rubbed hard enough, I could force the tears of frustration back into their ducts. "But you said I could trust him."

"You can. And you should."

"But look at what happened! We could have hurt you! Or Gege!"

"Ha," Behr snarled. "I would like to see you try, Little Ruler."

"I would never dare."

"Very well said." She rolled her shoulders, cracking her knuckles. "And now, you will get up, you will straighten your dress, which is almost coming off you, by the way, and you will attend the meeting you have called."

She offered her hand and pulled me to my feet. I felt dizzy, but my body was throbbing with energy. I felt more alive than I ever had. Like I could run all the way to Ender Stream and break the tunnels myself.

"Oh. Oh, wow. I feel amazing," I confessed, bouncing on the balls of my feet. "Like...really, really good."

Behr smirked. "Of course you do. Being close will have that effect on you both, just as staying apart will drain you. But—and listen to me Ruler—you must not break the lines of the map. Do not do this at the meeting. Discipline yourselves. If what happened here happens at the meeting, I will not be able to spare you from the consequences."

I swallowed. "What are the consequences?"

"That is not my story to tell."

"Whose story is it then?"

"Remember not to bow when you stand before the other Rulers. You are equals. If anything, you are their superior. A Magna Ruler. And don't forget to keep your chin high. Think like Stjarna in that regard. Keep a weapon on you when you sleep. Trust no one except who you know to trust. And mind your food before you eat it, lest it be poisoned. Rulers will want to bed you. Do not let them. And be wary of playing games with tricksters. You will only have one chance to petition the Rulers, so choose your words carefully. If something is thrown, duck. If something is aimed, dodge. But if something is waged, defend. Other than this, do not fight. Not even for sport. And do not worry. You were born for this. Now go, or you will be late."

"Wait," I said. "How do I know where I'm going?"

"To the meeting."

"I don't know where that is, though."

Behr grinned. "Come on now, Aerixon. Haven't you realized? There's nothing you do not know."

Ep 80

Setting The Pace

Life Tip: If you fall, it had better be on purpose.

I was very lucky I landed on my feet. The floor was so slippery, I almost skidded right over the edge. It was made of the smoothest, milkiest metal alloy I had ever seen. Calcium for creamy whiteness, pyrite for streams of glittering gold, and iron for tints of orange.

This floor flowed, with no railing or boundary, hovering many, many lengths above Aarde. If I had fallen off, I would have careened to my death. *Or not. I do have my drakon.* But I would have made a spectacle of myself, that was for sure.

"Don't peer too far over the edge," someone said from behind me. "The marble is slick."

I turned to see a boy, a bit older than me, with pale skin and flaming red hair, smiling at me. He wore loose pants, the smooth cloth rippling in the high wind. His hand rested causally on the hilt of a sword on his hip.

"I won't fall," I assured him. *I almost just did, but he doesn't need to know that.*

"Of course not." He nodded his head. "I'm Mil."

"Oh." I didn't realize we were introducing ourselves. "Umm...Nexus."

"Good to meet you." He tilted his head, the light catching his sharp, elegant features. "I've never even heard of you. How can that be? I thought I knew everyone."

I shrugged. "I'm the shy type, I guess." *Or the type who's hidden away behind a wall for her whole life, pretending not to be Meta so she doesn't get her throat slit.*

"You don't seem shy to me," he replied, his eyes gleaming.

"Okay." Awkward. But I did not want to talk to this flirty red-headed boy, even if his sleeveless vest showed off considerable musculature and swooping markings in glistening gold ink.

"Well then." He sounded offended, but he didn't look it. "Shall I show you around? Clearly you've never been to the Fall before."

"I got it," I said. Of course, I did not 'got it,' but he didn't need to know that.

He turned. "If you change your mind, or if you get lost, let me know."

With him gone, I peered over the edge again. Clouds and fog impaired my vision, but far beneath us were dark green trees and a large body of water. The air was chilled. I wondered what part of Aarde we floated over. And even more so, what mechanics held such a large space up in the sky.

And the space—I didn't know what else to call it—was quite large. I stood before towers and towers of buildings staggered on plates of marble. Each roof was gilded with metal, and the walls were made with soft white antimony, so they reflected the rosy light of the rising sun.

Many people walked through the large gates that separated me from the buildings, and all had different clothing styles, haircuts, and writings on their skin. They talked and laughed, some hugging; and some even wrestled, coming close to rolling off the edges. But most seemed to know each other and to be happy to see one another again.

I prepared myself to do it all alone. To find my way to the meeting space and to stand before a bunch of strangers as an outsider. An imposter.

But midway to the gate, someone called my name.

"Nex! Nex, wait up!"

I knew who it was from the warmth that spread through my chest and arms. Like on a cold day, after being out in the rain, someone was wrapping me up in a blanket. I turned just in time to put my arms around her.

"I knew it! I knew it!" she said, laughing into my hair as she squeezed. "I knew you'd be here and *not* dead. Api owes me half a dozen copper coils."

"Stjar," was all I could manage. It was so good to hold her, to be held by someone without worrying about rules or wrecks, about Meta or the Fight.

From behind me, Woden grabbed us both in enormous, rippling arms and spun until we laughed. "Both my daughters," he said, his voice booming. "What a rich Ruler I am! Ha!"

When he set us down, I realized how many stopped to observe our display of familial affection. I smoothed my dress back down, a bit self-conscious. "What about Heim? The council? I thought...."

"You are my daughter, no matter what Heim calls you," Woden assured me. "Besides, this is the Fall. Terms set by those whose feet remain on Aarde do not necessarily apply here." He ruffled my hair, and Stjarna's too. "Now go and find some young Rulers to torment. I will find mead."

Stjarna rolled her eyes as our father lumbered up to a group of Rulers, throwing his arm around the waist of a slender woman, who laughed and smacked him square in the face.

Stjar scoffed. "Mead *and women* is what he means."

"Stjarna—"

She held up a hand. "I am glad you are alright."

"But...Nŭrén...."

Stjarna sighed. "It worked. Of course it worked. The drakon was magnificent. But...even though she sits on the throne of Shuï, her emperor father will attend the Fall and sit at the meeting, and Nŭrén will not. Her feet must remain on Aarde."

"So this could go very badly for her."

Stjarna nodded. "But Api and Klok are with her. And Na has joined them as well. At least she's not without help." She tossed her head toward the gate. "Are you nervous?"

"I am." So many unknowns. And I'd vanished again, leaving Dahn watching stones I had yet to return to, with Monny languishing in some underground prison, waiting for me to do this. *Plot*, I told myself, remembering Behr's words. *Use your head.* I steeled myself in preparation. "It will all be over soon."

Stjarna shook her head. "Soon? This will take no less than three days, Nexus. The Fall is never rushed. But don't worry. It is outside of time."

I blinked. "A three-day meeting? And it's...outside of...what now?"

Stjarna chuckled and slapped my shoulder with a heavy hand. "And today doesn't even count as day one. Let's find some mead and someone worth punching. We can't let the old man outpace us."

Ep 81

Sadness Himself

Life Tip: Not everything that hurts you means to.

The closer we got to the gate, the more nervous I became. Everyone around me walked with such...purpose. They kept their chins up, their chests out. They surveyed their surroundings like they owned it all. Really, they reminded me of Stjarna. Confident and rightfully so.

"You're going to be fine, you know," Stjarna said, locking arms with me. "Don't look so anxious. They'll smell it."

"Everyone here is so...."

"Powerful."

My sister wore paint like mine and had hair like mine, but she hadn't lived a life like mine. In the City, power was something to be hidden. To walk down Ender Stream, I needed to look small, not big. Now, it felt like I was too big for the City and too small for the Fall. I fit nowhere.

"Just be yourself, Nexus. You exude power. It's who you are, not how you walk."

I exhaled, trying to loosen myself up. The gate didn't help. It was gigantic—looming—all dark iron and sharp angles. Rulers formed a line at the entryway, and as I approached,

I could see why. Someone stood there taking the names of those who wanted to get in.

"What happens if they don't let someone in?" I asked.

"I'm not sure," Stjarna said. "I'm thinking an eternal punishment-type deal. That would be my guess."

Oh good. Yes. Why don't we just take a stab at it? Throw out hypotheses like 'eternal damnation' and such. That always calms the nerves.

The gatekeeper was a boy, younger than us, with hair as white as Stjarna's and skin that glowed like the moon. He looked about Clay's age and he had a sweet demeanor that made me wonder if he secretly collected lanterns too. We got to the gate, and he bowed, his eyes all black with no visible whites.

"Hello, Stjarna," he said, though he didn't look happy to see her. He didn't look unhappy either. He looked...blank.

Stjarna gave a polite smile. "Hello, Dallr."

The boy held a long staff carved of white and gray wood and, strangely enough, containing no metal at all. It was simply wood. Nothing more. But his fingers curled around it tightly. "State your name," he said to my sister.

I thought this was strange because he already knew her name and obviously knew who she was. But I watched, my curiosity keeping me silent for once.

"Stjarna Aerixon. She Rules Like The Stars."

The boy, Dallr, thrust his staff into the marble floor, sending a ripple through it. "Enjoy the Fall," he said with a nod.

Next was my turn. I pulled magnesium to my fingers as I approached the gatekeeper.

"I am Dallr Sēdiz. The Bright One Of Great Sadness."

I forgot what Behr told me, immediately at the very first opportunity, and bowed. It just seemed right at that moment. But when I stood up, I blushed and scratched my head. Then, I dropped my arms, because Rulers were supposed to be confident and certain of themselves and were not supposed to bow awkwardly and then wish they hadn't."

Dallr didn't smile, but the light beneath his skin increased slightly. "You are very new here."

"How can you tell? Is it the bowing or the trembling?"

He did smile at that, but so subtly, I thought I imagined it. "State your name for entry."

I chewed on my lip rings. "What if my name wasn't... registered...or something? Do I die forever, or do you throw me off or something?"

"Have no fear, Nexus Aerixon," he said. "Your name was placed here outside of time. If it was, it is."

Have no fear? People only said that when there was so much fear to be had. *Fear for everyone, on me. Pass it around!* "Nexus Aerixon. Daughter Who Connects The Rulers Of Forever."

Dallr hummed at the back of throat. "It is the right time for you to be here, Connector Of Rulers. You are well come."

I sighed so loud that I embarrassed myself. I moved toward the gate as the boy brought his staff down. But he grabbed my arm before I crossed through.

"Not everyone here will think you are well come, Ruler. Not all gold glitters."

I nodded. His touch was surprisingly cold. It hurt my arm, icy pain radiating through my body. But I could tell he didin't mean for it to hurt me. "Thank you, Dallr," I said. "I'll be careful. I owe you one."

"Anytime," he said, and then he bowed to me, not awkwardly, but with reverence. "I'm yours."

Ep 82

Like A Ball Of Light

Life Tip: A friend made is a friend kept.

Inside the gate, a rush of energy tickled the bottoms of my feet and made me clear my throat, flowing straight through me. I rubbed my fingertips against my scalp, but the sensation only intensified, like I was walking through an electric sea. Stjarna was easy to find once I started looking. The white paint on her face caught the sun. That, and all of her glowed. Literally.

"I told you it would be fine," she said, grabbing my hand. "Let's eat. And maybe...drink."

She pulled me forward into the crowd of Rulers mingling outside of the buildings and released me so she could jump into a cluster of them.

The young people laughed, erupting with a chorus of, "Stjarna!" and wrapping her in hugs. She motioned for me to come over, and I did. They were nice enough, all glowing and smiling and beautiful and brilliant. Stjar introduced me as her sister, and everyone marveled but quickly began talking about their realms and the myriad of things that happened the last time they were all together. After a few minutes, I wandered off without anyone noticing.

I traced my hand along the antimony walls of the first building of many, the white metal rippling under my fingers. The view was like nothing I'd ever seen. Months prior, I thought the City was all that existed. I thought hiding my Meta, my power, myself, was the only way to survive. I thought being with Onur was the only way to be happy. And as I stood on a floating castle in the sky, my drakon sleeping inside me, my metal at peace in my bones, I wished all the people I loved could feel so much like themselves.

"It's beautiful, isn't it?"

I startled. The scarlet-haired Mil had snuck up behind me. He smiled, his handsome face glowing just like all the other Rulers who'd crossed the gate.

"Yes," I said.

The boy tilted his head, the gold scrawled on his neck reflecting the light as he changed positions. "You don't prefer speaking with me, do you?"

I planted my feet as I turned to face him. "You seem very friendly."

"I seem *friendly*?"

"What do you want?"

He grinned and shrugged, but his eyes peered deeply. "To be friendly."

I crossed my arms, an involuntary form of self-defense. "What realm are you from, Mil?"

"Melhor. But that is obvious."

"Why would that be obvious?"

"My accent. My charm. Good looks. General superiority. The literal gold in my writings." He leaned against the antimony. "And you are from Heim?"

"What do you want?"

"Just...to know you."

Like a ball of light, a wide-hipped girl bounded up to us, inserting herself between Mil and me. She flounced dark, tight curls over her shoulder. "New girl!" And she kissed both of my cheeks. "Come on, I'll show you around."

I had no idea who the girl was, but she hooked arms with me and led me around to the other side of the building and through an open door.

"Careful with that one," she said, depositing me to a rough wooden table and pouring a large glass of a frothy drink—one for me, and then one for herself. "He's sneaky."

"And you aren't? How did you know to rescue me? Were you watching us?"

She blushed. "Nothing sneaky about me. I owed him one is all."

She downed the whole glass and poured herself another. "Owed...Mil?"

"No, I'm not stupid enough to let Mil do me a favor." She glanced across the room at the other door and then continued to drink.

I followed her line of sight. Standing just inside the door, Lórr pretended like he hadn't been staring at us.

"Gross. He sent you to keep an eye on me?"

She smiled. "What did you do to him? We've been friends a long time, and I've never seen him so awkward about anything before."

A tug. From the depths of me. Nearly dragged me off my chair and over to Lórr. I gripped the side of the table, trying to appear casual, and changed the subject. "So... what's your name?"

I sniffed the drink, and it smelled so sharp that my eyes nearly disintegrated. Still, I took a sip. It burned but also cooled. Not bad. So I smacked my lips and took another.

"Fiel. And you're Nexus? I heard you handed Huangdi his own arse."

I choked, sputtering as I forced the drink down. "I didn't...um...."

She raised her eyebrows, her round, soft face confused. "You didn't destroy the bridges of Shui with a fyre-breathing metal drakon?"

"It was...lightning. Not fyre."

Fiel giggled. "I see why he's in love with you."

"*What?*"

Her face fell, and she glanced at him again, as if she'd said things she promised she wouldn't. "What?"

"No, what did you just say?"

"How do you like the mead?"

I lifted my empty cup, examining the bottom of it. "Is that what this is? I've never had anything like it."

"Well, you're a natural." She jabbed her thumb at the brawling men beside us. "They're only one cup in."

I laughed. "Do you think we'd throw a few punches after a few more?"

"We're too sophisticated," she said, making a kissy face. "But we could find something fun to do. I feel tingly. And restless."

"Me too." I paused. "Wait, you mean like we could do something...together?"

"Of course! I wouldn't just ditch you. Why do you seem so surprised?"

I scratched my fingers along the side of the wooden cup, wondering where Stjarna disappeared to. "I'm not sure any-one has ever offered to spend time with me without being obligated or compensated in some way. I've always been either leverage or liability. Or both."

"What about Lórr?"

"He's more obligated than anyone."

"No, he isn't."

"He is. We're...you know...magnetized or whatever."

"That doesn't mean he has to like you. Some Magna Rulers try to destroy each other, you know. Repelling or attraction are still choices. And neither means you have to *like* the other person. Preference has nothing to do with magnetism."

I chewed on my lip rings. "Oh."

Fiel tapped her fingers on the table. "So...want to go have some fun? Or you guys want...you know...a moment?" She winked.

"No, Fiel, we can't do that!"

"I'd cover for you."

I laughed again. "Show me where this fun is."

Ep 83

The Stuff Of Legends

Life Tip: Discomfort breeds greatness.

"Okay, ready," Fiel said.

I loved the way she talked. Her words rolled off her tongue like a song. It made me realize how plain and restrictive my speech was. The City gave me no flare, no spice. I sounded like synthetix.

"What exactly am I supposed to be ready for?"

She hustled across yet another terrace, her wide hips winding as she went, short legs moving her body forward. Finally, we reached an enclave of sorts, secluded from the rest of the Fall by trailing vines over iron trellises. Two other people were already sitting on the stone benches, waiting.

"About time," one of them said. Then, he smiled at me like I was dinner, his flawless brown skin illuminated from the inside. "You brought the pretty one."

"Beijo, meet Nexus. Nexus, don't bother meeting Beijo. He'll try to bed you."

"I will not." But he didn't stop smiling. "Don't listen to Fiel. She's a prude." He patted the stone bench. "Sit next to me, beautiful."

"Ignore him thoroughly." Fiel gestured to the black-skinned beauty who sat silently, her hands in her lap. "My partner, Vertroue."

She nodded, her long, thin braids swishing over her shoulders. She looked like she was carved out of obsidian and grace, her motions fluid and effortless.

What should I say? It was confusing being with people who didn't have to spend time with me. "So...um...where are you all from?"

"You can't tell?" Beijo asked, still smiling as he admired me.

"I don't even know the names of all the realms. Sort of learning as I go here."

"New and gorgeous," Beijo said. "I'm Melhoran, just like Fiel. A paradise in the sun, our Melhor, especially compared to simple Heim." He chuckled. He flaunted the gold writings on his arms, to further prove his point. "No offense."

"Offense, actually," I corrected him. "Heim is beautiful."

"Oh really? Maybe you'll take me there one day."

"I can't," I shrugged. "I'm banished."

The smile fell off Beijo's face. I moved on before he could ask more questions. "And you, Vertroue?"

"Rykdom is my home."

Fiel chimed in. "She lives in a *volcano*."

A vague image of a mountain on fyre flashed through my mind and made me shudder.

"Yeah, a dormant one," Beijo said.

"My vulkaan is more alive than you can ever hope to be." Vertroue said it with the confidence of someone who knew they were always right.

"So, introductions made," Fiel continued, clapping her hands. "Time for the fun." She looked around, frowning. With every move she made, the slits in her skirt revealed tan thighs. "Where is the fun?"

Beijo groaned, rolling his eyes. "He's late."

Vertroue pulled a ball of metal to her fingers, flipping it from knuckle to knuckle. "He is *always* late."

"I'm not late."

Lórr descended from nowhere, landing black-boots-first on the stone bench. He hopped down, brandishing four murky glass bottles of liquid.

"The fun!" Fiel said. She swished over to Lórr, taking the bottles and kissing him full on the mouth. "I forgive your lateness."

He chuckled. "You're welcome."

His eyes met mine and lingered for a while. We said nothing. I didn't know why he was quiet, but on my end, I was pretty sure if I opened my mouth right then, it would just be to put it on his.

"Wow," Beijo interjected. "You could just find a room, you know."

Heat rushed to my face, and I shook my head, trying to clear it. "So we have more of this drink?" I asked.

Fiel giggled. "Nexus can hold her mead."

"There are only four bottles," Beijo complained, already guzzling his share. "And five of us here."

"We can share," Fiel said, nestling into Vertroue's lap. "Go for it, Nex. That one's yours."

I grabbed a bottle and drank. It warmed and cooled me again, settling my nerves and tingling my spine. I felt my drakon wiggle in response.

Lórr finished half his bottle before I looked up again. Apparently, he also needed his nerves settled.

"So," Vertroue said, her voice like silken ash, "I heard you mortalized Huangdi, Nexus. Is there merit to that rumor?"

"Himmin and hel, how do you all know about that?" I asked, my hand to my head.

"Because Huangdi is Aarde's largest arsehole," Beijo said, belching loudly.

"Because what you did is the stuff of legends," Lórr corrected. He sat with his elbow on his knee, bottle almost empty.

"I'm not entirely sure what that means," I said." What are legends?"

"You don't have *legends* where you come from?" Fiel asked, her eyes wide. "How do you know who you want to be like? Which qualities to pursue?"

I shrugged.

"Legends," Lórr explained. "People who do the impossible simply because it must be done. Their names are remembered forever, their courage and passion an aspiration for generations after they're gone. That's what you did at the Great Waters."

"Ha. No." I took another big sip and swallowed. "It wasn't all that. It wasn't a legend thing."

Lórr stood up, his eyes flashing. "No? What was it then?"

I lifted my chin. *Arguing with me. Again. Always.* "A friend needed my help. I helped."

"You didn't even know Nŭrén. In fact, Gege said she *kidnapped* you before appealing to you for help. She should have been your enemy. Yet you stayed and gave her aid to fight the Emperor." He moved closer, his words growing more passionate, more poignant. "Why?"

"The people—"

"Those were not *your* people, Nexus. Yet you risked your life for them. And your sister and friends trusted you, followed you. They fought because of *you*. Because you are worth trusting and worth following." He was nose-to-nose with me. "You didn't stumble upon greatness in Shuǐ. Or in Heim. Or in the City when you held three metal movers alive for hours, drenched in their blood. Nexus Aerixon does not stumble into anything. When you are needed, you come. That"—he jabbed his finger into my chest—"is the stuff of legends."

It was so difficult to keep from leaning into him. The pull between us made me feel like my heart would rip out of my chest and smack into his. But I held my ground, fighting the sway of my body in his direction. "Four."

"Four?"

"It was four Meta that I kept alive, not three. You counted wrong."

He grinned. "Or I just knew you would correct me."

"*Arsehole.*"

"I'm just trying to keep up."

And he reached for me.

"Goddess divine!" Fiel shrieked. The glass bottle in her hand splintered, and she tossed it just before it exploded into a thousand shards. She leapt to her feet and cleared her throat.

"Onward," she said, her fist in the air, "before the two of you kill us all." She turned to Lórr. "Check the map."

He glanced at his arm, cursed, and then vanished.

"I figured as much," she said with a nod. "No worries, he'll be back once the universe cools off." Then, Fiel grinned, rubbing her hands together. "Now that we're all properly drunk...we go *up*."

Ep 84

On Your Marks

Life Tip: Less rules, more fun.

I tilted my head all the way back and still couldn't see the top of the tallest spire. Night was closing in, and the clouds descended on the buildings of the Fall. The stars flaymed above us like we could pluck one from the sky.

"There are rules," Fiel said, the wind whipping her hair. "You can play dirty but never go for the kill. That's rule one."

I gave up on trying to hold my dress down over my thighs and let the wind do what it wanted. "You mean that metaphorically, right?"

"No," Fiel replied, shaking her head. "*Literally* don't kill anyone."

"Has that been an issue in the past?"

Beijo gave one short burst of laughter, and Vertroue smacked his arm.

"We don't talk about it," Fiel said. "That's rule number two. And number three. You don't have to reach the top first; you have to hold the spot by the end of the round."

"Okay. How do I know how long the round is?"

"The Highpoint Star has to be straight overhead. Make sense?" The brightest star in the sky glistened, as if on cue.

"It almost isn't fair," Beijo said, bouncing on the balls of his feet. "The chances of anyone but me winning are so slim."

"He has won precisely once," Vertroue said, her sculpted lips drawn into a frown. "Only a fool claims victory from the vantage point of defeat."

"Ready?" Fiel said, flexing her calves, her eyes already on the spire that disappeared into the clouds.

The game was to scale a tower and to defend my position at the very top. Oh, and to do it while intoxicated. When I asked if it was dangerous, Beijo had said, "The only way to live is to practice dying." A nonsensical answer, followed by a mead-tinged belch.

"Go!" Fiel yelled.

She and Beijo sprinted toward the spire. They were impossibly quick, the gold of their writings illuminating, increasing their speed as they went. Beijo pulled a strange metal to his hands, using it to claw his way up the spire. Fiel did the same but used her short, powerful legs to spring herself upward in great bounds.

"What is that metal they're using?" I mumbled to myself, watching from the ground. "I can't place it."

"It's a steel alloy," Vertroue responded. She was not in a hurry to get to the top. "They create it exclusively in Melhor. It is very...versatile."

"Won't they get tired, racing up to the top like that? It's so many lengths high."

Vertroue nodded. "They will slow down soon. And then I will win the game."

I looked sideways at her. "You're pretty confident."

"I suppose I am. I know what I can and cannot do." She blinked at me, her black skin darker than the impending night. "Do you know what you can and cannot do, new friend?"

"I'm still figuring that out."

"Then you are fortunate. Adventure awaits the lost."

Without warning, Vertroue twisted her body, and a tungsten blade appeared in her hand. It rotated until she levitated above me. Then off she went, headed upward.

I knew, of course, that I could use my magnet stones to simply appear at the top of the spire. But I wanted to have fun, not to win with no effort. *What do you want to do?* I asked my metal. They hummed within me, vibrating against the walls of my cells. They wanted to run. To stretch. To be used.

"Race you," Lórr said, appearing behind me. If I weren't so inebriated, I would have jumped. But my reflexes were slowed by all the mead I'd ingested. "Ready?"

He focused honey-bhee eyes on his destination.

"The others are already so far ahead," I said.

He grinned. "You know very well this race is between you and me, Nex." He stuck his tongue out, his platinum ring flashing. Then he laughed. "No holding back. Deal?"

Ep 85

Get Set

Life Tip: If you are going to ruin something, make sure it's replaceable first.

"Deal," I said.

And we were off.

Iridium sparked behind my eyes, rearranging my metal within me as I ran. Heaviest metal to the top, lightest to the bottom. And then the other way, with the lightest on top. Until the metals in me spun. Faster and faster in a cohesive circle. It propelled me forward and, with slight adjustments, upward so that I ascended the spire with ease. The antimony of the tower rippled under my hands and feet, providing footholds for me as I pushed myself faster than I had ever gone before.

I felt, all at once, my cells unlock and my heart float in my chest, suspended. I had the sense that my body was finally...*happy*. It was free. And so I let it be what it wanted to be for once—open and fluid, just like metal.

I grasped the tip of the spire fractions of a moment before Lórr. He wasted no time, lunging toward me with a fist full of aluminum. I ducked, spinning on the spire, my fingers gripping the thin pole, and aimed for his legs with a blast of magnesium powder. Once the powder coated his shins and ankles, I squeezed my hand into a fist, clumping the magnesium into solid form. I forced my fist downward, dragging Lórr toward the ground.

He used his fingers to grab hold of the antimony tower, disassembling the magnesium and preparing another fistful of aluminum.

I didn't notice the copper coil creeping up the back of my leg until it clutched onto me, squeezing and sending me flying off the spire.

I fought with the copper midair. It was loyal to Lórr and refused to listen to me. But after a moment, it yielded, releasing me as my boots hit the ground.

I thought for sure the others would have been fighting Lórr at the top, but they were still on the way up. *How fast did we go? Did we fly?*

I knew there was no way I would make it to the top before them, no matter how fast my cells spun. And, with a hasty glance at the heavens, no way I would get Lórr off that spire before the Highpoint Star was overhead. I had mere moments. And the magnet stones were not an option. I was stubborn about how I earned my victories, I discovered.

Don't plan, Behr said to me when we polished metal together. *Plot.*

And it came to me. How I could be the only one on the tip of the spire when the Highpoint Star was overhead.

I planted my feet, took an enormous breath, then another. And then I opened my arms wide. *Antimony*, I thought with all my intention and effort. *Will you come to me?*

With a terrifying quake, antimony proved more than eager to play the game with me. A thunderous cracking noise filled the night, and the entire top half of the spiraling tower lifted from the building it rested on. A quick flip was all it took for Lórr to lose his grip and plummet to the ground. The other three—Beijo, Vertroue, and Fiel—all slipped as well. The star would have made it to Lórr right then, crowning him victorious.

But I moved the spire, so it crossed the sky along with the star. I planted the antimony on the terrace where I stood and climbed to the top with a few leaps before the others even knew what was happening. My hand gripped the tip just as the star crossed overhead.

Winner.

"Cheater!" Beijo screamed, the mead overtaking him at last, his eyes red and his brown skin drenched in perspiration. "She cheats!"

Fiel smashed her fists into the ground in frustration. "She didn't cheat, Beijo. She won!"

Vertroue dusted her long dress. "Yes, she is the winner. That is clear."

Lórr was nowhere to be found. *I hope he didn't die or anything like that.* But most likely our time had expired, and the rules of magnetism urged him to vacate my immediate vicinity.

"Who in himmin and hel has done this?!" I swiveled on the spire to find a cluster of very old, very displeased Rulers. "Who has the audacity to destroy such *holy* relics? And to what purpose?"

I slid down the halved tower, misstepping slightly thanks to the mead in my bloodstream. "Hello, Rulers," I said, with a bow. "I suppose I am to blame here. I was"—I cleared my throat and, to my horror, hiccupped—"I was playing a game."

The oldest of the grouches pointed a shaking finger at me. "And who on Aarde are *you*?!"

"Nexus Aerixon." I remembered to put my chin up. "Of the City. And of Heim. Sort of. It's a long story."

The old man narrowed his eyes. "Who...*the hel*...let you in here?"

Ep 86

Go

**Life Tip: When negotiating global politics,
if possible, don't.**

The grumpiest of old men pointed a gnarled finger at me.
"Your presence is not permitted among us."

I swallowed. "But...I'm the one who called the meeting."

Gasps and murmurs from the growing crowd of Rulers
who'd come to see why a building was torn in half.

The old man's eyes widened beneath thickets for eyebrows.
"Call forth the gatekeeper!"

I idled for a few moments, pulling magnesium to calm
my nerves. From the crowd, I spotted Stjarna.

"What did you do?" she mouthed.

I nodded my head toward the spire behind me.

Her eyes grew as round as the moon. "Oh my goddess!
Nexus!" She put her hands to her head. "That's so...awesome!"

I snorted a laugh, and the old man grimaced so hard at
me, I was sure he strained a neck muscle.

When Woden appeared in the crowd, he did not look
as amused as Stjarna. His lips curved downward, his eyes
shining and stern.

Finally, Dallr approached, his small frame squeezing by the onlookers, his iridescent body brilliant against the dark of night. He bowed to me, and everyone gasped again. Apparently Dallr showing respect to Rulers was not something that happened often. I bowed back because...Nexus.

"What is the meaning of this?" the old man asked the gatekeeper, his voice scraping together like rocks pummeling a synthetix hull. "Why is this one here?"

Dallr, still holding his wooden staff, spoke up, his voice flat as water on a windless day. "The Magna Ruler made her own way. As a true Magna Ruler must."

"Her kind is not permitted at the Fall. She should not be among us. Look, already, at what she has done. The meetings have not yet been called to order! Yet holy relics lie as rubble. She is careless, reckless. An abomination to our ways. As we always knew she would be."

Always knew? How can someone who's never met me judge my intentions? My character? "Maybe I'm reckless sometimes, but I'm not careless. I care. A lot. Or I wouldn't be here. All I ever do is care. Who are you to assign my merit?"

More gasps.

"And why are you here? For some other purpose than to destroy?"

I exhaled. *Now is my chance. The chance to set a few things right. The chance to advocate for the Meta of the City. And to free Monny. And to win justice for Clay.* "I am here to petition you to lower the wall around the City. To let people come in and out. To let people *live.* There is no way the people can survive with limited metal. Not forever. They are dying. *We* are dying. The strain causes infighting. It causes toxic fending. We kill each other because there isn't enough for all of us. We form enemies out of families. But this can't be healed unless pressure is relieved. So...I'm asking you to let us out."

The old man heaved, his face growing white and gray. "Lower the walls? You have no metal because you could not stop abusing it. Because you could not bear to share with the rest of Aarde. It is just punishment."

"No," I said loudly—louder than I had ever spoken before. "It is just to punish perpetrators. Not to punish their children. Not their children's children. There are unborn babies—right now—crying out for metal they can't have. Screaming in their mother's bellies. Children dying in alleys, alone and confused and scared. Starving. What did they do to deserve that? Nothing! They only exist in a way that *you* don't tolerate. *You* refuse to make room for their existence. What was done to achieve justice is only causing suffering. And it is not their fault. It's *yours*."

"You know nothing. Nothing of the sacrifices paid to ensure that destroyers like you were kept behind those walls. Nothing of the sacrifices of your own mother. Of your own father."

My own father? I pushed the questions aside. *Focus, Nex. Focus.* "Again, it is not my fault that I have been kept in the dark. My ignorance is *your* doing. I can't be held responsible for being lied to. I can't follow rules you haven't told me exist."

"Not here," Woden spoke up from the crowd. "We must speak of these things in private." But the old man ignored him.

"Your mother knew exactly what you were when she fled with you to that goddess-forsaken prison you call the City.

At her own risk, she left us. And against our desires. For she was well-loved by all, and you would be the end of her. And where is she now? What has her sacrifice cost her? Cost us?"

My eyes stung with tears, but I refused to let them fall. Refused. "You're trying to tell me that my mother chose to take me to the City to keep all of you safe? And that makes *me* some kind of monster? You don't think a world that forces a mother to make that kind of choice is the real monster?"

"Those walls were built to keep *you* inside. Viveka should have left you there to die."

Dallr lifted his staff and drove it to the ground with an echoing boom. Everything fell silent.

"Daughter Who Connects The Rulers Of Forever is well come." He turned to the old man. "Burr, you speak with great conviction. And your sincerity is evident. But...it is time."

"I disagree with every metal in my body," the old man said, his long beard dragging across a full chest.

"It is not your place to agree or to disagree with this," the boy continued. "The Magna Ruler has made her way to the Fall. She has left the prison you built for her and those like her. And she is here to connect the Rulers at last. To create, one must destroy. To destroy, one must create. *It is time.* The only question is this. Will you resist the Goddess or will you join her?"

The old man snarled. "The meeting has not yet begun, Gatekeeper. You make rulings out of order."

"I say when it has begun. I say when it ends," Dallr replied.

The boy raised his voice to address all gathered, which at that point appeared to be everyone. "From the Caged Realm has come one who defies all rules and all Rulership. Daughter of Woden and Viveka. Granddaughter of Burr and Bestla. She has come to rewrite the rules for us all. Who will resist her efforts, and who will join her? Choose now, Rulers, and let it be known."

Stjarna shoved people out of the way to get to me. "Move," she huffed. "Move!" Breathless, she grinned, bumping shoulders with me. "Goddess, Nex, I take my eyes off you for one evening."

A few murmurs in the crowd, but very little movement. Finally, a redhead with gold lettering along his arms made his way to where I stood. Stjarna's smile fell when she saw him join me, but she kept her place at my side.

Fiel, Beijo, and Vertroue maintained their positions behind me as well.

I looked to my father, whose eyes bore into mine. When he opened his mouth, he had to clear his throat for words to follow. "Forgive me," he said. "I must remain neutral in this, my daughter. My support would only endanger you further."

I had no idea what he meant, but it made my stomach hurt. Or maybe it was the mead. Or maybe it was the fact that a glowing boy was having people choose whether to throw me back into a prison I used to think was my home or let me live freely.

Finally, with six of us against a sea of Rulers, Dallr turned and stepped toward me, facing Burr and those who opposed me. It was strange, yet comforting, to have the glowing boy stand with me.

Burr and the crowd did not think so. They no longer murmured and gasped. They exploded, outraged at his decision. "You cannot choose sides," Burr growled at Dallr. "You cannot!"

Dallr was unphased. "You cannot tell me what I will do, Ruler."

"Then it will be *war*."

War? What war? "What war?" I asked. No one answered my question. There was nothing titanium could do to slow my heart back down. I had only ever heard of the Old Wars. Of what they did to Aarde and the people on it. Vague whispers of humankind at its worst, before the City was the City. I learned very little of 'war' from the Wizens who trained us. Only that it was ancient and would never come again. It was not something I wanted. It was not something I even thought possible. "*What war?*"

Burr pointed a finger at me. "You intend to destroy us all, Nexus Aerixon. Huangdi trembles in his palace as we speak. Heim crumbled beneath your exploits. And here, again, at the very Fall, you have brought holy relics to your feet. At all costs, we will bring an End to you. This time, no cage will be fit to hold you. We shall put this City to rest at last. As it should have always been."

"Listen," I said, shaking my head, my mouth almost too dry for words. "I don't want to fight you. I don't even know you! I just wanted you to take down the wall. Or at least to let the Meta in the City leave. I want to end suffering, not increase it. I want to fix this."

Dallr sighed. "Do you set down your grievances then, Burr, as Nexus is willing to set down hers?"

"She is not willing!"

"Yes I am."

"You agree then, to go back to your City and wait for death with the rest of your kind?"

I almost screamed, my hands in fists. "You think 'setting down my grievances' is the same as consigning thousands of innocent people to their collective demise so you don't feel threatened by their power? To force them to endure lives of misery and torment without metal? To be victims forever? That's not 'setting down grievances!' That's a crime against humankind. I will not agree to that. Ever."

I stood straight, my eyes unflinching. No lover's hand in mine this time. My dress had no pockets, but I had no need to hide my shaking fists. The soles of the boots I now wore had never touched the gravel on Ender Stream. Instead, they sank down into the metal of the marble as it moved beneath me, praising the power rushing through my veins.

"Then we shall call it war." Dallr lifted his staff, "So be it," and then lowered it to the ground. The ripple on the marble sent a shockwave through the crowd, flinging our parties in opposing directions with some magnetic force the likes of which I'd never felt.

So, in one night, after a silly game and a bit too much mead, I, Nexus of House Aerixon, began the First New War.

Himmin help. Hel be warned.

THE END

don't wanna wait for the sequel?

season two of STS is live now on kindle vella

From the Mind of Teshelle Combs

Vellas
Episode by Episode

Slit Throat Saga | S2

Season 2 | Picks up where this book left off. Don't wait to continue the story. Go to amazon.com/kindle -vella and search for "Slit Throat Saga."

A **vampire love story** | Meet Aurelie and Alexander. But be careful...he bites. Go to amazon.com/kindle-vella and search for "The Underglow."

The Young Ones

Sociopathic kingpin rules the world | Raised—and rejected—by the most ruthless Insider alive, Charley Porter will do anything to win Everything. Go to amazon.com/kindle-vella and search for "The Young Ones."

Tuck Me In

The worst love story you've ever read | Don't smile. Don't frown. Don't eat. Don't worry. Don't wrinkle. Everything for beauty. You adjusted, millimeter by millimeter until you achieve perfection. But remember, whatever you do…don't. Go to amazon.com/kindle-vella and search for "Tuck Me In."

Books

CORE SERIES

Ava is the kind of girl who knows what's real and what isn't. Nothing in life is fair. Nothing is given freely. Nothing is painless. Every foster kid can attest to those truths, and Ava lives them every day. But when she meets a family of dragon shifters and is chosen to join them as a rider, her very notion of reality is shaken. She doesn't believe she can let her guard down. She doesn't think she can let them in—especially not the reckless, kind-eyed Cale. To say yes to him means he would be hers—her dragon and her companion—for life. But what if Ava has no life left to give?

The System Series

1 + 1 = Dead. That's the only math that adds up when you're in the System. Everywhere Nick turns, he's surrounded by the inevitability of his own demise at the hands of the people who stole his life from him. That is, until those hands deliver the bleeding, feisty, eye-rolling Nessa Parker. Tasked with keeping his new partner alive, Nick must face all the ways he's died and all the things he's forgotten.

Nessa might as well give up. The moment she gets into that car, the moment she lays her hazel eyes on her new partner, her end begins. It doesn't matter that Nick Masters can slip through time by computing mathematical algorithms in his mind. It doesn't matter how dark and handsome and irresistibly cold he is. Nessa has to defeat her own shadows. Together and alone, Nick and Nessa make sense of their senseless fates and fight for the courage to change it all. Even if it means the System wins and they end up...

well...dead.

Poetry

Thoughts Like Words

Let There Be Nine Series

- *Let There Be Nine Vol 1*: **Enneagram Poetry**
- *Let There Be Nine Vol 2*: **Enneagram Poetry**

For Series: Words laced together on behalf of an idea, a place, a world.

- **For Her**
- **For Him**
- **For Them**
- **For Us**

Love Bad Series: Poems About Love. Not Love Poems.

- **Love Bad**
- **Love Bad More**
- **Love Bad Best**

Standalone Poetry Books:

Breath Like Glass

Poems for love that never lasts.

Girl Poet

A collection of poems on the passion, privilege, and pain of being (or not quite being) a girl.

FRAMELESS

A collection of poems for the colors that make life vibrant, from their perspective, so we may share in what they might think and feel.

This One Has Pockets

Narrative poetry about a girl who is near giving up and the boy who tries to save her.

ON THE NATURE OF HINGES

A series of poetic questions from the perspective of someone who has been left behind more than once.

Gray Child

A unique expression of being more than one race, written by a Caribbean American woman, for anyone who cares to read.

Contact Teshelle Combs

Instagram | @TeshelleCombs

Facebook | Vella World Of Teshelle Combs

Acknowledgments

Thank you.

Thank you to Nate Combs, my editor and manager and designer and partner and great love.

Thank you to Forest, who read all my chapters before I even wrote them.

Thank you to Jaxter and Zephyr, for being resilient whenever mom was a little busy and for cheering me on while I fight hydras.

Thank you to the Kindle Vella author community, without whom this story would be lesser than. I never thought a group of inspirationalists could exist so communally in a virtual space. You defy the odds.

And finally, thank you to my readers. My friends. The champions of all my causes. You are world-class. Genius. Brilliant. And worth every second I spend with my fingers to black and white keys. I hope you make your own way, every day, and make a life as brilliant as you! I love you profoundly.

Yours,

TC

Made in the USA
Columbia, SC
16 August 2022

65473087R00283